INTO THE LAIR

JERRY BRIDGES

For Permission requests, write to:

YBR Publishing, LLC
PO Box 4904
Beaufort SC 29903-4904 contact@ybrpub.com
843-900-0859

ISBN-13: 979-8-9852082-4-5

YBR PUBLISHING, LLC

Jack Gannon – Co-Owner, Production Manager
Cyndi Williams-Barnier - Co-Owner, Marketing Manager
Bill Barnier – Co-Owner, Senior Editor
Loreen Ridge-Husum – Art Director

DEDICATION

I would like to thank my son, James, for his regular encouragement, and even more for his ideas. Many of the best scenes of this book came from his active imagination. I unsuccessfully tried a number of times to declare him the co-author of this book, because, in reality, that is what he is. His friend, Jamie, was an immense help as well, helping me reason through logic errors. Logic errors in a fantasy novel get real. The magic must be consistent, otherwise, things look contrived. Karen Eaker, a childhood friend, helped me by her encouragement at tough times. I have another big shoutout for Dave King, author of **Self Editing for Fiction Writers.** He helped me overcome several key issues in the first five chapters.

Finally, and quite seriously, this book would have never been written had it not been for several girls who spoke with me during the two years that I taught as a substitute. Over that time, they came to me individually to speak to me over my free period or lunch. They had each been molested, between the ages of three and seven. Over half of them were students at the Alternative Academy, because they'd been expelled for a variety of issues; being cutters, attempted suicides, failing grades, promiscuity (sex on campus), and other extreme behaviors. I was outraged for them. After hearing of those terrible things, I authored a short story, "A Beauty Unveiled", which became the basis for the chapter of that title. From there the story grew organically. **In an effort to bring attention to the violent and humiliating acts of war, oppression, and subjugation, I try to offer life lessons through the personalities and experiences of the characters in this story. There are acts of extreme violence, sexual misconduct and abuse contained in this story which may not be suitable for very young readers.**

One in nine girls and one in fifty-three boys experience sexual assault or abuse at the hands of an adult. Eighty-two percent of all victims under eighteen are girls. Thirty-four percent are under the age of twelve.

RAINN (Rape, Abuse, and Incest National Network) is a nonprofit organization designed to help with counseling and education for the victims and the unaware population. I intend for ten percent of sales of this book to be donated to this worthy organization.

REVIEWS

The action throughout is hard-hitting, as is the characterization. In fact, every part of this novel is outstanding; I suspect it will become a minor classic of its type in due course.

~Piers Anthony

"Into the Lair" is a rip-roaring journey into the worlds of magical creatures and mind-bending episodes that take the reader on a journey to unimaginable worlds. With an intricate plot line that will engage any fantasy enthusiast, coupled with characters whose weird, supernatural traits redefine the meaning of a living being, the book is a laudable addition to popular stories that recast the future. Bridges appreciates a humorous moment, injects spine tingling escapades, and allows for the pathos that suffuses memorable relationships. His work will undoubtedly appeal to a wide readership.

~Neen Hunt

Bridges has written an imaginative, colorful world filled with adventure. The characters have an emotional approachability that would translate well on-screen. This fantasy novel is a visually stunning mix of fantasy and sci-fi and would be amazing to see unfold. Audiences young and old would have a lot of fun watching this world come to life.

~ Tess Hogue
Screenwriter

Into The Lair by Jerry Bridges is a high fantasy military adventure situated around an elven Shala'lir warrior, his wife, and the family they build for themselves along the way. In a loss of control due to his elven wife Laurealis' estrus cycle that triggers supercharged pheromones, Kailynn finds himself at an unavoidable meeting convened in the midst of 'kaipoctouyevva'. It goes very badly and his powerful clan leader, who is also his grandmother, is not pleased. He is sent off to fight and try to save the dying remnants of the human species. Kailynn's wife is left to care for Raina and Duncan, two war orphans that Kailynn wishes to adopt but has no time to explain to Laurealis as he exits for battle. While Laurealis is away with Raina and Duncan, she fears Kailynn is dead until she is able to determine he is not with the help of her friend, Astoria. Kailynn is a Champion, and the one known to have been captured while fighting. The four of them venture to find Kailynn, alongside a dwarf named Fausto who journeys with them. Between the landscape, elements, and circumstances that conspire against them, all five also have emotional carnage to contend with. The mental demons that haunt their thoughts, feelings, and motives can be just as dangerous as the hybrid demon race ready and willing to stamp out everything that gets in their way so they can breed their way in.

Shifting points of view in the first person give the characters of Laurealis, Raina, Duncan, Astoria, and Fausto the ability to develop to near completion in Into The Lair by Jerry Bridges. Kailynn is also given some time in the point of view spotlight, as is the terrifying Queen of the Asmodians, Ereshkigal, and a couple of others. The novel is massive and a resolute commitment to continue as valiantly as Laurealis is required for the first sixty or so pages, which are notably prolix. The story takes a more comfortable stride after Kailynn is exiled and adopts a steady jog as soon as Fausto enters with a remarkably bitter outlook and the best book within a book ever: A Travel Guide for the Rough Country. Yes, the dwarf is armed with magic and a travel guide that helps them fight dragons. The title Into The Lair is a worthy indication of how crucial dragon facts will be. He's also got a whip of a tongue that can level anyone in a game of deadpan humor and sarcasm. Levity is not easy to find elsewhere as the weight of collective experiences is immense. Children are euthanized in real-time to end torture and suffering, incest is explicit, and the consummation of a union is literally consuming. The battles happen as the quintet journeys in Kailynn's direction and have the customary grit, but the former brutality is more brutal. The ending is satisfying and ties up loose ends but leaves a door open, figuratively and literally, so there's room for more. Recommended.

~Jamie Michele
Readers' Favorite, LLC

"Fantasy, if it's really convincing, can't become dated, for the simple reason that it represents a flight into a dimension that lies beyond the reach of time."

~Walt Disney

TABLE OF CONTENTS

Chapter Header and Back Cover Art By

CURTIS DRESSER

www.curtistriestocomic.com

Chapter One
Disaster
Kailynn

My five thousand years were telling on me. The last time I'd traveled so far by mundane means was while on campaign at the end of the Fourth Age, about twenty-six hundred years ago, when I was a much younger man.

At least the journey was nearly over. Six weeks of hard travel with the newly orphaned and wounded boy, Duncan, was exhausting, especially over a country that, while picturesque, was much easier to fly over than to ride through.

The horse beneath me plodded steadily on. My hips followed its movements instinctively, and my thoughts wandered back to the scene of Duncan's family's death.

I had been flying at about a thousand feet, looking for Taen, a significant Gaelaur Troop Leader, and my friend. The last time I checked up with him, he still had six of the huge great wagons his people lived in year-round. Modeled after the forty-eight-foot-long First Age trailers pulled by great ten-wheeled engines, the First Age artifacts had six large artifacts. They discovered tens of thousands of the artifacts as the ice sheets retreated. Given how quickly the world had descended into a new ice age after the moon of that time crashed into the world, most of them were extremely well preserved.

I thought back to how the people of the Fifth Age had developed in such a surprising new way. The Gaelaur moved north into fresh territory as the great ice sheets shrank. There they discovered the remains of huge First Age cities with names: Chicog, Cleaveland, Ann's Harbor. The one that was settled was Detrota. The Gaelaur learned to adapt what they found to the technology they possessed.

Made of an extremely light alum metal, the huge wagons were light enough to be pulled by teams of oxen. The Gaelaur Great Wagons were also forty-eight feet long, but they were much wider at sixteen feet. They were made using two of the huge, yet light, trailer frames welded together, with the living structure built above. The living areas of the Great Wagons were all made from eight of the great metal twenty-foot-long boxes used in such enormous numbers during the First Age. They were stacked two high, two deep, and two deep, with some space between for everyday living. However, instead of eight wheels, they had four six-foot high rollers with two four-foot-wide rollers to steer with. The great ten-wheeled engines were beyond the abilities of the Gaelaur to build or restore so the wagons were pulled by teams of up to sixty oxen or a team of four mammoths.

Taen also did something new. He tamed a cold drake to pull one of his Great Wagons. The beasts were extremely bad-tempered herbivores who grew up to eighty feet long.

The one he had was only about sixty feet long.

Approaching the camp, instead of Taen, I spotted a boy, about eighteen, dressed in a fringed leather long sleeved tunic, riding a sturdy dappled gray stallion...hard. Like most of his people, he was pushing seven-feet tall. He was whipping the horse occasionally with a stick, not something the Gaelaur normally did. They were exceptional equestrians and rarely pushed their horses so hard.

Tipped off by the boy's unusual action, I looked further east and saw smoke and a great horde of Skarg traveling west. It looked like they'd intercept the boy, and I couldn't let that happen.

I cast a *Long-Door* spell and a magical door opened in front of me. I stepped through the door from a thousand feet high to the ground a few hundred feet ahead of the boy. I knew seeing me would shock him to his core.

I'm an elf, with the long, distinctive ears and unique colors of our species. In my case, light green skin, sky-blue hair, and dressed in a dark green silk robe with a Magnolia flower sigil on my right breast pocket.

"STOP! I'm a friend!" I shouted in the Gaelaur tongue.

When the boy tried to ride past me, I saw a broken arrow or bolt protruding from his thigh. He was probably past reasoning for the pain.

I decided not to use my first plan to simply scare the horse into stopping; the injured boy might fall off. Instead, I lifted him out of the saddle by using air.

"Help! What are you doing? Who are you?"

"As I said, a friend. Stop struggling."

"My horse! He'll run off!"

"Not far, as I'm sure you know. He needs a rest anyway. Why were you pushing him so hard?"

The boy hung in front of me, his face pale with terror. I knew his people weren't comfortable with magic. I gently set him down, and he dropped to his knees.

"The demon-men are coming! Dad sent me out to warn other nearby troops. I'm on my way back!"

"Boy, I have bad news. Lie back so I can get that broken crossbow bolt out of you before it festers."

"But—"

"Now, boy!"

He nearly fell as he tried to lie back. I cast a spell to put him into a restful sleep while I removed the bolt and closed the jagged wound with stitches. With his leg bandaged, I woke him about half an hour later. I made tea with a simple spell since I wasn't about to make a fire here.

"Listen, your leg will be fine. Sit quietly and drink that tea, it will help with the pain."

"I have to…"

"Drink your tea, let the pain ease some. There is little time."

He glared at me and winced. Holding his hand on the throbbing wound, "Uh, well, for a few moments perhaps."

"Good. I'm Kailynn, and you are?"

"Duncan."

"Good. Duncan, I'm looking for Taen's Troop. Do you know where they are?"

"That's my dad! That's where I was going when you stopped me!"

I sighed and let my head slouch downward. This was going to be bad. "Duncan, I strongly believe the demon-men, or as we elves call them, soulless ones or Skarg, wiped out your father's troop. I saw smoke on the other side of a fast-moving group of better than a thousand Skarg."

"On the other side; but that would mean…"

When he realized the import of my revelation, speech failed him.

"Yes, it probably would mean that. We need to move south to avoid them, then back to the smoke. I have to know for sure what happened."

"Yeah, I can see that. So how are you going to travel? I don't see your horse."

"I've already called one. He should be arriving any time now."

"You called a horse?"

"One of my little skills. Ah, there he is."

A roan stallion with a white patch between his eyes cantered near us and nickered. I stroked his neck by way of introduction and looked him over thoroughly. Then I scratched his ear and looked into his eyes, "I think I'll name you 'Courage'."

Reaching into the pocket dimension, accessed through my left vambrace, the armor covering my forearm, I pulled out a blanket and reins. As they expanded into their full size and shape, the boy's eyes grew wide. I noticed his hands trembling.

"Duncan, call your horse to you," I said, to break him out of his shock. "We have much ground to cover."

Several hours later, we found the scene of the battle. There were well over a thousand dead Skarg lying about. I saw the great wagons, pointing out one that was still smoldering. "Let's look over there."

When we were close enough for Duncan to see the great wagons, he exclaimed, "This is my troop. See, there are the wagons we traveled in, gathered in a circle. The five we lived in are on the backside of the battle and the battle wagon is on the side facing all the bodies."

"I do believe you're correct. Stay mounted, I must do something."

Unlike some of my people who use symbols or words to focus their mana spellcasting, for the somatic portion of my spells, I use katas similar to my fighting katas. I dismounted and began my spell disguised as a dance. This spell enabled me to track someone I knew or had at least studied with another spell. I knew Taen, so I aligned my spell with him, which allowed me to see what he had seen, as though from a short distance behind him. I also pulled out my memory stone, so I could record what the spell showed me. If, as I suspected, Taen had died here, I knew I'd want to watch this later when I could properly grieve.

As the spell began taking effect, I knew where to go to begin following his trail from when he first saw the main body of the Skarg.

"Come with me, the trail begins over here."

As I reached the correct point, where he had been earlier in the day, the spell coalesced, and I saw what he saw.

The vision revealed a teenage boy in a hot air balloon tethered to the battle wagon who signaled by mirror to another boy at the base of the same wagon. That young man signaled back and sent another boy to run, coming to a halt just in front of Taen.

"Taen! Thousands of demon-men are headed this way!"

"You've double-checked, I'm sure."

"Yes, sir! Look! You can see the dark in the snow where they are!"

Taen leapt to the nearest wagon and climbed quickly to the top. From over his shoulder, he pulled out a long tube with glass in both ends and looked in the direction the boy indicated. His assured demeanor disappeared.

He looked around at the pastoral scene below him of thirty-five highly fertile and industrious families; their children of all ages, their small livestock, chickens, pigs and such, their greater livestock, the hundred mammoths, fifteen hundred longhorn cattle, and two thousand sheep and goats.

"People! People! People!" he shouted. Once he had their attention he said in a booming voice, "We have thousands of demon-men heading this way! Wagon Leaders, hitch your teams to the wagons. If you can't load them by the time the teams are hitched, leave what you can't load behind! Your lives are more important than your things!

"Duncan, Little Bo, and Tomathon! You're our lightest and fastest riders. You three go a half-day's ride to the nearest troops you can find. Warn them, then get back to us, remembering we'll be going due south to escape. These monsters are heading west, so we're going south. Duncan, you go west. Little Bo, you go south ahead of us. Tomathon, you're going north. Any questions?"

"No, Dad," Duncan and the other boys answered in unison.

"Then go! Grab food, water, and oats for your horses and move! Quickly now!"

The boys dashed to their mothers, who had begun moving to meet their needs immediately, while other men saddled their horses.

"Bo! Move the Battle Wagon up to the front to guard our escape. We may have to leave it behind, but the bulk of our families must have a chance to get out of here. I need ten men to stay behind with him."

The spirit of the Troop showed in that every single man stepped forward.

"Bo, pick who you want. Don't pick anyone with children less than five-years old, if you can help it."

As a clamor began around Bo, Taen spoke again. "I need the rest of the young men under twenty to drive the cattle into that mass. You go in light and fast, then I want all of you back here. I'm taking Skillet Head into the battle after he's pulled the Battle Wagon into place. I'll be in my armor to get you boys out of any trouble. Remember, no heroics!"

Taen's wife, Marta, stepped in front of him. "No heroics? So, what are you doin' then? Goin' to get yourself killed, is what you're doin'."

Taen's face crumpled.

"Marta, I'm the only one who can control that cantankerous old lizard. He still hates being driven, but he's not as easily riled as a large herd of cattle. I'm hoping that if the cattle's blood, and hopefully, a lot of the demon-men's blood gets him into a battle fury, he may be angry enough to break them. I know it's probably not the best plan, but it's all I can come up with that has a chance to save any of us. Tom said there's thousands of demon-men, and he's not prone to exaggeration."

"I know, it's just…" She choked up.

Taen wrapped his arms around her. "Yeah, I love you, too."

"I love you."

"I'll be careful."

"Hah! Like ya were when ya tamed that bloody beast. Then ya left Duncan to watch it and it got loose and chased him around till ya jumped on its back and raced up an' hit its great thick skull with a bloody hammer. Careful like that, ya mean?"

"And you then hit me in the head with your cast iron skillet. You laid me out as well as I laid out Skillet Head."

"Well…ya deserved it, didn't ya?" She turned serious again, "I want your promise, Taen. You'll be as careful as ya can. Right?"

Taen didn't answer. He just hugged his wife tighter.

After a minute, he said, "Please get my armor, Honey. I'm going to move the battle wagon."

Now that I saw what took place, I tamped down the spell to show Duncan what had happened through mundane means, like tracks and dropped pots. Taen had been a great friend and I was already dreading what I was about to see.

The three messengers had already raced off. The young men had herded the cattle into a nervous milling mass. A cattle stampede is more likely to happen when many are gathered together.

The battle wagon was pulled into place and the other wagons were hitched and beginning to move south. Instead of the normal four mammoths pulling a Great Wagon, they had eight cows, each hitched with the bulls in their natural guarding positions nearby.

Ten men, with Bo leading them, stood to the west of the herd and held a weapon used by no one else I'd ever heard of…muskets. After the young men began whooping and hollering to get the herd moving, the men of the battle wagon followed Bo's lead and fired their weapons in the general direction of the Skarg. The herd began moving as a group, first trotting, then running with the continued shouting of the young men. Another two rounds from the very loud muskets, they began a fear driven stampede.

The Skarg were about a thousand feet away by then, and the stampede was timed perfectly; the cattle owners knew their animals. Fifteen hundred half-ton cattle with horns six to nine-feet-wide can cut quite a swath.

However, about a tenth of the Skarg were equipped with a ranged weapon. The Skarg weren't handy with any crafted weapons because only a fifth of them had hands. Most of them had claws, pincers, and huge crocodilian mouths, depending upon whether they were more reptilian, mammalian, or insect. The insect Skarg ranged weapons shot thirty-two deadly chitinous darts from the ends of their arms. They could only shoot what they had grown, so it was an all or nothing shot. After that, it took a day or so to regrow a full set of darts.

The stampede plowed right through the Skarg with few losses until they ran into a unit of the dart users. The poisoned darts were fired in mass at about eighty feet and knocked most mammals out of the fight in about five seconds. However, stampeding cattle run at about twenty-five miles per hour, so they can cover about thirty feet-per- second. The front ranks rolled over the dart users before they passed out and were trampled in turn by those behind them. The stampede then turned to avoid the fresh cattle blood.

The riders saw this, and rather than turn back, chose to follow to keep the stampede going.

Taen was now fully armed and armored and mounted on Skillet Head. The two of them headed into the fray.

Many things happened at once. Six light green ogres, fourteen-feet-tall and seven-feet-wide humanoid monsters with skin as tough as chain mail, charged the head of the stampede and turned it north, away from the fleeing Gaelaur.

Ogres are solitary creatures, which led me to start looking for Asmodians. It would take their powerful charm spells to control something as sociopathic as an ogre. That they attacked at the exact point of greatest benefit for the Skarg was very suspicious.

One of the young equestrians, Lear, was Taen's oldest son. He was near the front of the stampede, trying to turn it back into the Skarg. An ogre charged him and hit Lear's horse. The horse flew over thirty feet while Lear flew high enough for Taen to see him.

Taen was wreaking havoc with his big cold drake. A fully enraged lizard that size is a fearsome beast. Its tail was nearly half his length, and the creature was using it with deadly effect. Taen was on top and firing arrows with great precision, targeting those Skarg who appeared to be giving orders.

At the same time Taen saw his son flying through the air, the cold drake's head exploded in a great cloud of blood and flesh. The screams of dying animals and the smell of burning flesh and pooling blood on the field of battle was becoming overwhelming.

The attacker was a Golem. A creature animated from material such as sand or wood, this one was clearly assembled from one of the Great Wagons. Its hands were giant rotating saws made from a single roller over a body made from much of the rest of the wagon.

Only an Asmodian could have made something like that. It took powerful magic to create Golems, and this one was very advanced.

Leaving the Golem, Taen leapt off his dying lizard and fought his way to his son. The Gaelaur wore armor copied from mine in ages past. They wore chainmail underneath for protection from arrows, while I relied on tightly woven silk and magic to protect me. The outer plate was lamellar, bands of steel fitted to the body, allowing more flexibility than any other type of plate. The Skarg darts bounced off him with no effect.

Taen's people are giants by other people's standards; a pretty typical response to very cold environments where extra mass is a heat-storing strategy. Seven feet of heavily armored warrior is hard to stop, especially when they wield great swords as well as Taen.

After he hacked and cut his way to his gravely injured son, he sheathed his great sword and drew his shorter longsword and the shield that hung over his back.

I knew I should have moved on to see what else was happening. I did notice that the cold drake destroyed the Golem in its death throes. But Taen's defense of his son was a feat worthy of song. I sped up the time, so I wasn't waiting so long with Duncan unable to see what I was seeing. I was glad that all this was being recorded in my memory stone.

Before long, Taen was ringed by piles of dead Skarg. His other son, Connell, joined him, and though he was unarmored, his speed allowed him to keep up with his father.

Until, that is, another unit of fresh dart users showed up. His speed couldn't protect him from the poisoned darts that took him down and silenced his brother within seconds.

Taen's revenge on those dart wielders left none alive, but his boys were still dead or dying.

The ring of dead around him grew higher and higher. It reached seven feet, yet the Skarg were still climbing over and dying. Taen began standing on the bodies inside the ring. Finally, he tripped in the mass of corpses, or a wounded Skarg grabbed his foot. Once he was off his feet, he was quickly overwhelmed. Shortly thereafter, one of the monsters held up Taen's severed head.

My friend was dead. I choked at the sudden emptiness in my heart, though I stopped my tears for a later time.

I had been noticing things I could show Duncan, so I could describe what happened in a more mundane manner. I didn't believe he would take to magical explanations any better than most Gaelaur.

When I stepped out of the spell at last, I showed Duncan the pile of bodies and how high it was, even after the Skarg had harvested the legs and arms of their own dead for travel rations. I explained how Taen and his sons were not similarly desecrated because, as evil as the Skarg are, they respected strength. None could deny that great heroes fought and died here.

After that, we moved to where the ogres had charged toward the others and met the battle wagon.

I hadn't seen it in my vision, and my grief was too raw to recast the spell, but the marks of the liquid fire shooter were still clear on the ground. I remembered my last secret meeting with Taen just a couple of months ago. He had been so proud of this, his most expensive Great Wagon, which he bought from the Dowarchy Clan. They only sold it to him because of the huge amount of prestige he had amongst the ranchers.

Knowing I'd need to understand what happened in detail, I gritted my teeth and recast my tracking spell. As it activated again, I saw the Battle Wagon in front of me surrounded by hordes of Skarg.

Like all the Great Wagons, with their six-foot wheels and steering rollers, the battle wagon's platform sat four feet off the ground. Instead of rooms, it had steel-reinforced alum walls eight feet high with arrow slits, which meant the top of the wall was twelve-feet above the ground. The steam engine and the water and coal reserves were in an armored room with a foot-high gap at the top for ventilation. Forward of the engine room was a covered smithy, including tools such as a trip-hammer, lathe, and drill powered by a long pulley shaft that ran along the ceiling from the engine.

The battle wagon's weapons included a liquid fire shooter on a raised platform at the far back of the wagon which shot out a heated semi-liquid tar mixed with steam. It had a maximum range of about thirty feet. Flanking the steam engine and smithy were steam cannons capable of shooting dozens of small one-inch diameter grapeshot a couple of hundred feet, or a single four-inch iron ball up to three hundred yards. It wasn't exactly accurate at that range, but with thousands of Skarg and five huge ogres for targets, it was hard to miss.

When one of the ogres' heads flew off, the rest changed their attention from killing cattle to charging the battle wagon.

One of them grabbed a younger cow by a horn; it was no more than five hundred pounds and threw her a good two hundred feet. It missed, but the other three ogres copied the idea and one of the flying calves hit one of the cannons and dismounted it.

They charged the battle wagon, covering the ground quickly.

"Man, the fire shooter! They'll be here in seconds! Fire the grapeshot!"

The ogres were met by grapeshot about a hundred feet away. One ogre was hit hard enough that it was thrown backwards, though it was merely stunned and lightly wounded.

The grapeshot did slow them enough for the fire shooter to let loose. The weapon swiveled easily, and the gunners engulfed all three of the others in flame that couldn't be put out.

Even so, it would take the ogres several minutes to burn to death. In the meantime, they wreaked havoc on the battle wagon. Enraged by the flames, they ripped the fire shooter off its mount and threw it hundreds of feet. The hoses feeding live steam and tar were ripped off and one of the attackers was blinded when live steam boiled its eyes.

Duncan's Uncle Bo, an expert longbowman, shot another in the throat. It didn't die right away, but it did sit on the ground while it burned and choked on its own blood.

The third ogre grabbed Bo and ripped him in half.

Two other men shot the ogre in the chest at point blank range. Even that wasn't enough to bring an ogre down immediately. It hit each of them with a different half of Bo with such force they landed many feet away. They didn't get up.

The remaining cannon was useless since the pressure was lost when the steam pipe tore. The crew was about to abandon the battle wagon when the remaining ogre, which had been blinded and bathed in more tar from the fire shooter, finally began feeling the effects of the intense flame bath and stood still, screaming until it died.

They turned their attention to the other ogre who was getting up slowly. It may have been dying, but it was still in a full rage.

The Gaelaur's full armor was of little value when facing the sheer strength of an ogre.

"Shoot for the throat like Bo did," one of them shouted.

The eight remaining men may not have been the experts with the bow that Bo was, but they were skilled archers. Swatting at the arrows, which only stung the ogre, it continued its slow advance. Finally, filled with numerous arrows imbedded around its throat, the ogre fell dead just short of the battle wagon.

The most immediate threat now gone, the men separated and ran to seal the broken hoses to return pressure to the remaining steam cannon. Two men loaded it with grapeshot.

The Skarg had dealt with the cattle by then and were running their way when the second crew repairing the steam line, announced, "Pressure's up!"

The weapon roared and thirty feet of the Skarg line dropped or flew backwards in a swarm of screaming grapeshot.

The other five men began shooting their bows as quickly as possible. For a moment, it looked like they might hold, especially when a second load of grape cleared another portion of the line. Had the battle wagon's walls been intact, it might have held.

However, at least five hundred Skarg quickly swarmed over the breached portions of the walls, climbing over the fallen at the front. The first wave didn't fare well, but their bodies provided the height for the others to climb over the walls from all sides.

Once on top, the men fought bravely, but the battle didn't last long.

The Skarg tore the defeated Battle Wagon apart, then raced after the retreating home wagons. The mammoth teams were running as fast as they could, but Skarg can cover thirty miles per hour. The mammoths, not so much.

The results were too gruesome to watch.

I showed Duncan where his family had been run down. They fought bravely, but there were too many for them. When I told him all, he dealt with his grief in his own way while I gathered the bodies of the fallen onto one of the wagons and set it ablaze.

The worst part was finding Duncan's little sister impaled through her stomach on one of the wagon's. Wounded a day earlier, she was already running a high fever and in terrible pain. I hated that the enemy was so obviously close, but there was nothing either of us could do. I was going to mercy kill her, but he insisted that he should be the one to send her to the spirit world. When he couldn't, I wrapped my hands around his, and, together, we ended her suffering.

As I did, I became aware that my fury had been building since I saw the smoke, and especially since I discovered the Asmodians presence. I kept it at bay, needing to understand the situation before I could act. But after we mercy killed Duncan's youngest sister, I gave in.

I sought out and destroyed the remaining Skarg, but that hardly began to slake my rage. I found and destroyed the Asmodian as well. After that, Duncan and I began our desperate dash west.

Chapter Two
Upon Disaster
A Dwarven Border Fortress

Kailynn

We had been seeing glimpses of the mountains coming into view before us for a week. We finally picked our path through the foothills at the northeastern edge of the range which contained the highest peaks on the continent.

Surrounded by the grandeur of the mountains; snowcapped peaks, sheer drops, forests on the western side of each peak, we rode on. Finally, the Dwarven border fortress came into view. Its features blended in with the surroundings in a way that only the Earth Children could manage. Their Earth Mages were tremendously artistic as a rule, as all of us who bend the Chaos to our will tend to be. But their fortifications couldn't be matched for sheer strength and durability. Looking with an experienced eye, the towers and archer slots were part of the broken terrain we had been traveling through for weeks. Beautiful work by genuine masters.

We'd taken an additional day to reach the fort, rather than the more northern human enclave, because my old friend, Tartarus, was commander there. The world, my people in particular, needed to know about the actual involvement of the Asmodians. In my nightly scouting flights ahead, while Duncan and the horses slept, I'd discovered news of an even more disturbing nature. I needed to report it, but I couldn't trust a human to grasp why it was so important, and act upon it without delay.

The human nations had suffered so many defeats in the last five years that it looked like they might soon surrender. Only one of the powerful human nations, Francesca, still retained most of its territory. Most of the other nations had already been eliminated, and a random portion of their populations caged and transported into slavery or worse by the Asmodians. Of course, enough remained that liars like my fellow elf, Dumas, could continue to argue that the Asmodians weren't involved. I hate the Asmodians with a white-hot passion, but traitors or fools like Dumas make me want to kill…slowly. Right now, a slow death over the next year sounded good for him and his allies.

The demoralization and surrender of the humans had happened at the end of the Fourth Age, and at the end of the Second and Third Ages as well. The victorious Asmodians had simply given the humans a respite to disarm them and manipulated their political situations enough to render further fighting virtually impossible. It still amazes me how gullible unlimited bribes make some humans, and some elves as well.

It was only after surrender that their inevitable and gruesome harvest for their horrid sacrifices to their demon god, Asmodius, would begin. I and my cohorts, the Elf Champions, tried and failed to prevent this twice before. The Second, Third, and Fourth Ages ended in the most abominable and horrifying massacres. The ten percent of the humans who'd survived managed to repopulate the world again and would be allowed to do so this time. That might be a consolation, but I could not see that happen one more time.

How Dumas could willingly support such atrocities was beyond my comprehension.

The gates of the fort were opening so we cantered through. I stopped in front of a commanding dwarf who stood in challenge, battle axe at the ready and backed up by a squad of crossbowmen with their weapons cocked and at the ready. The war had turned these men into doughty veterans. They may only stand four-feet tall, but they're as broad as the tall human boy who rode with me.

One doesn't underestimate the Earth Children's troops more than once. Over the last five years of this current End of the Age War, they had become seasoned veterans. They reorganized their units from the decanis up to the legion. They had also magically upgraded their basic shield wards to their knights' offensive weapons, with new spells and formations. Combined with their ever-maturing Earth Mage powers, the Dwarves had become a more powerful force to be reckoned with. If only their numbers were as great as their hearts.

In my haste I threw my leg over the back of my horse, Courage, for a moving dismount.

A bit too quickly! I realized all the dwarves within sight leveled their weapons at my heart. One more wrong move and I would be a pincushion. I held my hands open with my arms raised.

"No fear, friends. I bear urgent news. I need to see Tribune Tartarus immediately."

At that moment, Tartarus emerged with open arms from a door in the stone fort.

"Kailynn! So good to see you!"

As soon as he appeared, the centurion with the battle axe barked an order and the dwarves around me lowered their crossbows.

Immediately behind me, I heard Duncan whistling for Courage to come to him. Now that I knew I wasn't going to be shot, I grasped forearms in the Dwarven soldier's greeting.

"Kailynn, how have you been?"

"Rushed. I bring urgent news, old friend."

I noticed that he wasn't dressed in his armor. His expensive and obviously tailored uniform of red and green set off his military bearing well. Instead of a helmet, he wore a red beret. He must have been in the middle of paperwork, the bane of all officers.

Hearing my words, his friendly expression became all business.

"Come inside with me. Let me serve you a glass of wine while you tell me of it. Decanus, see to Kailynn's companion and their mounts."

I ducked through the entry to the low room and sat cross-legged.

"Tartarus, six weeks ago I found and disposed of the remnants of a unit of twenty-five hundred Skarg."

He nodded. "Not an outrageous amount. It could be far worse."

"It is. The bad news is that they were apparently joining with a larger group. At night when my young companion was resting, I scouted ahead and discovered several hundred thousand of the beasts."

"No! We killed close to a half million trying to get to our besieged fortress at Lookout Mountain several months ago. We won, but that army lost four out of five men, and we're trying to rebuild. We can't afford any more *victories* like that. Yet five years ago, no one had seen one. Where are they all coming from?"

"Well, that's the unwelcome news," I said. "There's worse."

"What could be worse? Not unless they're led by Asmodians!"

"They are." My friend's earthy-brown face blanched.

"They had a large dragon with them, obviously charmed. It was the largest dragon I've ever seen, and it wasn't a winged one."

"That means that it's probably one of the rare caster types."

"I strongly believe it to be the Chaos Dragon herself," I added.

"No!"

"The only person powerful enough to charm her would be King Nergalis. I didn't see him, but I just can't think of anyone else who could do it."

"What are we to do? There's no stopping an army like that. Besides, she hasn't been seen in over a thousand years! It must be another, weaker one."

"Here, let me show you. Perhaps new eyes can see what I've missed."

I pulled out the large emerald memory stone from a pocket dimension accessed through my left vambrace and held it in my hand. I caused it to project an image.

It showed the view as I flew overhead fifty feet above a massive camp with low fires burning and surrounded by hordes of the half-demonic travesties of creation named Skarg. The dragon was visible on the horizon, its glossy black form isolated by a considerable distance from the Skarg. It was curled within itself like the snake it resembled. One short, bright-pink leg was exposed, proving that it was indeed a dragon and not some new monstrous snake-like horror the Asmodians had summoned or bred, as they did from time to time.

This short-legged wingless form had only appeared near the end of the last age, about twenty-five hundred years ago. Prior to that, dragons only had one form, the one that developed near the end of the Third Age. They breathed fire, had larger legs and bat-like wings. Their king, a huge old beast, could be reasoned with if you were strong enough. The younger queen, who succeeded him just before the end of the Fourth Age, never came out of her lair. You can't talk with someone who never answers the door.

This form had no wings, but with their enormous magical abilities, they could fly better than their winged brethren. Unlike the winged dragons, whose magic was located in their impenetrable wings and indestructible bones, the non-winged dragons' magic was focused on the long white tendrils extending from just behind the nostrils and growing to twenty feet past the back of its head. Younger dragons had shorter tendrils. Little was known about such dragons, other than to fear them and kill them quickly. The extreme length of the tendrils and the dragon's sheer size made me believe this one was the dragon queen, possibly the oldest dragon in existence.

She'd seldom been out of her lair before, preferring to let her far weaker children do her battles. We knew of her only from talking to other dragons. If this was the Chaos Dragon, we were in trouble.

Dragons have *True Sight*, so this one could have seen right through my *Invisibility* spell, if it had happened to look directly at me. The spell is highly focused at the best of times and faded with distance. I certainly didn't want to face a dragon that size by myself, so I rose upward to about five hundred feet above the camp. The image became much smaller as I moved higher.

Several humanoid forms were speaking with her, Asmodians, from the look of them. Finally, between this and what I'd recorded at Taen's Last Stand, I had the evidence to bring my people fully into the war.

Tartarus raised his hand, and I stopped the forward motion of time in the image, then reversed it a few seconds before allowing normal time-flow to resume.

He leaned forward to better see the ancient foe. They were as multi-colored as my own people and as filled with magic. Since the Asmodians freely interbreed with demons and the other chaotic dimension travelers, their forms could resemble anything, from squid-like to crocodile-like to …

"Does that jet black one with the more humanoid body have horns?" my friend asked. "You know, head like a bull with big, long-horn cattle horns?"

"What?" I reversed the illusion again and moved it forward even more slowly.

"See, right there. He's almost invisible next to the dragon's dark skin."

I felt my face blanch. "By … the … Goddess. That's King Nergalis. Well spotted, Tartarus. Now I really must use your portal. The war just moved to a whole new level. If I can show this to my people, I can get us fully involved. I don't need to tell you how that could swing things back, even at this late date."

"Kailynn," he said with a slight smile, "you know we have no such thing as a *secret portal*."

I slammed my open palm down hard on his desk and stood, being careful to stoop over the desk so as not to knock myself silly on the low ceiling. This room was built for the dwarves, the shortest of the Free Peoples, not the elves, the tallest.

"Old friend, I'm not stupid! I understand why you can't let the world know you have a portal at every major fort. But this needs to be reported, now! So, stop pretending ignorance!"

He responded with a despondent look that made him seem even more rocklike.

"Tartarus," I said quietly, "I need to report to the Council and to my fellow Champions. You need to report to your superiors. My companion and I volunteer to be blindfolded, or whatever reasonable precautions you want, to protect your secret. But you must allow this information through."

Tartarus sighed heavily.

"You're right." He rubbed his head with one hand. "This information is worth the consequences. Though, thank you for volunteering to be blindfolded. How would you feel about a potion to knock you out?"

"If it must be."

"It must." He sighed. "Well, what's a career when there's a war to win, or at least not lose? You and your companion stand ready. I'll need at least a quarter hour."

"Tartarus, thank you."

"I may need more than your thanks. This violation of protocol will have profound consequences for me, at the very least a Court Martial under a charge of treason. Low treason, if I'm lucky, but still treason. I wouldn't do it if I didn't trust you completely, though I must ask; how sure are you? Is there any way this could have been a trick or something?"

His fear was almost palpable. I laid my hand gently on his shoulder. Low treason meant exile. High treason meant execution and could also extend to his property, leaving his wife and children paupers. I considered backing off. I looked at my friend, who was putting himself in grave danger.

"Tartarus, I saw all this with my own eyes, and I recorded the images in my own memory stone. I also cast a True Sight spell on myself. There can't be any doubt."

"I was afraid you'd say something like that."

With his head hung low, he waved his finger in the general direction of the door. I left, my heart heavy. The thought of destroying a friend's career and his life, even over something so vital, sucked away all the joy of seeing him. I held the door for a moment before sadly turning away to find Duncan.

A moment after the door slipped quietly closed, I heard it slam open and Tartarus bellowed, "Centurion!"

I found Duncan in the stables using a curry comb on Shadow. The stables were of Dwarven make, which meant they were organized, immaculate, and cut out of the stone. He asked me as soon as I joined him. "What's wrong? You look like your best friend just died."

"He may yet, and with me as the cause."

I explained quickly what would be required, and we waited quietly while a soldier I recognized as the Centurion in charge of ten centuries, gave us each a cup containing a bitter potion, then blindfolded us. I recognized the honor given us, even as my senses dulled to the point of not knowing my surroundings. I allowed myself to fall into the waiting arms of several dwarves who lowered me into a makeshift stretcher.

Well, the secret portal worked.

As my senses returned, I vaguely remembered being handed a cup of something to drink. I pried my eyes open and found myself on a travois being pulled behind a tough little pony. We were already in the shadow of the twenty-foot-tall statues marking each gate of the public portal of Anthopoulos, my home city.

A Dwarven soldier held the reins of our ponies, guiding us through the ever-present crowds of merchants and customers.

These portals, the Stort'dørnettverk, was a system built and maintained by one of the Dwarven clans and financed by human bankers. This was the same cooperative effort that built many wonders in this Fifth Age. Each Stor'dør had up to ten gates leading to places around the world. For a fee, one could walk or ride through and be instantly transported to another city. Given the number of Stor'dør spread around the world, the Stort'dørnettverk, translated as Big Door Network, could move people and goods quickly around the continent, and the world.

Each Stor'dør was powered by earth-nodes, not by a magician's personal magic, so anyone with a minor amount of earth magic could work them. The dwarves have such a strong connection with the earth that even their name for themselves, Dom'barn, translates as Earth Children. Any dwarf can control the individual Stor'dør. As a result, trade sped up enormously and has been a tremendous boon in the world-wide conflict.

"Kailynn, what happened? Duncan, on a similar travois next to mine, was coming around. "We were in a Dwarven fortress, and now we're in fields of crops and huge flowers."

"Magic, my boy, magic. I told you we'd be blindfolded and drugged. That was to hide certain parts of the route we took. I can't stress enough that our method of travel is a strict secret of the Dwarves, and its privacy absolutely must be respected. The Stort'dørnettverk is public, and that is what we just left behind."

As I feared, he blanched. His people have little interaction with magic and therefore fear it. The only magical items they've seen are finished products, like his father's great sword slung over his back. It requires no sharpening to maintain its razor edge.

I worried about what would happen to him when we reached my home. Everything from the Dendrocasa, the animated tree that was our home, to my wife's art, to, well, everything in Anthopoulos, is magical. One tends to overlook the commonplace, but our people are the most magical of people, as his are the least. It would not be comfortable for him.

Hmmm, speaking of magic, I needed to contact a priest or priestess to cast the spell necessary for him to know our tongue, or he'll be in for a rough time. If he learns two or more tongues at once, he'd sleep for a few days while his brain assimilated all the information. Hopefully, he will also become comfortable with all the magical workings and artifacts around him. Having someone magically mess with his brain wouldn't be very reassuring, though it was a hope.

We detoured to see an old friend who agreed to come by that afternoon to work the spell. He wanted to give Duncan long enough at my place to get at least partially settled, yet not so long as to give his ignorance of the language a chance to get him into trouble.

We were awake enough to walk, leading our horses, when our Dendrocasa, Ti-grogordahai, came into sight. As soon as he sensed me, he opened his dinner-plate-sized eyes and smiled. Duncan stopped dead in his tracks. I was half expecting this reaction and kept a straight face…almost. For me, this was home.

My wife, Laurealis, came running out to greet me with an exuberant kiss. I caught a whiff of something I hadn't smelled in ages. Something hauntingly familiar but just out of reach of my memory.

"I missed you so much!"

I wondered why the exuberance. We loved each other deeply, but after our daughter died over six hundred years ago, much of the raw passion had left our lives. Yet here it was again. As she rubbed her face over mine in a catlike manner, I realized what that fragrance revealed.

Laurealis! *"The kaipoctouyevva has come back upon you,"* I thought, through our marriage bond. At our wedding, parts of our souls were shared. When we were touching, particularly during kaipoctouyevva, we were mind-linked.

That one-month window is the only time that our women can become pregnant. The last time she was in kaipoctouyevva was before we conceived Aletha. Her gentle rubbing of her face against mine felt so good, so mesmerizing, so—

"Stop!" I held her out at arm's length and thought more rapidly than speech. *"Laurealis. Stop! I have proof of the Asmodians' involvement in the human's war! I have to present my evidence to the Free People's Alliance, then call a Council meeting."*

"But do you have to do it now?" She kept trying to reach my face with hers, which would continue to flood me with her pheromones, leaving me with little desire for anything but her. Already, I could feel my passion rising, and my conscious mind receding behind the ancient urges.

I again pushed her back and held her at arm's length. "Not now!"

Her face immediately clouded. The *time*, which made her need for release as strong as my own, was quickly becoming unstoppable.

"But, Kai', I thought you wanted another child as badly as I."

I sighed heavily. My forehead touching hers, I could feel her need. I hid my feelings from my dear wife, not wishing to cause a major argument.

"Honey, I was wrong not to be truthful with you. But since Aletha…I can't deal with the risk of losing my heart again. I don't think I could remain sane."

I couldn't find the words. I had to go. This was the wrong time, and I was doing this all wrong. I knew she felt the urgency of my desire to go, the frustration at being thwarted so many times by the more mercantile factions of our people. I knew I should have brought this up centuries ago, but it hurt so much to talk about.

Sobbing, she turned from me.

I stood, my arms still out where I had held her, not wanting to let her go, wanting with all my heart, soul, and body to hold her, but not trusting myself to not beget another child.

She turned back, rage distorted her beautiful features into a mask, "Just…just go! Leave me! If saving the humans is all you care about, then just GO!"

Ti'grogordihai's mouth opened. She raced inside, and his mouth snapped shut in my face. I took a half step forward.

"Laurealis! I love you!"

She returned my words with a horrid, illusionary stench.

I couldn't make this right, not now. I had a duty to perform. One of the human races that vanished with the last age had a saying, "Death is light as a feather. Duty is heavy as a mountain."

With my heart, broken and bleeding, torn in half by my longing for her body and my desire to end the bloodshed, I stumbled. Like the lost man I was, I wandered away from my home and my heart.

Finally, after some time, I picked up the mountainous weight of my duty. Determined to make the Congress see the truth, I turned to meet with the leader's representatives of the Free People's Alliance.

I ported back to Lergenze, the capital of Francesca, the most powerful and still the largest of the free human nations.

That is where I would have to present my evidence to my fellow Champions and the Free People's Alliance.

This Alliance was our continent's political body for coordinating with the international and interspecies community's efforts to fight this world-wide conflict. So far, my people had avoided efforts to bring us into the conflict.

I still found it amazing. Actually, it made me suspect treason within the ranks of the Elves. For some reason, our people still did not accept that this was anything but a strictly human affair. Sure, we're an insular and self-absorbed people, but all the Dwarves and the Sylvan Elves accepted what was obvious to me and my fellow Champions. This conflict was being backed by the Asmodians.

Somehow, they bred a new race, one that combined humans and demons. We also don't understand how they made them multiply in enormous numbers, overnight, in their glacial strongholds. All without anyone suspecting what was coming. But now that it was upon us, my people still did not believe such a thing was possible.

I'd been looking for five long years and finally had the proof I needed. Now I could barely think for the guilt of hurting my true love.

Blasted hormones!

I would have to contact Bedros, one of the other surviving champions. His specialty was teleportation and transportation magic. Our armor takes a hundred years to construct and each of the pieces has special powers. The helmets of each are connected by telepathic links, so we can communicate with each other anywhere on the planet. If we're within a mile or so of each other, we can talk with everyone within range at once. Forty-five warriors died in the last conflict with the Asmodians twenty-five hundred years ago, and we've only managed a single apprentice since then.

"Bedros, I have the proof of King Nergalis' active involvement in the war."

"Excellent! Where are you?"

A human bumped into me. "Leave me alone!" "Kailynn! What's going on? Are you in danger?" "No!" I screamed through our mental link.

"Kailynn, what's wrong with you? You're not like this. You're acting as if…as if Laurealis rubbed faces with you?"

"She did."

"You're serious? You're presenting your case before a meeting of the Full Council in the middle of kaipoctouyevva?"

"Yes!"

"By the Consort's Spear…"

After a long minute, Bedros said, "I'll port to you. Give me a minute."

Our armor would give him a fix on me. So, in just a few moments, he was there.

"So, here's what's going to happen. You're going to tell us your evidence and let us present it. It's obvious you can't. It's not even *legal* for you to go out in public right now! You might kill someone!"

"It's not the full effect. I stopped her in time. I can handle this."

"You realize you're trembling and sweating, right? You may be in control, but at best, it's only marginal."

"I can handle it!"

"Kailynn, it's too important to risk an episode."

"I can handle it!" His eyebrows raised high.

I took a deep breath.

"I'll admit it's hard. But I can handle it. If I, the one who did the recon, am not the one to present the evidence, some idiot might get it thrown out. It's happened before."

His hand found his way to my shoulder where he squeezed as the companion and friend he was. In the daze and rage of unfulfilled kaipoctouyevva, I nearly planted a fist in his face.

"Yes, some idiot like Dumas. He and his gang of merchants did that, just before you volunteered to go on another recon six months ago. If memory serves me correctly, that's the reason you left on your scouting mission."

"I can't risk it. Bedros, I just can't let the Asmodians eradicate the humans yet *another* time. Murder just kills the body. Let's be accurate; they sacrifice the humans' souls and bodies to that abomination, Tiamora, who they keep up in their ice fortress. Those sacrifices fuel that hideous monstrosity. It's what gave them the power to defeat us twenty-five-hundred years ago and killed forty-five of us. It's probably what's given them the power to do whatever they've done that keeps more of us from becoming Champions."

"I know all of that, and you're right. Well," he sighed, "let's keep you isolated till the coming Council meeting. You know getting them to meet before Monday is going to be hard. Why didn't you just wait till then? Given that Laurealis rubbed faces with you, I know what you should be doing.

He kept his hand on my shoulder, staring into my eyes, not letting me escape till I shared my reasons with him.

Sighing I turned to walk away, before turning back and laying my hands on both his shoulders. "Bedros, listen to me. I stopped her before I was totally lost in Kaipoctouyevva. Then I had to tell her the other reason I couldn't go with The

Time. And it's hard to say." I averted my gaze. "I haven't told anyone this, it's too personal. It was only today that I told Laurealis. And I didn't actually 'tell' her, it slipped through our mind link."

"So, what's your big secret? You know you can tell me anything." He again put his hand on my shoulder. "You've been my brother-in-arms for ages. We've saved each other's life so many times I've lost count. What could there possibly be that you can't share with me?"

"Bedros, I can't face possibly losing another baby." My voice broke as I continued. "She was so little, so precious. She was only chest high, just a little over seventy years old. She was only half grown."

I sniffed my tears back. My control was slipping. Damn! I hated what was happening to me.

"That went over well, I'm sure," he said with a perfectly straight face.

The little bit of humor coming through in his voice was just the edge I needed to regain control.

"You just can't imagine."

"You know, you're right. Pretty glad I'm not the one running out of the range of her illusions. A rejected illusionist wife is bad. Pancros taught me to not get her angry a long, long time ago. I bet a mad emotive dancer can throw a doozy of a tantrum.

"Actually, just before I ported up here, Laurealis transformed into an old human hag throwing rotten tomatoes that stank worse than you can imagine. I can still smell that mess."

He chuckled. "Oh, that's good. She's always had a great imagination."

I joined him in a good laugh. Just what the healer ordered.

Chapter Three
The Allies Conference Divided

Kailynn

The twenty-foot-tall sculpture that adorned one end of the meeting room showed an elf leaning out of a tree, a dwarf atop a fortified mountaintop tower, and several human kings on a landing atop a stair. A fitting representation of the races gathered at the various sized desks spread round the room, together supporting a huge emerald.

The glowing emerald was a memory stone that recorded and displayed scenes at the call of whomever had the magic to control it. The scenes were normally recorded on smaller stones and transferred to the large one so the entire Congress could see it as a group.

I tapped my stone, feeling my way through its slew of images until I found the image I was seeking. I projected it to the display table in the center of the room.

The collected representatives of the races; tall, slim elves, broad-shouldered dwarves, and humans in the dress of a dozen lands, gasped in collective shock.

Dominating the three-dimensional image was a huge black dragon with long white tendrils growing from just behind her nostrils and extending twenty feet behind her ears. Her short legs were bright pink, and unlike most dragons, she had no wings. That's because the Queen of the dragons, the Chaos Dragon, had magic powerful enough to enable her to fly without them. Her very existence was legendary. Yet, her image was in full glory before them.

She was surrounded by Asmodians, enemies of both dragons and the Allies. They were clustered in groups, but none were close to her. A careless move by a two-hundred-foot-long dragon could crush them, and she might not even notice. The various rainbow hues of the Asmodians' skin, hair, and clothing accented the deep black of her scales. Their clothing was only slightly less varied than the colors of their skins or the shapes of their bodies. Given their half-demonic heritage, lack of conformity was the most consistent aspect of their entire race.

I used a short light-projecting rod to highlight a jet black, broad shouldered Asmodian with the head and horns of a powerful bull.

"This is Nergalis, king of the Asmodians, and their most powerful magician. I have other evidence of Asmodian activity as well. Seeing him is why I had to come here and present this myself. I recognized him from the wars at the end of the Fourth Age. With him leading an army, there remains no doubt that the Asmodians have been directing things from the initial attacks five years ago. They've been hiding their involvement these past years to prevent all our peoples from uniting until it's too late. This has to be another *End of an Age*."

I paused, to allow the import of what I said sink in.

In this silence, the chamber door burst open, and Dumas stormed into the room. Heavyset for an elf, he strode toward Pierre, shoving people aside if they didn't move out of his way.

"Dumas," I said, my sarcasm dripping, "so glad you could find time to take part in such an important meeting."

"Important? Important for what, or whom? Are you still trying to convince these fine people that the Asmodians are involved? What a complete pile of rubbish!"

Pierre, the tall, dignified Chairman of the Free Peoples Alliance, and representative of the Northeastern Seaboard Nations, stepped forward placing a hand on Dumas' shoulder. "Friend, Kailynn has presented a thorough and quite convincing report confirming what many of us have been saying since Firenzia fell so suddenly five years ago."

Dumas batted the human's hand aside.

"I'm no friend of anyone supporting that leach. He's been trying to get us to go into harm's way for the sake of a few humans for close to five years now."

I stepped between Pierre and Dumas, "Dumas, this behavior is extreme, even for you. Now stop it!"

"Kailynn, you, and the people who support you have been feeding us lies, like this, for five years. All you can do is lie. Now, back off and let me see this *supposed* evidence."

Bedros, his red skin shading towards purple, stepped forward.

"Dumas, you can see the Chaos Dragon, and here is King Nergalis, the only one who could have possibly charmed her."

"Lies, I say!"

"Watch your tongue," Bedros said. "Kailynn is in the midst of kaipoctouyevva."

"So, he not only lies, but he also breaks one of our most sacred laws by coming here when he's not fully in control of himself. There's no telling how violent someone in his condition could become."

"The news he brought justifies his actions," Bedros replied.

"As soon as he arrived," Pierre said, "he let us know of his condition and offered to let others present his evidence in his stead. We voted to allow him to present his own report. So, if you must be rude, be rude to me."

"Why should I be rude to you? You're just the fool who believes him and has supported him all these years."

"He has a memory stone!"

"Which he has taught to lie! Or his wife, Lauri… Lauri… Laurealis, encouraged it. She's a tremendously talented illusionist. It would be child's play for her to change the images on this memory stone to anything she chose."

My anger turned to rage by his slanderous accusations toward my wife. A small rational part of my mind was screaming for me to retain control. But the powerful emotions of Kaipoctouyevva overwhelmed me. I was so outraged that nothing would do, but that I have the satisfaction of a duel to the death, immediately!

I went into the kata I used to control the mana.

Flinging my arms out, a sudden, powerful wind blew everyone, and all the desks, chairs, and papers against the walls, creating a thirty-foot wide void around a point centered between Dumas and myself.

I again raised my hands, and the stone under the cleared space rose ten feet into the air, forming a column of stone shared by only the two of us.

Several of the representatives gathered around Pierre who had hit the wall particularly hard. Others dug themselves out of the piled desks and chairs.

Everything I saw was tainted by a red haze of rage. Scarcely noticing the injuries I'd caused to long-time friends and allies, I had but one goal; to kill this pest who had plagued me for years and now had fallen to insulting my wife. Nothing would stop me from eradicating this putrescent filth who had caused so many innocents to die and had prevented our people from honoring our solemn treaty obligations.

I dropped into a forward fighting stance, ready for either defense or attack. A blazing red semi-circle formed behind me and spread rapidly to my sides, girdling my half of the stone, then expanding to a half-dome covering me, the classic opening move of a magical duel.

To accept, Dumas would have to create a matching half-dome to shield anyone but the two protagonists.

Dumas backed away, his face drained of all blood, "No, no, wait–"

Bedros leapt into the challenger's position that Dumas had just vacated.

"Kailynn, my friend, stop! You can't do this!"

"Did you hear what he said about my wife?"

Bedros took a step forward. "What of it? He's not worth this. He's a worm, and you're playing directly into his hand."

Slowly reason began to seep back in. Seeing my friend facing me, I realized I had lost control. I couldn't fight Dumas, not here, not now. I fought to gain control of the blood rage filling me. It was a difficult battle, fighting to find my center through the red haze filling me. But as my emotions slowly approached my center, I also regained control of the power flowing through me and out of me.

It was only as I calmed that I noticed the lightning flashing between my fingers to the ground and occasionally to my half of the ward.

Another of my brother Champions leapt into the ring, then another and another…the other four elf Champions who had survived from the Fourth Age, plus an apprentice. They, like me, all wore matching vests that flared out well past their shoulders and similar, though different colored tights and turtlenecks. I felt them pushing back against his efforts. Instinctively, I pulled my power back, making it easier to hold off despite the red mist dominating my brain.

"Kailynn, your control is admirable," Cougar, the animist, said. "But you must let go of your rage."

The four approached me slowly, like they were approaching a cornered, feral dragon.

"Our brother, calm down and we'll…"

At that moment, Dumas, who had been backing up in apparent fear, dropped to one knee, pointed his closed fist toward me, and released a bolt of fire. Growing from a ring he wore, not his fist or hand, it was a hot actinic blue, far more powerful than most fire bolts.

With reflexes honed by millennia of fighting, I dropped and rolled instantly, hardening the very air around me into an arcane shield.

Dumas' fire bolt splashed against the duelist's ward, straight through the area where I had stood. Enough of it ricocheted back to have fried me, had my shield not protected me.

Without thought, I was up and throwing a return lightning bolt at Dumas.

Armor covered the bodies of all four of the Champions in an instant. Three of them stepped into my lightning, deflecting it from Dumas.

Seeing my lightning strike my friends, even though they weren't harmed, filled me with deep regret. My rage against Dumas' slandering my wife's name was my only insufficient defense. I hung my head in shame.

Cougar turned to face Dumas and waved one hand. Roots sprang from the stone floor with magical speed and twined around him. In seconds he was covered, except for his eyes and nose.

Now fully in control of my emotions and my power, I released my half of the dueling hemisphere.

When the dust settled, Bedros raised his hand and addressed the assembly, "We will go now to our Elders." With that, all six of us disappeared.

Chapter Four
To Fall from Grace
Kailynn

Well, the Alliance Conference meeting could have gone worse, I suppose. I didn't kill Dumas. I even waited until he attacked me first.

Not that grandmother was going to like that excuse. At least she was giving me a chance to explain myself in private before passing judgment. Since that would be in front of the other twenty-two Family Leaders, including Dumas' father, we had to have everything exactly right.

I hate politics.

Her dendrocasa opened her dinner-plate sized eyes, her visible anger probably an expression of how

Grandmother was feeling. I groaned as I stepped through her mouth and into Grandmother's private audience chamber, the large one.

Damn! This was going to be bad.

Facing Grandmother as Clan Leader, not as my mother's mother, I dropped to my knees to show proper respect, since the choice of this room meant this was a formal meeting.

"So, grandson," she said, "what do you have to say for yourself? Going before the Congress of the Free People's Alliance while in the midst of kaipoctouyevva, was foolish in the extreme, though I partially understand why you did that. The information *was* that important. But to allow Dumas to bait you to the point of attacking him? You know the rule is to prevent just such an event from happening, the law *forbids* elves to appear in public while not in control of themselves."

I was already on my knees, so in my shame I touched my forehead to the floor.

She chuckled. "At least you didn't kill him." A spark of hope, a small one, grew in my heart.

"Although, given the many mistakes Dumas has made, perhaps his father is wishing you had. His younger brother is said to be far more competent."

She stepped down from her chair, which was held in the air by her will. She was the most powerful Air Mage of our people.

"Kailynn, I know your heart has been dark since Alesha died in your arms. I know your ongoing pain about her is part of what this is about."

"Bedros!" I muttered in a flash of anger. I was so out of control! I threw my head back down against the floor immediately.

She tousled my hair with a puff of air as she used to do five millennia ago when I was a child of Alesha's age.

"Dear child, I didn't speak to Bedros about Alesha, nor did he bring her up. You are simply transparent to one who has loved you and been a part of your life as long as I have."

My heart was warmed by the declaration of my grandmother's love. I stirred but remained prone. My iron control was gone.

"Laurealis has been longing for another child, of course. The signs are obvious. Equally obvious is that, while you were and would again be a doting, loving father, your heart is still too hurt. Had you been around Laurealis, she would have continued to be sensitive enough to your moods and your own needs to have seen this.

"Six months can fly by or creep as slowly as a century. For you, it flew. For her, it crept, and her need for a child has brought her to kaipoctouyevva. I know that brings you fresh pain. Still, reality is as it is, not as you or I would have it."

I slumped, half in relief at knowing, not merely hoping, that she understood.

"Child, you may kneel."

I lifted my forehead from the floor and sat back on my heels.

On her summoned cushion of air, she rose to her comfortable old chair. She looked thoughtful.

After a minute or two, she said. "Kailynn, to prevent any further embarrassments to our family, you will be exiled."

My heart stopped. This was severe, more so than I had begun to hope.

"The exile will begin immediately. I fear if you returned home, kaipoctouyevva would prove too powerful, even for your will, my dear grandchild. So, to protect you from yourself, you will honor the agreement the Great Families signed five years ago and fight with the human armies. The fighting will do you some good and your skill will do the humans even more. When things have calmed down, when Laurealis calms down, I will send word that it's time for you to return."

I bowed to the floor again, indicating my desire to speak.

"Child," she said firmly, "I will not change my judgment."

"Grandmother, I would not ask you to, were it not for a responsibility I took on before Laurealis rubbed faces with me."

"Another responsibility? My child, you have been busy."

"Grandmother, I brought a human orphan home with me. He is nearly of an age to be responsible for himself, but his entire extended family was killed. There was no time to look for more of his people to care for him, my news was too urgent. I have a friend coming to impart any tongues he felt the boy would need when I left for my meeting. After the business of informing our people and the Congress of Free Peoples was concluded, I was going to talk to Laurealis about adopting both him and the half-human girl we took in before I left."

"The boy will sleep it off. He will be fine. I will speak to Laurealis of this. She will care for the boy. The adoptions can wait."

"Thank you. Still, Grandmother, I would ask a boon of you."

She frowned, not a good sign.

I took a deep breath. "As you stated, he will sleep off the spell. He knows nothing of my exile, and I care for him a great deal. I would like to say goodbye to him, to greet him when he wakes. I would say my goodbye to Laurealis at that time as well." She closed her eyes and sighed.

"Very well. You will remain away from Laurealis until he wakes. It is still unsafe for you to be anywhere near her."

"Yes, Grandmother. Thank you again, Grandmother."

"My dear child, you are loved," she said, her voice cracking. "Return to me, to us, perhaps a bit wiser."

She caressed me with a loving breeze as her dismissal.

It would be hours before the High Council met to make the judgment of the Great Families. I spent the time in meditation. I needed control, now more than ever.

They would all be there. The mercantile House of Adrastos, Dumas' House, the House of Xyla, which produced mages whose strength was manipulating life itself, and many powerful healers as well. Grandmother represented our own house, Idzi, or shield in the old tongue.

Then there were the humans. How was I to approach them? It was time to shake things up and make the war turn in our favor for a change. The humans had their own mages now, weak by our standards, with only a marginal control of the Chaos. They had greater numbers. We had great control, but we were so few.

"All rise!"

I snapped out of my meditation. I'd been so deep I hadn't realized the Elders had arrived. They filed in, and I and Dumas both prostrated ourselves. I was curious to see what tactics Grandmother would use. The Adrastos had always gone easy on Dumas until he loosed a deadly spell at me without completing the dueling ring. He had broken a major law as well. His crime even worse than mine. I already knew I would be exiled. How Grandmother managed it was her worry.

After all were seated, The Xyla rose. The room quickly grew silent.

Grandmother moved a finger.

"Yes, Idzi?" the Xyla asked.

"I ask to be allowed first sentencing."

The Xyla looked at the Adrastos who nodded his assent. Hmmm. The last to speak had the best position, so I wondered why she had given up that advantage without gaining anything in return.

"Kailynn of the Idzi!" Grandmother said.

I felt myself blanch, like I was a little child caught stealing a cookie.

"What were you thinking? What excuse do you have for your execrable behavior?"

"Grandmother, I returned with proof that the Asmodians are involved in the current war." I paused to allow the inevitable uproar of denials to subside. "And what's more, King Nergalis has charmed the Chaos Dragon. This can only be another End of an Age."

More murmurs ensued. Grandmother continued, "I agree that this is significant. But was it significant enough to ignore our laws? That is what we need to judge now." Ah. So that was the plan.

The Adrastos was on his feet. "I object! He tried to duel with my son without cause! That is the only thing that needs to be judged."

"Without cause?" I screamed in reply. But my voice was gone before I could continue my defense. I realize the air from my lungs was no longer passing through my vocal cords. *Grandmother!* I found I had leapt to my feet in my rage. I looked at my grandmother glaring at me. I nodded curtly at her and slowly went to my knees as the supplicant I was.

"There will be order," The Xyla said. "Adrastos, am I clear?"

After an angry glare, he backed down. "Yes."

Grandmother paused a moment, then turned to me. I felt the air around me behaving normally again. "Tell the High Council what law you broke by presenting your proof and why you were so rash."

I flushed. I hated how she was making me look so out of control. After a moment, I realized that I actually was out of control. I counted to ten and began.

"When I arrived home from my long journey, my wife met me and rubbed my face, pulling me into the initial stages of Kaipoctouyevva. I had already arranged for a meeting to be called in Lergenze a few hours hence. Knowing the importance of that meeting, I stopped Laurealis before she could bring me fully into our passion."

"So, you appeared before a potentially hostile group of humans while not in full control of your emotions?" she asked.

"I was in control!"

"Like you are now?"

"Grandmother...I was in control." My voice dissipated again before I could continue. I waited.

"You have friends, fellow Champions. True?"

"Yes." I almost ground my teeth in my need to explain at the top of my lungs. A small part of my brain was telling me that I was not my normal rational self and to stop to let her lead me if I didn't want her to shut me up again. It took a strenuous act of my will to listen, but I did manage.

"And did these friends offer to help you?"

"Yes."

"Are they trustworthy?"

"Yes, without question!"

She frowned ever so slightly. I worked on my control.

"Then, why didn't you let them be your witnesses. It would have kept you from breaking our law."

"Because Dumas and his allies have been actively working to keep us from fulfilling our commitments as a people. Had I not been the one to present my evidence in person, he could have convinced some of the more foolish of the humans to throw my evidence out…again."

I glared at him. I opened my mouth to damn him for buying off some of the humans to keep his cursed trade going while his customers were being butchered. A breeze touched my lips. I looked back at Grandmother and realized she was right.

"Were you able to present your evidence?"

"I was."

"Were the humans warned of their danger?"

"Yes."

"If Dumas was such a threat to your presentation, why were you able to present it so effectively? Would he not have presented many obstacles?"

"He wasn't there for the presentation."

"He wasn't? Did you not give fair warning?"

"Of course, I did! Grandmother… I ask forgiveness for my outspokenness."

"Granted. So, even though you were in the throes of kaipoctouyevva, you were able to give a strong, logical presentation of your proof of the Asmodians' involvement in this war?"

"Yes, Grandmother."

"Child, why did you not come to the High Council first? Is this not Elven business?"

My rage at past injustices, combined with the effects of the kaipoctouyevva, overwhelmed me.

"House Adrastos has always prevented me from presenting any of the various proofs I've discovered in the past. Those price-gouging merchants don't care if all the humans die if their coffers stay filled! They should be lowering their prices, not raising them! Don't they realize how much they're hurting the human nations? Don't they care? It's wrong, I tell you! It's wrong!"

The Adrastos was on his feet as were ten others of the twenty-two great houses.

"Outrage?" he yelled. "I tell you of the outrage. He is! We've been helping the humans! It isn't our fault if some of them couldn't afford our prices."

All their voices dropped to nothing as if someone had cut a string. I strongly suspected Grandmother of suppressing the sound of their voices so hers could be heard.

"So," Grandmother said calmly, but her voice magically carried throughout the room. "You would have the elves put money ahead of lives? Since when has this been our motivation?"

"Magic items should be dear!" Abrastos replied.

I wanted to shout, but my voice was gone again. Then it occurred to me, she'd let me have my voice during my rant. Oh, yes, Grandmother was in control.

"And food, too?" she asked. "Why? Our food is free for the picking. We have no needs. You have sown extra fields, yet for several years, your house simply picked far more food than you should have. You sold it as well."

"Adrastos, is this true?" the Xyla asked, "We all knew you were harvesting more. We knew you were sending the extra pickings to the humans. My house even increased production to make up for what you were harvesting and shipping. I checked with the dwarves, and they were shipping the food for free. Were you charging for free food?"

"I had costs. I had to hire my family to harvest, pack, and ship the food." He pounded his hands on the rail in front of him. "This isn't the point! Kailynn attacked my son!"

"Agreed," Grandmother said, "that isn't the point at *this* meeting. I move that we meet on the next full moon to discuss this food business further."

"Second that!" I heard from the left. From my prone position, I couldn't tell which house said it, but I knew Grandmother could.

I noticed the Xyla looking around the room as she looked at the heads of each of the Houses for their vote, a nod of the head one way or the other. She then smiled grimly and nodded.

"So be it. At the coming full moon, the High Council will meet again to determine the details of charging the humans for the food and supplies needed for their very survival." She had stressed the word "survival" strongly.

The Adrastos did not look happy, not happy at all. He glared at his son. I was feeling much better. It was always a pleasure to watch Grandmother work. "Kailynn!" Oops.

"So, you had things under control till Dumas of House Adrastos showed up…late, I might add."

"Yes."

"So why couldn't you maintain control after he appeared?"

"He screamed that I was lying. But worse, he insinuated that Laurealis had changed my memory stone to present falsehood. That we would have stooped to altering evidence was, was…more than I could bear."

"Could Laurealis have altered the evidence?"

I took a deep breath. I focused solely upon her, mainly so I would not see Dumas. "Grandmother, I have already said what happened as soon as I arrived. I stopped Laurealis before she could complete the ritual; you can see that I did from the fact that I only have partial control. Yes, my temper is up, but you all know what happens when The Time is resisted. Had I allowed the full ritual to be completed, I would not have left my home for a month for any reason. Also, since the woman has no more control over *beginning* the ritual than the man does with completing it, Laurealis had no choice either. She was fully in the *time* before she even saw me."

"So, you argue that your wife had no control, but you did." The Raptos said, "What are you? The most disciplined man in Anthopoulos? No man stops a woman from rubbing faces. Why should we believe you?"

"Because, as he has stated, his actions are his proof." *Thank you, Grandmother,* I thought.

"But why would he resist?"

"In case you haven't been paying attention, he cares quite a bit for the humans. Perhaps if you and your cabal were less interested in profits and more in people, you would see the obvious!"

Grandmother turned to face The Xyla. "I believe we have reviewed all the pertinent evidence. I would pass judgment now."

"You may," The Xyla replied.

"Kailynn, stand to receive judgment."

I stood and faced the entire High Council, one at a time as protocol demanded, then turned back to Grandmother.

"Kailynn, you have acted with honor and compassion. It appears you have exposed a plot to slur the name of all elves. You faced an impossible situation to the best of your ability. I am proud of you.

"However, you broke several of our laws. You brought shame to our House. For this, you will be exiled for a period of no less than one month and no more than six years. During that time, you will honor our commitment to fight with our allies and begin restoring honor to our House and, *hopefully*," she paused to glare at The Adrastos, "to our people as a whole.

"You will return home, under guard, to gather those things you will need, and to say your goodbyes. Such is my judgment. Does it meet the approval of the High Council?"

I felt a lump settle in my stomach and a strange feeling begin at my forehead and wash through my entire body. Exiled! From now on I would rightfully be known as an exile. It may only be for a month, but I will always be an outcast. Could I ever recover from the shame?

In a fog, I heard The Xyla say, "It is approved."

I felt strong arms guide me out of the room in a daze.

Later, I learned that Dumas was also exiled. His father was in a rage about his humiliating the clan and stripped him of his seed money, a considerable amount his family gives when one of theirs reaches his or her majority. It was a far more severe punishment than mine, as he would be broke, or nearly so. His family measures power in money, not magical skill, as does mine.

Chapter Five
Back in Anthopoulos
Duncan

It was a little disorienting, waking up inside a living, talking, intelligent tree. It wasn't anything I ever imagined I would be doing.

Within an hour of arriving and unpacking in a room Kailynn's wife showed me, a priest friend of his cast a spell on me that would let me understand both his and the common human speech in this part of the world. It quickly put me into a deep sleep.

I awoke to Kailynn's friendly face leaning over mine and smiling. "Ah, I see you're awake. Good. Do you understand what I'm saying?"

"Yes. In fact, you don't have an accent anymore. Is this Shala'lir instead of Gaelaur?"

He chuckled, "Yes, we're speaking in my birth tongue. You may not realize it, but you said my race name correctly; Shala'lir instead of elf. You must be half-dazed with all the new concepts floating through your head right now.

So, it wasn't just waking in a tree that had me disoriented. "Uh, yeah. I do have an awful lot of words in my head right now."

He patted me on the shoulder and laughed. "I should guess so. Absorbing two full languages, plus all their nuances and meanings in a mere three days would be enough to fill anyone's head. Since those three days were spent in sleep, I should imagine you're hungry." Laurealis brought fruit and drink, and travel rations. "We don't have any meat, but this should get you going."

"Thanks. Uh, three days?"

"Yes," Kailynn chuckled. Then he turned serious. "Duncan, I have to be going. I'm going to the war. I waited only to see you awaken. Eat, then come down to the main room. You do remember my wife, Laurealis?"

I nodded. He carefully wrapped his arm around his wife's waist.

"With your family dead, we know you have no place to go. Stay here as long as you need."

Laurealis backed out of his arm, a look of surprise, then anger, washed over her face.

"But I just woke up. You're leaving already?"

He patted me on the shoulder again. "You'll be fine, boy. Laurealis is a fine woman. She'll take good care of you."

He slung his well-worn pack onto his back and left. Laurealis stood still for a moment, then rushed after him. I thought of my mother and knew a squabble was about to happen that I really didn't want to get into.

I realized I was hungry. It really had been three days since I ate. I practically inhaled the fruit and dug jerky out of my pack.

I stepped out the door to see him off when I heard his wife shouting. "You're leaving? You just got back three days ago after six months away, and you haven't spent any time at home! I only saw you for a moment and now you're leaving?"

"I thought Grandmother told you. I found and recorded proof that another End Time is upon us. I presented it to the Congress of the Free Peoples' Alliance. Everything was fine until Dumas made a late appearance. When we became a little...forceful in our disagreement, both Dumas and I were brought before the High Council. We were both exiled."

She blanched and fell to her knees.

"Exiled! Oh, Kai!"

"I'm sorry, my love. Dumas got into my face screaming that all the recent wars were simply human wars, and we hadn't really seen any Asmodians. Then he insulted you, saying you had changed my memory stone. I couldn't take his disrespect and insolence anymore. I challenged him."

She laid her hand on his. "But that's against the law around humans."

"I know. And I now know far better than I did three days ago."

"So, where have you been? I received word from your grandmother that you would be coming home today, and you had mentioned adopting both Raina and Duncan. I am to take care of him as our own."

I was so startled at that statement I almost said something. I'm glad I didn't.

"I'm sorry," he said. "I was partially in The Time and a little out of control. I know that doesn't excuse my actions. I'm just so frustrated from dealing with Dumas. He should have known that the Asmodians used misdirection when they rebelled and left our people fifteen thousand years ago, before they committed the Great Abomination. They have always used some form of deception. This shouldn't be a surprise."

"Then you challenged him and ended up exiled. That still doesn't answer where you were, Kai."

"I know," he sighed. "I was in custody, locked in a room at Grandmothers' place. My meals were delivered. I need to let you know what happened, the whole thing. All right?"

Rising, she only nodded with her arms crossed defiantly across her chest, clearly still judging him.

"I regained control when Bedros and the other Champions confronted me. Then, after I stopped, Dumas used a ring to cast a souped-up fire bolt. The backsplash it made against my shield was bad enough. It would have killed me had he accepted my formal challenge. That ring of his is a genuine step up in power. As it was, I dodged, and it splashed over my head."

"He tried to kill you?" Her concern changed from judgmental to worried.

"And failed. Part of my exile is that I need to go help the Francescans while there's still time. They're all that's left of the human civilizations on this side of the continent. Duncan isn't one of them. He's just a heart-broken young boy, a Gaelaur from the continent's center near the Inland Sea."

"But, but . . . you just got here."

"I know. I have to go. It has been ordered by the Council."

"Stay here for just a while longer as my husband. I'm fertile. I want another baby. It's been so long."

"I know you are. I knew the moment I saw you. That's why I must leave now."

"That's so wrong! You're going to war! You could die! Leave me *something* of yourself before you go!"

"I cannot."

"Why? Don't you love me anymore?"

"Darling, I'll always love you. My heart soars at the very thought of you." He hugged her and she cuddled up next to him. Then she playfully began walking her fingers along his arm to his nose.

"Then why can't you do this one little thing? I promise you'll have a good time."

"I'm not strong enough to remain. And if those invaders are not stopped, there won't be a home for us or our children."

"Strong enough? Honey, you're one of our people's five Champions. You single-handedly defeated tens of thousands during the End Times War of the Fourth Age. Besides," she added huskily, "what's strength got to do with it?" She played with his ear and reached up to kiss him.

He pulled her arm down and held her back. "Darling, the thoughts of losing our child, or worse, *you*, are more than I can bear. How can I father a child and put you at risk of childbirth before I go off to fight? You know how dangerous giving birth is for our people. We lose six percent of our mothers during childbirth. I love you so much. I want you even more. I'm just not strong enough to trust myself around you. I have to leave. I'll be back when there's no danger of pregnancy."

He gently removed her arm from his neck and fled. She stood at the door crying for a long time.

Even though it broke my heart to watch her cry, I decided that announcing my presence right now would be a bad idea, so I returned to my room. I only met her briefly; too briefly to offer any comfort. Besides, now that I understood what Kaipoctouyevva was, I didn't think there was much I could do for her.

Interlude One
Near the End of the Fourth Age

Far past the coniferous forests of the northlands, a grove of sacred mana-rich Talu trees flourished. Looking like luxuriant three-hundred-foot-tall coconut palms, the trees captured high concentrations of the primordial chaos matter from the atmosphere and soil. Substantial portions of the alien being who had collided with the moon so long ago had been vaporized and dispersed throughout the biosphere. This chaos matter, concentrated by the Talu palms, was the form the elves, and their descendants were able to use.

The trees modified the climate near them; the larger the grove, the more powerful and far reaching the effect. With a sufficiently large grove, any climate on Earth could be converted to the sub-tropical climate suitable for the germination of their young.

Upon realizing this, the Asmodians, with great magical effort, melted the ice and planted a grove north into the glaciers, isolating them entirely. The sub-tropical environment surrounding the Talu tree forests melted the edges of the surrounding glacier. The moisture, having nowhere else to go, traveled up, creating a wall of sheer ice cliffs at least a thousand feet high. The glaciers away from this influence quickly shrank to a mere few hundred feet thick, creating ideal watchtowers with minimal effort.

The Asmodians didn't simply leave their new homeland, with its numerous fingers reaching into the ice, unpopulated. With their half-demon blood, they were consummate dimension travelers and they walled off and populated the different fingers that extended into the surrounding glaciers with assorted monsters. One example was the terror lizards that once lived on this planet but died out millions of years ago, though they didn't die out in all the alternate dimensions. Other areas contained interesting things to hunt, like ice trolls or ogres. While hunting these terrors cost them a certain portion of their youth population every year, it taught them battle wisdom and gave them valuable fighting experience.

Another advantage to keeping terrible creatures in their homeland was with them nearby; it was ridiculously easy to deal with humans when the periodic purges and slave gathering times came. If a general proved to be particularly tough, teleporting an eighteen-foot-tall carnivorous terror lizard immediately behind him tended to make him become food for the lizard and his army became far easier to deal with. If that didn't work, a large pack, say a few hundred of smaller terror lizards, would do the job.

In the center of the largest central region stood the Paradise Fortress. Surrounded by tropical gardens of awesome beauty, it was an enormous palace made of black glasslike stone. To those with the eyes to see, it glowed brightly with powerful magic, almost blinding bright. For those of the clerical bent, it exuded monstrous evil of an order of magnitude not seen anywhere else on the planet.

Deep under the palace, safely away from the surface, the king, his wife, and her daughter Sharra were just finishing their wake-up ménage à trois. While superficially resembling their distant elven ancestors, their demonic ancestry showed equally. King Nergalis' color was jet black. He had the fangs of a vampire and a bull's wide horns to match his equally broad shoulders and splendid thighs.

Sharra

My mother, Queen Ereshkigal, was caressing that part of his anatomy that was well south of King Nergalis' waist, as she reportedly had for nearly ten thousand years. I tend to doubt anything said to me by anyone I don't absolutely trust. Trust comes hard in the Court of Nergalis.

My mother bore many children, only a little over half of whom were her husband's. While I was raised in his Court, I wasn't his child. Mother was a spectacularly beautiful half-demoness. A consummate diplomat, she sealed many deals with the other dimensional and demonic courts, by offering to bear children by them. For nine thousand years, she had been popping out at least one or more kids each decade. All but me are dead now, through either sacrifice or rebellion. She hadn't borne another in over a thousand years.

That put her in an extremely dangerous position. We females of the Asmodian Royal Court are expected to be broodmares, the queen most of all.

Mother has the wings and double fangs of her succubus mother as well as her mother's insatiable sexual appetite and need for variety. She doesn't have the other traits of a full succubus; an illusion to allow her to appear as whatever her intended victim is most strongly sexually attracted to and the ability to feed off his spiritual energy, his soul. She has the other traits in part, but I've heard her complain many times that, compared to her mother, she feels like a cripple. She loves the taste of someone's soul, but she just can't get enough to truly sate her hunger. She can only taste enough of their soul to whet her appetite.

She was from the first generation of Asmodians, the children of the third of all the Shala'lir who left that race to form a new one. That generation followed the demon Asmodius and his wife, Tiamora. The first thing they did was ban and kill any children from only elven parents. One parent had to be demonic, that is, from the chaos or demonic dimensions.

So, I, Sharra, her only remaining daughter, am the result of one of her innumerable trysts. In this case it was with another half-breed, an ice demon who had some blood of one of the guards in their underworld. The guards are like monkeys with a scorpion sting on the end of their prehensile tails. My tail is just like theirs, except that unlike theirs, mine is as hairless as most of my body.

Now, not to undersell myself, like my mother, I'm a true beauty, with a delicate triangular face, light blue skin, violet lips, and pure white hair. Other than my tail, I could pass as a true Shala'lir. Since so little of my demonic heritage showed, and that I had chosen to only show a little of my intrinsic magic, all people believed me to be weak. The only magic I allowed to be seen was minor regeneration and some control over the temperature in my immediate environment. I could lower the temperature in my vicinity, but I was far more comfortable on the open glaciers than in the warmer palace.

That was, of course, to stay as far away as possible from my parents. The more powerful their children, the more they wanted them around.

My Stepfather and my King wasn't so bad, I mean he wasn't my biological father, but he raised me as his own. Still, when his guards found me and "escorted" me back to the palace, I knew what was coming. By instinct I immediately made myself as much of a sex kitten as I could, figuring it was the best way to preserve my life, always a precious and an all too easily lost commodity here.

I had been dreading this since that terrible day four months ago.

"My King, I knew when you called me to your bed several months ago, you were preparing me to be a sacrifice. No," I said when he began to protest, "I know that with the recent defeats the Paladain have given us, we need a true vision. As is our custom and tradition only the heart's blood of a woman of the royal line can give that. It is also true that only a woman of the royal line," I glanced at my mother, "can read the heart's blood. You don't need to tell me; I've been trained as a priestess enough to know that today is the most auspicious day of the year for my sacrifice." I began walking my fingers up his thigh and smiling. "Now, while I am eager to help our people—" I had practiced this line a lot and said it perfectly "—on this, what is certainly the last day of my life, I have one favor to ask."

He pulled me to him for a passionate kiss. We all had an act to play out. I'm supposed to be a true sacrifice after all, one who is eager to give her life for her people's greater good.

He was to feel genuine grief about killing his daughter by another man from an entirely different dimension; such hypocritical lives we royal's lead.

When I was lying on his arm while his other hand was busy playing with my body, he asked, "What favor do you seek, my love?"

"Please don't give me to Tiamora. I know she's the embodiment of Chaos, and Asmodius' wife. She needs to be fed souls so we can make this planet a True Source of Chaos for our demonic side. But I also know the real reason for my soul to be fed to her is so she will consume it. That way, if I'm angry at my *willing* and sacrificial death, I won't become a malevolent ghost. It doesn't make sense, as I'm going in with both eyes wide open."

I turned in his embrace to look into his eyes.

"Daddy, I love you. I actually want to become a ghost, a ghost in love with you." It was my mother I was angry with, not him. "You can make my death ceremony quick and clean or as gory as you want. I really don't care which. I don't feel much pain, and with my simple regeneration, I've participated regularly in some pretty gory things over the last five hundred years. Done right, it's a real high. To the slaves who worship us, my primary aspect is submission, so the gore is fine."

While he was still digesting my request, I began crying lightly and moved down to his feet, looking him in the eyes with my most submissive gaze, one that drove most men insane with desire. Kissing his feet, I asked, "Please, please, don't feed me to Tiamora."

The Queen, my hated Mother finally spoke, "Absolutely not! I won't risk it! We cannot risk having a malevolent ghost to deal with! Not one already inside the castle's primary defenses! I will feed you to Tiamora myself!"

I favored Mother with a truly malevolent smile, "As you did my sisters?"

I settled myself in my stepfather's open arms before speaking like a little innocent girl with the wide-open eyes, "I'm pregnant with your child."

The Queen blanched and said very quietly in abject terror, "No!"

"What?" the King asked. He cast a spell upon me, then smiled, "My Dear, yes, you truly are pregnant."

I stung my mother with blinding speed as soon as her shocked expression showed that she'd understood his pronouncement.

Despite my deadly toxin, Mother was only slowed, not beaten. She always had defensive spells protecting her and one had obviously operated now to neutralize enough of my poison to save her life…temporarily. Preparations like that were why she had survived so many attempts upon her life.

I cast ice bolts at each of her wrists, badly bruising or breaking them and destroying what focus the witch had left. I then touched those joints and ice grew from my fingertips, freezing Mother's wrists in place. I quickly repeated the actions on her elbows, shoulders, hips, knees, and ankles, trying to freeze them in awkward positions so they would break.

Several of her bones audibly broke as more ice bolts hit them. The pain filling her eyes brought joy to my heart.

Ereshkigal protested weakly, "But you weren't that strong."

"Yes, I was. I always have been, but I hid my strength."

I looked around at the lit-up skulls mounted at various heights around the room, the empty craniums of my many deceased siblings giving the room a soft, subdued light. My mother's eyes followed my gaze.

I pointed to a snake-like skull. "Ninkarrak taught me. The strongest of us, she was your first sacrifice. I quickly realized that as important as the sacrifices are, they are a part of our duty, as fighting and dying in battle is part of my brothers' duty. But, Mother, you used, no, you abused them to weaken our family so no threats to you survived. Your duty was to bear and raise a powerful and numerous family; one loyal enough to take on all threats. Instead, you weakened us. Your treacherous actions meant that I have lost all my sisters with no truly meaningful prophecies! Now, mother, since we both agree that a sacrifice is required today and I'm pregnant and you're not, I very much hope that your sacrifice will give me a meaningful prophecy to give us direction again."

"You little hussy, I'll…"

King Nergalis grabbed a robe and as he put it on, he casually waved his hand and her voice went silent, despite her furious screams and obvious rage. He cast another spell and her body floated to about waist height. We began our descent into the palace bowels.

I found my robe and put it on. Mine was tailored to fit my tail.

We had been walking for a quarter hour or so when I realized something. I touched Daddy's hand to stop him.

We were still private except for the ever present and muted guards; muted, as in their tongues had been removed. They spoke fewer of our secrets that way.

I stopped him because I wanted to make a point to Mother. He was now my husband. By default, the heir within me made me his wife and his queen. I held the new life in my belly and knew that though we would have a formal ceremony, from this point onward, the man who had raised me would be my husband. I would be his Queen with all the power I could accumulate under his huge umbrella. My mother no longer had any royal standing.

I couldn't lose track of why I stopped him. I couldn't appear weak or unfocused. I'd seen him casually kill someone because they weren't focused when they reported something to him. He called it the "Law of Unintended Consequences".

"My Husband, would you release the silence spell? She needs to hear this."

"She can be rather loud," he warned.

He let my new name for him slide, meaning he had already realized what I had just figured out.

Mother's screams masked all conversation. I tried hitting her. When that didn't work, I broke a chair, so I had a makeshift cudgel and stood over her. I smiled wickedly, knowing that pinned as she was by the ice, even my powerful mother couldn't defend herself from me. Even with broken bones and trapped joints, I still didn't trust her. Her reputation was that she'd broken out of worse fixes than this. I couldn't imagine how, but I was her youngest child and had missed a lot of now unspoken history. Not only had she broken out of worse situations, but those also who had perpetrated those rebellions discovered just how slow and excruciating death over extended periods of time could be. When it came to inventive ways to torture people, Mother was a master.

Mother Dear looked at the club I held and quieted.

I lowered my makeshift cudgel. "Mother, you need to accept that I will soon be holding your beating heart while your heart-blood drains within the sacred Bowl of Prophecy.

I need your thoughts to focus on the prophecy, not on the unavoidable fact that you will soon die."

All the centuries my rage had built, at last I was finding release, living out a centuries old plan. Unfortunately, my plan hadn't really gone far beyond getting Mother into this position. I was just now realizing how deadly stopping my plans at this point might prove.

Still, my entire body was energized with adrenalin as the constant flexing and motion of my tail to the deadly threat in my voice made clear to me. I had to regain focus, though things had fallen into place so perfectly. I'd have time to organize my thoughts on the way to the upcoming ceremony.

Now that I had Mother's full attention, I moved around and knelt by her head and continued in a low, hate-filled voice. "Listen well, mother! If you choose to focus upon anything else and botch this prophecy, forcing me to wait until the girl in my womb is grown before I have the proper sacrifice, I will offer your soul to Tiamora as you offered all my innocent sister's souls to that necessary evil."

She just glared at me.

"Oh, Mother!" I chuckled, "Your anger pleases me! You know your soul will please and feed Tiamora far more than thousands of mere human souls."

I couldn't help myself. I slapped her as hard as I could.

"Think clearly upon what I say. Your people need this prophecy. The humans are holding out too long and we've taken losses from them. It is unheard of that miserable little humans could kill us! They killed Asmodians, not some filthy mercenary army! And what did you do?"

I slapped her again for her silence to my demand.

"Tell me, what did you do? You brought in your sole remaining daughter to kill her! That's what you did! Now that the table is turned, how does it feel? The Paladain are gone. We haven't received our army's reports yet, and all you want to do is kill your only remaining child! Shame on you! You should have been making more children, not killing us!"

Various priests in long ornate blood-red robes, had joined us, as did the more powerful nobles, office holders all. Their robes were blood-red because they were for blood ceremonies. The more important the ceremony. The more blood was required. The robes were gold embroidered. The more important the noble, the more gold and ornate the robe. But the base color was always the color of new blood.

I somehow managed to not show my shock at seeing them. I don't know how they knew something was happening; perhaps my father sent them a message somehow. Regardless, here they were.

"Your Grace, Your Holiness," I said to the Chamberlain, and to the High Priest as I inclined my head slightly. I no longer had to prostrate myself, I was their superior. But any weaknesses, perceived or real, were quite dangerous. My change in status had just occurred, but slips in protocol, no matter how recent, had often been the basis for executions, or accidental deaths, or lesser forms of revenge. For this ceremony, all protocols must be followed.

Ereshkigal, who had lived through two purges of the despised yet feared humans, was now resigned to fueling the prophecy that her people so desperately needed. She made no further protest. She was guided by four priests maintaining a light guiding grip on each of the limbs of her levitated body. They made their way through a large part of the palace so all would know of the change in the royal family.

Changes in status from assassination were not an uncommon manner of succession in any of the Asmodian families, from the lowest crafter to the royal family.

They simply had never occurred in the highest royal family, though that wasn't due to not being legal. It was simply that neither member of the royal family had ever slipped enough to allow anyone or any group to overpower them. Some of their children had fallen, but neither of them ever had… 'till now.

I couldn't help it. I giggled with delight. Between my long-time dream of replacing my mother, and the power I had gained; I couldn't help myself. But I needed to take care not to show weakness.

The large crowd gathered behind us while we traveled from the morning hours to early afternoon. New nobles or priests bowed deeply to Nergalis, as was proper, and slightly less deeply to me, as was also proper. At last, we made it to the Temple of Tiamora where my husband guided my mother to the ceremonial table, complete with drains for the bloodbath she would soon provide.

I tried hard not to smile at the thought of her blood filling the drains. My twitching tail was telegraphing my joy. I successfully brought my rebellious appendage under control.

Nergalis waved his hand and dissipated his levitation spell slowly, lowering her gently to the table. Perhaps a small kindness against the brutality that was to come.

He again waved his hand at the mass of undulating and occasionally heaving chaos matter. A bit of it, with lots of tentacles and eyes, jumped out onto Ereshkigal's chest. It transformed a tentacle into a heavy cleaver and sliced her chest open with a single stroke. He deftly removed her beating heart.

Arterial blood shot all over me, as I was the closest, holding my hands out to receive her still beating heart into my eager little hands. I made no effort to avoid the blood. In fact, I moved into the path of more of it to be covered in it. It was the only gift my mother had ever given me that I actually wanted.

When her heart was placed in my hands, I almost passed out from the exhilaration of holding her still beating heart as I placed it into the Bowl of Prophecy. I held my hands on her heart so I could savor every beat until they stopped. I was surprised when they didn't stop quickly.

I looked up at Nergalis. "Her heart is still beating. Is that normal?"

"The Bowl of Prophecy will keep it beating until after you've drunk every last drop of her heart blood during the ceremony."

"Ahh." I said, understanding. I left my hands as they were. I had worked too hard, sacrificed too much to let my pleasure end quickly. I watched the drama of the demon forming in front of me while savoring the beat continuing between my hands.

The demi-demon, formed from the primordial chaos matter of Tiamora, hopped into the blood-filled void in her chest and transformed into a heart. It connected all the severed arteries and veins to itself and absorbed all the blood filling her lungs without closing the massive wound in her chest. Her lungs inhaled again, weakly, but the former Queen was alive.

"Mother, I wanted you to still be living for the prophecy to know your doom. Let's see if you focused properly. For your soul's sake, I do hope so."

Her heart blood filled the bowl a little more with every beat. After a minute, the senior priest gently moved my hands aside and poured a powder on the blood. It made the steaming fluid flash with a dark violet light, turn dark, and begin moving like the seething mass of Tiamora.

"Now drink it," the High Priest said. "Drink all of it. It will be bitter, but you must finish it to the last dregs for there to be a prophecy."

I upended that bowl and drank all of the vile liquid, slowly so as to not spill a single precious drop. Nothing happened for several minutes as everyone looked on with unquenchable curiosity, the same curiosity they used to pay mother when she was the one called to prophecy.

Suddenly I collapsed.

After a minute or two of convulsions, from what I was later told, I raised up on one arm and said,

> *A queen before,*
> *Her vengeance abated,*
> *A queen again,*
> *Her vengeance now sated.*

> *Oppressor's Bane,*
> *Her blood did reveal*
> *When for the second time His bite she did feel.*

> *The Dragon's queen*
> *Bids her children to rise And by thus doing*
> *Brings about their demise.*

When I regained consciousness, I asked what I had prophesied. The priest who recorded it read it back to me.

As confused as everyone else, I said, "Mother, I warned you to focus. Now know the foolishness of your treachery!"

"But I did focus. It is a true prophecy!"

"Then tell me its meaning! The dragons don't have queens! The King's power was absolute, and he tolerated no challenges to his authority! And that was *before* you had us kill them all. According to *you*, all the dragons were killed. What's more, Oppressor's Bane was a Paladain weapon. We destroyed the Paladain, every one of them, from what your lying generals said. Two of my sisters were sacrificed to warn us of their danger. You heeded their warnings. Yes, they defeated us one last time, that's why you were going to sacrifice me. But you were to tell us something like the Paladain are no more, or something. Or where the last remnants are hiding! So, no more excuses! Tell me what it means! Tell me now!"

"I can't!"

"Then your soul is as forfeit as your flesh! I'm going to enjoy this."

I remembered the words my mother said over each of my sister's as she released the tightly bound demoness' power to eat someone's soul.

"Tiamora, as the Queen of the royal blood of Asmodia, I give you Ereshkigal's soul! Let us all witness you devour her very essence!"

A pair of eyes opened on her left leg, right breast, her right hand to the elbow, and of course, her heart. They all changed into various demonic forms with odd limbs to move them about. The leg was the largest by far and it grabbed the hand and quickly absorbed it while holding the heart and breast immobile. It looked at Nergalis as if asking him something. He shrugged affirmatively, and it absorbed the two smaller demons trapped within its multitude of tentacles. As their mass was absorbed into its own it grew by a corresponding amount.

Then it pulled something wispy out of Ereshkigal's right foot, gently pulling as if it were the finest of fragile threads. Ereshkigal screamed and tried to move, but I quickly renewed what ice had melted during our long journey here to lock her remaining limbs in place. The newly formed demon continued spooling the spider web-like ethereal substance out of its victim as quickly as it could.

Now that it had stripped the soul from Ereshkigal's entire right leg to the hip, that leg was numb and useless. It now moved to the left leg's stump that was kicking it with enough force to nearly dislodge its collection of her soul. Meanwhile I took Nergalis' hand as we savored the agony of her death, though the demon's body blocked a lot of it.

"Slow down," I said, "stretch out her death. Let us fully enjoy it for as long as possible."

My mother's shocked look when I said those words was sheer joy for me.

I said to my new husband, "Revenge is so much better when served up cold, isn't it?"

Smiling, he replied, "Oh, yes, much more enjoyable, particularly when you aren't the one being served up." At that comment, I was shocked by what I saw. She somehow managed to heal her broken bones and severed limbs.

"She'll be using a lot of mana, but it is serving the purpose and she stopped the arterial bleeding with those flash burns she cast upon herself. Our new demon is having trouble pulling her soul out of her chest. Look how she fights him. I do believe she is melting your ice, dear." He wrapped his arm around me, "Shall we let her continue?"

I stopped my happy snuggling to cast more ice bolts, looking worriedly at Nergalis before I did so. He shook his head "no" and continued. "She might give him a real fight for his freedom. They both need her soul; her to live, him to become a free-willed demon. I wonder, which one will win?"

"Is that a bet? If she wins, she'll be a true threat to us. We can't risk that, can we?"

"Oh, she might be, she might be. However, you won by our ancient laws, so you will simply have to ensure that you remain fertile. I like how you're beginning, but Ereshkigal was seductive at one time as well. She allowed herself to not produce an heir for a millennium, not by me nor anyone else." His voice became steel, "See that you don't repeat her error. I don't care who the father is as much as I care that you allow truly little time to pass by between pregnancies."

Fire flashed over her body once, twice, thrice, but weaker. Ereshkigal was free and she began strangling the demon with her left hand while trying to pull her essence free with her handless right arm. It was an exercise in futility.

"Look! Daddy, I mean, my husband, she's broken partially free, and the demon is spinning faster, trying to strip her soul from her before she kills it. It looks like its suffering for not having given itself a fighting form."

"Yes, it gave itself a form more suitable for the first task at hand; dominating and absorbing the other demi-demons, not realizing my dear former wife's tenacity. Of course, without her right hand, she may be larger than the demon, but her form is even worse for fighting than his is. Oh, this is good, incredibly good. Eresh, dear, a slight bit of help, perhaps a hand?"

She glanced at her husband of ten thousand years, her doubt of his intentions showing even through the pain she was enduring. With her momentary distraction, the demon successfully began spinning her soul's essence out of the stump of her right arm.

I had a grand idea. "Dear, why don't you give her a hand and free her right arm, while I sting her again? I'd really like to sting her again. Please?"

The demon glanced back at them and spun faster, causing the ephemeral material to catch around her shoulder so the smooth spinning was interrupted. Ereshkigal tried fighting harder, but her personal mana had been leaking out through her hastily constructed heart and it was clear that her struggles were weakening.

Nergalis replied, "Yes, I like that. I'm also going to give her some mana. Ready?"

"Yes."

"Now!"

We struck simultaneously, my terribly potent nerve poison and sting in Mother's exposed belly brought her fresh agony and temporary immobility, while Nergalis' infusion of mana, the freeing of her arm and creation of a magical hand gave her a fighting chance. The hand was better crafted than the heart was, so it leaked far less mana. He also repaired her heart spell so that it was more efficient as well. Another aspect of freeing her arm was unkinking her soul in the clutches of the demon so it was able to properly reel in her soul as it fought for its freedom. She fought for her life and her very soul.

We looked upon our work and smiled.

81

Chapter Six
School - What a Way to Begin

Ragina

I adjusted myself on the comfortable bench as the illusion filled my mind. The world faded away and I saw buildings like I'd never seen before. They were hundreds of feet high, and so little sky could be seen between their tops that I felt like I was in the Little Fox River valley, except that it was buildings instead of stone on either side of me. Some of the buildings were made of huge sheets of glass, and somehow the glass buildings were still standing. I couldn't see any bubbles or distortions in the glass at all.

It was weird. I couldn't believe how much metal had been used in some of the buildings. Others were made of brick, which at least seemed normal.

There were lots of strangely dressed humans, but no other races. One thing about these humans; they had a fold in their eyes, just like Papa's. These were the first humans I had ever seen with that slant eye that all the elves had. Their skin was strangely pale, too; every single one had black hair. Not at all like my home village where everyone but Papa and I had sun-reddened coppery skin and all manner of hair color.

There was one large sign among the many which had a cute guy dressed in a leather coat, though the rest of his clothes were strange: blue pants and the stupidest looking shoes I'd ever seen. But what caught my eye was that it looked like he was smoking something. It wasn't a pipe like Papa smoked or a cigar like other men in our village smoked, but it was tiny and white. The words were written in a strange script that I couldn't read, but the guy was quite attractive.

The wagons, that's not what they were, but I don't know what else to call them, were the most fascinating things. They didn't need horses, mules, or oxen to pull them; they weren't pulled by anything. And fast? Sometimes they stopped when lights on the poles or hanging overhead at every crossroad turned red, and other times they would go. I mean GO. They were at least as fast as I could throw a stone, maybe faster.

A bay, or ocean, was visible on one side, with metal ships and even metal boats. How metal ships could float was beyond me, but there they were.

There was a circular thing up high that I swear must have been a clock. It even had markings in the right places for a clock. If it were a clock, it was not only bigger than the biggest clock I could have imagined, but it indicated it was 8:14.

Then I noticed the sky up beyond the clock, and the buildings. The rings around the world were gone! Instead, there was one really huge white ball or something. It was nowhere as bright as the sun over on the other side of the sky, but it was much bigger.

Then, something black, but glowing brilliantly white and with a long tail, hit it.

By the Lady! It was breaking up, and part of it was falling right at me!

There were loud noises like crows cawing, sort of, but really loud. When the noise began, all the people were getting out of their painted metal wagons and running into the buildings.

Lots of burning rocks were falling around and hitting hard, too. A big one, almost as big as one of the strange wagons, hit a wagon that a mother was just getting out of with her little toddler. She was thrown straight into one of the posts and I looked away, because she was obviously killed. Her little boy was thrown right to my feet. He began gulping air like he was about to scream. I tried to pick him up, but my arms just passed through him. I could see my arms inside his body, but I couldn't pick him up.

Then I guess about ten seconds after he landed, he began screaming. I'm an only child. I didn't know little kids could scream like that.

I gave up trying to pick him up because another louder sound than the poor little kid was roaring overhead. The few people left on the streets stopped to look and point. It was a huge rock, maybe a small mountain. As it got closer, I realized it was bigger than almost any mountain. It was a group of huge black rocks traveling bunched together like a herd of boulders.

I heard them hit on the other side of the buildings in the water. Despite being in the water, the ground shook hard enough that all that perfect glass broke and began falling. I saw the glass hit people. It was happening everywhere, so I couldn't look away. I was surrounded by the horror. The wind began blowing toward where the rocks had fallen.

A huge flash of light came from where the boulder herd hit, and everything began blowing away from there. Everything was flying and burning: people, weird wagons, even parts of the buildings began breaking up. Strangely, I wasn't affected, though a big shard of black glass flew out of my chest and belly. I hadn't seen it coming; it hit me from behind.

I was getting really scared. Then I felt a hand, a real hand, on my elbow and another on my shoulder, "Raina, back up."

I was so lost in the horror of what I was seeing that the words didn't make sense. I recognized the words, but I couldn't put them together.

"Raina, back up!"

"Aaaiiiyyyyyeeeeee!" I fell to my knees as I saw a huge building melting and blowing toward me.

Suddenly the whole city vanished. I blinked because I could still see it in my mind. I couldn't believe how real that illusion had been. The others had been nothing like that.

Today's instructor was a young elf who was talking, but the words wouldn't come together into thoughts. I had been looking at regular people. One of them was even my milk chocolate color, something I'd never seen before. My instructor was red with green hair. All elves are brightly colored like that.

Some of the words began linking up, something about the "End of the First Age of Man," and thirty-five thousand years ago a comet destroyed the single moon they had at the time. But all I could see was the little boy I couldn't help, and how, when he finally began crying, I wanted to pick him up and hold him.

I began to cry for him, for all those people. What I saw was just too horrible, like when my family, my kingdom and everything I knew had been destroyed five years ago by armies, swords, and fire. That seemed kind, in comparison.

"Raina?"

I felt soft hands holding mine.

"Raina, dear, can you hear me?"

I stopped crying for the little boy and the destroyed city when I realized the lady who had been looking after me for the last six months was talking to me. My friends and I had broken out of the horrible orphanage, and she'd found homes for all the human kids, and made her home mine, since I was half-elf.

I sat up to pay proper attention to her. Being proper is particularly important to elves. Except when it isn't. It's very confusing. We may not understand why they have certain rules, but we'd better learn them if we want to get along with them.

What's worse than their rules; is when they can see how you feel by just looking at your aura. Sometimes that's bad, because the cloudier your aura, the more it means you're hiding something. I have a lot to hide. Other times, like now, the cloudy aura is a help. Laurealis knew why I was upset, so she was more compassionate than normal, which is pretty darned compassionate. But I hate wearing a sign that I can't hide, showing what emotions I'm feeling and what my basic personality is like. The very proper elves try to ignore an aura, which may be one of the things that makes them so proper. But when someone who is acting like your mother is concerned about you, basic courtesy goes out the window. As for the others, I know they aren't supposed to look, but I've caught too many guys sneaking peeks at pretty girls. So why would I believe that I'm not being looked at in an even more intimate way?

It's not fair.

Despite being uncomfortable because they could look at me in a way more intimately than guys ever could, at least elves don't pick on me because of my color, or when I slip up. They seem to dote on kids. I guess that's because they have so few of them.

"Uh, sorry," I said. "That lesson today was nothing like the other educational illusions. It was so real, so horrible. I just can't get it out of my head."

"I came as soon as I felt your terror." She was breathing hard; she must have run a long way. I know she can feel people's emotions, but I didn't realize it worked at such a distance. She must have been miles away.

I heard the instructor approaching us. Anger flashed across Laurealis' face. I saw it without having to see her aura.

"Bertram!" she shouted.

He turned to face her, his face as blank and emotionless as his speech.

"Did you show her one of the End of an Age illusions?"

"Perhaps," he said, as if it wasn't one of the most horrifying things he could have shown me.

Then her voice went deadly calm, which means the same thing with elves as it does with humans. "Was it by any chance the End of the First Age of Man? The destruction of Hong Kong?"

"All people should know their history. I talked to the other instructors, and they all said that despite being far behind in all areas of study, she was bright and well able to handle a lot of information."

"So, you just took it upon yourself to show her the most terrifying time in the history of the world?"

"It is merely history. Things that happened in the past cannot harm us; they can only instruct us to not make the same errors. The humans of that time, while they were making plenty of poor choices, died not from any fault of their own."

"And it just slipped your mind that she is a war orphan and has seen horrible sights, including the murder of her own mother." Laurealis held her hand over her mouth and turned to me. That's the last thing I saw for a while, my mind whirled into darkness.

Later, when I thought back, she may have been shouting, "No! Raina, I'm sorry." But I'm not sure.

The world faded out again, not from some magical working. My mind jumped back to that scene from so long ago that was at least as horrible as the scene I had just witnessed. It was cold, not like this place of trees and flowers that doesn't get cold even when the entire world around it is icy.

The Skarg were overrunning the countryside. Papa had been killed just two days earlier in a desperate fight with the rest of the remaining men. They were trying to give us women and children time to get further away, but we still had one more river to cross.

On the other bank were men with armor and crossbows and things coming our way. We were going to be rescued!

I saw the boats waiting on our shore just a hundred feet away, but the Skarg were right behind us. Mama and I were running across the last meadow with the last fifteen people from our village. All the men and wounded were already dead, either from fighting to protect us, or because they just couldn't run fast enough. We didn't want to leave anyone. The last few days we just ran, and those who couldn't run had fallen behind. I hadn't stopped moving or rested in two days.

I tripped in a rabbit hole and fell. Mama heard me scream and turned back to help. I'll see that damned Skarg, with its lizard-like legs, tail, and back, and horrible, cruel face till the day I die. Mama charged it with her bare hands while I freed myself. I started to run, but I couldn't as I watched that horrible, wicked sword swing ever so slowly. I don't understand how that could be.

It took an eternity for the sword to go all the way through Mama's neck. Her body kept running forward and her head flew off and rolled to my feet. The blood spurted straight up before her body hit the ground.

I looked at Mama's face, her beautiful face, and I couldn't move. I thought I saw her eyes recognize me before they went blank.

Hands grabbed my arms and dragged me the last few feet to the boat. I saw the horribly evil Skarg falling backward, looking like a pincushion with all the crossbow bolts in him. Behind him, the field was blanketed with hundreds more.

I was then in the boat leaving the meadow. All I could see was the image of Mama's head on the ground between my feet, her beautiful face, and her loving eyes...those wonderful eyes were always so joyful and loving, and now so empty.

I came awake curled up with my head lying in Laurealis' lap while her fingers gently combed my hair. My eyes were burning, and my throat was raw, so I guess I was crying. Strange how, when she dresses herself in nothing but illusion, you can see her outlandish outfits. But, when you touch her, you feel her warm, soft skin. It felt good, and I rubbed my face against it as I left the memory of Mama behind.

I was pulled out of my remembrance by her gently lifting me to be hugged, then held far enough away for her to look at me.

"Raina, Raina, I'm so sorry," Laurealis whispered. "I was stupid, bringing up that subject. I'm so sorry!"

She hugged me to her loving bosom while aiming a look so filled with anger and loathing at Bertram that he may have burst into flames. I was still having trouble sorting out the horrible scene of the past and reliving Mama's death, but I knew she was on my side.

Still upset, I began noticing the tiniest details while Laurealis continued venting at Bertram. We were lying on a comfortable bench growing from large branches reaching close to the ground. There were living chairs and a table. The outer bark was smooth and light brown, except where it had peeled off, revealing the smoother cinnamon-colored bark beneath. The flooring was the flaked off bark, the walls and roof were the dense leaf canopy of foot-long dark green leaves. It was still hard to believe that a place this peaceful and secluded could be the source of such horrible scenes, illusions or not. I began seeing the little boy's face again as he gulped in air in absolute terror.

When Laurealis seemed to be finished letting Bertram have it, she sat me up straight, took my hand, led me out of the leafy room and we left the Tree of Learning. When we got far enough away, I could see the huge trunk and higher rooms, the ones you had to climb to get to. The shape of the tree reminded me of the low, wide, evergreen oaks of the Firenzian coast. The elf children could scramble up the gently sloping limbs like they were highways, though I preferred the ground level branches. It wasn't really that hard to climb them myself.

I liked the way they taught here. Until today, it had been math and languages, or other things that weren't terrifying. They were hard because I wasn't used to them, though they didn't scare me. They'd used little illusions to help me understand math questions or science concepts.

"Laurealis?"

"Yes, Dear."

"Would it be all right if I did something else this afternoon, and maybe tomorrow? That End of the First Age thing, it, well…I don't know if I really want to come back here right away."

"Oh, yes, of course. But first we have to talk. Master Bertram told me he gave you a note explaining what he was going to do today. Where is that note he gave you?"

Oh, right. "Uh, I think I lost it."

"Raina, had you shown me that note, I would have been here with you today. We would have let you be educated on this matter in another way. You are the size and shape of a small adult woman, and people naturally treat you that way. Even though your education was interrupted for years, we must act responsibly."

I hung my head knowing the truth in her words.

"I can taste how distraught you are still, and I was thinking…you've been good about coming to school and studying hard for the last six months, so would you like to go to Lergenze and go shopping?"

I grabbed her arm, instantly excited. "Lergenze? Just the second biggest market in Merica? Would I ever!"

Relief flooded through me when she hadn't mentioned Koranidor, the actual biggest market in our part of the world. Francesca was big, but that was just in our corner of this continent. Koranidor was a true world market. It was spectacular and beautiful. It was also where I spent five long years as a whore and slave in that *orphanage*. I hoped to never see those perfect streets and perfect buildings again. Everything perfect, including perfect law enforcement to keep me a slave for as long as I lived.

"You sure?" she asked, though her brilliant smile proved she was just teasing.

I hugged her, "Hmm, going shopping at the world's biggest fair, or facing more lessons from some stupid boring instructors who like seeing people killed? Oh, this is so hard. Yes! Today?"

"Don't you think we should pack? I still have to tell Duncan, and we have lots of work to do to be able to stay away for as long as I'd like. I want to be gone for at least a month, maybe two. I know you're having problems adjusting here, and I'm missing my Kai' so much… he's just gone, and I need him badly."

The loss in her voice was terrible to hear.

"I just know he'll be at war for a long time, and I'll have to learn to accept it. I'm hoping that maybe a shopping vacation will help with that. What do you think?"

I bobbed my head up and down as fast as I could while saying in my most sober voice, "Oh, I agree. Shopping will definitely help. I know it'll take my mind off studying."

"Well, you run along and start packing. I have to find Duncan."

"I wish you didn't have to bring him. He's so…down. I know his family just died, so he can't help it. But I guess it'll do him some good, too."

I ran back to Laurealis' dendrocasa, which was amazing. I mean, I grew up in the Mist Forest with its twenty-foot-wide trees, and we lived in a home carved out of one. It was just a tree though, a big tree, but still just a tree.

Tigro…something or other, it went on for four or five more syllables. Naming the tree *Ti'*, for short, was so much easier. His gender was clear, others were female. He was smart, too. Losing a game of Knights and Mages to a tree would be embarrassing but losing to Ti would be a challenge and an honor. He's like a person, even though he has branches and twigs instead of hands. I love how he grows flowers out of his bark at his windows and his other decorative places. He changes them most every day, just to be fresh. He grew a room for me up his trunk. It took him about a month and a half before it was big enough to move a bed inside. It's still growing, but it's all mine.

The elves…well, they do things differently. They don't seem to mind how long it takes to get something done. That's because they live so long, I guess. But since they do take so long to do things, they do them really well. They have magic, lots of it. They do non-magical things well, too, like mind games and satire. It takes some getting used to, but their hearts are good. I'd bet even that boring instructor has a good heart, just not much sense about what's terrifying. He looked really young, although for an elf, centuries-old is still young. Laurealis was right; if I hadn't lost that note, the day would have been different.

I found Duncan in a forest with hickory, oaks, and chestnuts. There were bearing fruit trees growing in the brighter areas, so I picked an apple and watched Duncan for a minute or two as he walked slowly by a small creek in front of a clump of rhododendrons. Their large, dark leaves highlighted him perfectly. Good-sized moss-covered boulders were all over the area, peeking up through the shield ferns, and beauty berries, and ginger. I used to collect that for Mama. I loved how it's white-striated, almost black-green, heart-shaped leaves were barely able to cover one's toes with their cool comfort. They were competing in the natural way, like Mama taught me, with trillium, shade stretched mint, and a dark green evergreen plant that bloomed from winter to late spring. That's where the rhododendrons, bay, ferns, and blueberries didn't completely shade out their smaller cousins. I really love the way the elves worked herbs and food crops into the natural environment without making it look fake.

Duncan was completely lost in his bagpipes, a strange instrument that his people use, playing a soulful melody that reminded me of wind and waves. I sat on one of the mossy boulders on the other side of a clump of rhododendron, out of sight, but well within hearing range of a beautiful haunting song that reflected my own mood. Sliding my shoes off and slipping them under me, I let my toes play with the moss while lying back to absorb his music. I'd tell him about our shopping trip soon, but this soothing melancholy music was just what I needed to hear.

As I learned the tune, I hummed along with it while considering the events of the past few days since Kailynn, Laurealis' husband, had brought Duncan to stay with us. Kailynn is tall, well over six and a half feet, but Duncan is a full head taller.

Kailynn is a light sage-green with plumbago blue hair, like a clear summer day in the mountains. His eyes are so vividly lavender that you're drawn to notice them, especially if he locks that look of command on you if you resist doing something he feels you should do. He's a Shala'lir so his ears are about four inches long and stick out well past his long flowing hair.

Laurealis looks good with him, with her lilac skin and shocking pink hair that hangs almost to the ground, if she hasn't done it up in some extravagant arrangement. Her deep green eyes and lilac ears just peeking through, with illusionary clothes that go perfectly with her colors... or theirs, if he's with her. She's a wonderful artist, sculptor, singer, and dancer.

Duncan is pure human, from his sandy blond hair hanging loose to mid-back, to his peach fuzz beard and his icy blue eyes. Where Kailynn is deep-chested and well-built, Duncan is built more like a mountain, with a barrel-like chest and a neck that looks like a ham stuck on top. He's so much bigger and meatier that he makes Kailynn, well anyone I guess, look small by comparison.

I'd known Kailynn for a week. He and Laurealis, with their friend Astoria, found me, after I'd broken a lot of us orphans out of that terrible place. With no place to go, he offered to take me in. Then, a week later, he came home all agitated, then left for a scouting mission.

After six months, he returned home for mere minutes, then didn't come back till three days later. While he was there, the tension around him was so strong it felt like there was another person in there with him. I heard he and Laurealis loudly fighting the last time, which left her in tears. Then he was gone, and she cried off and on in the four days since. I've seen enough of them to know males can be jerks by nature. I hope I never have a man who treats me like that.

She finally told me he had gone off to fight in the human's war against the Asmodians. Those are the evil people who worship the demon Lord Asmodius. I'm thankful that I wasn't shown how the last three Ages ended. It would have been awful; all three ended with the Asmodians killing off or capturing nearly all the pure humans. No one knows why they did this; I sure don't. Most people, most human people that is, think that we're in another of those end times. The elves believe it's just another human war, and they don't bother with human wars.

I heard Duncan stop playing to sob out the word, "Aisling," the name of a family member, I'd guess. More words followed, but they were in his native tongue, which involved a lot of growling deep in his throat. When Kailynn brought him to Anthopoulos earlier this week, a priest friend had come by, and cast a spell to give Duncan the ability to speak our language. But he still speaks his birth tongue when he's alone.

I felt his grief in my heart, remembering my pain of five years ago. I know the Skarg killed his family and his Troop, the group of people he traveled with in their great wagons. Both our losses were caused by the damned Skarg.

I didn't know whether to go to him or not. I spent a lot of time in tears when I was where he was in grief. Sometimes I wanted company, and sometimes they just rubbed me raw. I found myself hopping down from my rock to go comfort him.

I walked around the shrubs and saw him sniffing a sachet, a tiny bag filled with fragrant herbs. It had a crudely embroidered flower on it, like what a little girl might make.

He saw me looking at the sachet and hastily shoved it into his satchel like it was a treasure too precious to share.

"Go away," he snapped.

I looked at him, still thinking he might need company.

He glared back, then turned away and laid his hands on either side of his satchel. It was actually big enough to be called a pack…placed on a big rock. His bagpipes were between his feet, and his father's huge two-handed sword was leaning against a neighboring rock. He took in a large ragged, calming breath and sniffled quietly one more time. Then he said with threat in his voice, "Raina, please, just leave me alone."

Yeah, that wasn't going to happen. I touched my hand to his back, as high as I could comfortably reach, since I'm just short of five feet tall.

"Duncan," I said, "I know the pain you're feeling. The damned Skarg murdered my family, too. If you want to talk about it, I'll listen."

He spun around, "I doon'a want ta talk about it!" His brogue was getting thicker as he got more upset.

"But you need to unburden your heart!" It was a little dangerous to be shouting at someone who could break me like a twig. But I was fairly sure of what was going on.

He closed his eyes as he took another calming breath and said quietly, "I canna…not right now."

"But Duncan, it's the only way to get better. I know this, believe me."

He turned away again and hung his head.

I quickly moved to his side and took one of his large hands in both of mine. "Duncan, let me help you." I remembered how hard a surviving mother, one of our neighbors, had worked to get me to talk, and how it helped. She ignored my anger and my pain. I was determined to work just as hard for him as she had worked for me.

"Aaiiye!" He flung his hands over his head and back down, moving slightly to avoid hitting me, for which I silently thanked his thoughtfulness, even in his grief.

I smiled broadly and put my hand in the center of his big chest, "Please, you need this."

"No!"

He stormed away ten or fifteen feet and back again, saw me and repeated it. Then, he snatched up his pack and bagpipes.

I dashed in front of him, blocking his path, remembering the neighbor doing the exact same thing with me. I briefly wondered why people in grief were so predictable. I was sure this was the last fight before he would break and talk it out.

I grabbed his arm since his hands were full. "You need this."

"Doon't tooch me!" His brogue had gotten really thick. Not long now. "I doon't want ta talk ta some gurl with funny ears what looks like some brown cat or somethin'. Just leave me alone!"

Well, that was…he wasn't supposed to do that.

And the brown cat remark? All I could think about were the kids who wouldn't play with me, or would shove me into mud puddles, or other things while saying horrible things with so much hate in their voices that I either ran away in tears or started swinging. "You cat eared half-breed!

You're so brown, and you look like mud, so swim in it. Take your pick, since they used every animal there was. I've been in a lot of fights."

True Shala'lir ears are only three to four inches long, and they're tall, so their ears aren't so big by comparison. Papa was Tala'lir or Sylvan elf to other species, meaning his six-inch long ears showed up even more on his four-foot-tall body. With ears that big, they have to be protected, so the ears are covered in fur, usually the same color as their normal hair. Mine are fur covered, too, so that gave them even more reason to pick on me.

Everyone's skin in my village was Mama's coppery red color. My hair didn't stand out so much; being black with blue highlights. Their hair varied from a buttery yellow, to black with highlights or undertones in shades of all the primary colors. In a larger city like Koranidor, I sometimes saw mixes of those other colors; green, orange, and purple.

Sylvan Elf colors are earth toned, so we blend in, unlike High Elves whose bright colors make them stand out. Papa was mahogany-colored, so I'm in between. High Elves are so magical that standing out isn't such a problem. If something spots them, one good lightning bolt and zap, dead.

I mean, hiding helps when your best weapons are just really good bows.

My folks said I was a light milk-chocolate, though the village kids thought of me more like mud. Oh, joyful day, to be born a half-breed in a one-race village.

I looked up and noticed that Duncan was gone. Well, good riddance.

I walked to where he'd been pacing, intending to soak my feet in the creek, when I noticed his father's sword. He must have been upset. I'd pushed him hard, like Miss Maria had pushed me. I hadn't thought he was upset enough to forget his father's sword, a special link to his past. I was hurt and angry from his stinging remarks, but I had to take it to him. I shouted for him, but he didn't answer. He might have been out of hearing range, or he might have been too upset. I'm always suspicious of how poor human hearing really is because my hearing is so keen, the one good thing about these ears.

Well, mad as I was, he really needed the sword. As upset as he was, he didn't need to be frantic over losing it. I jumped down and dried my feet with my hands and the bottom of my dress and went back for my shoes.

I picked up his sword and was surprised by the weight. I'm ninety-five pounds soaking wet, and the sword was HUGE. It was indeed a great sword, fashioned for a seven-foot-tall mountain of a man, so it was about seven feet long as well.

I managed to hold it against my belly to let my strong stomach muscles help me. I walked a few hundred feet before my arms gave out. I wasn't about to quit, so I grabbed the hilt with two hands and dragged it backwards.

That was working better as I pulled it along the stream bed, until I tripped on a hidden branch and fell butt first right into black, stinky, mud.

Great! My best dress was ruined, and we're going to the big city tomorrow.

I sat on one of the rocks and fumed for a minute or ten. He was going to owe me big. Not only was I going to drag that two-ton sword the five miles back to our home, but I was also going to have to spend a long time cleaning my dress, before I began packing.

I finally figured out how to pull the two-ton thing. I heaved it onto my shoulder and dragged it behind me. I learned after the first rest stop to not drop it to the ground; it was too hard to pick up again with the way my arms were turning to dough. I leaned it against a tree.

I couldn't believe its heavy weight. When I watched him practice with it, I thought it was six or seven pounds…most swords are two to four pounds. I still had a mile or two to go. I repeatedly thought about dropping it and going to tell Sir Muscles where it was and let him find it. Then, I'd remember the brown cat comment, and there was no way I was going to let that stupid, pig-headed, bigoted, stupid, conceited, stupid, rude, arrogant, stupid, little, well all right, big, BOY get off without owing me.

When I was within sight of Ti`, I imagined what I was going to have him do. I didn't get past massaging my feet when I gave up. I knew I was going to need massaging all over, and there was no way he was going to touch me anywhere but my feet, and maybe not even them. I set the ten-ton hunk of metal against a tree and rested.

"Good evening, miss," Ti said. "You're rather later than normal this evening. Ah, Duncan's sword, he's been searching everywhere for it. Shall I inform him as to its location?"

I was too tired to be gleeful, but a plan is a plan. "No, I'll tell him, but I'd like to rest a few minutes first."

"As you wish, m'lady." He opened his mouth, centered in his fifteen-foot-wide trunk, revealing the first floor, the forty-foot-wide den, and art gallery. Yes, he's bigger on the inside than the outside, like so much about the elves I don't understand. Laurealis didn't go for formal entries like so many elves; it was all one spacious room. All elves were somewhere between eccentric and crazy. She went for eccentric and comfortable. I stepped through, glad that she had so many cushions covering the floor instead of tables and chairs.

I dragged that fifteen-ton chunk of metal and dropped it with a clang just inside the entrance. I plopped my worn and weary carcass onto one of the piles of cushions a few feet away and closed my eyes for just a few minutes.

Duncan

I'd been looking all over for Glenfallis, my father's magical great sword, ever since Laurealis told me we'd be going to the Francescan capital. I was excited about finally having a chance to do something, especially if it didn't involve people I simply couldn't understand. Packing wasn't a big job since I was able to bring so few of my things with me in that six-week long race across the prairie, badlands, and foothills. Some extra small clothes, my pipes, and I was done. Oh, and my father's sword, of course.

It didn't take long to realize that Glenfallis wasn't here. There just aren't that many places to misplace something the size of Glenfallis in a room with a bed, a chest growing out of a wall and a six-inch deep closet that grew a little deeper every day. It would be large enough to put things into by the time I had things.

I wish I could figure out how Dad would have done it. He had been one of the primary leaders of our people for decades, and one of our most honored generals. He achieved this by being both decisive and effective, by listening to everyone, and by not opening his mouth unless he had something worthy of speaking. I, on the other hand, needed a great deal of practice.

This first week had been such a disaster. I tried hunting. Game was plentiful, and I hadn't realized yet why animals were not afraid of men. After I killed and field dressed a deer to provide my share of the food, I discovered that elves couldn't eat meat.

Several words appeared in my head when I looked at the dressed carcass, though, all of them involved waste and none of them involved food. That's when I realized they're herbivores, like horses. They can't eat meat, though the humans they came from can.

New concepts like that had been in my head since I woke from the language spell. It's annoying to have thoughts popping in my brain that don't come from me, though they do let me understand these strange people better. The rain the day before yesterday brought to mind all kinds of new words for rain, about how it feels to the plants, how it changes the air, how it smells depending on the season. It got me to think of rain in a whole new way. I tried thinking of snow from where I'm from, just south of the big ice sheets. We have twenty-eight words for various kinds of snow and snowfall. They have four.

When I walked in with that deer over my shoulder, and Laurealis actually threw up, I finally understood why Kailynn always ate separately from me. He never fussed about my eating what was normal for me, but we never shared meals. We were so rushed he always made eating separately seem necessary for one reason or another. I never gave thought about why. By the time I was healed from the crossbow bolt wound, I had accepted it as our pattern. I barely noticed that he never ate the jerky we'd salvaged from my family's stores. I simply assumed his trail food was similar to mine, but his tasted better to him, or something.

I wish that he'd been able to stay after I awoke. I missed him, and his wife's disgust at my food was getting old pretty fast. I understand the expression, "If looks could kill" so much better now. But she wouldn't have hidden my sword, would she?

Small as it was, I tore the room apart, and no Glenfallis. I must have left it somewhere.

Think, Duncan, think.

By the Ancient One's beard, that's where I left it! It's by the creek where Raina got so pushy. I raced down the stairs spiraling down the central core of Ti-grogordahai four at a time, flipped over the rail once I got all the way into the den and hit the floor running.

And there was Glenfallis, by Ti's face. How…?

Oh.

Raina was asleep face down on some pillows. Normally she was immaculate, but now she was filthy, especially her behind. Cute behind, too, especially the way that black stain highlighted the roundness of it. She must have dragged him here. No wonder she's worn out; she couldn't weigh more than a hundred pounds and Glenfallis was ten pounds by himself, twelve with the scabbard. And a mile and a half, well, that's a fair piece to haul him, backwards, by the condition of her dress.

She had dropped him on the floor instead of laying him on a table or even just placing him against a wall.

I snatched Glenfallis and examined his scabbard. The toe cap was worn halfway through on one side, and the leather was scuffed and scarred, as if it'd been dragged for miles.

I glanced back and noticed the poor, bedraggled, exhausted girl sleeping there and realized what had happened. She'd found Dad's sword and realized that I had foolishly forgotten it. The tiny lass couldn't just pick him up and carry him, so she'd lugged him here. Of course, his scabbard looked like it's been pulled through the forest for miles.

"Ti," I whispered.

"Yes?" he replied, also in a whisper.

"I know yon tiny lass likes tea, but not how she likes it. Do you?"

"Of course, young sir. I pride myself on knowing the personal preferences of all my people."

"Laurealis makes drinks over at that cupboard. Would you help me make some tea for her?"

"Why certainly." He cleared his throat. "Should you choose to return to your room and restore my interior to some order, I would be most appreciative. I shall certainly inform you promptly as soon as the ah hem, *tiny lass* begins waking."

Ti's stiff manner put me off, as it often did. But I understood what he was saying about wanting me to clean up my space and did as he wished. A short while later, Ti's eyes opened in my room. "Young sir, the young lady is awakening. If you wish to greet her with hot tea upon her rising, I suggest haste."

I love having a reason for a good race. I dashed down the stairs again, this time slowing as I reached the second floor, walking silently but quickly down to where I jumped before and doing so again. Upon landing quietly, I checked her out once more.

Good, still sleeping, but definitely signs of stirring. I winked at Ti's big face. He smiled and winked back. He closed his eyes, and to my surprise, tiny emerald-green eyes opened just over the basin at the cupboard. I closed my mouth that had fallen wide open, and he smiled ever so slightly.

I can stalk quite well, and with no leaves, bracken, or other noisemakers to avoid, I moved quickly and quietly. As I arrived at the sink, he motioned with his eyes to the cabinet with the cups. I chose a kettle and cup with some nice blue flowers somehow painted into the glass... or whatever the translucent material was.

Oh, porcelain, whatever that was. I got an instant mental definition of porcelain, as if I wanted it. Having a language implanted was taking some getting used to.

Anyway, the cup looked sufficiently girly.

He guided me through all the steps to making her tea, though I must admit I almost blew it when I pushed the twiggy looking knob down and water came out. Not only that, but the water was also so hot that it scalded my fingers. I can't figure how he did that trick, but it sure did save time. I'd been fretting about why he hadn't told me to put some wood into the stove right away to heat the water. Raina groaned a little when I'd hissed in surprise at the scalding hot water, but I was nearly done by then.

I hurried over to the cushions on the other side of the low table from her and placed the kettle and cup down quietly, waiting for her to come fully awake. She even stretches like a cat; beautiful and graceful.

Then she jumped back. "Ack! How'd you get here?"

"Peace?" I said as I poured her a cup of tea. I had already put three spoons of honey in the cup like Ti told me, so I just stirred it and handed it to her.

She didn't smile, she only took the cup and sniffed it. She smiled a little and took a testing sip. Her slightly broader smile proved that it had passed the test.

Then her smile disappeared. "Why peace?"

"Because what I said was wrong, and I want to say I'm sorry."

She stiffened so slightly that only a hunter might have noticed. It reminded me so much of a deer catching a whiff of danger that I wondered briefly if she was about to bolt.

"You're sorry," she said neutrally.

Well, like Dad always said, *Shoot to the heart.*

"Raina, what I said back there was wrong. I was really upset, but what I said was wrong."

"You're just doing this because I brought your father's sword back here."

"Well, yes, that's part of it. After I saw it over there, it made me think about how hard you had worked getting it here. That reminded me of us back at that creek. Then I remembered your *eyes* when I called you a brown cat. I don't really know why it was so bad, but it was. I hurt you. I saw it in your eyes and your stance, though I didn't think about it 'till after I was calm. I hurt you, and you were just trying to help."

She took another sip of tea without saying anything. She looked so tiny and defenseless, and I felt so horrible, like that time I lost Mom's favorite teacup and had to tell her. I wished she'd accept my apology, or shout at me, or something. This waiting was killing me.

I tried to think of something else I could do…but hunting and roasting anything didn't seem to be an option. She had her tea. It was warm outside, at least for mid-winter after the solstice, so getting her a blanket seemed pointless. There was nothing more I could do, and I couldn't think of anything else to say. She was still sitting there studying me over that cup of tea.

It was finally empty, and she placed it carefully on the table.

"You really think you're going to get out of owing me a big one just because you brought me some tea?"

"Huh?"

"I bet Ti told you how to make it, too."

"Uh, yeah, I asked him." Where was this going?

"Apologies aren't real, especially from boys. You'll end up wanting to kiss and make up next, then do more than I'm ready to do with you yet. Well, you're not! And you still owe me for lugging that fifteen-ton sword back here!" She turned and raced up the stairs.

"Wait, I know I owe you for bringing it back, but why would I kiss you? We aren't even engaged!" "Ooh!" was all the answer I heard.

I stared slack jawed at where her feet had disappeared. By the Tester, what brought that on?

Chapter Seven
Off to the Big City
Laurealis

We were all outside of Ti' watching Duncan pack our luggage onto the wagon. I was thinking about how much easier this job was with someone like him doing the packing. I told Raina, "He's not only strong, but he's also organized. Don't you just love watching men work?"

"Well, sometimes, I guess," she answered distractedly before surprising me with a different topic. "Laurealis, I've never had more than one or two dresses at a time in my life. I just can't imagine having as much clothing as you. I mean, I think you have more clothes than my entire village."

"Dear, I've been around for a long time to collect things, and Ti does an excellent job of taking care of clothes and such."

"But those clothes are so well-made. They must cost a fortune. It's more money than I can imagine."

"But, dear, they didn't cost me anything."

"Huh?"

"Our people frequently don't use money with each other. We barter. Since I am the most popular, well, one of the most popular emotive dancers of our people, I give concerts regularly. It's only natural that when one particularly enjoys something, one gives the performer something of equal value. We have many talents amongst our people, and by human standards, we are all quite wealthy. It's common for us to sell a few of our items when we go to a human city to get coins in their type when we first arrive. Other than Koranidor, Lergenze is set up better for these exchanges than anywhere else I have seen for the last couple of thousand years."

"Couple of thousand years?"

"Well, yes. The Fourth Age had some wonderful people, but they weren't quite so…mercantile."

"The Fourth Age? Laurealis, how many Ages have you seen?"

"Oh, just this one and some of the Fourth. I'm really not incredibly old."

Raina became quiet, and her thoughts tasted very calm and pensive. I returned to helping Duncan by giving him suggestions to help him pack, until I tasted his agitation rising. It was as if he was upset by my suggestions, but that's just not possible, it must have been something else.

Then I went back to say goodbye to Ti'.

"It will be quiet without the young ones here, m'lady. I will miss them."

"Oh, Ti', we'll miss you, too. We plan to be back before the spring is over."

"You have always loved spring best. Well, till then, travel safely."

It was lovely, traveling across the breadth of Anthopoulos. I lived in the shady, ferny lowlands that were mostly shades of green, and this bright area of orchards, cereal crops, and sun loving flowers was beautiful in a far more vibrant and colorful way. Both children livened up, their issues with each other from yesterday lost in the beauty of the scenery surrounding us. The sheer strength and variety of their emotions reminded me strongly of our little one who had died, 634 years ago the nineteenth of last month.

We rode through the beautiful countryside, pensive and quiet. Duncan is quite good with animals and is also an accomplished driver. My friend Ailos, who traveled with us, was surprised at how skilled he was when Duncan finally talked him into letting him drive after hitching his horse, Shadow, to the wagon. I was surprised as well, as I had assumed that the steppes barbarians from just south of the ice sheets knew little more than riding horses and killing animals, not that they actually had wagons. Civilized people used wagons, not savages.

The road wound gently along in the Elven way, avoiding steep slopes by curving with the land. There was a nice way-stop, complete with benches and a wayfarer tree. I chuckled as Ailos startled Duncan almost out of those horrible leather things he calls clothes when he pulled on one of the tree's many knobs to fill the watering trough for the horses. I can't imagine what Duncan expected, but it obviously wasn't water filling what to him must have looked like an extra wide branch shaped like a boat, or something.

Raina, already knowing what a wayfarer tree was, had collected cheese, and grapes, and warm bread from the preservation box. After Duncan recovered from his shock with the watering trough and Raina passed out the food, nothing would do but for her to show him the preservation box. Ailos and I chuckled quietly as the barbarian opened and closed the box repeatedly; pulling warm or cool things out that people had left there for wayfarers to use.

Finally, Duncan appeared satisfied with whatever had piqued his curiosity and looked out to the horizon where a formidable structure arose from a nearby slope.

"Laurealis, what's that?" he asked.

"The Stor'dør."

"Oh, so that's what it looks like from outside. When I got here with Kailynn, I barely had a chance to look around before we dashed off to see you. All he talked about was seeing you. He reminded me of my father and some of the other men when we were returning from a hunt. All they would talk about was their wives and families."

I hate it when he talks about killing things. He could pass for a civilized person until he says something like that.

I felt the wonder in his eyes as he studied the Stor'dør. Tasting his wonder made me look at the Stor'dør afresh. It was less than a hundred years old. Built by dwarves and financed by human money, I think from Bourbesonne or one of those cities of this age. It was a massive structure, consisting of ten gates, one for each of the four largest human cities on this side of the continent, four more elsewhere on North and South Merica, and the remaining two on other continents. The ones of most interest to me were Chorisala, the Dwarven capital, Anthopolis, our own City of Flowers, and Koranidor, the city of all peoples, which the dwarves built on the coast. It was where Kailynn and my best friend Astoria and I found our beautiful and adorable Raina, as well as a few dozen others.

Our gate was the entrance to the entire complex. One passed through a sculpture of a beautiful Elven couple holding their hands over the guest's head as they entered. Of course, the statues were scaled to be high and wide enough for large wagons to pass under. A blooming Talu tree, the source of our mana, was behind the woman. Our bountiful fruits, bottles of wine, and books surrounded the couple's feet. These were the products of which our people were most known. Other generally unique products were found at each of the other cities' portals. The sculptures' colors were beautifully done, and except for scale, were quite lifelike.

"Those guard towers are impressive," Duncan remarked.

His comment infuriated me. He sees a beautiful work of art and all he can see are the guard towers where those awful soldiers were stationed. The very thought of soldiers in our peaceful city was simply wrong.

"Didn't you even notice the beauty of the Stor'dør?"

"Well, yeah, of course. It's just that after seeing the way my family was wiped out, and I understand Raina's was, too, I like seeing protections around something like this, since all doors can go both ways."

"But they're soldiers!" I protested.

"What's wrong with soldiers?" Raina asked, more aggressively than I liked.

"They kill people. It's wrong to kill people."

"I was sure happy to see the soldiers who rescued me," she said quietly.

Soldiers are evil, or close to it, I thought, but she had a point. I kept my mouth shut.

Just past the entrance, we were stopped. A typical dwarf, short and stout, with a beard braided to mid-chest, greeted us from a small building, "State your destination."

"Lergenze."

"Just the three of you?"

"No, the non-draft horses as well."

"Is the wagon coming, or just the luggage?"

"Just the luggage."

"Unload it on the scales over there and step aside."

After Duncan and Ailos unloaded, I paid the toll and waited. I hugged Ailos goodbye, and we waited. While I was still quietly in the throes of kaipoctouyevva, it was hard to merely hug any man, especially an elf. But Ailos was a gentleman and kept it quick and chaste.

It took at least another hour 'till a small army of dwarves assembled around our luggage and brought it to the Lergenzian portal. The arc over the entrance consisted of a judge holding a book of law overhead and a farmer holding a sickle upright. We stepped through and saw…walls.

I was shocked. Massive walls filled with alert guards surrounding the entire portal complex. This hadn't been here the last time I was here, just fifteen or twenty years ago. Of course, those ugly towers at our Portal hadn't been there either.

More dwarves quietly gathered our luggage, and with my approval, loaded it onto a waiting wagon. The road within the Portal area was as perfectly smooth as a calm lake, but that changed as soon as we crossed through the massive gate. The humans of Lergenze used cobblestones as their paving. While that prevented mud, it was anything but smooth.

Conversation was rare, as no one wanted to bite their tongue on the bumpy ride. I was thankful we were in a Dwarven wagon. Their wagons were expertly made, and they did something to make riding in them much smoother.

Still, the city with its fairly uniform architecture of red-brick lower floors, white stucco upper floors with diagonally crossed dark timbers and red-tile roofs, was quite attractive. It was even clean for a human city. The draft animals had bags to catch what they voided and there was some basic plumbing, so it smelled nice, unlike the overwhelming smell of the animals' droppings that was so common in some of the human cities I have visited over the millennia.

We traveled to the Elven embassy where I planned to stay. I knew that vacant Dendrocasa would be available and eager for guests since they can get as lonely as anyone else. The embassies have been bred to not be as attached to their people, which of course meant that they wouldn't be half as helpful or comfortable as Ti'. But we wouldn't have to stay, and worse, eat in a city full of animal eaters.

As soon as we entered the gates, I could smell the Sacred Grove with its ever-blooming Talu trees providing a background of the pollen we elves require for long-term health. To an elf there exists no fragrance as sweet as the Talu blossom.

Another sweet thought was that my dear friend Astoria was in this city and would also be staying here. I hadn't seen her in months, though we correspond regularly. Perhaps I would run into her tonight. I couldn't wait for some real visiting time.

I noticed something strange in the Dryad grove that marks the entrance to every embassy. The Dryad statues, each by their special tree, were closely following us with their eyes, particularly Duncan. What concerned me even more was that Duncan, and Raina to an even greater extent, were beginning to become quite distracted.

Real Dryads inhabited the surrounding trees; the statues were simply decoration. Now, one of the real Dryads, a lovely girl whose skin and hair were the same shades as her ancient oak bark and leaves, stepped out of her tree and approached us.

"My Lady, you may not enter here with the two strangers."

I was taken aback, "And why not? I've been here twice before."

"The strangers will fall victim to the Dreams. Were you not with them, we would simply allow them to become lost in their dreams and release them outside the gates, which would not open for them again. However, you are with them, so, to defend ourselves, you will not be able to enter again while with them."

"But they are my guests…"

Duncan had hunkered down and was holding his

head, obviously fighting influence. Raina was just lost in lala land.

"What is happening to them?" I asked.

"The dreams. You've never experienced them since you are Elven, but all others who enter our haven face the lusts they are most susceptible to: sex, money, and power. They eventually give in, regardless of the lust, and become completely lost in their dreams. We bind them and allow them to believe their dreams are being satisfied for a time, making them more pliable, then leaving them with a geas to ensure that they will never willingly enter here again. Of course, we also ensure that the gates will not open for them, and the walls are quite secure. Were you not aware of these basic defenses?"

"Uh, no. No, I wasn't. We'll be leaving now. Raina appears happy, but Duncan is fighting your dreams quite strongly. I wonder why."

"As you wish, my Lady. I will release your companions and escort you to the exit."

Well, this was an unwanted complication. Still, I had enough money to see us through for a while, so we went looking for lodging elsewhere. We traveled to an area on a hill overlooking the two rivers Lergenze is built between. The area was lovely, filled with picturesque bridges and numerous statues. Simple light spells within the crystalline statues made them appear to glow from within, a beautiful effect. It was not only more effective and safer than torches, but it was also far more artistic. Most impressive.

I chose a large hotel that a local constable had recommended, which went by the ostentatious name of "A Noble Rest". The sign was painted with a man in a ridiculous hat lying on a pillow. Humans, the things they must do, since so many of them can't read.

Anyway, the foyer was quiet, though the smells emanating from the tavern where we were supposed to somehow eat, were nauseating. Burning animal flesh! How supposedly civilized people could eat flesh was beyond me. However, the place had a feeling of peace, so I decided it would do. A feeling of unrest would do far more to upset me than eating in my room. Still upset by the rejection my own people gave us, I paid the exorbitant monthly price for a suite of rooms, and we proceeded upstairs.

Our rooms were small, and while not extremely cramped, I was forced to leave two of my six large chests in Raina's room. Fortunately, the bed was long enough for my six-foot frame, as I am a head taller than most human men and far taller than the women. Poor Duncan, I expect he'll have to sleep diagonally across his. The weight of the quilts and drapes covering the windows and bed served to let me know that the room wouldn't be as comfortable as Ti' kept our home. Even the cheerfully crackling fire only brought slight warmth to the room.

I shivered, remembering the thick snow and icicles adorning the landscape as we stepped through the Portal. It's one thing to paint or sculpt a winter landscape, but quite another to experience it. Though one of my jewels controls the temperature immediately around my body, seeing through the window how the people were bundled up against the cold and scurrying along made me shiver and stretch out my hands to the fire.

After a few moments of comfort, I tried to find a suitable spot for my morning stretches and exercises. There wasn't enough clear floor space in my room, so I went to our floor's common room. It was much larger, half the size of my den, and there was a nice clear spot in the far corner away from both the fireplace and the open doorway. The fireplace was huge, I guess at least eight-feet wide, and there was a fire roaring, filling the room with its beautiful golden light.

Unfortunately, not only were Duncan and Raina present, but several other guests whom I had not met were there as well. As people will do, they all turned to see who had entered the room. I turned away from them enough to hide my flicking wrist as I cast the spell necessary to taste their emotions.

Frankly, I was shocked; most of the men were offended by my mere presence. I realized by the amount of gold braid and brightly colored bits of cloth and metal that these men were not only soldiers, but officers. I hold murderers such as them in equal disdain.

I began my stretches, glaring at the officers from time to time. It only took a little while before they left, and I was able to relax. The kids, particularly Raina, studied my moves. After a while, she settled in beside me and we did my morning routine together.

"I'm going to go explore the area around here," Duncan said.

"That sounds good. Come back when you're hungry, and we'll see about lunch." I realized that I would have to let them eat down in the inn's common room while I ate fruits and vegetables up here. If I were lucky, there would be a restaurant in this city that catered to elves. That would definitely be something to look for.

Duncan spent less time out than I expected; I keep forgetting how much he eats. Kailynn brought him home only a few days ago and he almost immediately had our friend Makiek cast a spell to teach him our tongue and Francescan, as that is the common trade language.

I was still bitter that Kai' left shortly after Duncan awakened from his three-day nap. He clearly pointed out that saying goodbye to the boy he had thrust upon me and going off to war was more important than spending time with his wife who he had left for six long months while in the need of kaipoctouyevva. I was even angrier that he was only then telling me he didn't want another child. He'd had over six hundred years to express himself and he'd chosen not to let me know how he felt. How male.

We entered the dining area, and I motioned for one of the serving girls to come to the door. She came to us and curtsied, "Yes, m'lady?"

"Can these two eat here and the bill added to my room tab? I am staying in room 412."

"Yes, m'lady. May I see your key?"

I quickly handed her the key. The smell of burned animal flesh coming from the dining area was nauseating.

"That will be fine. I'll take care of them. May I direct you to that smaller room across the hall where we serve elves? I apologize for the smells in the hall, but you will be well taken care of there."

"Thank you," I said as I hastily retreated.

I felt much better after eating a fine meal, a meal made all the better by a spell that protected this room from smells. Noticing a man in the room, I was glad the spell also masked the smell of the pheromones I was emitting as I was enduring unfulfilled kaipoctouyevva. Elven men have an exceedingly tough time resisting the call of the pheromones and had he responded to me, I would have responded to him. I wouldn't have been able to prevent myself.

Still, I sat and dreamed of making a baby, then having a child to hold close to my heart again. Unfulfilled kaipoctouyevva is a difficult burden to bear.

I waited 'till the children found me a good while later.

"Was it good?" I asked.

"Very," Raina replied.

"It really was the steak…oomph!" he said as Raina elbowed him squarely in the stomach.

"What was that for?" he complained.

"Don't bring up meat to an elf. It's considered extremely bad form."

"But—" she glared at him. "Oh, all right."

I was quite thankful for Raina's prompt action since the man sharing the dining room with me was just getting his meal. While none of the offensive smells made it into this one room, there was no reason to remind anyone of what would hit them the moment one stepped out.

I hadn't spoken with him; I was having a hard enough time dealing with my condition as it was.

"Duncan, did you discover anything interesting during your explorations?" A quick change of topic was definitely in order.

"Well, yes, in fact, I did. I saw some jewelry shops not too far from here. I know my mom loved jewelry and gold. An uncle made it in his spare time and taught me some things about setting gems."

I was again surprised. My opinion of his people went up quite a bit. I hadn't realized they were able to make jewelry. No telling what the quality would be, but at least they're capable of making it. I feared they just stole it or something. I mean, he is a barbarian. By definition, which is just above a savage beast.

"We can go look at it if you like, but I prefer jewelry in the Elven style."

Holding the straps of my off-the-shoulder dress in place, I plucked off the large ruby securing it, and held it in my hand. "My big red beauty, I just love the way you catch the light."

It flashed its appreciation to me, and I set it down and moved a few feet away. It promptly rolled toward me, and I placed it back atop the shoulder of my dress where I could feel it attach itself to me through the dress with its indigenous magic.

Duncan, eyes wide, backed up immediately and made a sign.

Raina said, "That was weird. How did you do that?"

I chuckled, "All Elven jewelry is like that. We don't like to pierce our bodies like humans. Self-inflicted pain, ick. So, we make our jewelry slightly intelligent and able to move. If your jewelry likes you, you can't lose it, even if you're as absent-minded as I am sometimes."

"I'm impressed," Raina said. Duncan just stayed quiet; he seemed quite unnerved. I don't believe he'd been exposed to much magic.

"What about clothes?" I asked. "Humans are always so innovative, and I've always loved their ability to create beautiful new types and styles of clothing, especially for their ruling classes."

"Uh, I didn't see anything like that, but I didn't get very far away."

Scooping both our arms in hers, Raina said, "Well, we're here to go shopping, let's go!"

We walked the streets for just a short while before I saw an old man talking to a group of little boys. He had a kind face, wrinkled, and gnarled with age, with few teeth and little hair, but his face had character. Though disheveled, his clothing was in good condition and his lap was covered with a colorful quilt. A happy little boy about half his height was sitting in his lap while he spoke to a group of like-aged boys. I decided his face was so interesting that I just had to sculpt a bust of him, and maybe a larger statue which would include the boy in his lap. Before we reached them so I could ask his permission, the boy hopped off and took him by his hand, leading him away.

"Grandpapa, we need to be getting back. We need to eat."

The old man chuckled with a natural good humor. In an ancient voice he said, "Sonny, it's you who's needin' to eat. I don't eat so much these days."

"Oh, Grandpapa, you have to eat, too. Mama says you must stay strong, and it's my job to make sure you come 'ome for lunch."

I stepped a bit closer. "Excuse me," I said.

"Eh, who's that?" his ancient voice croaked. His palsied hands shook as he put on a pair of the spectacle's humans used instead of a healing spell to correct poor vision. His watery eyes appeared enormous behind them, and he seemed startled by what he saw.

Then his face clouded in anger pointing an accusing finger at me, "Eh, Sonny, this here's one of them elves. They's the ones what says they'll 'elp us, then all they do is bring groceries, expensive groceries at that. If'n they'd done as they said they'd do after Bourbesonne, why I reckon the war'd be over by now and your papa 'ould be 'ome."

The nice little boy turned to face me angrily and demanded, "Is that true? Did your army stay 'ome, so my Papa has to stay away all the time? I've only seen 'em twiced in my whole life. Why are you so mean to us? What did Papa, or me, or Grandpapa ever do to you?"

I was flabbergasted. I didn't know what to do. I noticed angry glances a couple of times while we walked. Now it seemed like everyone was closing in on me. I couldn't think. I was surrounded by such negative emotions. I wished I hadn't cast that spell to increase my sensitivity. The strength of their anger and hatred felt like a dam bursting, and the entire ocean was pouring over and drowning me. I broke and ran for the refuge of my little room in the hotel.

Duncan

I was watching Laurealis over the heads of the dense crowd, still amazed that there could be so many people in one place. The only time I had ever seen this many people at once was when I went to Detrota a couple of years ago.

Among my people I was a little taller than average, but here I was a giant. She was talking to an old man, and everyone around her began getting their feathers ruffled about something. She ran away in haste, clearly upset.

I moved toward them, not being mindful of my size. "I'm sorry. I didn't mean to step on you."

"Watch where you're going, you big oaf," some irate man yelled after me.

"Duncan, can you see Laurealis?" Raina asked.

"I did, I was, I mean, she was there, then she went behind a wagon, and she was gone. Did you see her talking to the old man over there? She ran off after talking to him." "Damn, she went invisible." Raina exclaimed.

"What? Went invisible?"

"Made herself clear, like glass, so you can't see her."

I only half heard her because the voice in my head was explaining the term at the same time.

"Duncan, you find her and get her back to the hotel, or at least wait for her at the hotel. I'm sure that's where she'll end up. I'm going to talk to the old man. I'll see you there."

I headed back to the hotel, looking for our lost caretaker, wishing now that I hadn't come with Kailynn after that horrible time back home. I pushed my way through the crowd, like wading through a chest deep river, sometimes against the current, sometimes with it. I kept seeing a tall woman with a dress the same shade of bright blue that Laurealis was wearing this morning.

I wonder…yes, she ducked into an alley and when she came out, her hairstyle and dress had changed to blend in better with the crowd. At least she was still tall. I began wading faster. More curses followed me. Curses were just words, and I had to trust that they had no power. For now, I had to reach Laurealis.

Still fretting about the curses, I was gathering and hoping they were powerless, I closed the gap with her. Near the hotel, I closed to within ten feet, kept my distance, then followed her up to her room and slipped in right behind her. She immediately realized that I was there and turned to me, shocked.

"How did you do that?"

"Do what, follow you?"

"Yes, you weren't supposed to be able to do that," she sounded confused.

"What was hard about following you, other than getting through all those people?"

"But I changed my appearance," she protested.

"Not enough, I saw you right after you ran, then again when you changed to blend in better. I don't understand how you changed like that, but I saw it."

"I'm an illusionist; I can make people see what I want them to see. How do you see me right now?"

"As a tall human woman, in a nice blue dress. Come to think of it, not only is the dress like others I saw, but the color is also exactly like them. It's like a cornflower blue."

"You're very observant."

"I'm a hunter and I was on your trail. Of course, I'm observant."

"You were hunting me like I was one of your animals that you murder and eat?" she demanded, shocked and angry.

"Huh? No, no. I was following you because you ran away like you were afraid of something. Tracking is a skill used in hunting, but I was concerned about you."

She accepted my answer and calmed down. I leaned back against a wall and studied her.

"So, tell me why you were running?"

A scared look flashed through her eyes, and she turned her back to me, though not in anger. I gave her time, and after a minute or two, she answered.

"Those people, they really don't like elves. When the Asmodians attacked the human cities and completely destroyed Bourbesonne most horribly, we promised to help them." After the briefest of pauses, she added hastily, "and we have. We've sent them food and other supplies. But they believe we should have done more. They think we should have sent our people to be killed and to kill others. Don't they realize that our people are peaceful?"

"Are you really?"

"What? Of course, we are!"

"Kailynn killed over a thousand Skarg after he found me. Seems to me that some of your people are fully capable of helping the people you promised to help."

"But only a few of our people butcher other sentient beings like that!"

"Is that what you think of your husband? That he's a butcher?"

"Yes!" she said emphatically. A second later, her expression became aghast. She covered her mouth as she realized what she said, "NO. No, I don't. He's gentle and kind, at least he is when he's with me."

"Yet he can be strong enough to protect you like a man should, even kill for you, and that scares you."

She opened her mouth to answer. I waited for her.

She walked around the room, tidying the clean room some more. But she didn't ask me to leave, so I continued to wait, leaning against the wall.

"Killing is murder; how can it be right?" she asked.

"My dad explained it this way. There's a right and a wrong reason to kill. Killing for food, please don't give me that look; our people are different, like cats and horses. Cats and horses are both beautiful and wonderful creatures.

"There's a right and a wrong reason to kill. Killing to stay alive or to protect and keep others alive is right. Killing for pleasure is wrong. The Skarg killed Raina's and my people for no reason; we hadn't done anything to them. Killing all of our people was wrong, evil. My mom and dad, my siblings, and our whole troop, killed hundreds of Skarg in self-defense before they died. That was right. Kailynn, when he killed the ones that got away, better than a thousand, he said…well, I haven't quite figured that one out yet."

I paused, thinking it through, "That was war, I suppose. I know, he said the reason he did it was so those can't kill any more innocents. So yes, that was protecting the innocent. It was war, and I can't see anything wrong with war against the Skarg. They kill with no purpose, except to destroy."

"Well, maybe. I'll meditate on what you said. For one so very young, you are wise. You said your father taught you that. Was he always so wise?"

I answered hesitantly. "Dad was…Dad. He had lots of sayings, and most people listened to him. He loved to play, but he had a temper that was bad sometimes. With us, with all kids really, he doted on us and usually had endless patience."

"But not always?"

I chuckled. "But not always." A knock at the door interrupted us.

"Who's there?" Laurealis asked.

"Raina. I have someone who wants to speak with you."

"Who?" she asked, but Raina was already opening the door. The poor old man and boy in their disheveled clothing stepped in right behind her.

The old man bowed, and the boy did, too, after the old man nudged him. Laurealis sniffed the air ever so slightly and immediately relaxed. I stayed in the background, just watching to see what happened.

"M'lady, Raina here, she's 'elped us to understand we was wrong. I never knowed you elves had menfolk what fought. She's given us ta understand that your Champions are some kinda powerful. Not only is your man one of 'em, but he's out fighting with the army an 'elpin' us. Well, we sure do appreciate it. We gonna spread the word that some of you elves is all right."

"Thank you. And thank you, Raina," Laurealis replied.

The old man ducked his head and backed out. Laurealis, who had been lost in thought, looked up as the door was closing. "Wait!"

The old man looked back in and asked, "Yes, m'lady?"

"I was wondering. Well, the reason I started to talk to you is that you have an interesting face. I was wondering if you would let me do a bust of you and your grandson. I'd pay you for the privilege."

The old man's voice wheezed out in alarm, "You wantin' to bust me? Eh, what're you meanin' by that?" His face hardened and his fists clenched.

"Bust you?" she chuckled, "No, no. I want to do a sculpture of you, maybe just of your head. That's known as a bust, a sculpture of just the head, or of you with your grandson. I really liked the picture I saw when your grandson was sitting on your lap."

The little boy began tugging on his grandpa's shirt. "Grandpapa, Grandpapa! You said we was needin' money. She said she was gunna pay ya."

He scratched his head. "I don't know."

Laurealis has a really beautiful smile when she wants. "Please?"

"How much money?"

Laurealis began pulling off a jewel when Raina quickly stepped in front of her. Raina turned her head to me and whispered, "Give me a second, please."

I knew Ma generally did the bargaining, so I figured the same was going on here. After all, if her people didn't really use money, they might not really know its value. I stepped in front of the door, blocking the view and probably most of the sound.

After a couple of minutes of hurried whispering, Raina touched my arm as she stepped around me. Offering a small gold coin, she asked, "Would this do for a few minutes of your time?"

The old man and the boy's eyes grew large as the grandfather said, "I reckon. Now that's jest for a few minutes, mind ya. My time ain't cheap."

"That's fine, just fine." Laurealis said. "Would you mind sitting over here?"

It was the work of but minutes to get the two of them arranged, including pulling the colorful quilt out of the boy's pack to lie over his grandfather's lap. Then Laurealis cast a spell through one of her diamonds and walked around them while pointing the gem at them. Then she smiled and thanked the two of them.

Once they were out of the room, Raina asked, "So how did they sit long enough for you to sculpt them later? When you said you only needed them for a few minutes, I really didn't believe you."

Laurealis pulled the diamond from her midriff where it was a jewel decorating the bottom of the top half of her outfit. She held it in her hand and an image of the old man, and his grandson appeared in between us.

It startled me. I really don't like it when she does magic like that. My people don't do magic like that.

"Wow," Raina said. "Well, I wish I had taken you at your word, I could have gotten him to agree to do that for nothing, as ashamed as he was thinking so bad of you when your husband is a great warrior."

"Well, I'm glad I paid them. They looked so poor, and the boy kept emoting his hunger and the grandfather his pain. I'm afraid he won't live much longer. It'd be nice if my friend

Astoria could see him. That's why I insisted on at least the gold. They love each other deeply, and the grandfather will make sure the little boy is fed."

Raina looked like she was absorbing what Laurealis said, then her face brightened considerably.

"Well, you were asking about nice clothes, so are you ready to go shopping?"

"We still don't know where to go. I'll stop and ask at the front desk, I guess."

"Are you interested in where the local nobles shop?" Raina asked.

"Well, yes, did you find a place?"

"The old man knew. He told me on the way back here."

"You really are amazing. Do you know that Raina?"

"Uh, huh," she said, smiling brightly as she curtsied.

Laurealis kept her human disguise, except when she went to dine. Raina suggested that it would make life easier if they both looked like human nobility. The ladies spent time deciding exactly how they should look, so I took a nap in my room while they dilly-dallied in Laurealis' room. When they were done Raina finally woke me to ask how she looked. Without the ears and her brown coloring, she looked different. It took me aback.

"You look good, really good. But I kind of like the old Raina better."

She looked shocked, then she smiled and jumped really high, throwing her arms around my neck and her feet around my waist and kissed my cheek. I was bending over so her feet would touch the ground when she released her 'hold' as gracefully as she had jumped. Her athleticism surprised me.

Then holding my hand, she said, "Thank you."

I don't know why she made such a big deal out of it. I don't do changes very well, and once you get used to the brown cat look, it's kind of cute.

The place we ended up in was amazing. Buildings like these were in themselves amazing. These folks would call my people's few cities nothing but towns or simple villages. Our largest city is nowhere near this huge.

Except for our mining towns located at the edges of First Age's great cities, we mostly live in great wagons that are forty-eight feet long, like the great wagons we found in Detrota, Chicog, and the other great cities. We use huge alum wheels instead of the eight narrow wheels made of a material we can't duplicate. They take up to sixty oxen to pull, and we ride horses to care for and protect our herds.

Since the great wagons are so exceptionally large, families of up to thirteen kids are the norm and can live in them easily. Still, everything is designed for storage and taking up as little space as possible. Mom always said, "A place for everything and everything in its place," when she'd scold us for our messes.

This place, this store, well, I don't know where to begin. It wasn't like that at all. It was cluttered with rich stuff everywhere. Some of the really nice jewelry was displayed on gold cloth; the cloth was actually made of gold, of all things. I checked. It really was heavy like gold.

Raina kept going all bug-eyed at the jewelry. She was like a kid in a candy store. Well, maybe she was.

We looked around for a while before moving on to another across the street, one that specialized in clothing. While Laurealis and Raina were looking around I wandered to a different section, one set up with all manner of clothing. The fabrics were thick and soft, not at all like the wool cloth I knew.

A man walked up to me. "If you're not buying something, I can show you to the door."

"I'm with them," I said, pointing to Laurealis. She was engaged in an active conversation with another man who was holding a piece of clothing against Raina.

"I see," he said, looking satisfied that someone really was where I was pointing.

"I see that you're wearing leathers. We have some rather fine leathers over here. If you would follow me."

He asked more questions, becoming interested when I mentioned that I lived near the ice sheets and a couple of thousand miles east northeast of here. Before long, he had me in a fine vest that actually came close to fitting me. When I asked if my family's crest of a green falcon like the one adorning my breechclout could be added, he beamed proudly. "Well, of course! It might take a day or two longer to have it beaded like that one. May we take this purchase over to the lady to confirm it?"

The salesman and I went to where Raina was wearing a new dress and holding her hands to her waist while looking into a glass, not metal, mirror. It was red and made of a fabric that clung to her like a second skin. The color looked good on her, but I didn't really like her wearing it. She'd always struck me as tiny and vulnerable, like she needed to be protected, and that dress just made her look too good, if that's possible. I was surprised, but in the last few days, she had really grown on me. And that dress, well, I just don't know. It made her look like she was showing too much. Her shape showed through perfectly, even to her…well don't look there. We aren't husband and wife. My people never wear things like that.

She saw me and excitedly ran over to ask how I liked it.

"Fine," I lied, and she was almost squealing in delight as she raced to Laurealis. "I've worn things like this, but never had anything of my own anywhere near this nice. May I have it, please, please, please?"

Laurealis talked to the clerk and was shocked at what he told her.

"Raina, dear, you really do look marvelous in that silk dress, but I could buy you an entire wardrobe, a large one for what that costs. Are you sure you want that one?" "Oh, yes. I do, I do, I really do!"

Laurealis glanced back at me holding the vest. "Really, Duncan, can't you at least pick something to WEAR that didn't involve killing? It's absolutely obscene using parts of murdered animals as," she actually shuddered, "clothing."

"Um, I like leather. It protects me and it's what I'm used to wearing."

"Oh, all right! Put it on. Raina, would you be a dear and see how it looks. I'm sure I wouldn't be a proper judge of such things."

Raina winked at me and nodded for me to put it on. She pulled me in front of the huge glass mirror. My people have steel mirrors, but they're small. I only had to duck a little to see all of me at one time. Amazing.

Raina said, "Look's good. A little tight around the chest, but you're a big guy."

You know, she's right, I decided. Her saying that made it much better. I don't care much about clothes but having her approve was…nice. She's pretty all the time, but when she smiles like that, well, it takes my breath away.

I decided right then that I'd really like to see her smile like that more often.

I handed the vest to the salesman. "I like it just the way it is. Thanks for the suggestion of the falcon, but it can wait."

He took one look at Raina and gave me a quick smile. I must have been easy to read.

They ended up buying the dress and a coat that looked nice to go over it. The dress was so thin and skintight over so much of her body that it wouldn't have done at all wearing it outside without more protection from the cold. Raina handed me the coat as soon as we entered other buildings, preening her, uh hmm, well, interesting areas much more than she should have. She was displaying herself in ways that definitely had mine and every other man's attention. It made me uncomfortable, and I could feel my hackles growing like a dog ready to attack in order to defend the pack. The feeling was strange. I just wished she'd leave the coat on. I was going from disliking the dress to hating it.

The second store we went into had a weasel looking man hanging around who kept eyeing her. I didn't trust him at all. He was well-dressed, but I didn't like his eyes or his smile when Raina was displaying herself. I hid while his attention was focused solely on her. She and Laurealis disappeared behind a corner, and I caught him by his shoulder as he was sneaking around to ogle her from around the corner. I saw a bulge confirming he was armed with a dagger at his waist. It was but a second to have my hand over his mouth and my skinning knife at his kidney.

"If I were you," I said quietly, but with an edge of threat, "I'd leave and not trail her again. Now get out of here. If you see us again, turn around and go another way. If I see you again, this little sticker will carve a new hole in you. Nod if you understand."

He nodded, and I stayed to watch him leave. I picked up Raina's coat and rejoined the ladies. When I handed her the coat, she looked caught and embarrassed. I think she heard my discussion with the weasel-man. She snatched the coat and put it on immediately, wrapping it tightly around her. She behaved much more demurely after that.

We shopped at more places but didn't see anything else that caught our eyes. Now that Raina wasn't being so…immodest, I could relax.

I found it boring, but I was incredibly happy for the warmth of the new vest. The snowstorms here in the south, the ladies think of it as northern because their world is mostly south of here, are far milder than back home. There, most kids have, or know someone who has, stuck their tongue to a bit of metal in the winter. Then they're stuck 'till their tongue can be melted free. It's a common trick to play on the uninitiated. I found the snowstorm a bit brisk for true comfort in just my leather jerkin and wool shirt, but not worth all the comments I was getting about being crazy or foolish. Still, the vest was definitely nice; warm is good.

The next morning, I got up early and found Raina already up, though not very talkative. Later that day, I realized that she seemed upset, but I was having problems being stuck inside walls and I had to get outside. I wish now that I had done more than just ask her to make a lunch for me.

She did make a nice big sandwich. There were preservation boxes that we'd stocked with our own food, so we didn't have to eat in the expensive restaurant downstairs. The main reason was so Laurealis wouldn't have to smell cooking meat. It was a wonderful idea. It saved her money, and I respect how disgusting normal food must smell to her. Anyway, I had a lunch packed, and I'd told Raina I planned on being out till late afternoon, as I explored the city.

Chapter Eight
A Beauty Unveiled

Ragina

I woke in the middle of the night, so disturbed by the looks men had given me after I put on that red silk dress. The worst had been from that weasel Duncan chased away. He's so sweet. Those looks brought back the memories of the five long years I spent in that horrible so-called orphanage where I was forced to be a whore. I kept thinking about Laurealis and how men looked at her respectfully. For the last months everyone I saw gave her the greatest respect. Yesterday, was different. They looked at me like I'm the dirt I am, nothing but a half-breed whore.

"Speak of the devil," I thought, "and she's at the door." Being in the common room right in front of the fire there was nowhere to hide. I hunkered down in the huge chair hoping she would pass without seeing me.

A moment later I realized that I'd had no such luck. I heard her step into the big common room. Bitterly, I thought that all I deserved were the daily beatings I got for years, and here she is being nice to me. I don't deserve nice.

"Raina, what's wrong? You're trembling." She carefully placed her hand on my shoulder.

I hunkered down further, wishing she'd just go away.

"Dear, where is that dress we bought yesterday? I'd like to get it washed today. The first washing is the most important."

I was so miserable; I couldn't think of an answer, so I didn't.

"Dear, did you hear me?"

Sighing, I mumbled, "I heard you."

"Then where is it?"

"I burned it."

Her hands that had been gently massaging my shoulders stopped. "You what? Raina, I told you, I could have bought you an entire wardrobe, a nice one, for what that one dress cost! How could you?"

"I couldn't help it." I knew it was wrong, but I had to do something. The shame of yesterday was just overwhelming.

Spinning up and turning to her, her arms had already opened wide to receive me, like she was anticipating my need to hug her. I just cuddled and cried on her shoulder for a while, sobbing for my very soul. I wanted to die, and I think she knew it. I felt that I shouldn't let her comfort me; I was too filled with my own shame. But her comfort, warmth, and love just felt too good to let go. I needed her love right then, more than I've needed a lot of things, like air, or food, or water.

"Dear, what's wrong?" she finally asked me. "Yesterday, you loved that dress. I would never have bought it had you not been so enthusiastic about it. Why, I think you liked it even more than Duncan liked his new coat that some poor creature died to have its skin used for…oh, it's just too disgusting to talk about."

Of course, Duncan isn't civilized. He's a barbarian from the prairies. Killing that deer and offering to cook it got them off on the wrong foot, and she's not letting him live it down.

But, with me she's been different. She's been so good to me for the past half year. When I escaped, she was there with Kailynn, and Astoria, and Zreetor, because of Astoria's dream. Since then, she's tried as hard to help me as Mama would have. I wanted to open up more to her but…I couldn't. I was scared to trust again, though the kindness Laurealis has given me these past months should have earned my trust.

I backed away from her embrace, looked her in the eyes, and set my shoulders determinedly. It's time to trust again.

I tasted the word I hadn't said since I watched Mama's murder five and a half long, horrible years ago, "M—Mama. Can I call you Mama?"

Laurealis hid her sharp intake of breath behind her hand before she replied, pausing several times appearing to gather her thoughts, "Honey—I—I know I can never replace your parents, but if it pleases you to call me Mama, then by all means, do so." She wrapped her arms around me as her own tears flowed, matching those I had been shedding since long before dawn.

After a few moments, she asked, "Is that what this is all about? Missing your parents? I know they died, what five, maybe six years ago now. I certainly understand…"

"No! It's not about that!" I shouted.

Then I turned my head away, and without realizing I was saying it instead of just thinking it, "All you have to do to survive being orphaned is to sell your body for the night... I know, I remember. The night after night, never-ending hopelessness of it. The chains, the beatings, the…worse than that. All because I'm a half-breed. And probably because I'm pretty. I hate being pretty!" Laurealis' body stiffened as she heard me bare my soul.

I looked Laurealis square in the eyes, deciding that honesty was the only way to explain. "It's…men. Why are they so…evil? After I got dressed up yesterday, I could feel their eyes and their hands all over me, like I was a whore again at that awful *orphanage*. So, I got up in the middle of the night and burned the clothes. It didn't help. I can still feel their hands all over me and know, really know, that I'm nothing but pig crap. I feel like I should be wallowing with some dirty pigs on a farm."

"Oh, dear," she gasped, holding her hand to her mouth. "I'm so sorry." Taking my hand, she led me to the couch and took a seat, inviting me to do the same. She then took both of my hands in her own and prayed.

"Dear Blessed Creator of us all, I beg you to give me the wisdom to help Raina. You have shown me over the past six months how strong, kind, and resourceful she is."

What? No, I'm not.

"You have also shown me her unimaginable pain."

So little of it. So truly little of it.

"It went so far beyond what I had thought," she continued in her prayer.

If you only knew.

"You know Kailynn and I would do anything for her; love, hold, and protect her for the rest of her life, if that is what she needs."

Please do! I screamed silently inside my head. "We also know you need your women to be strong."

Strong! Who's she kidding?

"But Goddess! She's so hurt! I'm no priestess. I can't deal with this kind of pain! Elves don't know of this kind of evil. I'm just a dancer, a singer, an entertainer. I tell stories through my dances."

I pressed her hands hard, willing her to hear the words I felt, but couldn't force myself to say. *But you love me*! I thought, wishing I could say the words.

After sitting like that for a long while, she said, "Yes, All-Mother. I will seek out Astoria and her wisdom. Together, we will help little Raina get through this."

When she looked up, a teardrop hanging from the tip of her nose, she touched her lips to my hands and said, "Raina, that friend that I wanted to see, Astoria?"

"Yes."

"Well, we're going to see her and talk this through."

Astoria

I was deep in my morning meditations when Laurealis was announced by Jin-ta, my guest Dendrocasa. I dashed downstairs, delighted at such a wonderful surprise.

"Laurealis! I didn't know you were here! What brings you so far from home? You never travel!"

We spent several hours in my hotel room visiting and catching up. She presented the problem that brought her to me without going into details. She wanted my first impressions to be unbiased.

We left to talk with Raina. When I met the girl, I saw she truly was a lovely young lady. Being half-human and half-elf was a problem, though not one that she caused. I eased into a light trance to study her aura.

Her basic aura was red with yellow tones, indicating that she was a doer, and yet sensitive by nature. My kind of girl. But it was also cloudy and near black in several areas. This girl's soul was close to necrotic. I wondered if she was ready to kill herself. It's what I feared, but first I needed to determine if she was ill with a dreaded disease.

I hurriedly cast a diagnostic spell and approached her.

"Sweetie, this won't hurt a bit, but I need to check something out."

Her pallor indicated that I had frightened her, but I had to know if she was horribly ill, evil, or had been terribly abused. The blackness of her aura was frightening. One normally doesn't look deeply at auras; it's just not courteous. As I scanned her with my spell, I was relieved to learn she wasn't physically ill. I feared she was eaten up with a horrible disease and I only heal trauma not disease, at least not very well.

I felt none of the repulsion that evil gives me. This poor girl had been horribly abused. I suspected she might become suicidal if she suffered any more major abuse or shocks. At least that wasn't likely to happen with Laurealis.

I prayed briefly for wisdom and sensitivity to meet her needs. Poor dear.

I indicated Raina's bed for her to sit upon, while I sat on one of the large chests of Laurealis' that I recognized. I motioned at the bed beside the girl for Laurealis. I wanted Laurealis' emotional support close at hand for this very disturbed girl. As we settled ourselves, I cast another spell, a variety of charms to make Raina comfortable with me and to help her feel I was a friend. I didn't like the manipulation, but her anger and pain were seething, and she needed to be calmed so we could explore her deepest memories.

"Sweetie, we need to talk. Has my dear friend Laurealis old you who I am?"

"Uh, a priestess, but not much more than that."

"Well, that's a lot right there. We do many things, we who serve the Lady. Tell me about yourself. You're from Firenzia? Did you lose many people when it fell?"

"Everyone. Everyone, I loved, and almost everyone I knew, died."

"Oh my! How horrible. How did you feel about that then, and how do you feel about it now?"

"How do you think?" she said with anger. "I felt abandoned, and angry at the world, and the Gods, and everyone."

Gratified the charm had worked, we continued in this way for quite a while. The picture of a horribly abused young lady was built more strongly. She quite justifiably had learned to hate men. As we continued, I thought and prayed about how to deal with that issue. Hatred, anger, and bitterness are killer emotions.

"Raina, you will find this hard to believe, but over time I have seen that most men are good, not like those monsters who did those horrible things to you when you were a teen."

She crossed her arms and stated with great conviction. "Men, good?"

"In fact, I have found that men want, and need three things," I continued.

She cupped her breasts, "Yeah, and these are two of them. The third is—"

Quickly, I reached over and laid my finger upon her lips.

She glared at me, then sat back.

"All men need a battle worth fighting," I replied. "Yeah, a battle over these."

"Stop it!" My, was she stubborn!

"Only after you prove that at least one man is interested in something other than these!"

I looked at the couch and realized we were both now standing. I slowly sat, and she followed suit. Taking a deep calming breath, I said, "You win. Tell me something, though. What is your favorite memory of your father?"

I saw by her expression that it was the right question. "Thank you, My Lady," I silently prayed.

She had a couple of false starts before answering. "I guess it would be the look in his eyes when he called me his 'Little Frog'."

"Little Frog?"

"Yes. You see, in Papa's native language, Raina means gem-frog. That little frog is unbelievably beautiful and is common to his native forests on the southeast side of Merica, where he grew up. That was four thousand miles from where he met Mama in the mountains of Firenzia, so I've never seen one. When he would describe its colors, a deep blue like in my hair," she flipped it with its blue highlights, "with bright yellow stripes that glowed in the dark, and chartreuse eyes! His eyes would glow as he remembered the joy he had raising them as a boy. He loved them. When he called me his *Little Frog*, his eyes glowed the way I always imagined they did when he was a little boy, the way they did when he looked at Mama when she didn't know he was there. Then he would tussle my hair or give me great big hug or something."

She opened her eyes again after reliving this cherished memory. It was nice to see something of an enjoyable time in her life. This was going to hurt, but it needed to come out.

"What happened to your father?"

Her eyes filled with tears, but they didn't quite spill over. Laurealis had cast a temporary spell to make her more emotionally sensitive to allow the rot to easily come out of this horrible emotional wound. She's tough. If it weren't for that spell, if she went through this at all, she'd say it without tears. Of course, she'd stay deadpan, hiding her pain so deep I couldn't deal with it. This girl had suffered so much, and I admired her will and strength. It seemed unfair to make her more emotionally vulnerable. Still, if we could lance the emotional boil, it would be worth it. Lots of tears are a good way to clean old wounds.

"He led the men from our village, and eventually from all the other villages and towns on our way to the border as they fought the Skarg that overran our home."

She stood and walked over to a table that held water and glasses.

"Dear, Skarg is a vulgar term," Laurealis said as Raina was pouring a glass of water. "They are 'Soulless Ones'."

In a flash of anger, she slammed the glass down hard enough to spill water everywhere. Spinning around, she screamed, "By the Lady, no! Maybe you haven't seen them, but I have! They're Skarg, horrible crossbreeds between men and demons, and that's all I'll call them! Papa was fighting them, circling behind and in front of us, always on the move! Then he, with a couple of hundred men from all the villages we had run into, made a stand at what he called a *highly defensible location*, a place in the mountain filled with caves. It looked good for a day, 'till the next morning when all we could see were thousands and thousands of Skarg. The men sent all of us kids and our mothers away. The Skarg charged like a wave, pouring over our papas, and we ran and ran. We ran into a Francescan army two days later. Papa fought those horrible things for a month, and they murdered him two days before the Francescan army found us!"

Her rage broke and tears began flowing as she muttered quietly, "Two lousy days."

My heart melted hearing her story as probably the whole floor heard her explanation. Humbled by her pain, I asked, "So he had a battle worth fighting?"

I began helping to clean up the mess which she made and was trying to clean, but she was so upset that she just couldn't. Laurealis pulled her into her shoulder where she quietly sobbed.

After just a moment, she sniffed and said, "What? Well, yeah, I guess he did. He tried so hard to get all of us out of there."

"A battle worth fighting is the first thing good men need. All men fight, but *good* men fight for a reason." I put a strong emphasis on the word good, hoping that concept got through.

"Wait. Are you saying that women aren't brave enough to fight?"

"No, no," Astoria said with a smile. "Women are just as brave as men, but we generally express that courage in separate ways. One, men are more ready to fight physically; it's in their nature. Second, they are stronger and generally faster than women, so if the fight is physical, men are more able to fight. We elves are blessed in that we are magical enough to have means to fight other than the strictly physical. You know, with swords and such. But with the humans you grew up among, that isn't true. In your culture, the women kept the house, and the kids and men did the hard, physical labor of farming and things."

"Well, of course, they did. Momma had a profession with her healing herbs, but most women did just like you said. Women just aren't strong enough to work the fields or handle swords and other weapons like a man."

"There's nothing wrong with that, but with the elves, the genders are more balanced since physical labor isn't the most important attribute to surviving. With humans, it takes a lot of strength to farm or blacksmith or most any of the more valuable jobs. It doesn't make women's roles less important to society, but it frequently masks our courage. It is a rare man who can handle a home and ten kids. It is a rare woman who can lift a hundred-pound load of anything. We are different. But as you said, women are rarely strong enough to defeat a man with a sword. It's not courage; its strength, and men are predisposed to enter a physical fight. Women aren't likely to fight unless it's for something they really love, or for those who are weaker, like their children."

"So, while all men are itching for a fight, you're saying that good men don't just fight each other for fun and to beat women. They fight for a reason, like protecting what they claim as theirs."

"Uh, that's not quite what I meant. I don't think that good men claim their families as property, as you seem to be saying. 'Good' men," I said, stressing the good strongly, "love their families and will jump out front to protect them.

Not from a feeling of ownership, but out of love. They willingly sacrifice themselves to save those they love."

"You mean there are men who treat women like women treat each other? Like people? Sorry, I don't believe you."

"Yes, that is exactly what I'm saying. Your father was one like that. He, like all those other two hundred men, willingly gave, no, sacrificed their lives so you and the other women and children had a chance to escape."

She opened her mouth to argue but stopped. After looking at me for a moment, she nodded as she unwillingly gave me the first point. Her anger had an explanation, though not yet a cure.

"The second thing they need is that reason," I continued while she glared at me, "someone to fight for, a princess or beauty to rescue. A purpose."

Her expression hardened again, then lightened. I supposed she was thinking about her father a moment longer. Good.

"Have you noticed how often boys show off when you or other girls come around?"

"Well, yes. I always thought they were silly."

I chuckled, glad for a lowering of the tension and drama. It was enough that she was able to let go of Laurealis' shoulder, though she ducked under her arm to snuggle next to her support.

"Well, they can be, but it's the way they're made. Good men fight for their wives and families," I said. "They're demonstrating their skills to impress possible wives." Reinforcing that point was pretty important, I believed.

She turned to Laurealis and asked, "That's why Kailynn is off at the war right now, isn't it, Mama? That feels right, calling you Mama."

"Dear, it feels right for me, too. Yes, that's why Kailynn is off at the war. I realize that now. Like most of our people, he was sitting out this war, since the Asmodians attacked only the humans. But something happened when he found Duncan on that six-month long patrol. He found Duncan gravely wounded and Duncan's family, and so many of his people, killed by the Soulless Ones. I could feel his agitation through our marriage bond even thousands of miles away. All the time after that event, I could feel how upset he was through our bond. He was like a wild animal trapped in a cage. I've only seen one other time when he was more upset. His agitation tasted like it did that time long ago when we lost someone incredibly special to us. As you know, after leaving Duncan with me, he went straight to aid the humans."

"I heard. You were both rather vocal," Raina said. "His leaving really upset you."

"Yes, I was wrong, but it hurt so much that he would leave me alone so quickly after being gone so long. There's no way of knowing when, or even if, he'll come home again."

Raina looked at her curiously. After a moment, she shrugged, but such a little shrug that I almost missed it. *Something else that Laurealis didn't tell me,* I wondered. *What's been going on? That must have been some fight.*

"And Duncan's silence doesn't help, does it?" Raina asked while taking Laurealis' hand.

Her perception surprised and pleased me. "He hardly ever talks. It's been four days, well now five, and he's hardly said a word, except for that day we fought. He said a lot then, too much actually. I know I don't know him, but something's eating away at him, and I think it's something more than losing his family. I know, oh, Goddess, I know how hard that is. That's all it is, but it seems deeper. The other day when he was moody, he'd screamed out in his sleep the night before, I saw him holding a little sachet. It's very crude, like a little girl made it. He was playing that wonderful haunting song on his bagpipes. It makes me think of softly flowing water or wind."

I pledged to ask about this boy later. I understood why Laurealis took in two war orphans. I was so proud of her. There were so many, and these two obviously needed her help.

"You like those pipe things?" Laurealis asked. "I hate them. I have to get out of hearing range when he plays that thing. I know he has a lot of pain to release, I heard him scream, too. I held him 'till he calmed, and music is one of the best ways to do so. That's why I haven't said anything, but his music sometimes makes my skin crawl. Those minor chords, yuck!"

She took Raina's hands in hers and pressed them against her cheek. "Yes, Dear, I know he's hurting as badly as you. I can feel his pain as strongly as I feel yours. I worry about him, too. All Kailynn said when he brought him to me to talk about taking care of him, was that Duncan was a heart-broken little boy. That 'boy' is so big, almost seven feet tall and all muscle and appetite, it's hard to think of him like that sometimes. I know most human cultures think that males become men after their sixteenth to eighteenth birthdays instead of being just a few years out of diapers, but still…something's wrong and he won't talk about it. All he does all day is eat disgusting food or practice with that huge sword of his father's or play awful music."

We were getting the emotional garbage out of both my old friend and my new one, but I needed to regain control of this conversation.

"So, men need a battle to fight and someone to fight for. The last thing they need is to live out an adventure. They can't stand things too safe and settled. They go 'stir-crazy' and have to go off somewhere and do silly daredevil stunts. They have to go exploring, slay the dragon, or lead the way into danger. Even their games have to involve danger. Sensible Elven men need this as well, though less so than humans. It's part of the way their bodies and minds work, not something they generally realize, much less try to control."

"Yes, that part I see. Papa was a mountain guide on the far eastern side of Firenzia. We lived on a mountain under the eaves of the Mist Forest. Our house was carved into one of those giant trees and had been lived in for generations. With those twenty-foot-wide trees, you could see a long way through the forest in between them, if the mists weren't too thick. It was filled with wild boar, bears, and even forest dire cats."

Raina paused, left Laurealis' underarm, then asked me. "Well, I can see all of those things, but what about women? Don't we have needs, too? Didn't the Creator, in Her Wisdom, give us needs as well? Different ones, I mean.

I've fought, I've killed even, but it was to get free of that 'orphanage', and I certainly don't crave it."

I smiled, noting that she was becoming more comfortable, "That's an incredibly good question. I believe the Creator did also give us needs. In fact, I believe them to be the corollaries of what She gave the men. As men fight better and try harder for the approval of women, especially for that special woman who becomes more beautiful for the right man. Think of any wedding you have attended. Have you noticed how all women, even plain ones, become beautiful, even radiant, on their wedding day?"

She nodded "yes".

"And women love to be the princess rescued and to be chased by the right man just as in the stories they were told as young children. They need to be romanced, to be noticed and valuable. Did your father chase your mother or rescue her from something, or just be romantic?"

"Well, she didn't need rescuing, but he did romance her."

Laurealis is so good with people. She just adores love stories so much that her attention pulls more out of the storyteller. She crossed her legs, resting her elbows on the couch in front of her knees and smiled radiantly, inviting Raina to continue.

Reacting to Laurealis' interest, Raina smiled and began, "Well, like her mother before her, she was the village herbalist. She was also known as *La Belle Nigre*, the Black Beauty, after our hair."

Raina got her fingers stuck in the tangled mess that her hair had become. Laurealis grabbed a brush and moved behind her to work on it, just naturally pulling the story out. It's always amazing to watch how easy and natural she is with people.

"All the men for miles around, indeed from several neighboring towns, came to court her. She wouldn't have anything to do with them. She said that all they wanted was her body and her cooking and cleaning. She knew her value and she was going to wait for the right man."

"So, what was different about your father?" Laurealis asked.

"He was patient. For months, he would leave flowers, or bunches of fragrant herbs, or delicious and exotic snacks or meals, where only she would find them. Then, after she began anticipating them and looking for them when she went out, he would come out of hiding only after she picked up his gift. He started just barely in sight and vanished after he knew she had seen him. Then he kept moving closer each time. Finally, he spoke. Another month and they were holding hands. In another year, they were married. The way Mama told it was so beautiful."

Raina asked so quietly it was barely audible, "Do you think I could be beautiful like that someday, and someone as wonderful as my Papa would romance me?"

"Why of course! Why couldn't you? You're beautiful when you don't let yourself be hidden by anger and fear," Laurealis answered.

"No, I'm not. I'm ugly and cheap!" Laurealis jerked on a tangle in reproach.

"No, you're not, Raina. You're beautiful and precious, like your mother."

"I'm not like her, I'm dirty," Laurealis jerked at a tangle again.

"I can't ever get myself clean." Raina held her hand to her chest, her voice close to tears. "I've tried, but baths aren't what I need. Inside here, I'm dirty. Nothing can change that."

My heart was breaking just hearing her. I couldn't imagine the hell her life had been. I took a drink of water to hide what I was feeling and prayed for guidance.

Laurealis studied her for a long minute and then hugged her, whispering in her ear. "Dear, you won't ever,

ever have to go through that kind of hell again. You're safe here for as long as you need."

"And remember," I continued, trying to move her past this emotional knot. "Not just your mother, but all women, including *you*, have a deep beauty within, just waiting to be unveiled. And the Creator has a man for every woman if she is patient and perceptive. A man who can accept her as she is, baggage and all, so she can set aside her shame, despair or whatever hurt her, no matter how much she might bring with her."

After a while, she looked up at me from under Laurealis' comforting shoulder where she'd found herself again. "Thank you."

"Back to your father, so he rescued her from the wrong kind of attention and romanced her. I'm glad he was so wise, but what else would one expect? He was a Blessed One, one of the elves. As such, he was probably wise enough to continue romancing her after he won her heart."

She looked at me strangely, like I'd said something wrong. I paused, trying to imagine what I could have said wrong. Her father was wise, and what else would one expect from a Blessed One, even a lesser Blessed One, like a Tala'lir.

"Anyway," I continued, "the final thing women need is an adventure to share. We are nurturers, and men are protectors. In the muscle-powered human cultures, they tend to be the providers as well. We, men and women, are the opposite sides of one coin. Neither is at their best without the other, though both genders can do just fine alone most of the time. Men need women, our nurturing, more than we need them in most situations. But, as you know, it was the men who died to protect the women and children in your village."

She seemed to accept that a little better, having thought about it carefully.

"We need to share an adventure. So, your mother shared the adventure of living on the outskirts of that dangerous forest. Also, from what you have said, I'm sure your father helped your mother with her herbalist practice, right?"

"Yes, when he guided people through the Mist Forest and the surrounding mountains, he would usually come back with fresh herbs that could only be found in the forest. It pleased him to provide for her."

"And they also shared duties with raising you, correct? Your mother probably nurtured you more, and your father disciplined you more. He taught you right from wrong, where your mother just loved you for you, and that full acceptance helped build your self-esteem. You knew you were loved for being you, not for anything you did, but just for being you. I don't mean that exclusively on either parent's part, but in general, that's why it takes two to really raise a child."

"So, you're saying they shared the adventures of living in that beautiful, dangerous forest, running the shop, and raising me," Raina concluded.

"Exactly. We women need to be romanced and to be shown we are cherished. We need to share an adventure with, not just any man, but with a good man. And we need a man we can become the 'beauty unveiled' for, to bring out their courage. I'm sure, as a little girl, you played games that were meant to get you noticed."

She absorbed that for a moment. "Well, yes. I, and some of my friends, would run into rooms where one or several of our papas were talking or working, and play, twirling our skirts or jump on a table and sing, or something.

I see what you're saying."

Laurealis, who had heard this before, interjected perfectly, "Sweetie, our needs are complementary. It doesn't make us weak or them strong. Both genders are weak and strong in their own ways.

I could never do what Kailynn does. He's a Champion of our people, a magician capable of wielding the very elements as weapons and a warrior extraordinaire. When our own daughter died, he nearly died, too. That's the other time he was even more distraught than when he brought Duncan here. Though she was only sixty-nine when she crossed the Veil, she was comparable to a human eight-year-old. That's because we age more slowly than humans, though after we mature, our aging really slows down. It was my love that brought him back from that grief cave in his soul that he retreats into."

Raina cocked her head thoughtfully at Laurealis as she digested that revelation.

"That's beautiful, the way you describe how people support each other and have separate roles. I never thought of it that way. I can see how my folks did that. Thanks…Mama."

After a pause, she looked at me and added, "And thank you, too, Astoria."

Laurealis laid her hand on Raina's arm and looked her in the eye. "Do me a favor, don't ever, ever ask Kailynn about Aletha. I don't know what he might do. He's so strong and resilient in so many ways, but in his pain, he's brittle and weak. He's put his pain aside, but I fear he might shatter if something really brought her strongly to his mind again. If you're curious, ask me."

She winked conspiratorially at Raina. "And now, we need to pack."

She turned serious again, "I thought bringing you two here to a human city would distract us from Kailynn being gone. I'm sorry, but I was wrong. It may have been more to distract me. I miss him so much. We'll leave today."

Regina

After Laurealis and Astoria left, I went to our balcony. The snow and the cold helped me focus less on my heartache and more on Laurealis' and Astoria's words. I watched the crowd while thinking about all Laurealis and her friend just told me.

I saw Duncan standing head and shoulders above the crowd. I couldn't believe it as he took off the vest he had been preening in so much yesterday and put it on the little boy he was speaking to. It didn't come close to fitting; it swallowed him. Wrapped around his thin body several times, I'm sure it did help him warm up. He smiled gratefully at Duncan.

Then I noticed the waif was also eating the sandwich I made earlier for Duncan. I also saw the older boys lurking, ready to take the vest from the boy, leaving him exposed to the snow and cold once more. It didn't appear that Duncan saw them. He stayed and talked to the boy for a while, to let him finish the sandwich.

I don't know where Duncan picked his knowledge that too much food eaten too quickly could kill someone near starvation. Duncan gently stopped him after each bite, by taking the sandwich back and taking the smallest bites he could. The little waif could only eat a bite or two at a time, and judging by how thin he was, it was the first decent food the kid had eaten in weeks. I remembered when it was me down there. The vest almost dragged the ground and looked ridiculous on him. It would keep him warm if he could keep it. After he finished eating, Duncan playfully ruffled his hair and turned back toward the tavern, so I went with Laurealis downstairs to wait for him while we each enjoyed a cup of hot chocolate.

Duncan came into the common room and went immediately to the fire to warm his hands. Laurealis looked from Duncan to me and back again. Then she asked, more firmly than was her intention. "First Raina and now you. Where is that horrible leather vest I bought for you yesterday?"

Duncan, who hadn't seen us in his haste to reach the fire, straightened up so fast that he looked as if a red-hot poker had just been slipped down the back of his jerkin.

When he turned to face her, he was blushing furiously. "Well?"

"I, uh, set it down on this wall and, uh, when I went back to get it, it was gone."

"You set it down on a wall," she said neutrally.

"Yes, I did. Yes, that's what I did," he answered quickly, too quickly.

"Why?"

"Uh…"

I scornfully asked him, "Duncan, you do realize those older boys surrounding you and that little boy you were talking to, are probably already beating him up to take your vest from him. Some 'hero' you are, leaving a waif something valuable, something he isn't strong enough to keep. And while he's huddled in some corner, bruised and bleeding, he'll still think pleasant things about you, I'd bet."

Duncan's eyes grew wide as saucers as he realized what I was saying.

"Older boys around us," he said, "beating Quirino. No!"

He burst through the crowded common room, knocking chairs and people over and crushing two tables to splinters by jumping on them as he raced to the door.

I don't know why I had to be so hurtful. I watched Duncan do for that boy what no one ever did for me. He's good and I'm not.

"Raina! Couldn't you have been a little nicer to him? He obviously hadn't thought everything through, but he wasn't trying to get the boy hurt," Laurealis scolded.

I hung my head. "You're right. I don't know why it bothered me so much. It made me mad that he was so nice to that waif, I just wanted to scream."

"Could it be because no one was that kind to you when you were a waif?"

I stared at her for a second, wondering if she read my mind. I wondered if maybe she was right?

"I'm going back upstairs now," I said. We have to pack. He'll be back soon, I'm sure."

"No, I'll leave a note for him to pack, and I have to pay for his damages. Then we're going back out to get you something other than those old rags to wear. I respect your pain, and we won't get anything too nice, or that would show off that wonderful figure of yours. But it will do you good to wear something that doesn't look like it belongs on a trash heap."

I thought, *That's why it's on me.*

"I suspect he's going to thrash some bullies and thieves badly," she continued. "And he may bring the boy back for us to find a real orphanage. I know of one near here, but I want you out of this city as soon as possible."

She dragged me back to the market to get something *nice*. I let her get whatever it was she liked. I couldn't have cared less. I was in a fog. I barely remember it.

We were returning by way of the Stor'dør. The huge square around it was usually filled with shouting venders selling all the newest and freshest stuff, from produce to fashions.

Now though, the venders were silent, and wounded soldiers were getting off their wagons. It seemed like every one of them had blood-soaked bandages or worse, missing an arm, a hand, a leg, or more. It looked like the only whole people were carrying the ones who couldn't walk, and even they wore bloody bandages. There were very few wearing the green of healers. It was horrible.

The stench was even worse, especially from the gut wounds. When I stopped gagging, I noticed Laurealis talking to someone. She was frantic. She was shouting at this poor man missing his right arm, as if he were talking too slowly.

She was screaming, "You say you saw an elf Champion in green and blue with a magnolia flower sigil on his breast! What happened?"

"I knew him. His name was Kailynn."

Laurealis flinched like he had hit her, and she turned white as a ghost, covering her mouth with her hand.

"Was?" I heard her ask very quietly and fearfully as he continued like she hadn't said anything.

"He just met up with us a week ago, and from the first day, he fought like a man possessed. He would disappear in the night, and shortly thereafter we'd see flashes in the dark. Only then would he rest. The entire army became animated as we advanced. He was doing a far better job of scouting than our own scouts had been doing. He came back every night. Ours frequently didn't. We pushed the Asmodians into a boxed-in valley where we could eliminate one of their armies, something we've never been able to do.

"Then, in that huge battle just two days ago, he saved the whole army, m'lady. We were ambushed and losing badly. He flew up to the top of the trees in front of us and wrapped himself in a whirlwind to protect himself from arrows. He was tossing fireballs and lightning bolts like I would throw gravel. If I hadn't seen it with my own two eyes, I wouldn't have believed it. He broke charge after charge of hundreds of thousands of Skarg with his magic. We'd been retreating and were about to break; there were just too many of them. Then the Asmodians summoned demons to attack him. He had to devote himself to them and leave the Skarg to us, but by then we'd rallied. Seeing him in danger galvanized us. We began driving that damned horde back ourselves. General Ghourdy led us on the left and General Bisenhiem, he was on the right and—"

"Kailynn was my husband, you fool! What happened to my husband?"

"Oh, my, I had no idea! My sincerest condolences."

"Yes, thank you, but if you would—?"

"Oh, yeah, I'm sorry—"

"I know! Just tell me about my husband!"

"Well, he was beating the demons with that weird kind of double billhook he uses. You've seen it, I'm sure."

"I KNOW. JUST TELL ME WHAT HAPPENED!"

I had never seen her like that. She was always so compassionate and respectful.

"I am. I am. You see, that's when a huge demon began tearing apart the enemy lines from behind. He flew down and began throwing lightning bolts at whatever it was that was throwing pieces of our men and Skarg dozens of yards with each blow of its huge black swords."

"By the Lady, no! Then what happened?" Fear was replacing the urgency in her voice.

"I don't know exactly. The lightning began gathering around him, while he kept shooting at the demon. It was like the lightning built up to a point where it all exploded. When we could see again, the demon fell dead, and Kailynn was nowhere to be found. It must have completely destroyed his body. I'm sorry, M'lady, I really am." He reached to touch her shoulder sympathetically.

"I don't think our entire army could have beaten it. It was just that terrible.

After the demon fell, we tried to get to where the battle had been to see if there was anything left. We fought hard, as much for him as for the king. I lost my arm in the third charge.

I understand we won the day, so the site is being searched intensely for his body. Of that, I am sure. The nation owes you and your husband a huge debt. If there is anything that I or my men can do for you, please allow us that honor."

I don't think Laurealis heard him. She had collapsed, and her eyes glazed over at the news.

"MAMA!" I screamed, rushing to her side, and hugging her, hard. When she did nothing, I shook her.

She said very weakly, "No." Her eyes were so glazed over that I don't think she saw anything in this world.

I reached out and began hitting the soldier as hard as I could. "What did you do to her?" I demanded.

Crying out and closing his eyes in pain, he grabbed me with his remaining arm, holding me off. I stopped instantly, still angry, but even more fearful of hurting him further. He must be under a really good pain control spell, I thought.

He spoke after a minute or so, "Little Lady, I—"

"I'm not your 'Little Lady'! I'm Raina, her daughter! Now what did you do to my Mama! Why did you have to tell her of her husband's death like that? Couldn't you have been nicer, gentler?"

"Raina. I'm sorry. But news like that, well, there's no uncomplicated way to tell it. I had no warning I would run into *his* wife now, of all things."

The crowd was like a herd of cattle. They were pushing in on us and actually about to run us over. Not intentionally, just like a herd would behave.

"Corporal," the man called to someone who only had a noticeably short, bandaged hand.

Oh, my, I thought as I realized that his fingers were missing. His face was gray from his pain, unlike this man whose right arm ended in a bloody bandage just short of his shoulder. Yes, this man had to have a really powerful pain control spell on him. Of course, he was an officer. "Give me a hand getting this woman up."

"Yes, sir," the man said listlessly.

"Corporal, this Lady is Kailynn's wife."

"Yes, sir, Kailynn's wife. So what?"

"Kailynn is that elf Champion who saved our butts."

"Him! He's here!"

"No, man! He's dead! This poor woman is his wife, and she just found out about her husband's death. Now help me get her up!"

The corporal called out to another of the less injured men, "Rolf, over here! Now! Help me get this Lady up! This 'here's the wife of that elf what saved our butts!"

Together the two picked her up gently while a buzz arose amongst the men. Before I realized what was happening, men were dropping in an expanding wave to one knee, some with tears in their eyes, while the closer ones were kissing the hem of her dress and thanking her. Lost in her own world, she saw nothing.

The man giving orders dropped to one knee. Looking me in the eye, he said, "Raina, I am Captain von Teutendorf of the 15th Heavy Lancers. Are you from this city? Or rather, in this crowd, can you find your way home?"

I looked around. With so many tall men around, I couldn't see a thing.

"If I could see anything, I could."

"As I thought. This man, Corporal Schmidt, is from here. These two men will escort you wherever you need to go." He pulled out a huge amount of money and put it in my hands. It was more money than I had ever seen at one time. "Now here are five gold Marks in case you know of a healer. If not…" He turned and faced the corporal, "Corporal, do you know of a healer close by?"

"Yes, sir, I knows a healer what's had some dealings with wives in shock. She helped my sista-in-law when my brother done paid the Tillerman last ye-ah. We'll get 'em to where they need to go, and I'll fetch her."

"Very good. Now, Raina, until the wounded are evacuated, you won't be able to use the Stor'dør to go anywhere. But they should be through by late this afternoon. After that, I imagine the backlog of civilians who will be using the Stor'dør will be significant. I assume you'll be taking her back to Anthopoulos?"

"Yes, I will. At least, as soon as I can."

"Good, come get me, and I'll move you to the front of the line and pay your fare. Now, do you remember my name and unit?"

"Yes, Captain von Teutendorf of the 15th Heavy Lancers."

He smiled at me and laid his hand on my shoulder. "Good, now all you have to do is ask any soldier where the 15th Heavy Lancers are billeted, err, staying, and they'll help you. By this afternoon, I'm sure the whole army will know the plight of your mother, the wife of the elf who showed up and saved all of us here. Once they know who you are, your only problem will probably be too much help. On another note, I know by your accent that you're from Firenzia. You're obviously a war orphan. I spoke to your adoptive father several times, and this is something I want you to hear with all of your war-ravaged soul."

He took my face with his left hand and his right shoulder moved as well. He gasped in pain and took a minute to compose himself before continuing. I regretted my earlier attack even more.

"Listen to me. Really hear what I am about to tell you. He was a Prince. Whether elves recognize such or not, I don't know. I was in on the relief efforts in Firenzia back in the spring of '02. I saw how bad it was when it fell. But as hurt as you must be and as wonderful as your parents may have been, you are now the daughter of a Prince, which makes you a special person, a Princess." He then bowed, and everyone around him bowed as well.

The only thing I could think about was not being worthy of being close to royalty, much less be one.

He grabbed my arm before I had begun to turn to bolt. "Raina, I see you're having a tough time accepting this, but it's true. Any man in the Army of the North would do anything for you."

He nodded toward the murmuring and pointing men who had opened up a respectful space around us. They were still bowing or smiling at me as they continued on their way.

"By the end of the day, I'll wager every man here will know you and your mother's description. We all owe your father our very lives. That means our wives and children do, too. Raina, my children owe you for them not becoming orphans. You know better than I how much pain you have saved my little girls and their brothers. So, lift your head high, Princess."

I didn't care what he said, I'm no Princess. Kailynn, I could accept as a Prince, and even Laurealis as a Princess…but not me.

He told the men to escort us home. I remember telling them at what inn we were staying, but not much else about that nightmare morning. We got Laurealis to our room somehow. The men had to physically carry her, which woke her. She began fighting them as we got to her room.

"Get away from me! You, you… humans. It's all your fault that my Kai' is dead!"

The men ignored her comments. Rolf got a good grip on her, while the corporal ran off to get the healer. Laurealis looked insane. Her eyes were rolled back, and her immaculate hair was wild from her struggles. The other man was only barely able to hold her while I ran to bolt the door.

I turned back to see if I could do anything to help when she looked right at me and screamed accusingly, "You! You're from Firenzia! They did something to start this war! It's all your fault! Go! Just leave me!"

I fell to my knees and grabbed her hands, "No, Mama! It's your grief talking. It'll get better over time; it does. In time you won't hurt so badly."

She shrieked, "Leave! I can't stand the sight of you! I hate you!" She broke free and slapped me before Rolf could pull her back and trap her under him.

Something in me died. I backed away. I tripped on something and fell. I just kept backing away from this person I no longer knew. When I felt the wall behind me, I stood and rushed to the door. I broke several fingernails trying to unlatch the bolt that had slid in so easily an eternity ago. Finally, it came clear, and I ran to the top of the inn. There were some chairs and a table up there on the roof, so I put one of the chairs under the doorknob so I could be alone.

I sat on the ledge, hugging my knees to my chest, and trying to go through it all. I kept rocking back and forth, trying to make myself as small as I could, thinking maybe if the wind would just blow a little harder it would sweep me down the four floors to the street. Dying would be so much easier than living. I kept trying to tell myself that it was just her grief talking, but she must have had those thoughts all along. The nonsense about me being a princess made no impression; I simply couldn't accept it, and finally decided to end it all and jump. I set myself for a long jump, since I would have to clear the balconies jutting out four to five feet from the walls.

I had just put my hands on the ledge, when the door sounded like it had exploded.

"A little frog, how cute," Duncan said.

I had heard Papa saying the same thing when I was a little girl. I froze. I looked at my hands and feet and realized that I really must look like a frog about to jump. The next thing I knew, Duncan's huge hands picked me up as if I were a feather and carried me back inside the parapet wall rimming the top of the tavern.

He sat me on his knee and looked at me strangely. Reaching out to my face with one of those enormous hands of his, I saw my chance. I whipped my leg onto his and leapt over the ledge.

My face hit the wall after that huge paw caught my ankle. He jerked me up and over the wall where I landed against his other arm, hard. He picked me up again and sat me down on his knee again, hard. His hands never left my waist.

He glared at me, and I glared at him. Finally, he spoke. "You looked like a frog, so I don't think you'd fly like a bird."

"I would have if you hadn't crashed me into that wall." I touched my nose to see if he'd broken it. He hadn't, though my hand was wet with all the blood from the scratches. The stucco was a little rough and scraped my face a lot. I pressed my dress into my face, trying to stop the bleeding and not caring if I ruined the dress, since it was Laurealis who had bought it. After what she'd said, I didn't want it anymore.

"You might have soared like a bird, but the stop at the street would have been a bit hard."

"Exactly what I wanted." I shouted. I glanced at the yellow dress quickly. Damn, with that much blood, I'd wear those scabs for weeks before they healed.

He looked at me, gentle-like. After a brief time, he said, "Look, that guy told me what Laurealis said. And I'm sure she didn't mean it, she just…"

"How do you know that? Were you there?"

"No, but—"

"Then shut up and leave me alone."

He shut up, but he didn't leave me alone. He just held me there with those huge paws of his and wouldn't let me budge, no matter how hard I tried. He did move his legs together after I kicked him as hard as I could between them, but his hands never left my waist, never flinched when I kicked him.

Yet as strong as his grip was, it was strangely gentle. Men can't be that gentle. He wasn't letting me hate him for hurting me with his strength.

It wasn't fair. I wanted to hate him. I hurt so deeply that I wanted to hate, to hurt someone; myself, him, anyone.

His eyes never left mine. I had never realized 'till I had to look into those pale blue eyes for so long, how much pain his eyes also held, despite the blackening eye and the scratches that probably matched mine.

He spoke in that incredibly deep voice of his, "Would you like to hear about my homeland and family from… before…while they lived?"

As his voice broke, I realized that he really was hurting as badly as me. "Yeah, sure, I'll listen."

He talked for hours. We missed supper while he spoke of his life. His empty stomach grumbled, but he just kept on talking.

When he told me about the beautiful horses of his native prairies, this look of wonder filled him. It was so intense I almost wanted to see those endless prairies, just to see them through his eyes.

He explained that there normally weren't Skarg around, demon-men as he called them. In the five years since they'd first appeared, they had learned to fear his people and avoided their territory. He'd never seen such numbers of them before, but it looked like his people were just in the wrong place at the wrong time.

He told me of his dead family and his older sister who was engaged and was planning to marry the man at the winter solstice celebration that would have been about six weeks ago. He talked about his brothers, also; two had been growing in their father's likeness, like he was. Another had become a priest and wasn't with his family when they died.

He was so proud of his papa. He sounded like an awesome warrior and a fun and loving father and leader of his people. He talked about his mother, and how she trained him and his siblings with a spear, small sword, and shield. And about how stern she was, but how he knew she loved him all the more because she was so firm. That all hurt, but I knew something far worse was eating at him.

"Kailynn found me wounded and dressed my wound, a crossbow bolt through my leg. I'd been riding hard to bring warning of the demon-men to more of the Clan's Troops, so I was away when the attack came."

He went on to describe how together they read the battle of his Troop's, his family groups' last defense. There were bodies everywhere, hundreds and hundreds of Skarg, and a few hundred of his Troop. The ravens were already feasting, though they scattered as the two roamed the scene of the massacre. He believed that Kailynn's ability to read what happened from tracks and signs might be even better than his papa's.

He described how the herd of over fifteen hundred cattle, with their long horns between six to nine feet wide on both genders, had been stampeded into the Skarg, killing many of them.

Then, the great cold drake, an herbivorous dragon-kin his papa had somehow tamed and used to replace one of the mammoth teams, had been set free to wreak more damage and confusion in the Skarg ranks.

A group of ten of the young men had been guiding the cattle stampede into the confused mess. After ogres broke up the stampede, they retreated. That doesn't sound like much, but they charged with their huge two-handed swords and retreated with bows. It is an effective attack since he brought it up. I wouldn't know, but he was proud of their efforts.

Next, he talked about one of the wagons with one of his people's weapons, something that shot out liquid fire that couldn't be put out, and killed lots more, including all the ogres. I lost track of his story while I tried to imagine what could shoot out liquid fire.

When he found where his brothers, Lear and Connell fell, I was all ears again. He described where his papa made a stand over Connell's body. There was a ring of bodies as tall as he was surrounding his brother's corpse where his father had made that stand. Possibly Connell wasn't dead yet and that was the reason for the desperate fight. The Skarg harvested the legs and arms of their own dead for their abominable travel rations. What a fight that must have been!

They went to where his mother and sisters had fought and died. He described what they did to his mother, and my anger burned as I realized that the same thing was probably done to my mother.

I remembered the scene of her death. When I told him why I hadn't heard him and wanted him to repeat himself, he laid a sympathetic hand on mine.

He continued talking about how his sister's body was gone from the scene of the battle. Kailynn explained the reason the men's bodies weren't butchered was the respect his father and the rest of the men of his family had earned by their prowess as warriors. Evil and cruel as they are, he explained, The Skarg respect strength. He said they normally take young human women with them instead of eating or butchering them on the spot. They are never seen again. So, he'll never see Marsha again.

The practice of capturing only the young human women is one of the mysteries about the Skarg, along with where they came from and how there came to be so many so quickly. Kailynn felt the two mysteries were related.

Duncan finally came out with what had bruised his spirit so badly. What had been eating him alive the past two months, was his other sister, his little sister. He tried to shy away from speaking of her, but I could tell that he needed to share his grief.

She was a young girl, only eight. He spoke for at least an hour about her. I could tell he knew everything she did; that he doted on her. They were obviously so close. The look in his eyes when he spoke of her riding on his shoulders everywhere, said a lot. Then he described how she would climb into his lap and hug him for a long time, either falling asleep or playing a game of peeking at him. If his eye met hers, she giggled and hid her face in his shoulder.

As he told me of this his huge shoulders began heaving in great sobs. Finally, he stopped, and I swear I never knew that two eyes could express such absolute misery.

"Raina, this is hard to say, but, but—I had to kill her."

My hand found his arm as I gasped, "Why?"

He sighed, "When we found Aisling, she'd been impaled by a spear through her belly on the side of one of our wagons. She was still alive, so they left her to die, just to be cruel. She was a girl, not a woman; she was a long way from having her monthly. That seems to make a difference to them.

She woke and gasped as I pulled the spear free, and Kailynn caught her. He examined the wound and told me she would die, regardless of what we did. She was already burning up with fever and in terrible pain. Her unavoidable death in several days would be filled with senseless agony, and since there was nothing we could do, he would do the mercy stroke."

"But why did you give it instead?"

"I felt that a kinsman should be the one to send her to the Spirit World. It just felt like the right thing. I couldn't think; everything was numb, but I knew she should go by my hand, with my love."

Duncan bowed his head and sighed before he continued. Kailynn offered to play a final song for her, but she said, "Duncan, I'm so scared. Play *The Wild Wind*. Then just do it. I keep seeing when they did that dance imitating ravens and wolves eating me." She turned her head into my elbow hiding her face. "I just keep seeing that over and over. If you can't save me, then just end it. I hurt so bad, and I don't want wild beasts to eat me.' Then she cried and I thought I would die."

I hugged him briefly, then taking his hands in mine, I asked, "Duncan, is the Wild Wind that song you were playing by the creek?"

He just nodded curtly and continued, "I found my bag of pipes in the great wagon and inflated them. While I was doing that, Aisling laid her head on Kailynn's lap, and he just stroked her hair gently while I played. His eyes were shut, and he kept calling her Aletha instead of Aisling, while he sang some song I couldn't understand. I told him several times that her name was Aisling, not Aletha, but he seemed lost in his own world."

I put my hand on his arm to interrupt him, "Duncan, he had a daughter named Aletha. In the years of the elves, she was about your sister's age when she died."

He mouthed a big "O" and sighed, "Then the rest of what happened makes more sense now."

"How so?" I asked.

"When I finished playing The Wild Wind, we played it a second time with Kailynn doing a spontaneous harmony on his lute. She said, 'Duncan, you've always been my favorite brother. I love you. Now do what you must. I hurt so bad. Let me join Mommy and Daddy and Connell and Lear and roam the Wild Winds.' Raising her clenched hand, she whispered, 'I made this for you when you left to go warn the Clan, but you were gone when I finished it. Mommy said I could give it to you when you returned.'

"I took her first sachet filled with the fragrant herbs of our homelands and tried to do as she asked. Raina, I couldn't do it. I laid her out and kissed her forehead and placed my skinning knife to her throat. But when she looked up at me and smiled so bravely, I just crumpled, hugging her, and crying like a baby. Kailynn left me for some time. When he returned, he pulled me up and placed the knife back in my hands and directed my hands as we ended her suffering. Then he disappeared."

"He walked off, leaving you there like that? How cruel!"

"No, he didn't walk away, he disappeared. He did some spinning move and said something and just disappeared in front of my eyes."

"Oh, Laurealis said that he's a magician; he must have teleported."

"He returned sometime later, flying this time, and said, 'They're all dead, all of them. I killed them all.' I asked him who was dead. He said, 'The damned demon-men. I couldn't bear it anymore. They've hurt too many. Now those will hurt no more innocents.'

"'But that's impossible,' I'd replied. 'By their tracks, it was a huge group, better than a thousand.'

"'There were, but no more,' he replied. 'He stood tall over where I was still holding Aisling in my arms, singing to her corpse. Boy, I am an elf Champion. A mere thousand of the Soulless is no challenge for one such as I. Now let us see to your people's death ceremonies. Your people burn their dead, so their spirits can roam the Wild Winds?'

"'Yes, we can stack their bodies on the Great Wagons and burn them all.'

"Then he used his magic to lift the bodies of my family and the other Gaelaur dead and move them to the wagons. He asked me if I had any last words or anything I needed from my Great Wagon. I took my father's sword, which passed to me as the last member of the family, and Marsha's horse blanket she made to demonstrate her womanly skill.

"When I went to gather my father's armor, Kailynn said, 'No, that'll slow us up too much. When you're ready for armor, I'll make sure you have the finest.'

"I don't know why I accepted his word. Our armor is very finely made and so is our horse's barding. It's tremendously valuable. Anyway, for whatever reason, trust in him I guess, I left it. Then I said some last words over everyone. Kailynn did more magic, and all the furniture and combustible stuff on the wagon burst into flame.

"While I watched it and my family burn to ashes, he stood beside me, supporting me with his presence. As the last flames died while the sun was just lighting the horizon with the red light of dawn, he asked, 'You ready to go?'

"We mounted and pushed our horses as hard as we could for a month and a half to some fort in the mountains. My wound pretty much healed over that time. He would wash it and change the dressings every time we stopped, but that was the only time he let us slow down. Then we used the Dwarven Stor'dør to travel here in a day. He said we had covered as much ground in that one day as we covered in the previous six weeks of hard travel.

"Raina, I still can't believe they're all gone! And I killed my own sister."

He let out a great blood-curdling scream I swear could have awakened the dead. I saw a soldier peek in shortly after that.

I think I'm the first-person Duncan had been able to speak to, with more than a few necessary words, since I first met him a week ago. He allowed me to hold him for a long time while he released his pain.

Then I opened up to him about my past. He became furious when I told him I wasn't worth worrying about, that I was used trash.

"Raina, it doesn't reflect on you at all; what others did to you while you were helpless. The only thing that matters now is that you not let your past destroy you."

He told me how his people gave rapists over to the women. Enforcing natural laws, the men would deliver the *hideous beast* bound and the worse for wear.

"The beast cannot run if his legs are broken," he explained.

His people traveled through the year in groups of four to eight enormous Great Wagons, which took teams of sixty oxen to pull. They lived in them year-round.

In one of them, they carried their blacksmith's forge. They would stoke the forge, leave lots of horse and ox "chips" for fuel, and lay all the blacksmith's tools out, ready for the women's use. Then they moved a distance away with all the men, boys, and young girls to a temporary camp out of sight, but not out of hearing. Several days later, when the screams faded, they would return with the fathers leading their boys. They would walk past the horribly mauled remains of the rapist while the Head Woman spoke in witness. "This is what happens to those who take by force what should be given in love. Behold. Learn and be wise."

The last act was to bury the body. Duncan actually shuddered a little. Since the criminal wasn't cremated, his soul couldn't soar free. Burying the dead tied them to one place and is the equivalent of our Hells. He said the last rape he knew of had occurred when he was a little boy. I finally accepted that he saw me as he said he did. That he wasn't lying just to make me feel better about him.

I realized that he was nothing, if not genuine. It was a wonderful, freeing feeling. I'd never felt anything like it. I felt special.

All through that long winter day, he never let me go, though I finally got him to get off the wall with that freezing wind and settle against it while I nestled against him. With him taking the force of the wind, I was glad that he had recovered his vest, though he was sad for the waif.

He insisted on wrapping his arms around me so I wouldn't do anything foolish again. It felt good when he wrapped those strong arms around my waist. I felt safe, like nothing could hurt me. It wasn't like when those beasts used to hold me as they lied to me and used me. It felt, well, clean. He didn't even try to squeeze me. It felt so good that I tried to "reward" him by shifting so he could squeeze me if he wanted. I knew that's what all guys want, and for him, I didn't mind.

He lifted me again and held my waist. They sure raise them differently on the prairies. I finally, simply settled and relaxed in his comforting embrace.

I awoke as the sun was setting behind us to see Laurealis standing amidst the splinters of the door Duncan had destroyed to reach me. Her eyes were red and swollen. I cringed, backing into the safety of Duncan's arms.

"I came to beg your forgiveness," she said. "When they told me what I said…it was so horribly wrong, and I'm deeply sorry. That I lost my mind for a while is my only pitiful excuse. I hope, but without real belief, that someday you'll forgive me.

"Now, seeing the two of you here, with him asleep and you just waking, it's so beautiful. I want to remind you of how Astoria told you that your beauty would be unveiled one day. It has been. Right now, you seem renewed, and incredibly beautiful, *a beauty unveiled.*"

That huge block of ice trapping my heart, my soul, was finally cracking. It had been hit hard so many times this horrible, wonderful day that a little sunshine was beginning to peep in. For the moment, I was at peace.

Chapter Nine
The Dance of Dreams
Laurealis

When I saw Raina sitting in Duncan's lap, I felt peace returning. I still couldn't believe that my beloved Kailynn was gone. Raina's cringing from me told me, more than anything else, how deeply I had hurt her. Well, I'd deal with that later.

I was barely coping with Kai's death. It would have been incredibly difficult at any time, but now, while I was in the middle of Kaipoctouyevva, and my emotions were always a swirl, I didn't know how I would handle myself. That must be why I hadn't felt his death through our link. I hate this unfulfilled Kaipoctouyevva.

I walked over and tousled Duncan's hair to wake him. While near the edge of the roof, I saw Astoria below running toward me, her green healer's robes flying out behind her. They were darkened in places like they were covered in what might be blood. She was shouting, "Stop! Don't do it, Laurealis!"

I was confused, do what? I turned and saw Duncan and Raina entwined in an embrace with their eyes lost in each other. In my mind's eye I saw Kai' and I in the same position. My fragile peace and acceptance of my Life Mate's death was shattered. I felt myself shrinking, my clothes falling off me, and growing the butterfly-like wings that are part of my most powerful form of the emotive Dance of Dreams of which I am one of my people's masters. In that form I am no taller than my hand is long, and I fly with beautiful butterfly wings of lilac and pink, like my skin and hair.

Without my willing it, I began projecting my awful grief. I saw Raina and Duncan crumple with the weight of the emotion. I fluttered higher and away.

"Laurealis!" I looked back. Astoria was there; somewhat protected from my emotions by a spell, its white glow was clearly visible.

"Laurealis, no! Come back. You're in a human city. You'll kill people. I know you're upset…"

Her words were barely registering as I sank deeper into my darkness. I flew on, lost in my grief. I remembered Aletha and the afternoon that Kai' brought her to me broken from her fall…

Astoria

"Please, m'lady, we need you to keep healing the men!" an officer pleaded with me.

"The Lady has spoken to me, and I must leave, NOW!"

"The Lady?" he asked.

"The Lady, the Goddess we elves worship. The one who sent me and two more of Her healers currently in this city to heal your soldiers. Now, release me!"

I cursed the delay he'd caused. I raced to the area of town where the better hotels were located. I knew the Goddess would guide me as I got closer.

Unfortunately, that delay meant I was just in time to see my vision come true. Laurealis changed from her natural form to a sprite and flew off. In that form, she can receive emotions and redirect them; modifying or strengthening them as she chooses or project her own emotions to everyone within miles. It is normally done as entertainment within the confines of special meadows and arenas in or near Anthopoulos. A Master such as she, can project so powerfully that untold damage could be done to the unprotected.

I knew from my vision that something terrible had just occurred, almost certainly to Kailynn, by the power of the dread I felt. I raced to meet her, following the promptings of the three-form Goddess, only to arrive too late.

GRIEF!

The overwhelming emotions just poured over me, filling me inside and out. Its power was irresistible.

"Papa!"

"Little Johann!"

I collapsed from the sheer power of the emotion. It had blown through the protection spell that I always had up in strange places, and I noticed that it wasn't just me. Everyone had collapsed, many of them crying out names, obviously of someone dear to them. I noticed most of them lost in tears, and one old man held his chest and his left arm. I tried struggling to my knees to reach him to help through his obvious heart attack. I couldn't make it. I saw him relax in death. The rage I felt at the needless death gave me the strength to actually make it to my knees.

Now that I could draw breath, I focused on the chorus of one of my favorite hymns because singing my prayer spells focuses them, giving them far more power. It was a song of light entering our hearts as we fight darkness, fear, and evil so courage also fills our hearts. I set my voice free to sing of hope in the midst of such darkness:

> *Let there be light; let the darkness be shaken.*
> *Let there be light; let our hearts be awakened.*
>
> *Let there be light; let the darkness be shaken.*
> *Let there be light; let our courage be awakened.*
>
> *Let there be light; let the darkness be shaken.*
> *Let there be light; let our souls be awakened.*
>
> *Let there be light!*
> *Let there be light!*
>
> *LIGHT!*

At the song's crescendo, I was standing tall, my forefinger pointing to the sky, a brilliant white light emanating from my fingertip. As the spell developed, the light grew into a sphere surrounding me.

I felt confident that my spell would surely cancel the magical effects of Laurealis' dance as it bathed the street around me in its brilliance.

It didn't.

The spell wasn't strong enough to entirely cancel the dance's power; it merely allowed me to think while her remarkably potent spell leaked through my strongest Sphere of Protection. Looking around, I wished I could expand the protection my spell brought me, but that wasn't possible. Every spell has its limits.

My head still clearing from my dear friend's unintended, but enormously effective attack, I realized that I should move on to a song of praise commonly sung at our funerals to celebrate the deceased's life and our relationship to the mother. It might get Laurealis to focus on me and allow direction to her grief before half the city joined that man who had just died in my sight.

> *How deep the Lady's love for us, Her children She adores.*
> *How Her wide and open arms invite*
> *Not loss, but transformation...*

I tasted the flavor of her dance changing.

As my mind cleared more, my song grew in power. I naturally widened my prayers to include the city, naming as many specific groups of people who would be sensitive to the grief of the recently bereaved as I could. I sang in prayer for the Goddess to be merciful to the city of a half-million unsuspecting humans.

I felt the Mother's Touch like an ethereal hand resting on my shoulder. Eyes closed to focus on my extemporaneous song, I gasped when my subconscious desire was granted.

She allowed me to see how her Blessing was protecting the widows and widowers, the orphans and parents grieving their loved ones lost in the horrible war.

She showed me the soldiers, especially those who had just lost dear friends in that terrible battle up north.

I understand that soldiers and warfare are necessary at times. But the loss of life is extremely upsetting. I hadn't truly realized how soft their hearts could be for the innocent.

Laurealis, like so many of our people, saw soldiers as monsters, except of course for her own husband, guilty of all the violence and bloodshed of war. I don't remember when that point of view came about, since we used to be a nation of warriors. It was when so many of our malcontents, and our bravest, became the germs of the Asmodian race, then later more became dragons.

Then the mother showed me the acts of heroism, which mattered little to me, and the acts of compassion to children and families off the battlefield, which mattered a great deal to me. She showed me their pain, and I, who had always felt that in some way they reveled in causing pain, came to know just how wrong I had been. With tears of remorse streaming down my cheeks, I included all She was showing me in my prayer. I felt Laurealis pick up my prayer in her Dance. She pulled the raw emotions from those who were actively feeling them and broadcasting them across the entire city. I became a conduit for The Mother's concerns.

As Laurealis adapted her Dance to what The Mother was feeding me, The Mother next let me see those She allowed to give in to their grief and cross the veil, leaving this life, with all of its pain, behind. Through Her, I felt a number of lives end peacefully. She even allowed me to see them greeting the ones waiting for them as their souls approached the Gate. Again, Laurealis picked this up through her receptiveness while performing her Dance. She projected it with the Lady's promise of peace and hope to come.

Renewed, I continued to sing of the cycles of life and death, new life, and praises to The Mother. Laurealis' dance picked up another note, as the Consort joined The Mother. His masculine presence led us to remembering the terrible outrages of the first attacks and the destruction of Firenzia when the Soulless Ones first appeared. We remembered the Rape of Bourbesonne, that beautiful Arcean seaport that will never be habitable again. Outrage filled all of the city's hearts. A terrible rage brought me to my feet. I saw the raw emotions filling the eyes and body language of those around me as the entire city remembered that terrible time of five years ago. Then She filled our minds with True Knowledge of what the Soulless Ones were actually like. How cruel and cannibalistic they were. How they weren't truly human, but a horrific cross between men and actual Chaos Matter, the stuff that demons use to grow from.

I was shocked. I recognized the demonic connection from what I had heard about them. But it never crossed anyone's mind that they were partially formed from actual Chaos Matter. I thought it was too rare and precious to use like that.

She gave us another shock, filling our hearts with the knowledge that this war was another of the End Times. If it could not be stopped, virtually all but a few full humans would be killed, again.

There was an added urgency because of the new element of the Soulless Ones. If the Asmodians won this war, it might not be just the humans that were eliminated; all the Free Peoples would vanish as well. Our world would somehow become a land of Chaos where demons could exist freely. We saw a vision of a pool of a living, multi-hued viscous liquid of pure Chaos Matter in a huge castle far to the north in the ice sheets where the Asmodians lived. Due to the order of our dimension, demons had not been physically present, and were bound to whoever summoned them. In the Chaos Dimensions, demons were free and fully physical. The Soulless Ones were only able to exist in our dimension because an element of Chaos Matter existed here. This was a war to the death of both the Asmodians and their minions, or of the Free Peoples.

Next, we saw a vision of how the demons sent the Chaos Comet in an attempt to destroy our world. Instead, it hit and destroyed the single moon of that time, creating the rings and nearly destroying all life on the planet.

This dance was trampling all over my long-held beliefs. There was no time to examine them, the Dance rolled on.

The Consort joined, linking His strength to The Lady's in Laurealis' Dance. The rage cooled to a tempered steel that would stop at nothing to right the wrongs. This city, like our own, had grown weary of the cost, especially in lives lost or ruined, and in the treasure this war had already squandered. From what I was seeing and feeling, I knew their spirit had been renewed. I felt the overwhelming desire to do anything to right the wrongs and soundly defeat the Asmodians, no matter the cost, no matter the time, no matter ANYTHING! We stood strong! The Soulless Ones and their subjects, we would beat back and cure or kill. But their makers, the Asmodians, we would utterly destroy.

As this tempered emotion settled over my shoulders like a coat of armor, I knew it would not fade quickly, as it was Goddess and God-touched. I also had the strongest hunch that Laurealis was going to need my help now. She would be over there, near that tree.

I was exhausted by all the mana drained by my long prayer and a day of surgery and healing. Drawing on the last of my strength, I staggered as fast as my robes would allow me and saw her flutter weakly down, like the butterfly she so strongly resembled. She saw me and smiled as she lit on the palm of my offered hand.

"Well done," I told her.

I quickly grew worried. I noticed her ragged breathing and her pallor as she collapsed on my hand into the sleep of complete exhaustion.

I became extremely concerned. I realized it was less like sleep and more unconsciousness, as she grew back to her normal size without subconsciously clothing herself with illusion. She hadn't had a chance to ground herself before her grief took her, and she had worked such a powerful magic. I was quickly suspecting it was mana deprivation shock. Her life was in danger! This condition was rare because all of our people are trained from childhood to instinctively ground before working magic. I had to save her. It's what I do. It was why the mother had directed me there.

Her pulse was weak and unsteady. Knowing it was pointless, I tried channeling some of my mana into her. She had never learned to channel mana like priestesses and priests do. I knew her body, even if it had been conscious, was probably unable to receive energy this way. As I'd expected, the blue energy I sent her from my hand over her heart simply shot out in all directions, wasted.

I then thought; if I could get sweets for energy, and some pollen from the Talu palm into her quickly, she should recover. I avoided thinking of the result if it didn't work.

I looked around, hunting for options in this strange city. I was so tired; I could barely think. I noticed several men ogling her. No! The lechers saw only her lack of dress, not how ill she was.

Humans! They breed like rabbits and think like them, too! Unlike in our home of Anthopoulos, a woman as beautiful as Laurealis, with her perfect shades of lilac skin, pink hair and long, slender ears rising through her hair, cannot sleep on a human street dressed as she was.

I could, I thought briefly. I'm ugly, overweight, and ochre yellow with yellow-green hair, wishing for the millionth time that I could have been born more attractive.

Unfortunately, I have no skill with illusion, so I did the best I could. I covered her in two of my colorful, sheer, fine linen outer robes and glared at the lechers who ogled both of us until they grew bored and left. I tried to spot someplace that served sweets. I saw an inn, then a constable, whose rotund form led me to believe he probably knew where all the local sweets and confections were served. I shouted, "Help! I need to get her inside that inn and get her something sweet to eat. Please, she is quite ill."

He began walking toward me when his look changed from compassion to alarm when we saw an enormous young man charging us, with Raina right behind him. The constable did what any sensible person would have done seeing someone the size of that young man charging. He drew his club from a ring at his waist.

He stopped when Raina shouted to the constable, "That's our mother! I don't know why she's out here, but we're going to take her to her room there."

The constable stepped forward, protecting Laurealis. "Who are you and why should I believe you?"

Raina stepped in front and said to the constable, "I'm Raina. And this is Duncan. She and her husband, Kailynn, adopted us. We heard someone; it sounded like you were shouting at her, then she turned tiny, with butterfly wings and her clothes fell off. She flew away and we were knocked out somehow by grief. Her clothes are still up there. I don't understand what's going on, but she's hurt somehow. We're taking her back to our rooms and getting her some help."

Duncan reached down to pick her up and the constable shouted, "Halt!"

I spoke to reassure him, "No, I believe it's all right. I met the girl this morning and I know of the boy, Duncan. What she speaks is the truth." I hadn't finished with what I was saying before "the boy" swept Laurealis into his arms and was trotting away like she weighed nothing.

I offered my thanks to the constable. He looked relieved that he hadn't had to fight the young giant. I think we both believed that it wouldn't have been a contest; the young man just looked tough. I added the worn out greeting that had meaning to only a few these days. "Remember Bourbesonne."

His reaction was startling; it was like the interceding years had fallen away. His eyes flamed in righteous anger and his posture straightened, "I remember."

At last! I now knew why the Goddess had sent to me that vision. It wasn't to stop Laurealis. It may have been partially to help her afterward. It was primarily to pray for her to be guided by the mother. This war was in the Gods' hands, not ours. I only hoped ours were the stronger Gods.

"Raina, would you take me to Laurealis' room? I assume that's where that young giant has taken her."

She smiled, then her eyes hardened with a calculation in them that I didn't understand, like a young and very jealous lover, and something else I couldn't put my finger on. I vowed to watch these two. Laurealis said nothing of it that morning, and it certainly didn't come out in our talk.

"Yes, she replied. I'm sure that's where he's taken her. Even though he's a man, she's perfectly safe with him." Her voice dropped to a whisper, "He's…different, safe somehow. I don't understand. Come, I'll show you."

I was curious. This girl had gone through a lot, which I knew. But what did that comment mean? That was strange… like she was just putting radically new thoughts together.

When we got to their room, the door was closed with him standing guard outside. The young giant had a sword that was huge enough to match him, held point down, but ready to use. I felt no aggression from him, only honorable resolve.

He smiled gently at Raina and stepped aside. She tried to hold an arm, but he shrugged her aside and nodded "no." Then he motioned for her to join me inside. His smile only lasted a second, but it spoke volumes.

I checked Laurealis from head to toe. No physical injuries but it was obvious she was losing her battle to live.

"Raina, Laurealis is in shock and slipping away. I need you to fetch fruits, honey, sweetbreads, and sweetmeats, anything sweet. Now go!"

"Could she die?"

"Yes!" I snapped, "Now go!"

She ran off like a demon was after her.

Well, maybe one was. I sure snapped at her. I was becoming dizzy and my stomach heaving. I, too, was having a low mana reaction. I'd healed 'till I exhausted my mana, then did surgeries all day. Oh Lady, give me strength.

I dropped to my knees, as much to not fall on my face, as to properly pray. Her power and peace flowed into me, steadying me. I felt just strong enough to realize what a fool I had been about others, including my best friend over on the pillows. Like so many of my elf friends, I believed, since the Soulless Ones appeared a few years ago, that they were not truly evil. They were merely controlled, and we should give them more time before condemning them. But the Lady shattered those suppositions as powerfully as lava flowing into the ocean.

Poor dear, I thought as I checked her pulse again. I hope those sweets get here soon. The sweets would get her blood sugar back up, but she needed it sooner than later.

"Thank you, Lady," I prayed briefly as I realized my mana was back to workable levels.

Now that I again had mana to cast a few spells, I chose a diagnostic spell. My hand glowed blue as I ran it from her head to her feet. As I thought, my spell confirmed the dance had dangerously exhausted her natural mana. She had performed her dance from her personal energy, not from the surrounding fields.

Her grief wasn't helping either. When couples marry, their internal magic meshes their souls together and many times a surviving mate has died from shock when the other dies suddenly. Her shuddering, groaning, and occasional thrashing was probably at least as much from her grief as from low blood sugar and mana. Either could kill her. Both most certainly would.

She had known better than to take up the sprite, but bless her, her heart was broken. As suddenly as she took off, I suspected she was as surprised by her reaction as I had been.

I was still too weakened to think properly. I was missing something, something vital. I had no doubt about one thing I had to do; I must feed her straight Talu pollen. I tried finding her Talu box, which she always kept close. The Talu was the tree that absorbed mana, allowing the elves to use the Earth's magnetic fields to perform our spells. Minor spells could be run safely from our body's indigenous mana, but major spells, like her Dance, required an external source of power. Powering it from personal mana could exhaust energy quickly. My supply was back at the embassy. There just wasn't time to get it. If I could find hers, her extremely low mana would no longer be in danger of killing her.

The little mana I tried to channel into her out on the street hadn't worked; she wasn't skilled enough at channeling to absorb enough to help, even if she were conscious. Besides, I was too drained to give her much, even if she could absorb it. I searched urgently for her box. I knew what it looked like since I had given it to her a few hundred years ago. It looked like she had travelled with all of her clothes. There were four large chests in the room plus the normal furniture one would expect in a high-quality hotel like this one.

I could ask the Lady. She seemed to be paying a lot of attention to me lately…

I heard a loud gasp as Laurealis woke. "Astoria, I can't believe he's gone," she wept.

I didn't know what to do. Her grief could kill her, and so could her low energy. I let my intuition guide me as I held her, helping her to cry out a little of her grief.

After only a minute or two, I interrupted her to ask for her Talu box and she pointed to a drawer. I returned and opened it for Laurealis to lick her finger and hold a pollen laden finger under her tongue. Inhaling it is the fastest way to get it into the blood, but, oh my how it burns when you do it that way. Under the tongue works well, also, so she would be doing better soon with such a straight shot of mana going directly into her blood. Being magical in our very nature, mana is as important to our short-term health as sugar.

My worry about her low mana abating, I held her in my arms again and let her cry. As I comforted her, I examined what the mother had just revealed to me about soldiers. I was grappling with the thought of soldiers as protectors from violence, and often not the cause of the violence. I mean, I knew men were protectors, but soldiers, too? I needed to be honest. Soldiers could be protecting their loved ones, the same as Raina's father who had died protecting her. They must be as strong and cunning as their opponents, without reservation.

I wouldn't have thought it possible, but it made me feel even worse about the four boys I lost earlier. I realized that I had been as guilty of forgetting the cause of this horrible war as anyone else.

Lost in my thoughts, I was startled when Raina returned, followed by several serving girls, two men holding a serving table, and the manager with enough sweets to feed an army!

"We remember," the manager said in that unique way as he indicated a place for the table. The men put the table in place and bowed. The girls set the table with practiced ease into a handsome arrangement, complete with fresh flowers. I wondered where they came from in the height of winter. The girls then curtsied and backed away to stand in front of the men in a respectful maneuver.

The manager said, "Please, if there is anything else you need, anything at all, just let me know. It is all complementary for the one who returned our hearts to us."

He then bowed and everyone left. I was amazed at the seemingly choreographed performance I had just witnessed. I had forgotten that mere humans could be so charming, graceful, and competent. There was much I needed to meditate upon. I looked upon Raina with an appraising look, and she just shrugged her shoulders and smiled. Looking back at Laurealis, I wondered if the huge appetite she should have was making itself known, or if her grief was masking her basic needs.

Of course, for my exceptionally emotional friend, it was grief.

I spent several minutes, with Raina's help, coaxing Laurealis to eat. I cast a spell to relieve her nausea. With Raina's strong will and intimidating looks promising all kinds of trouble if she didn't eat, Laurealis slowly extended a shaking hand for a sweet. Once she took the first bite, her body's hunger asserted itself and she ate as she should after such a huge, ungrounded magical effort.

I stepped back, watching Laurealis begin to go through that mountain of sweets, sweet breads, and sweetmeats. Just to be sociable, I gave in to my special weakness for sweet breads with cinnamon. I had an excuse; I had also put out a lot of my own mana all day, though I had been properly grounded, Then I noticed some real chocolate! By the Goddess, nothing would do but having some. I monitored Laurealis' eating while enjoying a not so small snack myself. Satisfied that she would recover after more to eat and sleep, I looked for a place to get comfortable and rest. I noticed a pin on the dresser, one of Kailynn's clasps for his cape. I picked it up… PAIN!

Gut wrenching pain exploded within me. The field surrounding me held me helplessly away from the mana that

I could sense all around me while I experienced a vision of chains which held me suspended over a deep chasm in total darkness inside a cave.

I screamed and collapsed. When I came to, the young giant, Duncan, was holding me with a worried look filling his face.

"Are you all right, Priestess?"

I noticed the mess of the table and its contents strewn across the room. Though still a bit disoriented, I tried to get up, supporting myself on his shoulder. I fell back, the memory of the pain Kailynn had been in was still intense, and I'm nowhere near as graceful as Laurealis.

I smiled and nodded my thanks to Duncan. He helped me stand. When I was on my feet, I held up the pin wrapped in the end of my sleeve for Laurealis to see.

"Laurealis!" I shouted happily. "I just had a vision of Kailynn and he's alive!"

"What? Oh, Goddess be praised! Where is he? How is he? Is he injured?"

"I touched this clasp and only saw him for a second. He's held captive somewhere. Let me get a bowl and some water and do a proper scrying, and we'll see just what happened to him."

Laurealis continued eating from the plate she held, though her eyes were locked on me, waiting for the news my scrying could give us. There were still some of those wonderful chocolates on the table, even though most of the sweets were strewn about. It looked like the young giant had charged into the room with a single-minded focus. Good to know that he acts like one of the long-lost Paladain he so strongly resembled.

Those chocolates were so good! I found myself munching on a handful while looking for that bowl.

"Would this do?" Raina asked, offering a suitable bowl.

"Sweetie, that's perfect."

"Then let's go get some water and leave some of those sweets for Laurealis," she suggested.

"But I didn't eat that much," I protested, which was met with "the look" from both of them. I know I'm fat, certainly by Elven standards, but they were right. I followed Raina to another room, filled the bowl, and began the necessary meditations and prayers.

Raina stepped beside me, and Duncan gently held her shoulders and looked over both of us. Laurealis wasn't strong enough to join us yet, but I wasn't worried about her. If she should appear, she knew what I was about to tell the children.

"Children." I felt them stiffen at the word. Well, they *are* children. "Raina and Duncan. My consciousness will be going into the water to look for Kailynn from that clue I saw when I touched his pin. You may look, but whatever you do, absolutely do not touch the water till I come back out. The results could be…unfortunate."

Raina said, "Look, but don't touch. Gotcha." Duncan nodded.

Satisfied, I began humming, then singing very quietly. The water in the bowl grew cloudy, then cleared. I felt the impression of "east" unmistakably. I saw mountains, though I didn't recognize them. There was a single, distinct, cone shaped mountain with three additional cones rising from the sides, which I still didn't recognize. I really haven't traveled much, except to the semi-civilized human lands. In a vision, I rushed inside the mountain, and traveling far too fast to recognize anything, I saw Kailynn hanging from chains face down in a cavern over a lake. The chains were held to the walls by glowing red crystals, which were obviously generating a spell of some kind. I was above him, and he was in a craggy, wet area with lots of cliffs. He was nude, so his Champion's Armor, which could do anything, was elsewhere. With that gone, his power was reduced, and was preventing him from rescuing himself. He was suspended hundreds of feet high in a hole or chasm a couple of hundred feet wide. I felt a deep foreboding about this water!

Suddenly I was thrown out of the vision, faintly aware that a hand had touched the water. My head hurt so badly in reaction to being thrown out of the spell that I couldn't recognize the hand that had broken the spell. I threw up the sweets I had just eaten, then curled up into a tight ball holding my aching belly and throbbing head.

"Astoria! Astoria!" Laurealis cried, "I'm so sorry, it's just that I saw Kai' and I had to reach out to him."

I couldn't speak, I couldn't do anything except be miserable. At least I knew what happened. My dear friend had, once again today, lost another battle to her emotions. I couldn't very well blame her; today had to have been one of the worst of her life. I felt myself being picked up and I threw up again. Duncan placed me on a bed of pillows, and Laurealis wiped my mouth clean, then bathed my forehead with a cool damp cloth that she rinsed several times in the bowl I'd used for scrying.

Laurealis stayed with me all night. The next morning, she asked, "Will you be able to scry again soon?"

I felt like in another week I might actually feel like living. This must be what a hangover feels like to a human.

My voice sounded horrible even to me, "What are you asking? Can I scry again? You know I can only scry something once, especially after how I was jerked out of it. That's the way the Goddess works."

"But you didn't get a full view. We don't know where he is."

Oh, her high-pitched voice hurt. I held my aching head, "Laurealis, whose fault is it that I didn't get the full vision the Goddess sent me?"

At least she looked abashed. "Mine," she replied.

"And why do I feel like death warmed over?"

"Me…I'm sorry. But can't you try?"

"No!" I shouted, and immediately regretted it while trying to curl into a tighter ball and holding my ears to shut out the horribly loud noise of my own voice. "Just go. We need to go east. Get maps and some people to go with us and we'll find Kai. But I can't go anywhere for now, not till tomorrow morning or even tomorrow night.

Duncan spoke quietly, "Raina and I will go with you. The four of us can travel quickly and lightly."

From where in the Mists of Heaven, did he appear? Oh, Raina's here, too.

"Whatever, just leave me alone and close the shutters. The light hurts."

Laurealis tucked me in, and everyone left.

Chapter Ten
Delays, Delays
Duncan

Why is it that three women can take longer to get ready to travel than it took me to load the four horses and that cantankerous mule?

"Ladies, are we leaving today? Laurealis, I would have expected the least delay from you. Are you ready?"

"Yes, sweetie. Just load those two bags for me, would you?"

"More bags? I thought the hotel manager was going to send your extras to your friends in Anthopoulos."

"Well, I am sending one case over there to them."

"No, Laurealis. I'm going through your things myself and reducing them to one pack. Why do you need so many clothes anyway? The clothes you wear and the ones you packed are made of linen so fine, so sheer, that you might as well not be wearing anything, unless you have layers of it on, like Astoria wears. I can see adding some cold weather gear, but we have to travel light. Do you understand?"

"I am traveling light!"

"With all your gear, I'll have to have a second mule. I hate mules. One is bad enough; there's no way I'll go with two. They're slow, cantankerous beasts."

I gestured to the hotel's bellman, who was to help with the luggage, and we left. After Raina spoke with him, the manager had been kind enough to donate food and cold weather gear to us. When we reached the stables, we dropped everything to the ground and went through it all. The ladies arrived when we were halfway through discarding most of the extra clothing and nonsense gear.

"But a lady needs to carry changes of clothing," Laurealis protested.

Astoria placed her hand on Laurealis' shoulder. "Laurealis, what he's saying makes sense. Though he may think you're wearing those outfits, I know, except when you're going where you might be in contact with lots of people, and your illusion might fail as a result of being touched too often, you generally don't wear anything but illusions. Just leave the clothes here. You have your jewel to control the temperature around you, so you don't need your heavier clothing for the cold. Here, I'll help you pick out two outfits, one for really freezing weather, and one for being around lots of people."

"But..."

With Astoria taking charge, I turned my attention to Raina's bags.

"What are you doing?" demanded Raina as I threw another bag of strips of cloth bandages into the discard pile.

She grabbed them and tried stuffing them back into her much lighter saddlebag.

"By the Ancient One's beard!" I shouted in frustration.

My explosion got the attention of all three women.

"I'm trying to keep you alive! We're going into extremely dangerous country to rescue a man who killed a thousand Skarg like it was squashing bugs! If he couldn't fight off whatever got him, why should we be able to? Speed is likely to be one of our best defenses, for reasons that I'm not going to go into right now!

"Raina, you did pretty well.

"Astoria, you did even better. I had to think twice about some of your stuff, but you needed that bowl for your, what'd you call it, a scrying spell? I assumed that your extra stuff would prove useful, for reasons only you know.

"Laurealis. Except for your spell books, and what looks like it must be needed for your magic, I'm sending almost all of your things back. I've eliminated the need for the mule with what we're leaving here. Now, let's get started before you decide to stop for lunch or something! Aaaahhh!"

I hopped onto Shadow, the fine stallion I had caught and trained with Dad's help and waited for the others to mount. Watching Raina try to climb onto her horse, I discovered another problem I had never considered, since all my people are on horseback before they can walk. "Raina, have you ever ridden a horse?" "Uh, no," she replied sweetly.

"Great, simply great! Why didn't it occur to me that someone couldn't ride a stinking horse? All right, we'll move my gear to your horse, and you ride in front of me. I'll give you riding lessons when we can make time."

She just beamed that gorgeous smile at me. "I'm sorry for being so much trouble. I'll try to learn. It's just that they're so big and scary."

"Scary?"

How could horses seem scary? Strange, she seems so competent. She's a city girl, even though she spent a lot of time in the country when she was younger, so I guess that's to be expected. Still, if she can't ride on her own, she'll be a delightful handful riding in front of me.

Don't think like that, man. I'm not a man yet! Not until I go through the Ceremony of Manhood. Besides, we are not properly engaged! And just how is that going to happen? What's more, our parents died, and the nearest matchmaker was two months, maybe three, of hard riding away! I couldn't do any of the things I've been dreaming of doing unless I have a way to support her and any children that may come. And how would I do that?

My, but she was a pleasant handful. Easy on the eyes, too, even with those ears. They just looked good on her, made her look like a cat I'd love to pet, or…

But I couldn't do anything 'till we could be engaged, which would involve solving the problem of no Great Wagon and no herds and no way to get either of them. Of course, it would have helped if I'd gone through my Ceremony of Manhood so I could braid my hair into a queue as a man. I shouldn't look at a girl, since I was not properly a man yet. Two weeks before Winter Solstice and everyone I knew that could have declared me grown and ready for adult life, was dead. Well, two impossible tasks are just harder to do than one. Like Dad would have said, just put one foot in front of the other.

Food crossed my mind. Between repacking and ensuring proper shipping directions for the wagonload of stuff she had to ship back, it really was time for a satisfying meal before we left.

I was glad for Astoria's help. She seemed levelheaded, though her face was still pale. I knew she still wasn't over her sickness since she hadn't shown the slightest interest in eating. When I'd mentioned food, she just looked sickly green, instead of her natural yellow green. I got the idea real fast that all talk of food was a bad idea.

Still, I was shocked when I heard them fighting. I was still at the table in the common room, since Raina and Laurealis eat like birds, when I heard Astoria scream out in full-blown rage.

"You haven't tried to heal either of those children's obvious emotional problems because you don't like to feel negative emotions! Haven't you looked at their auras? By the Goddess, that has got to be one of the most selfish things I've ever heard!"

Laurealis said something, but it wasn't shouted.

"Yes, you're an emotive dancer! I know you're an emotive dancer. Laurealis, the special. Laurealis, the beautiful. Laurealis, the great emotive dancer. You're a performer, not a healer. I'll tell you what else you are. Laurealis, the spoiled. Laurealis, hang around with me to bask in my glory. Laurealis, you're my best friend. But dammit woman, you're a coward. You can actually feel their emotions! I can only sense something is wrong. I could talk to them, but it would be like using an axe instead of a scalpel!"

I heard Laurealis' clear high soprano voice cut through Astoria's alto. "Well, then, YOU do it! You're so damned competent in all you do, I'm sure you could handle that, too!"

"What? Yesterday, I went to help the human army and discovered to my horror that the way they deal with deep wounds seems to be by having a barber, a BARBER, by the Lady, cut off anything that was too serious to heal on its own. My Dear Lady of the Healing Waters! The outside of the 'healing' tent was lined waist-deep with amputated limbs. It looked like stacked firewood. So many of the 'doctors' victims were dying of shock, I spent all of my stored mana just healing the most critical of them to the point of merely surviving.

"I screamed at them to stop drinking their damned whiskey because they needed to use it to sterilize equipment and the wounds. I did a lot of screaming. I even ripped the green robes off one of them that reeked of whiskey.

"After I stabilized dozens, it seemed more like a thousand of the victims of human 'medicine', I couldn't rest. It was only after I was exhausted and almost drained of mana that I had to do surgeries on the serious cases that had been treated by a damned drunken BARBER!

"Aargh! They had hacked off limbs for no medical reason! I finally had to stop when I passed out on someone. THEN the Lady informed me that you had a crisis and I had to help you!"

"But you're a healer! You're supposed to want to help! You don't know how much negative emotions upset me!"

"WHAT? You think you're the only one who must deal with negative emotions! You don't think negative emotions upset me as well? How in all the various Hells of all the Gods of all the world do you think I felt yesterday when I was trying to get that arrow out from right beside that boy's heart. I slipped and, and I cut his aorta, and he died right there in front of me. I had no mana left to heal the artery."

Tears flowed freely down Astoria's angry face.

"I was shaking with my exhaustion! Then to top it off, a nurse showed me the letter he'd been having read to him before I got to him. It was from his wife telling him of the birth of their child! And you don't think I feel? I lost four, count them; one, two, three, four boys yesterday! Then I found out that those boys weren't the bad or misinformed people, they were the good people!"

Astoria was crying, and I didn't know whether to go to her or not. I started toward her when I heard, "Don't touch me! Yes, I feel. I feel like death right now. I failed those boys, the Lady as well. I know I killed those boys because I was too damned exhausted to keep going, and there were too few of us. We needed someone with your skills to help us with the ones who simply couldn't go on anymore. It was their emotions that were wounded, not their bodies. With your gifts, those children, need you to help with their emotional scars. You're being a COWARD! This is WAR, woman! I didn't truly realize it till your dance yesterday, but we are all in this, for better or worse, 'till it's finished.

"Now the Lady tells me we have to find and rescue your husband, so I can't help healing the wounded here. You have to grow a backbone and help where you can, Laurealis! And don't go mouthing any of the stuff we've told each other for so many years about how the soldiers caused all this. After what you and the Lady and Consort wrought yesterday, we all know those were just lies, possibly fed to us by Asmodius and His minions!"

Laurealis said something else, too quietly for me to hear.

Astoria's rage was quieting as well, though her voice was still projecting loudly enough to hear. Her compassion was also there. "Laurealis, I really don't know where you'll find the courage. You can ask the Lady for some. I find it when I see people hurting, I just want to stop it. That might be a good place for you to begin."

There was a long pause, then Astoria continued, "No, don't touch me. I love you, but I'm too angry at you still. Just, just leave me. Just go."

I had heard enough. I had just left the dining room with Raina and bumped into Laurealis. She glanced up at me and ducked her head, crying as she ran away. When we passed in the hall on my way to her room Astoria was also quietly weeping. I didn't know what to say, but Astoria came to me and cried into my shoulder.

This was beyond me. How was I supposed to deal with three emotional women on a journey into dangerous territory? All three of them have been terribly upset in the last two days, and with just cause. It's not like they were just being emotional. They had real reasons to be upset. My mother would have known what to do.

The image of her dead, mutilated body flashed through my head.

My head bowed over Astoria's shoulder as I comforted her, but I realized she was comforting me as well.

Oh, Lord, help me. That was too much. I hoped the elves could ride. Wouldn't that be just grand, riding a wagon instead of a horse? And what was that about healing me emotionally? She'd better not. Dealing with Aisling's death once was bad enough. But if she makes me feel what I felt again, I didn't know if I would stay sane. Just one day at a time, like Dad always said. "Tomorrow's problems will still be there tomorrow." Still, I doubt Dad ever faced anything like these three!

Chapter Eleven
On the Road, At Last
Duncan

The next morning, going after Kailynn immediately was not going to happen. Astoria was still too sick, though she recognized many of her fellow priests and priestesses coming into the city. When she asked them what was going on, they began describing the same thing we had all felt, but without the initial grief that knocked out Lergenze. The elves' Gods made Laurealis' dance into an event that was felt all over the civilized world. Healers were pouring into the city, so Astoria was no longer needed. She had been terribly worried over it, however. Facing the odds, I was sure we were facing, I was pleased we would have such a skilled healer with us.

I calmed as soon as I got out of that city. As towns and cities go, I'm sure Lergenze is a fine one, with all those white walls and red tiled roofs and all. It's just; all those walled rooms instead of the open plains. The animal sounds and the wind are shut out with walls around the houses, walls around parts of the city, and finally, the giant wall around the entire city. It was just too much. I felt like I couldn't breathe, like I was suffocating.

We made suitable time traveling through the easy country in the heart of Francesca. We were in a huge north/south valley running between high mountain chains. Since we were heading east, we followed the stone-paved highway to the well-guarded pass. This is where Francesca's presence, both in the good roads and inns, and more particularly in the police presence, quickly fell away. There were settlements away from the metropolis, even a couple of pretty large towns, small cities, mid-sized cities, or villages. Where they had once been around farms and ranches, now they were around the mines. It seemed the area across the mountains was as rich in minerals as the valley was rich in crops.

There was almost no wild forest, just little areas a few miles square in between the croplands and two ancient ruins of once mighty cities, the kind you see from time to time from previous Ages, probably First Age. They died so long ago that their names are lost to history.

I didn't see the expected mines around these ancient ruins. My people's largest cities, Detrota and Chicog, were built around the eastern and western remnants of an ancient city, or maybe it was several such ancient cities that had grown into one huge one. The ice sheets are slowly melting and retreating north and have, over the last couple of hundred years or so, exposed more of remnants of the ancient cities on the southern side of the Great Inland Sea and to the west of the Little Sea. We mined wonderful and often mysterious machines, metal, glass, and other resources. These southern lands were far more heavily populated than my own people's area around the great inland seas and the eastern and northern parts of the great prairies. The people must have already mined out their own ruins in past Ages.

There were no mountains anywhere near my homeland. I realized that our city people's strength in metals was due entirely to our fortune of being located near a city that hadn't been mined out during an earlier Age. The ice sheet had protected the resources that were now our strength.

My family was from our frontier, so we were nomadic ranchers who had far larger wagons than anything I'd seen here, due to the resources from Detrota. I wondered if these people were closer to the norm for most cultures, where mine, with our use of ancient resources, were more like what it was like during the earlier ages.

We were making good time while I was lost in my thoughts.

The second night, I had the middle watch. The night before I explained why we had to keep the fire low and never look at it so as to not ruin our night vision. I was enjoying the cool night, a good one for chewing on my thoughts. I thought about the last couple of days, and about Raina…especially about Raina. The end of my watch arrived all too quickly, and I woke Astoria for her watch. For years I have always said good night to the horses and made sure all was well with them before I rested.

Sometime later, the horses' nervous nickering woke me. I got up, and in the stillness of the snow-covered forest, I heard something strange.

It sounded like something kept falling in the snow, but I couldn't imagine what could be causing the sound. Astoria looked askance at me, but I just shrugged my shoulders.

Whatever was making the sound was approaching the camp. I thought of something walking with a limp, but the sound also kept making me think of a heavy chest hitting the snow when we unloaded a wagon in the winter. I just couldn't place what could make such a sound.

Swish, swish, whump! Swish, swish, whump! It kept getting closer. Astoria nodded to me, and I woke Raina, and she woke Laurealis.

I had prepared some makeshift torches of pine boughs covered in dead tufts of needles from near the woodpile earlier in the evening. Now, I pulled them beside the fire. I didn't want the extra light yet, but I knew it might be needed quickly. I readied my sword, and Raina pulled out two knives.

Laurealis whispered, "What is that? I think, no, it couldn't be. Even humans wouldn't be so foolish."

"What do you see?" Astoria asked. "Oh, my…I see."

I thought I had great night vision, but I still couldn't make it out. The light of the three lunar rings against the snow provided some light, but not enough.

"What do you ladies see?" I asked, having already realized earlier in our travels that elves, and even Raina, a half-elf, have far better night vision than mine.

"A wooden chest. A walking, limping chest," Raina said.

"What? A chest, walking and limping?" I repeated, not understanding. "I was taught your language with a spell; I must have misunderstood you. Did you say…By the Ancient One, it's a walking, limping chest!" I relaxed, chuckling, and knelt, my sword sliding through the snow to the ground.

The chest stopped, turned to face me, and charged! I backed up, startled beyond thought, and tripped on a piece of wood. Laurealis did something, and a gem placed in her belly button flared to life. The surroundings changed, so we all looked like trees. It was an illusion like she'd explained to me.

The chest stopped charging me and moved to her in mid-stride, bowling her over. Several ropes popped out and began stripping off her magical jewelry and gems. Drawing my sword, I had to check my swing, because she was pulled around quickly as it grabbed her hands to strip her fingers of rings.

With my sword momentarily still, more ropes swung out and grabbed it. The thing had a tremendously strong grip and pulled both the sword, my hands, and arms to the open chest top. I wouldn't let go, but it was so surprisingly strong that I was being dragged, piling up snow against my set legs.

One of the ropes had finished stripping Laurealis' rings right off her hands and threw them inside what was now looking more like an open maw to me than an open chest. I was jerked so hard that my sword was halfway inside. I was bracing my feet against its side and pulling.

Then the lid slammed down on my forearms. Good Lord, the thing had a powerful bite. It could have broken my forearms. It would if it hit me enough times. I let go of my sword and ran back. The thing let go once it had my sword inside.

Laurealis screamed, "My babies, give me back my babies!"

It looked like she was talking about the gems that she played with and talked to all the time. They were magical and would follow her around or stick to her where she placed them.

I jerked away and backed up in disbelief, still unable to do anything because my forearms were still hurting so much from the bite the chest gave me.

Astoria had backed away and was screaming, "It's going for our magic! Duncan, Raina, we're magical creatures. Help Laurealis! Grab her before it eats her!"

Indeed, the thing was pulling like it wanted her, to store her, to eat her; I don't know. I just wrapped my arms under her armpits and wrapped my wrists across her chest and pulled for all I was worth. I slowed her, but not enough. My feet were sliding through the snow. I couldn't get something to really push against. It was pulling us to its open lid, and she was screaming in absolute terror and kicking, fighting to keep the chest from taking her inside.

I again set my feet against the edge and pushed with all I had. I just barely had the strength to hold her out. My grip had changed as we closed on it. It had her arms and legs, and I had her waist. Feeling the powerful muscle in that skinny little body of hers, relieved me. I was scared that if I could actually keep her out, simply the force of being pulled in opposite directions would hurt her badly.

Raina dived in and cut the tightly stretched ropes, which thankfully weren't magic or hard to cut; they were simply good hemp ropes. It looked like it was ignoring her non-magical blades. Freed so quickly of the ropes, we flew back about ten feet. I rolled and dropped Laurealis and raced to the chest. Grabbing my axe from the wood pile, I attacked.

"Eat this!" I screamed as I proceeded to chop it to bits. Raina had thrown the pine boughs on the fire when it first bowled Laurealis over and now was chunking the pieces I cut off into the fiercely burning fire.

"It stole everything, all my babies!" I vaguely heard

Laurealis scream. When the thing stopped moving and most of it was burning, I noticed Astoria attending to Laurealis. She was fine, simply scared.

All of her gems were rolling their way to her. She was greeting them by name, telling them how beautiful they were and how worried she had been for them. She was obviously answering them, as if they were complimenting her in return.

I asked Astoria, "Priestess, what's going on? Is she going crazy or something?"

She was chuckling quietly and shaking her head. "No," she replied, "it's just elven jewelry. Humans pierce themselves to ornament themselves. Elves don't like piercings, so we make our jewelry slightly intelligent and able to move a little. If your jewelry likes you, it can't be lost because it comes back to you, unless you tell it to stay in a special place, like a box. It also will compliment you, so it's great for people used to being the center of attention, like our friend over there."

Laurealis was sitting, with all her gems gathered in a circle, chatting with them. All thoughts of her trauma had obviously vanished.

I remembered Laurealis explaining that to Raina and me earlier. The gems had already rolled to Laurealis, but many pieces of jewelry were being held back by the weight of the metal, I guessed. The more metal a piece had, the less mobile it was, for sure.

I grabbed Glenfallis and sheathed him. Raina was just finishing fishing out of the ashes the last of Laurealis' rings and bracelets for her toes, fingers, ankles, wrists, and of course, several necklaces, including a really big one for her waist. As she caught or gathered the slower moving jewelry, she chunked them near Laurealis, where they joined the circle of *friends*.

"What was that thing?" I asked when we finished with our little chuckle at the scene unfolding before us.

"Looked like a walking chest to me," she replied.

"I'm serious."

"I am, too. We are in human country, and human magicians are…careless. They don't perform well-crafted magic. That was an animated chest with a broken leg. The strange thing was how it obviously was going for magical things, your magical sword, Laurealis' gems, and jewelry. They're all magical tools, enhancers, and aids to her illusions. Finally, it went for Laurealis. Thank you both. I would have been next."

I rubbed my wrists, not at all liking the thought of what it could have done to the two ladies.

Raina chimed in. "Look at the other stuff that was inside. I found a broken wand, the remains of several bottles that could have held potions, and a ripped scroll. Here, Mama. Here are your rings that didn't go to you."

"Those two aren't mine."

"Oh, goody, treasure. Can you tell what they are?"

"No, sweetie, I don't know how to do that."

"Perhaps I can help," Astoria said. "I can use my scrying bowl to help figure out what they do. You'll have to help me by thinking of yourselves putting the ring on and trying to use it."

Raina chose one and put it on.

Astoria said quickly, "I said to just think of putting it on, not actually doing it. What would you do if it were a cursed ring, and you couldn't ever take it off?"

"Well, I, uh, I, well, I get what you're saying. So, I'm imagining shooting a fireball from it.

Astoria chuckled. "You know, letting me get set up to actually use my scrying bowl would probably do better." Raina sighed and sat on the log on one side of our campsite. She became bored pretty quickly and went to the remains of the chest.

"Oh, look, there's another ring in here!" She picked it up, but this time she didn't put it on immediately.

Laurealis asked, "How did you see it?"

"There was this red aura around it."

"Red, so that would probably be a weapon spell. That could be useful," Laurealis surmised.

I couldn't help myself. We had a few conversations over the past weeks. "Laurealis, I thought you hated all offensive spells."

She blushed. "Well, everyone can make mistakes, can't they?"

"As long as they realize it, yes they can."

Astoria did her preparations and looked into her bowl for several minutes after asking us to picture using the rings. After a while, she began chuckling. We all looked up at her when her chuckling intensified.

"Astoria, what's so funny?" Raina asked.

Our answer was a full-on laugh as she fell over holding her belly.

Raina stood over her, "Care to share what's so funny?" She obviously didn't see anything amusing.

"It's just, hee-haw," she snorted like a donkey. "It's just …" She shook her head in disbelief and humor. "I'm sorry. It's just so funny."

"What's so funny?" Raina was definitely not amused at being left out of the joke.

"That thing that almost ate Laurealis is an escapee from a trash heap. The ring that was invisible is a ring of invisibility that was made wrong, and the ring was turned invisible, not the wearer. The …" She stopped to get control of her laughter again. "The one you were pretending to put on, Duncan, was a ring of foolishness or bad advice. I'm glad you didn't wear it. It was cursed to not come off, probably because it was supposed to be a ring of wisdom for a foolish son. Raina, you have the only thing of any use, sort of. Your ring is a ring of detect aura, except it detects the wrong aura, so it showed that ring of invisibility as a weapon."

I was confused. "So, you're saying that we had all that trouble from something that escaped from a trash heap?"

"Well, basically, yes." And she broke into laughter again. I wanted to get upset, but her chuckles infected me as well. Pretty soon we all had a good laugh.

After our laugh, and the ensuing talk about the foolishness of messing around with powers that one barely understood, we were preparing to return to our sleeping mats. I noticed that not only was Raina's hand in mine, but she was right in front of me. I let go, and she wrapped her arms around me and queried, "Good night kiss?"

"Uh, sure, I guess."

I had intended to give her a quick peck on the cheek, but she caught me with her mouth. The kiss became far more than I had intended it to be, but it felt wonderful. My hands began to wander, and she just melted into me and even pulled my hands to explore her beautiful body.

"Stop it!"

"What?"

"Stop it. This is wrong! No matter how much I want to, I can't do this right now!"

"Why not?" She looked really angry and hurt.

"Raina, I'm sorry. It's not you. I really, really like you. It's just some things I have to do first before it's even proper for me to look at a woman, especially one I like as much as I like you."

"Like a vow or something?"

"Uh, not exactly, but close enough. A code; The Way."

"This isn't life-long or anything, is it?"

"I certainly hope not!" Even I could hear the frustration in my voice. It must have convinced her to wait for me though.

"The Way is life-long, but as you pass certain milestones, things change. Some things are allowed, though other things may become restricted.

"Well, this can wait, but don't be surprised if I keep 'motivating' you to finish your, 'not exactly a vow'."

She smiled, and we parted for our sleeping rolls. She was sleeping peacefully long before I was. I realized that she was the hunter, and I was the prey. As beautiful as she was, I wasn't sure that was an altogether bad place to be, though it was certainly different. In my culture, the males were the hunters. I hoped that she was hunting me because she saw something special in me, not just my size and ability to protect her. I know I'm not much, certainly not to look at, but she's so tiny and cute and sometimes beautiful. She's been through so much; she needs a protector.

Still, I knew I couldn't continue this relationship until I had gone through the ceremony of Manhood. I just couldn't figure out how to make that happen. I couldn't continue until

I found a way to support us. A man absolutely does not seek a wife until he can support her. For my whole life, I had pictured doing it as my father and his father before him had. With the help of my family and friends, I would build or inherit one of our great wagons and work for years to earn enough of my father's herds of oxen, cattle, horses, and other animals to make it on my own. Then I would travel with him while the first children came along so the women folk could help each other if there was trouble.

Eventually, I might start my own Troop, but that was sometime far in the future. Now, I was lost. My family was dead; their herds scattered or in Skarg bellies. Her family was dead and their source of income, collecting and selling herbs, destroyed. What could I do? I chewed and gnawed on the problem for hours, like a dog with an old bone. I finally gave it up and nodded off to sleep sometime near dawn.

I dreamt of killing Aiden and woke up in Raina's arms. My voice was raw. I must have been screaming. I was crying uncontrollably. Raina just held my head to her shoulder and rubbed my hair.

"Calm down. This will pass. It's difficult, but it will get better in time."

I don't know what caused it, I guess the stress from the night before, but I was glad she was there. She could be a comfort sometimes.

When we stopped for lunch the next day, she got up right behind me and immediately began rubbing me with her hands and body, which disturbed me even more. Since I shouldn't do anything about it, she was making it clear she'd be fine with anything I wanted to do. It got a lot more intense after we got back on Shadow, and she began settling my free hand on her thigh or other places. We were holding hands all the time now, and I kept finding interesting body parts gently colliding with me, and especially with my hands. This was the kind of things dreams were made of, but it wasn't supposed to happen 'till we were engaged. When we stopped to walk the horses, I tried explaining my problem with how fast this relationship was going.

"Raina."

"Yes?"

When she smiled like that; as bright as the morning sun coming out from behind dark clouds, my words just left me. All the careful speech I had been practicing for the past hour just flew away like a mockingbird.

"Raina, we need to talk."

"Uh, huh, so talk."

I stared; I couldn't help it; she was just so beautiful. "Uh."

She pulled my head down and kissed me like I have never been kissed or even dreamt of being kissed before. It was several minutes before she finished, and when she was done, all I could do was stare. When I found my hand touching my lips, I realized I had absolutely no idea what it was I had been doing or thinking before she kissed me. I remembered vaguely there was something I needed to tell her, but for the life of me, I couldn't remember what it was.

As we rode together, I finally got out part of why we needed to wait and just be friends for a while. I couldn't bring myself to tell her I wasn't yet a proper man, so I tried argument two. She just couldn't understand why I needed a matchmaker to let us become engaged, and her attentions were driving me to distraction.

I explained that we had to rescue Kailynn, but right after that, we were going to the plains. Any priest or bard of any of the Gaelaur clans could do what needed doing. Once we found them, my Clan would help out with starter herds and building a Great Wagon. I might have to work for more years than Dad would have made me, but it would be doable. I hoped.

As I explained problem two to her, I was debating if I could find a way to go through the Ceremony of Manhood. It would sure help, at least buy some time. I just couldn't bring myself to explain to her that my people didn't yet consider me a man, despite her efforts to prove otherwise.

I finally got through to her when I explained that we would be traveling into extremely dangerous territory soon and that simply surviving would be difficult enough. But surviving with only half of my attention to keeping us alive, could prove to be impossible.

She slowly slid my free hand back to a more appropriate place and left me in peace. I found myself, the bad person that I am, still longing to explore where her hands had been guiding mine.

Interlude Two
Near the end of the Fourth Age
Settling an Old Score
Stanley, The Primordial Fire Drake

Much to my delight, my old friend Ereshkigal, the Asmodian queen, appeared on a shield in my lair. Ha, lunch on a half-shell. I remembered fondly the beautiful shield she appeared on, which once belonged to some long-forgotten soft-skin hero who lost it here, along with his life. He'd been a rather crunchy breakfast as I recall.

Even more interesting, she came surrounded by a strong nimbus of chaos magic left over from her deposition from the throne by her daughter. She'd been terribly wounded, with a huge cut in her chest and several missing limbs that had been replaced by magic. Even her heart was missing, replaced with a well-constructed magical pump.

"Ereshkigal, my dear. You don't look as lusty as is your desire."

"Damn you, Stanley. I need your help."

Picking her up by the shield and bringing her up for a sniff, I said, "You come here near death and curse me while asking for my help. Give me one good reason not to allow you to become lunch. Your magic, mixed with your fresh blood, smells so, so…appetizing."

"Because, if you heal me, I'll agree to anything you want. I just want my revenge."

"Ah, revenge. So, you've been deposed. Well, in that case, you did well. You survived, for a little while at least. You survived long enough to become my lunch."

I held her close and licked her remaining foot while she backed to the far side of the shield. The shield was small enough that her knee still hung over the edge, though her foot was hidden. "Just a taste? A small one?"

"No!" She tried to pull her knee inside the edge of the shield. I carefully pulled her foot back out over the edge. She knew how the game with greater powers was played. That was how she'd lost those missing limbs.

I remembered the Court of Duke Ashicaru as if it were yesterday. There she was in all her arrogance, informing the Duke of what he would do for the Asmodians. Unexpectedly, she was quickly surrounded by his guards while her guards lay dead all around her.

"Overextended yourself just a little, haven't you?" the Duke asked, his legendary anger just barely held in check.

She dropped to the floor and prostrated herself. Then she rose to her knees and extended her left hand.

"My Lord, you are wise. I have overreached. Take my hand that I might not ever forget myself again."

The Duke was taken aback momentarily. He then smiled viciously and replied, "I agree. But I want your right hand, not your left. I want the lesson to hurt enough to sink in."

Without hesitation, she stood, walked to the Duke, and knelt again. Humbly, she held out her hand with her head down. It was so nice, seeing such arrogance humbled so completely.

"Look at me while I take your hand."

She looked him straight in the eye as he took her hand and wrung it off, slowly.

Her only reaction was to gasp, the pain had to be insane.

The Duke threw the hand to her. "Tell the cooks how you want it prepared. For your arrogance, that is your dinner. For your courage, you will live."

I saw her flash-burn her stump of an arm, but only to the point of not bleeding. She left it raw 'till after the meal, and she ate her hand as if it were the greatest delicacy in that dimension. Afterward, she negotiated for a trade agreement and the two kingdoms became close to each other.

She's one tough lady. A bold one. Of course, anything less, and she'd have died. Maybe she's just a realist.

She sighed and relaxed, pushing her leg further out, offering it to me.

"Fine, but only the foot and only after we conclude our negotiations."

"No, the entire leg, but I'm willing to wait for you to negotiate me not eating all of you."

"Deal."

I did enjoy the completion of negotiations, even if I didn't get the full prize.

"What do you want?" she asked.

"To have lunch, what else?" I answered, amused at my own rather considerable wit. "And you don't want to become more than the snack you've already given away. I win." I opened my mouth wider. Her squawk was so enjoyable.

"No, no! I know from my sources that you have been hoping to reproduce the dragons. But without a mate, you can't. What if I become your mate? You can have fun, of a different sort than what you're thinking of now and meet your long-term goal. That's two good things from one decision."

I set her down so I could think.

"Your idea has merit. So, the queen responsible for killing all my children and mates is willing to replace them from her own body. Bringing up your treachery, in the painful state you are currently in, took great courage. It brings up all the old pain."

I remembered my dead wives and my favorite children. I roared and thrashed about until I realized I might accidentally kill her. Now, I might desire that she live.

While in disguise, I had enjoyed her several times at various courts, without her knowledge of my identity, and she was an extremely lusty and enjoyable bedmate. That was one of the reasons she had been such an effective queen for so long; that and the courage she had to accept harsh terms and sacrifices to achieve her goals. Of course, when she had the upper hand, she used others as ruthlessly as she had allowed herself to be used. She was also a powerful enough caster to become a dragon.

However, my rage was fully engaged, the smoke venting from my nostrils obscured my view of my foe. "I will agree, but there will be more conditions."

I waved my hand and a contract of gold appeared in the air between us. It already had our current conditions engraved upon it.

"Name them."

Another wave of my hand and a fiery pen appeared by the contract, ready to record the new conditions.

"To make you more colorful and for your limbs to be of matching colors, you will lose all your limbs. Since I'll be limited to only one mate for quite a while, I'd like that mate to be as colorful as possible, and I really don't care how much pain it causes you. For bringing up my old pain, you will endure your dismemberment without pain relief. You can stop the bleeding like you did for the Duke, but that is all. I want you to taste a tiny portion of the pain you have caused me. You and your demon race killed all of us but me. I, the first dragon, am the only surviving member of my race. I saw the destruction of all I hold dear." "I will accept that condition."

The pen recorded our statements.

"Two, you will be my absolute slave no matter how much I humiliate you."

Her face began to surrender, but suddenly hardened. "I'll be your queen, your brood mare. I'll bear you your offspring. You will NOT humiliate me."

"Yes, I will. As often as I choose, I will bring you as low as I possibly can in front of as many people as possible."

"What? This spell may make me accept that for a season, a long season, but after my will returns, you realize that I will kill you. Don't you?"

"I look forward to it, my bride."

"Huh? You want to die?"

"I am over twenty thousand years old; old, and I tire of this life. I have seen all I really want to see, except for the repopulation of the world with dragons. You will make my final years lusty and filled with descendants. Then, when I am again ready, I want to go out in battle. When that time comes, you will have developed enough that the battle will finish your development. Whether you are truly willing or not, we will have a vast number of offspring by then, and my death will make you capable of leading them. And who knows, you might spark the desire to live again in me and I will grow to love you and treat you so well that you choose not to kill me."

She mulled that one over for a minute or so, so I continued.

"Oh, also."

"What now, Stanley?" she asked, quite irritated.

"You must focus, truly focus on submitting wholly to me as your Master as this spell develops over the next year."

"I've agreed to be your brood mare! Isn't that enough?"

I chuckled before letting my temper show again, "I, Ulu-pierotikon the Magnificent, whom you knew in my Elven form as Stanley, have watched you for millennia. I don't trust you anymore than you trust me.

"Therefore, part of my spell transforming you into my mate will be a Geas of Submission. Now, it is true that a genuinely deep commitment on your part to joining with the Geas will make it become a deep love for me. It will of course, lengthen the time of your bondage to me.

"But listen well, for this is the caveat I'm throwing to you. It will save your life."

"The transformation spell will already do that without more humiliation! You will have my body, but not my soul!"

Smirking, I said, "But Dear, your body was already mine the moment you appeared in my lair uninvited. However, that's not what I was referring to."

Confusion flooded her proud features. She was terribly weak to not hide her emotions better.

"Surrendering completely and voluntarily will do so much more. One; the extra time will mean that when your inevitable rebellion occurs, you will be past the hatchling stage and be closer to holding your own against me physically. Two; your magic in its new form will have matured as well. That is even more important than you realize. Three; when your memories of this conversation return, meaning that the Geas has dissipated, I want you to kill me quickly without a chance for the survivor to be maimed or possibly both of us dying. If you have been a wonderful mate, I likely will not defend myself. If I am angry at a half-hearted mate, I doubt you will survive, even with the strength that maturing as a dragon will give you."

A snort of steam escaped my nostrils as I showed my scorn for the chances in battle of an immature dragon against me.

"So, wait and plan for the perfect moment, then strike hard and sure. Consider my words as you dwell within your egg for the next year."

"It takes a year?" she asked, her voice quivering. She really must be near the end of her strength.

"My future queen, the changes are rather significant. Don't worry about your sanity, though. Your mind will be asleep most of the time. But, if you are wise, your conscious thoughts, when they occur, will be of active surrender and submission."

As her expression and body language showed her acceptance of my words, I gloated inside. Soft skins can be so naïve, even ones as ruthless as my betrothed. Don't I wish I could cast a Geas spell that complex. But her active focus on modifying the spell can accomplish what my spell can't. So, by her own actions, she will bind herself to me for a millennium or more. Oh, life is becoming interesting again! "One more question. Why?" she asked.

"Why? Oh, for one, it will be interesting. This is basic to the nature you are about to embrace, even more so than for the nature you are abandoning. I'm strong and you're not."

She looked me in my eye for quite a while; I was too close for her to see both of them at once. Suddenly, she smiled.

"Agreed. Seal the deal," she said as my courageous new queen continued looking me in the eye, not backing down. She laid back and lifted her whole leg, wagging it fetchingly, offering it to me eagerly. Oh, the next few years, while she grew up large enough to mate with, couldn't pass quickly enough! I scratched my forearm and dropped a little blood onto the golden parchment, sealing the contract from my end. Then I pinched her proffered leg off and dropped some of her blood onto the parchment to complete the blood identification portion of the spell.

I quickly ate first her leg, and her other leg's stump, and finally her arms to seal the deal and to punish her, I wondered where the strong infusion of chaos magic had come from. Tasting the powerful chaos in her flesh made me realize that she might not become fire based like all dragons had been before, but a new kind, a chaos dragon, perhaps? Hmmm, what kind of children will I have with a chaos dragon? Life should prove interesting again, at least for a while.

Chapter Twelve
Wolves
Duncan

We were finally in true wilderness. I was so relieved to be completely away from walls. Sundown was still a couple of hours away, but I noticed a defensible site just off the road.

"Let's set up on that hillock. It looks defensible."

Laurealis complained, "But we need to move on, don't we? We have to reach Kailynn."

"All of us need to reach him; we aren't going to lose anyone along the way due to foolishness," already guiding Shadow up the gentle slope. "See, others have used this place as well. There's firewood stacked neatly near a stone fire ring. We'll need to replenish the wood, but this looks good."

The others followed me, and we set up the camp quietly. After I finished setting up my tent, I used some of the fine Elven rope to set up some noise-maker warning traps around the camp and the horses, to give us notice of something three feet tall or more. I didn't want to be awakened for every rabbit or little animal, but I worried about the larger predators. I also set out noose traps to catch some small game. The elves might not like meat, but I sure did.

We cooked an early dinner over two campfires, and Raina and I enjoyed a fine rabbit. We then put out the extra fire, made tea, and told stories. Laurealis was an excellent storyteller, but Astoria had the better stories. She'd lived a long, interesting life. Raina sat by my side the entire time. It was peaceful.

I took the middle watch, which I figured was the most dangerous. I was up in a tree, looking over things, when Shadow quietly nickered up at me.

Shadow didn't spook easily so I dropped down silently. I stepped up beside him, calming him.

"What is it, boy?" I whispered, "What do you smell?"

A bush rustled. I looked over and saw a wolf!

"Wolves!" I screamed, drawing my sword and charging.

The hateful beast backed off and ran a short distance away.

I heard Raina shouting, "Laurealis! Astoria! Get up! Now!"

"Raina, build up the fire!" I yelled. "There are wolves around us!"

"Aww, wolves are cute. In Anthopoulos, they're like big dogs," said Laurealis.

"Maybe there," Raina snorted, "but here, they'll eat our horses if they don't eat us, too!"

"What? That can't be!" Laurealis said in disbelief.

I saw the eyes gathered round us. I counted eight, but I was probably missing a few. I stayed near the horses.

Suddenly Shadow kicked out behind him, and a wolf yelped in pain. I dashed past him and decapitated the vermin. One down, seven to go.

"Girls, prepare to be attacked. Laurealis, if you continue to act the fool, maybe I should let your horse be eaten. I could cut her loose and she'd run, pulling all the wolves with her for an easy meal."

"Don't you dare!"

I held my sword in one hand and pulled my dagger, preparing to cut her horse loose.

"All right! All right. I guess you're right. Give me a minute."

"A minute we may not have."

Astoria yelled as she held out her hand in a fist and the wolf fell. "Her magic takes a little time to set up! Give her the time she needs!"

Three of the wolves converged on me as I guarded our horses, the primary reason they were converging on us.

They growled menacingly at me, so I returned the growl. They charged as one. I stabbed straight ahead, preparing to get hit from both sides. My sword was caught in bone in the back of the skull of the center wolf. The wolves on either side hit me hard enough to knock me down with my sword still stuck, so I dropped it.

The one to my right yelped briefly as a huge hoof collapsed his skull and another hit his side, probably breaking ribs.

However, I was down, with my sword gone and holding the wolf going for my throat in my bare hands.

Suddenly, a tree exploded near me from a lightning bolt. The wolf ran.

I set my foot on the shoulder of the one I'd lost my sword in and finally freed it.

Armed again, I entered the forward stance as I scanned our surroundings, only to see them running away from us.

Just to be certain, I stabbed the throat of each of the downed wolves. I hate wolves, though I have to admit they are fearless in battle.

Just as I was about to stab the one Astoria had put down, she said, "Stop, he's just asleep!"

I stabbed quickly; fearful he might awaken.

Now I had a furious Astoria in my face. Well, a foot below my face, but she was angry.

"I told you he was just asleep!"

"Well now he'll just sleep a little longer."

"You killed him!"

"I exterminated vermin, livestock killers. I protected our horses. We cannot survive without them."

"The sleeping spell would have kept him at bay until we were gone. You killed a defenseless animal."

I sighed and dropped my head into my hand. "Astoria and Laurealis. Raina, you, too. We need to talk about some things."

The fire was still blazing because Raina had shown the sense to build it up quickly at my urging. We gathered on the logs we sat on earlier.

"Ladies," I began, "I don't know where to begin, but this is important. We aren't in Anthopoulos anymore. It might be safe there. Raina, you know how dangerous a city is, much better than I do, I'm sure. But I know how dangerous the wilderness is. A wolf may be cute in Anthopoulos, but out here, they are deadly. You must wrap your heads around that concept."

"But…" Astoria began.

"No, I won't listen to anything 'till you all get that basic concept down."

Raina immediately spoke, "Duncan is right. The city is dangerous, like you said. But this isn't some walk in a city park. We could have all died tonight, or at the very least, lost our precious horses"

Then she curled up against me. While I enjoyed her attention, that's not what I wanted. I wanted the two elves to realize how dangerous this was, and they had to be ready at a moment's notice to help.

"Astoria, that holding your fist out thing…"

"A *sleep* spell."

"All right, that *sleep* spell was great. We were surrounded by better than eight wolves and that took one down immediately, until it could be properly disposed of."

"He wasn't PROPERLY disposed of! YOU killed him!"

"Of course, I killed him. He was vermin. That's all wolves are."

"But, but…"

"Laurealis, that was great, that illusionary lightning bolt. You saved my life."

"You really think so?" she said with wonder in her voice.

"Yes, I think so. No, I know so. Wolves are smart and work in packs. With me down, one or two would have dragged me away from Shadow's protection and I would have died."

She looked thoughtful, not arrogant for once. "I guess you're right. I may not like it, but we have to be ready to kill and to be attacked at any time. What do we need to do to prepare ourselves?"

I couldn't help myself. I leapt high and shouted, "Yes!" from the bottom of my heart. We had a fruitful discussion on tactics. Generally, I would take the front. Raina would watch the fire and use her knives. Astoria would put enemies to sleep and Laurealis would use her illusions to fool or chase off as many enemies as possible.

Unfortunately, I had to make an agreement with the elves. Like a true compromise, neither of us were genuinely happy about it, but both of us would honor our word. I would kill animal vermin without any hesitation or later fussing from the ladies. I would leave human vermin, bandits, thieves, etc. alive. I don't know why, we couldn't transport them, but the elves were adamant on this point. Hopefully, we wouldn't run into any human vermin.

Chapter Thirteen
Behind Walls Again
Duncan

We had been on mostly level ground for only a few days. After that, for three weeks, with a day at the end of the week to rest the horses, we were always going uphill. The short winter days were much longer here than up near the great ice sheets. We were fortunate in that we only had just the two fights. Over the past two weeks, we had been able to spend the nights at inns or waystations, which was undoubtedly the reason we'd had so little trouble. We'd been told the end of the easy travel would be coming when we reached a Dwarven fortress, Fort Blue Canyon. Of course, then we'd be at the crest of that road and would be moving down into a huge basin between ranges of mountains. This region was so different from where I was raised.

Virtually all the people traveling on the road were groups of freight carriers with their wagons heavily loaded and covered. From what I had been told, the incoming wagons had metals and gems and outgoing wagons were loaded with what the miners needed. It seemed so…mercantile. I didn't see any families, except in the settlements. They were nothing but fat merchants who wouldn't know what to do if real trouble hit them. My people had to be much more aware of the dangers surrounding them, especially since they carried their families with them.

The road was good. It was built over a First Age road, although many buildings had long since collapsed. It was just such an easy grade and had been cut straight through the mountains rising on either side of us. We reached another pass cut into the mountains. This one was higher, and the walls seemed…shaped. They were slightly more regular. There were still bits of the stone jutting out, but now that I'd seen another Dwarven fort, I realized those hid openings for crossbows to shoot from.

We finally made it to the fort I had been hearing about. I was amazed. Like the northern fort that I had been through with Kailynn, this one seemed to grow out of the rocks. There were weeds and small rocks scattered around, for effect, I assumed. If it weren't for the dark holes of arrow slits and the gate with the perfectly smooth road leading up to and through it, I could easily have imagined rocks rising up at the same time the smooth cliffs on either side rose up, blocking the way.

"Astoria, I can't believe how well that fort up there blends with the natural rocks around here."

She smiled. "Duncan, you've obviously never seen earth mage work before. We haven't been in 'natural' areas since we first entered the pass this morning. The Dwarves are nothing if not thorough perfectionists and artisans. In a pass this important to Chorisala, their home, every bit of rock had been fused and made impervious to earthquakes and attacks of any kind, magical or otherwise, all the way down to and including the bedrock. They take care of every detail before they even begin construction.

"You see where all the wagons disappear as soon as they enter this area?" She stopped to point. "Then over there where they all go afterward as they leave the first area?"

"Yes."

"The first is where the drivers and crews are all inspected quite thoroughly. The next is where they wait while their wagons are inspected. I'm sure they separate the crews from the wagons for that inspection. They will be completely assured that everything is to their satisfaction before the merchants are allowed beyond this fort."

A short, very wide man stepped in front of us. Other than his proportions, which were like the dwarves up north, the most notable things about him were that his chain mail and a wicked looking axe looked very well cared for. His braided beard was so long that its two tassels extended to his waist. A wave-like motion overhead caught my eye, bringing notice to the considerable number of crossbows aimed our way from the natural-looking wall across the pass.

"Halt!" he shouted.

After a few seconds of thorough visual inspection, he asked me, "Your business?"

Before I could answer, Astoria sighed and pulled out a letter hidden in her robes and handed it to him.

The guard read it and gave it back. "Safe passage, sir and my ladies. The letter said that you were to be offered any reasonable assistance. You will be escorted to the commander to explain your needs and he will determine what is reasonable. That is what will be given to you. This way please. You will leave your animals over here and I will escort you to him."

Everything was so formal and well done. It was strange, though I did notice that normal looking men, not these wide, short dwarves, staffed the stables. I've heard of dwarves all my life. Now, in just a few weeks, I've seen two distinct groups. Though they only came up to my ribs, their shoulders were as wide as mine. They also looked competent with the way they handled their weapons. Astoria's translation of their name for themselves, Children of the Earth, or Earth Children, sure made sense.

I never went inside the other fortress; at least not while conscious, so I was looking at everything around me.

We walked through corridors that were so low in most places I was bent nearly double. The warrior in me recognized this as part of a deliberate strategy to weaken the attack of larger folk.

The floor had ribbons of colored pebbles, or possibly glass, contained by twin bands of colored metal. Flattened marbles! That's it. They looked clear, like colored glass or gems, but that many gems would be insane. They must be colored glass ovals!

Inside the ribbons of colored marbles were sigils with complementary colors of the ribbon the sigil was in. I noticed a hall with a sigil of crossed axe and sword on the wall outside the opening to that hall. Some of the ribbons that had that same sigil in their stones flowed into the hall and others came out of the hall of blacksmiths, I believed, and joined the one we were on. Then we passed a dining room decorated with a plate, knife, and fork like the path leading up to it, and the door was painted the color of the glass beads on the path. It was framed in the color of the metal containing the beads with the details like the little, lighted sculptures providing light matching the outside band.

I asked, "So which of these colored paths are we following to your commander?"

The man gave me a sharp, suspicious look and said nothing. After a minute, he glanced back with less hostility.

"So, where have you seen the work of the Dom'barn before, human?"

"Never. The purpose of the colored bead walks is obvious. It's ingenious and looks great. I was just asking."

After another minute or so, he said, "Dark blue, gold, silver."

"And his sigil, the pattern within the path?"

"Hmmm…" He glared suspiciously at me a moment, then he pointed to the sigil of a helm with a pair of horns in a dark blue, gold, and silver path.

"Thank you."

We walked in silence. When we approached the commander's door, our guide knocked and announced us.

"Come in," I heard a tired and impatient voice.

We entered a room where a dwarf in uniform, not armor, sat behind piles of meticulously organized papers. He glanced up and turned the paper he was reading face down. I cautiously glanced up to see if I could stand and was glad I did. There was a beautiful mural painted on the low ceiling. I was beginning to dread the ceiling height as my head hurt from too many encounters with door jambs and ceilings already.

The commander looked up and scowled at us, as if irritated for interfering with his work. He motioned the guide to bring our papers to him, reading them quickly. He sat back and steepled his fingers together, thoughtfully beating one index finger against the other.

"What am I to do with you? A Shala'lir elf, a Hama'lir elf, a half human/ half Tala'lir elf, and a full human bearing a letter of introduction and safe passage from a Francescan general, though none of you are Francescan. It wouldn't matter so much to me, but the letter also includes instructions that you are to be given all reasonable aid. Help me to understand *why* you need aid or what type of aid you might require, and I might provide it. Make it good, I have truly little time."

Laurealis spoke up immediately, "I, my family, and my good friend, Astoria are going…"

"Ha! That's good! Your family? Elves are the most arrogant bunch anyone knows about their racial superiority. Blessed Ones, hah! These two most certainly didn't come from your womb! Try again, but this time stick to the truth, your time is half what it was."

"My husband, Kailynn, is a Champion," The commander didn't guffaw, but he did cross his arms and scowl.

"Sir, he is," Raina said, all in a rush. "Duncan and I are both war orphans, he's from the far north and I'm from Firenzia. My family was murdered by the Skarg five years ago. His people are the Gaelaur. He was wounded by the Skarg while his people were massacred a dozen miles away from him. Laurealis adopted me last year while Kailynn was out on a patrol. Kailynn found and adopted Duncan just a few weeks ago. There was some huge battle up north and Captain Teutendorf told Laurealis and me of how Kailynn gave his life saving the army. Then Astoria, a Priestess of the Lady, discovered that he wasn't dead."

The commander had glanced down at the guide who signaled something. The commander relaxed, but his arms were still crossed.

"I have a gift," Astoria said. "Sometimes I can touch things and feel things about the owner. I touched a pin belonging to Kailynn and knew he was alive. I did a scrying and discovered he was to the east in a mountain with three spires or volcanic columns or something. It was surrounded by a huge lake, and he was suspended high over a body of water in an area with lots of cliffs. The water was foreboding, but I don't know why."

"Sir," I added, "I know Kailynn killed over a thousand Skarg by himself. Whatever has him, has him bound, to prevent him from using his magic. His armor and weapons are gone, or I'm sure he'd have freed himself. Sir, the help we need is to find him and get him safely out of the cliff area."

He extended his arms, resting his fists on his table.

"The arrogance of the elves continues to amaze me," he said contemptuously. "You enter into alliances with other people, then fail to honor them. Your promised armies never showed up, yet here you sit expecting me to help you, when your people never help others."

Laurealis objected, "What about all the food and supplies we've sent to you?"

"Humph!" he snorted. "What about it? At the prices you charge! It's criminal! It's fed those who could afford it, but that's just the government and the rich! Besides, it's the Dom'barn and yon humans who have done all the fighting and dying. You elves seem to think you're too damn precious to risk your own necks, but you're happy enough to feed those of us who do, IF they have enough money!"

Laurealis leaned over to get right in his face and screamed, "What about my husband, a Champion?"

The commander stared hard at her before admitting, "Well, ye got a point there. They haven't played a big part in anything since the wars at the end of the Fourth Age. Still, from what I've heard, those Champions were incredibly tough. But still, we Dom'barn and the humans are doing all the bleeding and dying. Your people aren't doing *anything* that we can see."

"Astoria is a healer. She was healing dozens of humans after their big battle just a few days ago." He became very still for several moments.

"A healer…well ain't that just sweet? So, you just decided to show up and begin doing a little healing, eh, sweetie?"

Astoria blushed and nodded yes.

In a sudden fury, he screamed, "Then where were ye when my brother died at Lookout Mountain? Where were ye then, ye skilfin? I bet, good as your healing was, ye was the only damned elf healer there. Tis the same ole story, too little too late. Just go, get out of my sight!" In his anger, his almost unnoticeable brogue, similar to, but different enough from, Duncan's, had become thicker as his tirade continued.

Laurealis knelt and said very humbly, "Commander, you're right."

He closed his mouth tightly while his eyes flashed wonder before the anger and skepticism filled them again. The pile of papers he had picked up as if to throw, he set back down then glared at her.

"Our Gods, the Lady and her Consort, brought to the attention of the whole Shala'lir nation, how wrong we have been about a great many things. As I was leaving, nearly two hundred healers, which is virtually every healer our people have, showed up in Lergenze to continue healing the wounded. Commander, I am terribly sorry for your losses. Our people number very few and fewer of us have counted military skills to be of much value as we focused on other things. Will you accept the apology of our people? I know, after what we experienced just three weeks ago, we'll do better as a people toward you and the other warrior nations." She held her hands out towards him, waiting for his answer.

He snapped, "Apologize, yes. As well ye should! A day late and a pound short..." His eyes searched hers for several minutes while she maintained her humble smile with open arms. The tension in the room was so thick, it was palpable.

Finally, his angry scowl softened, he said softly, "But your people never showed up," in a voice that was breaking with grief. "Our lads held out for seventeen months before the fortress fell. We were hard pressed all over, and so were the humans. Lookout Mountain was too far for any of our other armies to reach in time. We and the humans tried but were turned back. We needed you. In our moment of need, you failed us, and my brother died."

"We were wrong. All our healers are now working. I don't know about the Champions, but one at least was captured while fighting."

I stepped forward. "Right, and he took out—"

Laurealis motioned urgently to Raina to quiet me, and she put her hand over my mouth until I stopped trying to speak.

I don't know if he even heard me. All his attention was on Laurealis who just stayed quiet. My need to break the silence, which was stretching into long minutes, was killing me. But Raina and Astoria both kept looking back at me as if they sensed I was the weak link. Neither Laurealis nor the Dom'barn commander spoke, he just glared at her while she held her open pose, inviting forgiveness.

Finally, he sighed loudly and said, "Oh, lassie. Aye, I'll forgive ye. But ye better get ready to give that pretty speech a lot. There's a lot of righteous anger toward your people. But, if your Gods spoke and you listened, well, what can a mere man say to beat that?" He turned toward me. "Now, laddie, what under the three rings possessed you to travel with three women? One's bad enough, but three? That's either just insane or a fine way to get there. They'll assume things you haven't done or talk you to death. And that's just one of them. Three of them together? Well, better you than me."

"Uh, well," I put my arm around Raina to gather my thoughts. She snuggled tightly to me and wrapped her arm around me as well. "Raina and I are war orphans. She was down in Firenzia…"

"Bad bit of business, there," he interjected. "Damn Skarg, thick as flies. Kept my axe busy for quite a while. Lassie, I'm sorry for your losses."

"And my whole extended family was also wiped out by Skarg just two months ago. Kailynn and Laurealis adopted both of us."

"I see. So, this Kailynn is yours and the little lassie's daddy, so to speak. Well, that makes a tad more sense. Where does the Hama'lir come in?"

"Laurealis' best friend and the only source of knowledge about where we're going. She seems to be on particularly good terms with her Goddess."

He paused before answering, "Again, I can see that. It would be an incredibly good thing to have someone able to speak to her Goddess and get answers you can act upon. But I still say you must be daft, traveling with three females. One can drive a man daft, but three?"

"All the soldiers in Lergenze were wounded or taking care of the wounded, sir. We were hoping that you could provide an escort for us. Freeing Kailynn would do the forces of the free world a lot of good. Like I said, he killed a thousand Skarg like I would squash a bug."

"If the Skarg comes against us in force, we'll kill a lot more than a thousand. That I can promise you. I have no men to spare. Still, an elf Champion…well, I have a lot to think on.

You will be assigned rooms in the third hall, purple, and green, green with a bed. Guido will assign someone to assist you. You're dismissed."

Laurealis said, "But sir! We need to rescue Kailynn as soon as possible. We should continue traveling this afternoon."

The commander sighed, "My Lady, I'm sure you mean well, but he'll be in even deeper trouble if you go off half-cocked. A crossbowman waits patiently for the proper moment…and so shall you."

"But…"

He stood and slammed his fist down hard enough for his papers to jump off the heavy desk, "Enough! May the Smith take all elves!"

He glared at Laurealis. His expression and obvious lack of patience intensifying. "Go now, or you'll find what one of our jail cells looks like," he said with finality, and he sat to resume his work.

He glared at her 'till she backed down. His expression then relaxed just enough to show he wasn't truly angry; he just looked that way. I used to see the same expression on Dad's face.

We bathed and changed in a series of baths that was way beyond anything I could have imagined. First, we separated by genders and disrobed in a large room where lots of little niches held our clothes.

There were a series of baths, the first was warm and strictly for bathing. The second a hot one for soaking, and the third was a comfortable temperature for swimming. I was amazed.

When I met the ladies again, I saw Astoria in her layers of fine, sheer linens. She wore five to six layers of different lengths and colors, so the effect was very feminine, but modest. They went well with her ochre yellow skin, gold eyes and green hair with its yellow highlights.

Laurealis wore something completely different than she had worn traveling in, which just emphasized that she was wearing nothing but illusion. She never dressed modestly, which was only accented her form, since everything she wore had no back. After watching her turn into that tiny butterfly-person and fly out of her clothes, I could understand the why of that.

However, I was finding that the more aware I was of her illusions, the less I actually saw them. Her clothes had always been only one to three layers, or illusions of layers of sheer fine cloth. Sometimes she added bits of opaque material, thrown in for effect not modesty, only without road grime and in changing colors.

Now bathed and fresh, her dress was made of a single layer of some shocking pink shiny material that clung to her like a second skin. It had a huge cutout that extended from her exposed back to under her left breast well down to her left hip that covered little more than the absolute minimum, leaving only a quarter-inch strip of pink connecting the upper and lower parts. Her right leg was bare from well above her hip and her left leg was covered in a pant leg. Her entire belly, except for that tiny strip down her side connecting the top to her left leg was exposed. Little bells lined the edges and circled her right ankle, drawing even more attention to her. My wildest dreams could have never produced anything like it. When she walked past me, only her left leg and buttock were covered. Her outfit was absolutely scandalous! Only an illusion of clothes could stay on her body. There simply didn't seem to be enough material to stay in place.

Now her outfit was sort of visible, like I knew what it was supposed to look like, but it was really not much more than a mist. I don't have the words to describe it other than it was translucent, like a pink fog. The closer I was to her, the clearer I could see through it, just like fog. It didn't hide a thing. Except for the bells, which were formed around her jewelry and the gems were the exact color and location of the illusionary bells, so they looked solid. Sincerely, she was beautiful. Leaving nothing hidden, except by a misty haze, it was difficult for any male to resist staring.

"Laurealis, why are your illusions so much less real than they once were?"

"Sweetie, that's just because you know what they really are. Since you saw what I wore in here and what I'm wearing now, it's not as real to you. You're obviously intelligent enough to not be fooled easily by illusions. I'm guessing that all you're seeing is a hint of pink in all the right places. Is that right?"

"Well…yes. Sort of, anyway. It's more like a fog and the closer I am to you, the less I see even of the pink color. I can hardly see the fabric at all. It's scandalous." She giggled just a little.

"Oh, that's fine. We elves don't have nudity taboos like most humans. Except for you and probably Raina, and of course, Astoria, everyone else sees the full illusion. But if they don't, so be it. It just doesn't matter that much to me. I am who I am and if you see all of me, that's simply fine with me. Just so you know, if my clothing being fully opaque is important to me, I'll use a more powerful spell that should fool your perceptions as well. It should at least be solid enough for you to be comfortable with."

"Uh, I see, I think." The women of my people would be hopelessly scandalized and shamed. Their husbands would also take strong measures with them in private; she appeared to be shameless.

My stomach rumbled loudly, and Raina chuckled. "Duncan, I know you're hungry. That guy at the entrance said that if we followed the brown, cream, dark brown path with the beer stein, we'd find food and beer." Chuckling, she added, "I'm not sure which he thought would be more nutritious, the way he was carrying on about the beer."

Astoria put her hand on Laurealis' shoulder and nodded no.

"Uh, Duncan," Laurealis said, "go on ahead of us. Raina, could the three of us have a little talk?"

"I didn't do anything," she said guiltily, looking like she'd been caught at something.

Laurealis said, "Oh sweetie, we know. You've been through so much and it's affecting you a lot. We're completely on your side and just want to help."

They each locked an arm about her waist and walked away with her.

"Wait! Where are you going?" I asked.

They stopped, turning to smile at me in unison as Laurealis said, "We need to have a talk with Raina. We'll catch up with you."

Laurealis patted my cheek, "It'll be fine. We'll be a little while, but we'll find you. Go along."

I didn't like us separating in a strange place, but I accepted it. With a last glance at Raina, I asked, "Uh, how do I pay for supper?"

Laurealis tossed me a couple of coins from a purse that must have been hidden by her illusions. It looked like she'd pulled it out of the big necklace thing around her waist. It disappeared after she took out the coins, but I had the coins to get a meal with.

I couldn't understand how she hid the purse, especially since just before we left the baths her outfit had changed to a two-inch wide and maybe eight to ten-foot-long blue and pink ribbon that appeared to simply be loosely wrapped around her body and pretty much covered it. It only wrapped around her once up top and twice below with a loose end over her shoulder and the other between her legs or just loose. The wind blew it realistically. It was extremely distracting. I wondered how the Dwarves would react to it.

I'd just have to get used to the way she dressed. I hoped I did a better job of that than she did with me eating meat. I just wished she realized I was as disturbed by her dress as she was by what I ate and wore. Of course, being honest, if I had gone through the Ceremony of Manhood, I would feel a lot freer to look. But for now, that was forbidden.

"I'm going up to see Shadow for a bit, so it may be a while before I get to the meal area, if that's okay?"

"Sure, sweetie. That'll be perfect."

I'd been getting nervous inside all this stone. It wasn't just Laurealis' way of not dressing modestly, that just added to the stress. I like the free open spaces. Walls were bad and these walls were very thick, and the ceilings were extremely low.

I began following the dark brown and green edged path but stopped and asked someone how to get to the stables. As I entered the stables and was able to actually stand tall, I snagged some oats and hid them in a pocket. Shadow whinnied when he saw me and as I greeted him, he sniffed around me 'till he found the oats. I fed him out of my hand while scratching his favorite spots. Finally, I just laid my head against his to enjoy his comforting presence. He lay his head over my shoulder and back and hugged me. He didn't know why I was so tense; he just knew I was.

We were still inside, between those accursed walls, but I could see the outside and feel a slight breeze, and it helped. I knew he had been ridden hard the last three weeks and could use a rest, so instead of taking him for a hard ride like I wanted, I finally said my goodbyes and walked outside, but within the walled-in area immediately outside the stables. Watching the sun set over the mountains helped my balance return.

Going back inside and following the correct path, I found a place where the wonderful aroma of roasting steak filled the cavern. I was nearing the end of my meal when I heard Raina crying in the street, "Duncan, Duncan!"

I was awfully glad I paid for my meal in advance because I bolted out the door.

She saw me, ran the last few yards, and clung to me, trembling, and crying as my arms wrapped around her.

"What's wrong?"

"Hold me."

I picked her up and carried her to a swing in front of the tavern.

I asked again what was wrong, but she just nodded no and wouldn't speak. She curled up into a little ball and whimpered every so often.

I was ready to hang Laurealis out to dry. What did she do to Raina?

I saw Astoria guiding a weeping Laurealis down the street. They were looking for Raina, because when they saw us, Astoria smiled and left Laurealis for a moment while she ran to us.

"Thank the Lady she found you! The healing session uncovered some awfully serious stuff. While it went well for as bad as it was, poor Raina just needs you to comfort her. Hug her or whatever for however long she needs you, like Laurealis needs me."

"What did you two do to her?" I asked perhaps a little too accusingly.

Laurealis, who was at least twenty feet away, let out a loud sob. Astoria turned to her briefly. "I promise I'll explain everything tomorrow. We lanced an emotional boil that was unbelievably bad and emotional rot went everywhere. But like a lanced boil that hurts terribly for hours, it heals afterwards. Trust me."

Raina looked up and saw Laurealis and exploded! She ran to Laurealis and held her hand back to slap her, then reconsidered and simply screamed, "I know humans see me as nothing but a half-breed. I've had that screamed at me all my life. But now you? You called me a half-breed as well. That's all I ever am to either side. Can't either of you see me as me? I can't help that I'm caught in the middle!"

She returned to me, and I gathered her in my arms where she began crying again. I held my head down over her, like Shadow did with me; suddenly glad we were spending the night here, even if it was under tons of stone and walls. I stroked her hair and her back which seemed to calm her some.

Sometime later I noticed by her even breathing that she had fallen asleep. Even later, music, from a neighboring establishment filled the air. Very lively music from instruments, some of which I had never heard before, drifted into the night.

Raina heard it, too, and stirred. She stretched mightily, and noticing where she was, pecked my cheek and lay her cheek against my shoulder. She felt so good right there, smelled good, too. The music was so lively that my foot began tapping in time.

"Honey, let's go dance or listen to the music…"

She pointed down and smiled, "Your feet wouldn't have it any other way."

"You, all right?" I asked.

She gave me the funniest look, like someone just showing normal concern for her was surprising. "Sure, I'll be fine."

We took several steps when she stopped me, and taking both my hands, said, "Thanks for asking."

That confused me even more. What else would I do? She was obviously out of sorts.

"Raina, I heard what you said to Laurealis and Astoria. You're just *you* to me. You're unique, but that's just who you are. Ok?"

She hugged me tightly. "Thanks, I needed that."

We went in and had a wonderful time listening to a group of Dwarves playing instruments I was familiar with, and one I had never seen before. It could play fast, and you just wanted to dance, but when it played slow, it had a mournful sound like nothing I had ever heard.

Laurealis and Astoria arrived shortly before the band took a break and sat with us. None of the ladies would talk about or even acknowledge what went on earlier that evening. When the player of the strange instrument approached our table with his hat out for a tip, I motioned for him to sit after putting my change from the meal in his hat. He smiled and sat.

I stuck out my hand, "Name's Duncan."

His handshake was firm. "Fausto."

"I liked your music. What was that instrument you were playing? It looks a lot like the lute that my people use."

"A fiddle. We got it from the elf instrument they call a violin, but we play it differently. They use a bow to play it and, while we might use a bow, usually we strum it like how your people play the lute. When we use a bow, we hold it differently."

He glanced at Raina, "I noticed you and your lady enjoying yourselves on the dance floor."

"Yes, we did. Fausto, this fiddle intrigues me. What I play is a bag of pipes and it's too large to bring with us. I also play the lute and drums some, but I lost everything but my pipes a couple of months ago. My pipes are with my gear."

"You're a player, too?

"Hey, guys! We have a player out here. He left his bagpipes in his room. Marcus, give him your bagpipes and let's see what he can do."

I was amazed. "You have a bag of pipes?"

"You're from those plains people, the ones who travel all year following the herds, right?"

"Yes, the Gaelaur."

"That's it, the Gaelaur. Our people have had dealings with yours for hundreds of years. There's a good chance the meat we're having tonight came from your people. We have a Stor'dør near one of your cities, Detrota, I believe. I've heard of the Bu Clan from some of my kinfolk who've traded with them."

"Bu Kearney was my favorite adoptive uncle." I couldn't hide the sadness in my voice.

"Was?"

"Two months ago, he and everyone else in our traveling group, basically our extended family and friends, were wiped out by the Skarg."

He nodded his head, acknowledging my loss. "I'm terribly sorry, Duncan. Most everyone here has lost people to those vile creatures or to the Asmodians themselves. We all wish we knew where those things came from. Five years ago, no one had ever seen or heard of them. Then they were all over the place, from Firenzia in the south and now to your people up north.

"Ah, I see Marcus is back. Play with us. It's the least we can do since I brought your pain back to the surface." He finished his beer and the extra one that I'd noticed always seemed to be delivered, like he always ordered two beers at a time.

I followed him back. I examined Marcus' instrument. It was a beautiful piece.

"Thanks, Marcus, this is much nicer than mine."

He said, "You're welcome. Go ahead and get comfortable with it, it's been at least a month since I've touched it."

I inflated the bag and while playing a few notes, I noticed something and paused before beginning again. "This piece is higher pitched than our people's bagpipes. By at least a full step."

Fausto smiled broadly and said, "Well, since you obviously know your way around the pipes, now play for us and the second or third time around, we'll accompany you."

I looked at Raina. She smiled and whispered loudly, "The Wild Wind."

I began, losing myself in the lilting sway of its melody, so much like the winds through the tall grasses. I used to love to get up high on a wagon or even a tree and watch the wind play with the tall grasses in late summer 'till the first heavy snowfall. Fausto joined in almost immediately with that wonderful "fiddle" of his. Marcus on the drums was only a little behind. The lute and tin whistle joined in near the end of the second verse. It was so much richer than by myself, I was transported back to the good times with Dad on the drums, Bu Kearney on his lute and Dom Camlain on the pipes he taught me to play.

I realized how good these guys were as we moved into more songs. Raina just sat and listened to me play, a content smile on her face.

After a while, I asked, "Fellows, would you mind if we played something more suitable for dancing? I'd like to take a break with Raina. This room is tall, so maybe we can learn one of your people's group dances."

Marcus laughed. Fausto actually hesitated, then pointed me towards Raina.

I stood and approached her with my hand out. Her smile was so bright; it just took my breath away.

"They're going to play some dance songs for us. I mentioned maybe showing us some group dances or something."

"Sounds good to me. But give me a second. I'd like to talk to them for a few minutes."

Like she said, she was just gone for a few minutes.

"Do you know how to group dance?"

"Uh…I can do Gaelaur group dances."

"Well, we'll do a few group dances. They'll have to teach us, then I'm going to show you a few dances that we do in Firenzia that my Mom taught me.

"Sure. I'd love to learn how your people do things. Teach me something new."

She just smiled. She took care of getting a woman to help us learn their dances as Fausto and Marcus played. Raina is just so amazing. She learned the dances like she was born to them. She was graceful and happy floating between partners. She always had a special smile for me as we passed each other.

Between learning new dances and avoiding the ceiling or the noticeably short tables, I was a klutz. She didn't laugh at my clumsiness too much, even when I forgot and rose on my toes a little and bonked myself on the head. We had a wonderful time.

Then Marcus announced, "Raina here," he said as he gestured toward her, "is from Firenzia. She wants to show us a couple's dance from her homeland. So, couples, join up and let's be as gracious in learning a dance from her people as she has been with learning ours."

There was some polite noise, clapping and such. Before I knew it, Raina grabbed my hand and placed it exceptionally low on her back. Then she took my other hand and held it out before saying, "Now that you're holding me properly, I'm going to do your part, the lead. As soon as you think you have it, let me know and you take over. This is called a waltz and it's a three-step dance.

"So…one, two, three. One, two, three."

It really was fairly simple, and it was just a dance. I'd danced lots of group dances, so why was this one, holding Raina so close, doing such strange things to my mind?

She stopped from time to time to teach the Dwarves, or sometimes me, fine points of her waltz. She spun while I held her tiny hand over her head to balance her. She came close to me and spun out and then back into my arms.

The musicians had a good feel for what Raina wanted and as long as they kept to the three-beat music, Raina kept coming up with more innovations. The fast tunes were fun and exhilarating. The slower ones were…simply great. She was messing with my mind the way she kept my arms wrapped around her lower back.

After one especially fast tune, instead of spinning back in my arms, she shouted, "Catch me," then leapt over my head so I had to catch her. She somehow spun down to land in my arms and gave me a quick kiss before leaping down to the floor to go back to the basic one, two, three steps. I called for a stop.

I led us over to the table with our drinks and sat. She chose to sit on my leg instead of the chair.

"So…what do you think of my people's dances?"

"Uh, wow. I never knew dances could be like that. You're so full of surprises."

She just smiled a special, a coy, smile. Before things could go any further, Fausto interrupted things, by banging a chair on the floor till the room quieted.

"It's time for a special song to remember our losses from this war."

"Shush. What's Fausto doing?" I asked. "Do you know?"

"No."

Fausto stood and approached an old man, saying, "Gabinus, it's time. Would you mind joining us?"

I expected his voice to be weak, but it wasn't. He stood, and grabbing a cane, the room was transformed. He was shown the greatest respect as everyone quieted. The serving girls quickly brought fresh mugs of ale to everyone, removing what they had been drinking. I realized why they were treated with respect; unlike what Raina had described was the norm within Francesca for barmaids. Each of the girls was wearing a Torc, each of them unique, and not unlike what my own people exchanged upon marrying. Most of them moved to wrap an arm around one man who was wearing a matching one. Two women who wore Torcs and dressed all in black, one of whom was pregnant, stood by themselves, but they had received the largest tips the entire evening.

It must be the Dwarves were honoring and helping widows with extra tips. Sure beats what Raina had to go through.

Raina and I were seated at the table near the open space. Gabinus pulled out an unused chair and turned it facing everyone as he supported himself on its back. While Fausto strummed rapidly a sad, slow solo on his fiddle, the man sang in a fine strong bass.

We shall meet, but we shall miss him. there will be one vacant chair. We shall linger to caress him while we breathe our evening prayer. When a year ago we gathered, Joy was in his mild blue eyes. But a golden cord is severed, and our hopes in ruin lie.

At our fireside, sad and lonely, often will the bosom swell at remembrance of the story how our noble Hero fell. How he strove to bear our banner thro' the thickest of the fight, and uphold our people's honor, in the strength of manhood's might.

True they tell us wreaths of glory ever more will deck his brow. But this soothes the anguish only sweeping o'er our heartstrings now. Sleep today, O early fallen, in thy green and narrow bed. Dirges from the pine and cypress Mingle with the tears we shed.

We shall meet, but we shall miss him. there will be one vacant chair. We shall linger to caress him while we breathe our evening prayer.

(The Vacant Chair was written by Henry Washburn about Lt. William Grout during the War Between the States. It became a favorite of both the Union and Confederate forces.)

When he finished, he stepped beside the empty, but spirit-filled chair, as the spirit of the missing loved one filled it in my mind. He raised his mug in salute. "To Modius, my beloved grandson, Battle of Sasquaan River, oh four." He stepped back; his head bowed.

Fausto played softly and another man stood forward and called out a name and relationship, friend, brother, father, a battle, and a year, then stepped back. As each man repeated this ritual, sometimes for several names, occasionally their voices broke and their comrades on either side would lay hands on their shoulders in support, giving them the heart to finish. The solidarity within the room was as thick as stone as the litany continued. The two single serving girls were both widows. The ritual went quickly for so many, but still took an exceedingly long time. I noticed that Lookout Mountain had claimed a lot of men. I understood the commander's initial hostility much better now.

Everyone else had finished and Gabinus looked me in the eye, "Boy, you're human, so I expect you should join us. You, too, girl."

Raina shoved me forward when I hesitated. I raised my mug as I had seen them do, "To my father, Taen, son of Camlain, son of Donneal, General of the Loch Clan of the Gaelaur; my brothers Lear and Conner, my mother, Marta, my sister, Lily, my sister…" I couldn't go on.

Then Raina wrapped her arm around me, lending me her strength. Gabinus stepped forward and laid his hand on my shoulder. I took a ragged breath, "My younger sister, Aisling, and the rest of my troop, all my extended family, all several hundred of them. I don't know if the battle has a name, it just was." I stepped back, glad to not be talking anymore.

Raina stepped forward, raising her mug, "To my father, Cireno, a lone warrior of the Tala'lir who tried so hard to save my village, to my mother Rachel, and to most of my village, the Fall of Firenzia, oh two."

I noticed many looks of sympathy for both of us. Gabinus glanced at Laurealis and Astoria, not expecting anything. He was shocked when Laurealis stepped forward and said, "To Kailynn, my husband as well as Champion of the Elves, some battle up north two weeks ago." Astoria remained silent as looks of amazement filled the room.

"Would that be the Battle of Kailynn's Gorge?"

"I, I don't know. I never heard the name, but Kailynn is…was, my husband. He may still be alive, but I don't know. I just don't know."

"Laurealis," I said, "I talked to the soldiers who were with you. They named it after the tremendous heroism of your husband. It had been an unnamed gorge until then."

"Oh, well then, to Kailynn, my husband. The Battle of Kailynn's…"

She broke down on Astoria's shoulder. Looks of sympathy filled the room. While she may not have seen them, she quieted shortly thereafter.

She looked up, drying her eyes with a napkin, and Gabinus took control again, "To our noble dead," and he saluted with his mug held out again and drained it in one long drink, as did everyone else. Raina, a couple of the women and old men put their mugs down, but no one said a word. All the mugs were empty, and conversation began again.

Many people surrounded us, offering words of comfort, and understanding. I felt soothed as I hadn't felt since the nightmare began two months earlier. The war had hit these people as hard as I'd been hit. I felt the resolve of Laurealis' dance settle deeper in my belly.

When the music began, we had a round of drinks to calm ourselves. I needed calming. Neither of us were up to dancing, the ceremony we had just performed brought back memories that were too recent. But the looks and comforting comments Raina and I were receiving did a lot to help. When we went back up to the platform, I could sense that the crowd was one with us, even though we were so different.

The next song was lively to bring on a round of clapping in time with it. They were boisterous people. After how somber they were a few minutes earlier, it surprised me with how lively they'd become again, as if they wanted to forget their sorrows.

That thought, forgetting their sorrows felt right. I looked around and noticed how much ale and hard liquor was being served and disappearing as quickly as it appeared.

The foot stomping and clapping were so loud I didn't see how they could hear anything, but it certainly dispelled the gloom.

When Fausto and the other musicians came back to join us for a break, I said, "I'm amazed by how similar our music is."

"Duncan, you're a fine musician, but like all your people, you know no history." Marcus said.

"Huh?"

Fausto slapped me on the shoulder with a force that almost staggered me, "You people know us and the elves as the elder races, but we're not. Our cultures are old because ours haven't been destroyed by the Asmodian purges. But we're offshoots of humans who developed as we began using our sources of magic. We Dom'barn use the earth nodes, chunks of the Chaos Comet itself, the Lir'folk, the Talu tree and its products. Magic is nothing but the ability to tap into and direct the power of the worlds' magnetic…well, you don't know that term. The earth has a lot of power circulating through and around it. Magic is the word for tying into that power, which we call mana, as it has been altered by the Chaos Comet. Only the magical races have been mutated enough by the Chaos Comet to have extra organs to manipulate the mana. The gods that have developed through worship are apparently another reservoir of power that some, even humans can use."

"I've never heard any of this."

He pulled a chair to the table and motioned to the barkeeper for rounds all around. For him, two beers and two shots of something harder that he had begun drinking after the song Gabinus led. During that ceremony as it were, we learned that he was a war orphan like Raina and me. His father had been a general at Lookout Mountain.

"Not from yon elves, I'm sure, with their high and mighty ways. You humans are the original race, the one all the other races branched out from. The Asmodians have tried to wipe you out many times. Every few thousand years, they wipe out every one of you they can find. I sometimes think the *magic* of you humans is your resiliency. Well, that and your reproductive speed. Ye breed like rats. But your survival has come at a terrible cost, your heritage. Each time you come back; new aspects of your race come out."

Marcus said, "The Paladain best exemplified the true nobility of your race."

"The Paladain? Who were they?"

Marcus continued, "They were destroyed twenty-five hundred years ago at the end of the Fourth Age, the last purge.

We helped them, too, but their magic was too weak. 'Tis why I am so delighted to see your bright wee lass. You humans need the magic of the elder races in your blood to fight off the Asmodians and crossbreeding with the elder races will do it. She probably has the organ needed to respond to the Talu tree. When you go making babies, some of them just might have that ability as well."

"Babies!" I sputtered. "I've only just met her!" But I noticed Raina's eyes flash and she smiled ever so briefly. It was so quick; I would have missed it if I hadn't turned to face her in my shock at the thought of babies. Still, she'd be a nice one to make them with.

Astoria and Laurealis had wandered over and Astoria objected, "But look at how careless the humans are as they do all that crossbreeding! Their half-trained magicians have created abominations like the various merfolk and centaurs. They have created diseases of plants and animals with their careless magic. They don't know what they're doing!"

"Aye, I agree. But did the Paladain hold out as long as Francesca? Individually, they were better fighters. Their generals may have been more brilliant, but they had no magicians of their own. You Lir'folk did actually help in that war, unlike this one. But there are never enough of you. Their magicians may not be a tenth as good as yours, but they have more than ten times your number of magicians and, unlike you, they're fighting. So, I ask again, did the Paladain hold out as long as Francesca has?"

"Well, no." Astoria said, "They fought with even more spirit, and they never quit while one still drew breath. But the magic and demons of the Asmodians just overwhelmed them within three years despite the powerful enchantments of their Hero's Weapons. Their worship didn't create powerful Gods like our Lady and Her Consort. They empowered various weapons and their King's Crown, though those wondrous, supremely powerful weapons are now gone. The Asmodians destroyed them long ago, or perhaps they were lost."

"Exactly," Fausto said, "the humans this time have the magic fully on their side. Poorly controlled, even more poorly understood, but there. That's the difference. They have so much more than merely enchanted weapons. The centaurs, especially the horse centaurs are great heavy cavalry and horse archers. Some of the others, like the spider centaurs, have gotten several of the Skarg generals and even some Asmodians."

"They are an abomination!"

Fausto yelled, "Did a third of them leave their race and breed with demons like a third of the elves did? Boys! A round of cheers for the damned elves and their children, the Asmodians! Oh, and let's not forget their other children, the dragons!"

He drained his shot glass. "What? No takers on my toast? My, my, I guess you elves have worn out your welcome, no matter what my uncle may say."

Marcus stepped in front of Fausto and shouted, "Fausto, stop it! You can't afford another incident!"

"I'm right and you know it"

"Yes, you're right. So, what! If you get yourself banished!"

He pulled out Fausto's seat and the other two musicians pushed him into it. Fausto had drained his last beer so he snatched and chugged Raina's who had gone to the lady's room just before the incident. He was so quick about it that it was done and over before I could react.

"You see how it is, Duncan? A man tries to drink a toast, and everyone gets on his case. Anyway, we Dom'barn have always supported you humans. We know how tough it can be starting over. The dragons taught us that."

He stood and staggered towards the bathroom. He passed Raina and turned around to point at her saying, "That's why humans breed so fast. With women like her." In a slurred, loud voice he asked, "Lassie, I wonder what your price tag might be?"

Raina turned white as a ghost. The entire room went silent as people nudged or hushed each other in an expanding circle, watching the slim, outraged girl and the drunken fool standing behind her.

After waiting nearly five seconds, with blinding speed she spun around while whipping out a knife hidden in her sleeve. She grabbed his beard and sheared both braids off in two swift strokes. She then pranced to her chair, half dancing and melodramatically laid his braided beard in her seat and sat on it. In the totally hushed room, she loudly proclaimed, "More than you can afford."

One of the men at the bar shouted, "Hey, Fausto, you look like a boy now. Guess the girl showed you who's in charge."

Fausto turned beet red. I saw the vein in his temple beating strongly.

Marcus leapt in between them, "Fausto, wait!"

"Young lady! Young lady! I see what you may have thought he meant, but what he meant was your dowry…"

A dowry, well that makes sense. Unfortunately, Fausto hadn't waited. I was waiting to hear what Marcus was saying, hoping to defuse the situation as well. Fausto began chanting something I couldn't understand.

A chunk of the wall cracked and began moving! A manlike thing walked away from the wall. It wasn't solid like the stone it had been a few seconds earlier. It was sandlike with lots of pebbles and fist-sized rocks. It was so different from anything I had ever experienced; I couldn't figure out what to do.

I reached for my sword, but it wasn't there. We'd been told not to bring any weapons larger than a knife anywhere we went inside this stifling cave. Instead, I grabbed a chair and broke it over the rock thing. It only noticed it enough to hit me in the belly with its forearms hard enough to send me flying. Fortunately, I had both arms down and crossed in front of my belly or I would have been seriously hurt. I rolled and came to my feet in time to see what happened next.

The Elven ladies ran out the door and the rock man threw a table after them. It barely missed them. Then Commander Marcellus arrived just in time to be met with another table. He went down…hard. A couple of men went to check him out while the rest of the room looked at Fausto with accusing angry eyes. Fausto was looking at his uncle and the tears began flowing. He made a chopping motion, and the rock man froze, and the light went out of its eyes. It then dissolved into a pile of rocks, gravel, and sand.

He stumbled over to his uncle whom he had just killed or seriously injured and collapsed to his knees. Everyone else gathered round to give him time for his grief, but it was plain that he was going nowhere.

Suddenly the commander's body disappeared, and the ladies reappeared in the far back corner. Everyone was shocked, but someone said, "One of them is a damned illusionist. Well, Praise the Smith, Marcellus isn't dead. But Fausto, you're still in a pile of trouble. I know you miss your

Lucia. But drinking away the fact that she loves another isn't helping you. Come now. It's the brig for you tonight."

The man, burly even for a dwarf, escorted Fausto away while he mumbled in disbelief, "My beard! She cut off my beard! It finally grew long enough to braid, and she cut it off!"

The spirit went out of the room. We quickly left for our rooms to prepare for an early start on the morrow.

Early, startled out of sleep, I heard three sharp raps on my door then on the ladies' door. It sounded heavy, like an armored fist.

I grabbed my father's sword and placed it beside the door. Oh, the Dom'barn and their locks. I had to release the latch with one hand while simultaneously lifting the crossbeam with the other. I fell back, grabbed the sword, and waited for whoever woke me.

The door swung open slowly with such a complete silence that it was eerie. Dwarven workmanship never squeaks; I don't think it would dare.

Through the open door, I saw two guards peeking over their shields at my raised and ready sword, since the ceiling was too low for me to stand upright and slash.

"What do you want?" I demanded. "It's the middle of the night."

What?! I heard the commander just before I saw him in the light of one of the glowing statues that serve as torches lining their halls.

"Whoa lad! Calm down, the ladies will be here in a moment."

I blushed and hastily put aside my father's sword, reaching for my jerkin. I turned as I was pulling it down to see who had just entered the room.

Of course, the two soldiers I had already seen were flanking the door. The commander, accompanied by a miserable Fausto, was standing against the empty wall. As I finished tightening the lacings on my knee-high moccasins, a furious Laurealis entered dressed in a full length, opaque, blood red and black gown. It matched her mood well. She was certainly an unhappy lady. It felt like anger was radiating from her like heat from a forge. She nodded at me curtly and sat beside me.

Next, Astoria led Raina, who paused in the door for a huge yawn before sitting by my other side. Naturally, her yawn precipitated an equally large one from me. She nestled in beside me and Astoria sat at the foot of the bed on the other side.

The commander nodded curtly and motioned for someone to enter. A young Dwarven lady stepped in. Outside of the tavern, her presence made a much stronger impression on me. She was sturdily built, certainly of the same race as the men, but much slimmer. She was cute or even pretty, though she looked strong enough to break any of my companions in half without trying. Her very modest dress covered her, neck to floor. Its bright pink and blue colors stood out so strongly because the men's dress was so somber. Their artwork was anything but colorless, so the men just expressed themselves differently.

She pushed in a small cart loaded with all kinds of breakfast foods, eggs, ham, cheeses, biscuits, rolls, various fruits, honey, and my newest addiction since Raina introduced it to me, breakfast tea. She smiled and bowed to the commander who said, "Thank you, Rubra. You may go."

"Duncan," he nodded to me. "Ladies," he said, nodding to them, "let us discuss several things while we breakfast."

He poured a cup of the tea, without honey or that brown powder he called sugar or even cream, I noticed. He sipped it while we prepared our plates.

"First, I'm afraid I've been remiss in my manners. My name is Marcellus, and you may refer to me by name or by my rank of Tribune. I am already aware of your names.

"Our discussions of yesterday afternoon and yours, and Fausto's actions last night, have caused me a great deal of concern." Fausto glanced at his uncle's broad back and managed to look even more miserable. "I confirmed what you said yesterday. Yes, the elves are finally fulfilling their obligations to the Alliance."

He looked Laurealis square in the eye, "And you, my lady, if you're who I suspect, are either in a great deal of trouble or are a national hero. You may be both." He looked as if he was trying to match what his reports told him to what he saw in her.

"Regardless, your people are now fulfilling their obligations, so I will lend you what aid I am able." We all looked at each other and grinned.

He held up his hand, "Not so fast. If I'm right about your destination, what you need is an earth mage, a sober one, and at least one full legion of dwarven knights, not the legionnaires my cohort consists of. However, that is not possible. I need my men here. I have decided to lend you the services of a fully competent earth mage…my nephew, Fausto."

Raina stiffened within my arm. I glanced at Laurealis and began counting with my fingers, "One, two, three…"

Raina was on her feet screaming, "How dare you even think of sending him with us? Throw out your garbage with the other trash! We won't have anything to do with him!"

As Fausto began talking in his native tongue, I realized our languages were really quite close, as I understood a good bit of it…

"Uncle, I was fooled. She's got the…of a whore and she…like one."

Red flashed before my eyes. How dare he!

"How DARE you call Raina a whore!" I leapt up to defend her honor and… CRACK!

Laurealis

Duncan leapt right into the low ceiling and went down like a felled tree. Raina screamed, "Duncan!" and knelt beside him. Astoria pushed her back and lit up her fingernail with a brilliant point of blue-white light as she pulled up his eyelids to examine his eyes and the swelling knot on his head.

I felt my rage explode. I realized what that worm Fausto must have been saying about my Raina. I was about to stand and glanced at Duncan. Not wanting to knock myself out as well. I sat down and morphed into my sprite form.

I tasted Raina's near panic and Astoria's focused concern. Marcellus' eyes widened and he tasted of confirmation and a great deal of cautious, respectful fear. Fausto tasted of…a curious combination of arrogance a psychosis, lust, anger, love and respect, and fear, a great deal of fear, though not of me, of Marcellus. The guards were fearful of the entire situation and dangerously alert.

Astoria cautioned me, "Laurealis, be careful."

My anger spoke first, "How dare you? You slime, how dare you…"

The horrible little swine said, "How dare I what? Say what every Dom'barn who sees her…sees her dressed like that, knows? That she's nothing but a…"

"Fausto, quiet!" Marcellus cautioned.

"She's nothing but…"

"Fausto, STAND DOWN! Stand down now or I swear I'll use this and lay you out beside yon giant! Do you understand?"

Fausto mumbled something.

"You great oaf! This lady killed hundreds, perhaps a thousand people in Lergenze less than a week ago!"

Astoria was holding Laurealis in her hands and patted Duncan to wake, where he had collapsed onto the bed. "Laurealis, come out of it! Yes, you killed a lot of people, but they died with the Lady's blessing. You galvanized not just a city of a half million humans, you braced the moral structure of the entire Alliance, except the Dom'barn who are immune to our magic. Now, let go of the sprite and come back into your natural form."

I waited to change. I had missed what he said in the shock of learning of my killing so many people, how horrible! I wanted to be able to taste their emotions to make sure they were honest. While possible in my standard form, it was so much easier in this form.

"Did I really kill that many people?"

"You really didn't realize it?" Marcellus asked.

Hearing what I knew was the truth, I hung my head, my eyes closed while tears wet my cheeks.

I felt compassion pouring out from him. I would have never expected compassion from a Dwarf.

"My Lady, you are either a great criminal or a great heroine, probably both. You are certainly the most powerful emotive dancer of our Age. Do you realize that your dance reached from Bourbeson to the north, to the far southern end of your people's lands to the south? The resistance to the war from the humans and your people is over. The humans were about to sue for peace, which in each of the three previous Ages, would have ended with their slaughter within a decade. Now they will continue the fight.

"With the magic of their magicians and yours, they may survive. As a student of history, I'm so tired of the poor humans always ending up massacred. Each Age is defined by the primary human civilizations before the Asmodians chose to destroy it. This time, there's as many as five or six strong human cultures, of which Francescans are one of two on this continent. Destroying the humans only makes the Asmodians that much more powerful, sopping up all that death and murder energy for their foul spells."

He turned to his nephew, rage filling his face. "You, great oaf, need to realize that a Dancer that powerful could have killed us all with her anger. And I mean everyone in this fortress, not just this room. The only thing that saved us is that everyone within her range, including her adopted orphans would have died as well. You need to remember that she can kill you with a thought if you get her angry enough."

A much-chastened Fausto simply said, "Yes, sir."

Marcellus continued, "My Lady…"

Astoria interrupted him by singing,

By the beautiful shores,
By the deep, da-ark oaks,
Round the cool, mossy banks of Lake Maura.

I gave up my sprite form as she hit high notes of Lake Maura, and I joined her. It always gives her spells more power when she has accompaniment. She's a highly skilled alto, while I'm a first soprano. Together we sing a beautiful duet. When I'm aiding her in casting her spells, we sing in unison, not harmony. With this old favorite of ours, I took the liberty of singing harmony as I also cast an illusion of elves playing our beloved horns, harps, and bells. With the accompaniment, her spell swelled. The barely visible dark green aura emanating from her palms spread to her entire hands and kept slowly growing past them. Her eyes closed and she laid her hands over the top of Duncan's head. As the song hit the next crescendo, the aura exploded in a burst of healing mana that quickly gathered around and disappeared inside his head. She continued focusing as she manipulated the injury. With the healing mana around the wound, she could direct her consciousness to it and directly manipulate whatever was wrong. Still, it took time.

We waited as she worked. Within minutes, he stirred, and Astoria smiled as her consciousness returned to her body.

Raina had been doing her own worried chanting of his name and pleading for him to not die, until Astoria snapped that he was in no danger of death. She stayed quiet after that, rocking on her heels, and holding his hand. As soon as Astoria smiled, Raina leapt to his lips to kiss him.

"Gently, child. He's just been healed of a concussion. He's going to be sensitive for a few days as the spell continues to work. You'll have to take safe care of him. Be gentle about the head and I'd be careful of his neck."

Raina jumped back and said with almost too much earnestness, "Oh, I will. I promise I'll take good care of him.

I'll make sure he takes care of himself, so I can take even better care of him later."

I made a mental note to investigate that comment later. I was afraid she was being a bit hasty and foolish.

Marcellus said, "My Lady, Duncan, I'm glad you were healed. However, you really must remember the height of our ceilings. Hauling out enough stone for someone of your height would involve a ridiculous amount of labor.

"Now, back to what my tactless nephew was saying that angered you so much. There's a lot to what he said." Raina sputtered.

"Listen to me," Marcellus commanded firmly. "You have seen what our women dress like. Raina, what you wear is modest by human standards. I know. I've been to your Lergenze. But by our standards it is terribly immodest. While you obviously do belong to a man, you do not wear his collar. So, it is a logical assumption to believe an immodestly dressed, non-collared woman to be a sex worker, a light woman."

"Wait! Wait!" I spoke. "If I'm hearing you right, all women must belong to a man. We're nothing but property! Is that what I am hearing?"

"Well, in a manner of speaking, yes. Marriage is actually far more complex than that. A wife has complete control within the home, but rarely leaves that home without being accompanied by a male relative. And while I understand that your customs are different..."

"Different? By the Lady! That's barbaric. No wonder we civilized elves have never been able to get along with you dwarves!"

His eyes flashed anger before continuing, "Our customs are different, but no less felt to be honorable and just within our separate cultures. Young Rubra is being courted by several young men. If asked whether she feels that giving up her freedom to court other men and during the marriage ceremony puts on his collar is *uncivilized*, I believe she will answer a resounding *no*. She will exchange freedom to be with any man for security. It is a fair exchange, at least for our people."

"Barbarians!" I repeated. I heard Astoria murmur, "Men," quietly behind me.

"From your point of view, perhaps, but more to the point, I would suggest that at least while in dwarven lands you have Raina wear a collar."

Duncan sat up gingerly and asked, "Is this collar something like the marriage torc of our people, including my mother?"

Marcellus smiled, "I'm sure it is. Your people borrowed much more from us than just some of our language while we watched over you with the Watcher's aid. That time lasted for a hundred years or so after the end of the fourth Age, while you were finding your way. It could even be a sturdy necklace, with that beaded green falcon on your breechclout as an identifying decoration. The collar is always decorated and is quite expensive. It is often the costliest item a young man purchases until he buys or excavates a new dwelling to make a home for his wife and family. It's a demonstration of her immense value to him."

Pulling a wire out of my locket's pocket dimension, I hung it around Raina's neck and cast an illusion of something like that upon the wire so that the wire disappeared, and the falcon decorated torc was hanging around her neck. "Is that what you're talking about?"

"Perfect."

Raina held her hand to the collar and her eyes filled with terror as she said, "For five years I wore an iron collar. I…I'm…" Her eyes, her entire body grew calm as she stood proudly, saying, "I am NOT a slave anymore. I'll NEVER be a slave again!"

Then her fragile courage broke, and tears began running down her cheeks. She turned to Duncan, holding her arms out, "No, no, I can't. I can't! Duncan! Mama! HELP!"

Duncan held her close and whispered in her ear, "Honey, you aren't a slave. This is saying we're engaged to be married. A marriage torc is more ornate, but neither has anything to do with slavery. Can you just go along for a while and let's sort this out? I promise you; you'll never be a slave again. This is just an act to help Fausto act better. I don't like it because it means so many terrible things to you, this really isn't a terrible thing. It is a symbol of a particularly good thing. And we do need more help." He held her hand in both of his.

"For me, would you do this? I don't know what we're getting into, but I know some of Kailynn's power and if he was taken out by what we're facing, more help is good. We need to help Kailynn, but I'm scared of what we don't know. I know this hurts you a lot, but if it helps us to survive and to rescue Kailynn, wouldn't it be worth it?"

Her absolute terror was calmed by Duncan's steady strength. Shortly, her tears and terrified "no's" quieted and she threw herself around his neck and glared over his shoulder at Marcellus, then even harder at Fausto. Had looks been knives, Fausto would have been nothing but quivering little cubes of meat on the floor. They turned to face Marcellus and Fausto. Duncan's expression and his emotions were only a little less violent than Raina's. His need to protect was as great as her need for protection.

Duncan set her down and knelt on one knee, so his head was well below the ceiling. "Tribune, this is wrong. Why can't he just act like a normal man and recognize limits?"

Marcellus spoke softly. "Son, I understand your concerns. Raina, I'm sorry. Please step outside a minute with me, both of you."

They left the room and talked for several minutes. I was glad that my hearing was so sharp.

"So, what do you think will excuse Fausto's behavior?" Raina asked sharply.

"I didn't want to say this in front of my nephew, as some of what needs to be said would be more embarrassing to him than I choose to allow. This is a large part of why he is behaving the way he is toward you, Raina. Dwarven men outnumber women nearly two to one. In our culture, women are married by the time they are your age. For a woman your age to be unmarried is unheard of. The only thing I can think of that would be comparable in shock value to your culture would be if Raina were walking around partially or completely unclothed."

"Why, I would never!"

"I know," he said as he patted his hands palm down to tell her to be quieter. "That is why I said that; to give you a mental image of just how strongly your dress, and that you aren't wearing a torc or marriage collar…is hitting him."

"Then why aren't you and your men acting like him?" Duncan asked.

"Because we're older and have seen more, a lot more than Fausto. He's little more than a boy himself. Although he's older than you, in our years, you're older emotionally. He's also brilliant, one of the most promising young earth mages we've seen in hundreds of years, but that's intelligence, not wisdom. We don't want his foolishness to destroy him. He needs time and experience for that. I've thought many times that where most people have some balance between intelligence and wisdom, Fausto is all one and none of the other."

"Well!" Raina said, "He certainly proved that in the tavern!"

"Yes…yes, he did. That's why I feel it is imperative that you wear a torc. I really don't believe this will work without one. I'm sorry. I didn't know you were a slave, and I can see why this makes it almost unbearable. This is really about pretending that you are engaged to Duncan. The way I see you two interact, I expect you really aren't that far from engagement. His people, like mine wear marriage torcs, but it is exactly comparable to the rings other cultures use, representing a never-ending circle.

"If you can do this, I'll personally make it worth your while. He doesn't know it, but my nephew needs you, and you need him. If you're going where I fear you're going, you need every bit of help you have. He may very well save your lives, though you may want to strangle him slowly before all is said and done."

Raina breathed out heavily. "Oh, all right, I'll do it. But I'm not happy, not happy at all."

They stepped back into the room with us, Raina tucked tightly inside Duncan's protective arm.

I put my hand on hers. "Raina, I would like to do one more thing to your engagement torc. May I?" She scuffed her foot on the floor. "Go ahead." She held her hand to her neck.

"You just put it there. Did you just take it away?"

"No, dear. We can all still see it. You can't feel it anymore, though you can see it. It's a complicated bit of illusion, but I hope it'll help you tolerate wearing it."

She felt for it with her hand. The wire the illusion was built upon was real. For the first time, she smiled weakly, "Thanks, Mama. It does help…some."

"Now that that bit of nastiness is settled, is there anything else? Like, why do we have to take that beast with us?"

Marcellus thought for a second. "Well, for one, he is a very competent, though young earth mage. Two, I need to get him out of here, as you guessed. Three, I believe the women of your group will be able to teach him a thing or ten about women that he has chosen to overlook here. My hope is that being in the presence of three such strong women will help him grow up enough to allow a father to consider letting him marry their little darling. You see, he's gone to drink because no father will allow him to marry or even speak to their daughter, despite his competence as an earth mage. I see the strength in you. I believe if anyone can teach him how to behave, you three will. He wasn't like this 'till the news of Lookout Mountain arrived. His mother died birthing him and his father's death hit him hard. I'm his only remaining relative. The war has hit our people appallingly hard.

"I'll want to have a long talk with you when you're done. If he's learned humility, if he's showing more promise of being marriageable, I'll have a large reward for you. Duncan, your people follow our precept that you must be able to provide for your wife before you seek one, a home and profession, or Great Wagon and herds in your case, right?"

"Well, yes."

"Good, if you return my nephew back to me a marriageable man, you will be set, at least for the wagon. They're huge and quite expensive. It says a lot that your people are capable of building such large wagons. They are non-magical and the highest technology our Age produces. However, our people are great craftsmen as well. Your wagon will be magical, to make the frame for such a huge wagon more manageable. But I'll see it's done and to as great a degree as I can, to your specifications. He means enough to me to spend several years' wages on him if that's the case. If he's still not suitable for marriage, I'll still give you a large monetary reward for the effort. Raina, that means you'll get your man, as one of the things that is probably preventing his offer of marriage is his lack of a means of supporting you. Do I have your cooperation, too?"

"How big a reward?" she asked.

"I don't know. Say a minimum of ten Francescan marks? We'll discuss it and I'll be fair, at least within the limits of my income. All right?"

She nodded curtly, "A minimum of ten marks, you say?"

"Aye."

"Minimum, and that's to both of us, right?"

He looked startled and looked like he was about to protest. Then his eyes fell to her torc, and he stopped.

"Aye, lass, to both of ye."

"Humph," she said and turned abruptly to Duncan.

"Duncan is that true? What he said about providing for your family before you propose. Is that why you keep putting me off?" she snapped sharply.

"Partly, it's one of the two reasons. If the Great Wagon problem were resolved, that would leave only one nearly impossible problem to settle."

"What's the other?"

He stone walled. She gave up when it became obvious that he wouldn't say anything more. Since his lips were locked so tight the skin was white around them, she turned back to Marcellus. "Then, yes, I suppose. Does that mean I have to continue to wear this THING?"

"Yes, and it absolutely means you cannot kill Fausto, not even in his sleep. If he's not returned to me, I will be equally vengeful. I may be forced to exile him for a time, but he is still my nephew, the only living descendant of my brother. Do I make myself *perfectly* clear?"

"Yes," she sighed, "Yes, you do."

"Duncan, you must be the leader of this group. It would be unseemly for a woman, no matter how much older and more experienced she may be, to be the leader. I will send Fausto with you. He is extremely useful in mountains like the creviced areas you described, but he simply will not be led by a woman. It'd be like riding a horse. Dom'barn don't ride horses and they don't submit to women."

"Wait, what?" Duncan objected. "He won't ride a horse? Then how are we going to make any time?"

Marcellus smiled, "Oh, you'll see. You'll see. He is an earth mage after all. Do we have a deal?"

We all agreed and ate our now cold breakfast. Astoria insisted upon Duncan resting 'till that afternoon and possibly for an entire day, her decision, not his. I wondered what this afternoon, or possibly tomorrows' dawn, would bring with Fausto accompanying us.

Duncan chose that moment to begin getting to his feet.

"Thanks, Astoria, I feel a lot better."

"And just where do you think you're going?"

"Up, we have to get going. I'm fine, a little headache, but I'm fine. Like my Dad always used to say, "No time like now for getting started.""

"With a newly healed concussion? We'll get going soon enough, after lunch. But it's my choice, not yours."

Raina noticed what Astoria said, sat cross-legged on his chest and frowned at him. When he put his hands on her waist to lift her off, Astoria began singing a lullaby while her hand brushed his temple. It had a faint red aura, unlike the green aura she showed when healing.

"*Go to sleep, go to sleep, go to sleep now, my warrior,*" As his eyes closed, the aura now changed to green, "*Heal and mend, heal and mend, so you'll fight one day again.*"

Noting the gentle rise and fall of his chest, Astoria began arranging his pillow, but made way for Raina as she took over that job.

Looking at Fausto square in the eye, Astoria said, "Fausto, I generally spell fighter or warrior, F-O-O-L, but you make most fighters, this one, in particular, appear wise. You continue to mess up or bring alcohol with you and you'll find yourself dreaming, just like Duncan, while we search your gear. You smirk, trusting no doubt to your race's legendary resistance to spells, medicines, poisons, exhaustion, and in your case, common sense, but I'll let you in on a little secret…"

She leaned over and put her hand beside her mouth as if she were whispering a secret before continuing in a stage whisper, "During the last couple of years of healing soldiers, including dwarves, the Lady and I worked out a sleep spell that works consistently, even on you Children of the Earth."

Then she winked, "Just try me," and sat back.

Marcellus roared with laughter, "Astoria, you're all right."

Chapter Fourteen
Into No Man's Land
Laurealis

That afternoon, it rained heavily, melting the snow, and making it a miserable time to travel. We had planned to stay each night in one of the travel shelters built every ten or fifteen miles along this well-traveled road. With our late start, that wouldn't be possible. Considering Duncan's healing concussion, Astoria decided to have us wait until exceedingly early the next day.

After dinner, I approached Raina, "Honey, are you feeling better?"

She looked at me guardedly, obviously worried that I wanted to have another session of dealing with her past. She still didn't realize that those sessions were at least, if not more, draining to me as they were to her.

"Don't worry, Raina. Yesterday was…intense. I don't think either of us is up to another 'healing' so quickly.

But I couldn't let the issues that are causing you so much emotional pain, fester. They don't go away; they just express themselves in some other way and get worse. I'd love to leave them alone, but that would be so bad for you that I couldn't forgive myself if you succeeded in doing what you tried to do on the inn's rooftop in Lergenze." She nodded, but still looked worried.

"Have you spent any time meditating on the hatred between the races and why all of us need to grow past that? You really surprised me when you showed me my own bigotry. Again, I'm sorry and am actively working on that. With Fausto, he's so easy to dislike, but he's going to be with us, and I want to make sure you're ready."

"No. No, I haven't." she said cautiously.

"Really? What have you been thinking about?"

When she didn't answer, I couldn't blame the poor dear, yesterday was intense, especially considering the actual hatred she'd experienced from all sides as a defenseless half-breed child. The bigotry between the races that was displayed so strongly before, brought all that hatred to the fore. So, I decided to state the obvious.

"You're wondering why Duncan isn't responding to your sexual advances."

It was comical how her mouth dropped, and her eyes popped open in shock at my seeing the obvious. Despite all the pain she'd suffered, sometimes the little girl within her showed through. She was so adorable; I had to work hard to resist the urge to pick her up and hug her.

"Duncan is a good man, well, a boy trying desperately to be the man his father was and would want him to be. His moral character is extraordinarily strong, but you're a beautiful and exceedingly difficult girl to resist when you throw everything you learned over the last few years into it. It's his pain of missing his father, and the respect and love they obviously had for each other, that's giving him the extra strength to resist you throwing yourself at him so blatantly. He wants you with all his adolescent urges. What man wouldn't? But he knows how badly you've been treated, and he'll go to great lengths to make sure you know he would never use you wrongly. He's sensitive enough to your pain that he wants to do everything right by you, at least as he understands right."

"What's that mean… 'as he understands right'?"

"Sweetie, every culture and every person within that culture has their own concept of right and wrong. Sometimes it agrees with ours, and sometimes it doesn't. The Dom'barn, even with their virtual enslavement of women, respect the role of women with bearing and raising children, so much so they've ignored or forgotten how much more we're capable of."

"But Fausto didn't respect me—"

"Right, like I said, he's so easy to dislike. That's the exact point I wanted to make. But remember, he's still a boy without much guidance in such matters. That comment about your price tag was…well, that was just ignorance."

I paused, waiting for her to make the obvious connection. "If Fausto weren't an isolated sick individual, but representative of his culture, what do you expect the others would have done? They had us outnumbered by a good bit."

"Well, if they all agreed with him, they would have joined him…then they would have all raped me. Over Duncan's dead body, I expect."

Laurealis said, "Yes, if they had been like Fausto, Duncan would have died trying to save you. I doubt that not doing so wouldn't even have occurred to him. He's developing strong feelings for you, but he's one of those who can't say it 'till something happens. His actions prove his feelings, instead of his words. If you need words, then you'll never be satisfied with him. Everything he does shows his budding love for you, including cracking his skull this morning when he heard Fausto calling you a whore."

Raina smiled, "Yes, I got that, but I do wish he'd say something. When he played a love song last night, he looked at me the whole time and I knew he was playing it for me. But I do wish he'd say something. I did like the dancing, though. He is an excellent dancer, well, once he figures out the steps."

"Give him time, sweetie, give him time. Fausto's an easy example. There will certainly be something cultural between you and Duncan that could drive you apart. That's part of why there's something else we need to speak of regarding you and Duncan."

She got defensive again; I could taste the sourness of it in her emotions. When she gets defensive, she goes quiet.

"Sweetie, you need to back off. Love is a journey; it takes time to sail the Sea of Love. Let him be your captain and you his first mate. Sex is a very enjoyable part of a journey that ties the two of you together, but it's only a part."

"He talks about 'womanly' skills. Mama, I only have one skill! Well, one 'womanly' skill, but I have other skills. You know Zreetor trained me to be an assassin, which is the only way we escaped from that *place*. I want to use those skills I learned to show Duncan how good I can make him feel. I can't cook, Mama showed me some, but I was only eleven, and I forgot. I picked up skills in sewing and of course, I had to clean, but all I really know is between the sheets. What else can I do? I'm not strong enough to do most men's work."

"Sail with him. The winds will blow as they will. Guide him gently when he needs it, help him, serve him, and he'll serve you in return, without boundary. He needs the time to grow with you as much as you with him. He knows that at a gut level, but he doesn't express himself well.

I suspect that in his culture, like in most cultures, the men do the chasing. You chasing him may actually scare him away, not catch him. Using your body's charms works sometimes, but only when that is all the man is looking for. I strongly suspect that Duncan is, in his own clumsy way, looking for far more than that. He wants a wife to share his life with, his joys and his sorrows, his children, and his old age. He's steady. Honey, you're so full of life and vitality. Steady men like him need your life and laughter as much as you need their calm and order. Trying to get his clothes off all the time won't catch him unless you end up pregnant. That's entrapment and can sour even the best marriage. Not a wise tactic."

By her expression, I realized that was exactly what she was trying to do. Fortunately, Duncan was a young man of extremely strong moral beliefs. But a small axe can chop down the largest oak, and when it came to exciting a man, Raina was more like a huge saw than a small axe. It looked like she was set on entrapping him, even though I'm sure she didn't realize how much a baby would change her. She obviously always lived by her considerable wits and figured to cross that bridge when she got to it. Well, truth would distract her from that goal; get her to catch him the right way. Poor girl; so much potential and so much baggage.

"Tell you what; after we rescue Kailynn, maybe we can all travel up there. It'll be a lot safer with him with us. And until then I can teach you cooking and sewing…well, that may have to wait, sewing stuff is bulky. Maybe embroidery. Duncan's points about packing too much stuff were right. Yes, we'll cook and do embroidery. Later, we can make clothes and cloth."

Raina looked closely at my fine linen, illusionary fine linen that is. "Cooking and embroidery would be great, but I won't be caught dead, well, outside of Duncan's bed, wearing clothes like that. I was forced to wear stuff like that. I won't wear anything like that again."

I laughed, "That's fine, I can make clothes like that dirndl dress you're wearing, but there are friends of mine who would be better teachers. I bet one of his kinswomen, when they discover that you're a war orphan aiming to catch one of their men, would be happy to teach you. That's probably the best, since then you'll know you'll be wearing what he's familiar with."

"I like that." I walked her back to our room as she leaned against me, inside my arm. That felt so good. I've missed walking with a child like that for so long, ever since Aletha…

The next morning, we left early and made suitable time. Fausto's mount turned out to be an earth golem with a basket on its back. It required no skill to ride, which was good, because he must have drunk all the whiskey left in the fort last night. Maybe it's bad of me but watching him suffer through a hangover that I thought Dom'barn didn't get made me feel good. By the Lady, he began singing. I cast an illusion over him of birds singing whenever he began that awful caterwauling.

Raina seemed to be taking my advice to heart. She was pensive, which was good. She had much to think about. I spent my time dealing with the bigotry I'd displayed when I was in shock, and again later when Astoria revealed what she thought about half-breeds. I was so ashamed, especially after I saw it from her perspective, with her emotions and past history of the racial hatred directed at her.

I was also pondering how to deal with what I saw about the whips, and knives, and chains she'd mentioned. That went on for a long time and she was always helpless. Such beasts! I'm so glad she shared with me how she personally killed that evil Count de Borgia.

Then I had to think how we would help turn that little beast, Fausto, into a civilized person. I noticed the birds have been chirping a lot. I laughed because I noticed that all of us had totally ignored Fausto and he was red-faced from shouting. I wonder if he has anything to say I would want to hear.

I suspended the illusion of birds chirping, keeping it ready in case he needed to be ignored again.

"I HAVE TO STOP AND I CAN'T MAKE THIS DAMNED GOLEM STOP WITHOUT SOUND! I HAVE TO STOP..."

"It's all right, you have sound. Why do you have to stop?"

"Damned woman! I have to piss! Now!" He told the golem to stop with words from his arcane tongue.

Raina said something and Duncan replied, "No, you never leave a party member alone without an incredibly good reason. He's just going to be a minute."

"Come on, Duncan. Gallop past him and scare him!"

"No."

"Party pooper."

The earth rose up, creating a private room for him. He came out and nodded to Duncan but glared at Raina. Oh my, those two were definitely complicating my life. Raina did not need to egg him on. Of course, if he would apologize for his outrageous behavior in the tavern, it would help.

We rode in peace, stopping late into the evening. Astoria started a fire while Raina, Fausto, and I set up the tents. Duncan went to take care of the horses. Duncan spent a lot of time with the horses. Occasionally, after all the beasts were cared for, I'd see him lay his head against Shadow and just stay there a long time stroking his neck, thinking. We all had a lot on our shoulders, and he was so young to be forced into this.

Raina and I made biscuits. When they were done, I let her work on loading some of them down with meat and cheese, while I prepared others with honey for Astoria and me. I then showed her how to warm the sandwiches, melting the cheese without burning the biscuits by wrapping them in green leaves. We filled plates with a good many of them and I nodded at Duncan with his head at Shadow's neck.

"Talking to you instead of to a horse would do your relationship better than acting like you want to strip and ride him any time he's around."

She smiled and carried the biscuits to him, which he accepted with an eager smile. They sat and began talking quietly. Thank the Goddess, she's keeping her hands to herself and they're just talking. He needs someone to talk things out with, and Astoria and I can't help but come across as more experienced in most things. She's perfect for him, exactly what he needs.

Things continued like this for several days and Fausto was acting like a person. He was respectful towards Raina, speaking only what was necessary.

"What's going on toward Raina?" I asked him. You're acting respectful, almost as if you realized that she's a person, not an object for your pleasure."

He glared at me. "Why wouldn't I? She's properly collared; I'd never mess with another man's woman."

"Really? I hadn't noticed that much restraint at the tavern."

"She wasn't properly collared then."

"She was still a person with the right to be respected."

"No, she wasn't. Only a whore would expose her ankles and breasts like that. Well, a whore or an elf."

"Women in the human lands wear shorter dresses than your people, and generally have a nice square cleavage in their blouses. It's just their fashion. It was the most modest outfit I could find that came even close to fitting!"

"What's a lonely man to do when exposed to that much female flesh? It's blatant advertising."

Biting my tongue hard, "I would suggest restraint."

"And what about you? You're not covering a thing with that fabric. Astoria wears stuff just as thin, but she's got enough layers on so I can only see hints of that gorgeous body underneath. You! You're so scrawny it's obscene, and you flaunt it!"

Shocked, I tasted his emotions as he looked at Astoria and felt the obvious lust. When he looked back at me, I tasted his obvious distaste. I was dumbfounded.

Astoria was fat, a cute fat, but still fat. Humans frequently think she was "built" and lust after her. Her colors were also unfortunate, ochre yellow skin and green hair. But he's not looking at her colors, only at her shape. I've always been considered among the most beautiful of my people and he thinks I'm ugly. I didn't know how to deal with that, and I rushed off. I know I'm beautiful. I've always been the most beautiful person around. I didn't understand…Well, I didn't want to attract him anyway! But I won't be thought less than what I am, so I'll make a change here and there to "lower" the tensions in the group.

I worked with my cosmetic illusions, changing the way my body looked to be more like Astoria's. I altered my clothing as well, so that my beauty was only visible in the strongest sunlight. I then went back to see the little jerk, Fausto.

"Is this better?"

"What? Another illusion? You elves are unbelievable. If I didn't know what you look like, it might help." He sighed as his anger calmed, "But for another dwarf, you won't start out on the wrong foot. It is much better."

I stared for a second, not trusting my ears. "Thank you."

Duncan

Hugging Shadow around his neck has always been calming for me. I love the earthy smell of his soft coat. I tried thinking about everything that had been happening lately.

The ladies calmed down, thankfully. Raina was wonderful since she backed off some. I saw Fausto doing something as well. He wouldn't be so bad if he weren't so self-centered. He doesn't see past his own desires to the ignorance of his actual needs.

Raina came up beside me and gently placed her hand on the small of my back while softly rubbing Shadows lower neck.

"Duncan, Shadow's deep brown in front with white spots on his face and chest, and white in back with deep brown spots. Why did you name him Shadow?"

"Well," I chuckled, "you see, when I was befriending him in the time-honored way, with apples and other goodies, he always hid in shadows. He's really a smart prankster. After I began trying to ride him, he would hide, especially in shadows, where he can virtually disappear. He playfully pushed my back hard enough to make me stumble from the shadow of a huge tree. Not hard, but definitely hard enough to get my attention. I'd walked right past him and not seen him, the big rascal."

I had to pat his shoulder at the fond memory.

Fausto shouted, "Duncan! Over here!"

When Raina and I approached him sitting in his basket in that stone golem 'man' he created. I asked, "Any news?"

"Pretty large group of armed men up ahead. We need to stop to let them pass."

"Describe them."

"Slavers."

Raina gasped and stiffened.

He glanced at Raina, "Too large a group for us to handle. There are at least fifty, maybe a hundred of them not including their captives. They're heavily armed."

Raina turned to face me, "Duncan, we must save them!"

I was aghast. "We do nothing! Five against fifty to a hundred, no way! We still need to rescue Kailynn."

Raina looked into my eyes. Seeing my resolve, she turned to Fausto. Using her most sultry voice, she asked, "Fausto?"

A stronger man would have fallen prey to that smile of hers and Fausto struck me as anything but strong, "Yes, gorgeous?"

I didn't like the way she was talking to him. I realized I was jealous. We seemed to be getting close quickly. That feeling of being hunted came over me so strongly, I almost missed their next words.

"How many slaves were there?"

"I don't know, looked to be at least a half-mile of 'em strung out two-wide. But like your lover-boy said, 'five against fifty, no way.' I wholeheartedly agree."

"But we have an earth-mage on our side. I'm sure someone as powerful as you, Fausto, could lessen the odds, couldn't you?" she asked in that sultry voice that just did things to me, and probably to Fausto, as well.

"Sure, I could drop the mountain on them. Of course, the slavers could ride out of danger while the slaves, being all chained together, would die. A quick death would be a blessing. The mines are just a death sentence anyway, and that's probably where they're going. "Besides, once a slave, always a slave. Right, Raina?"

In a flash Raina dismounted and drew those knives she always carried. It was like she's a member of the Society of the Snake.

He called out a couple of things in that strange language he used for his magic. Out of the corner of my eye, I saw Raina rearing back to throw one of her knives with blinding speed.

"Raina! Don't!"

I reared up on the stirrups and hit Fausto's chin as hard as I could. A fist sized bit of stone formed in front of my fist, crumbled under the force of my blow, and disappeared. He flew out of his basket, hit the ground, and didn't get up.

I knocked out that arrogant fool, or so I thought. I hoped I didn't break my hand on that hard head!

While I was distracted rubbing my hand, 'Rock Head' rose from the dust and came right for us.

"Raina!"

Shadow liked that rock man as little as I did and was backing away quickly. We turned and dashed toward Raina. I held my good hand out while controlling Shadow with my knees. She reached up and hooked my hand and I landed her in front of me upon the horse. Astoria and Laurealis were facing us, and by the dark look on their faces, had seen the whole thing.

I raced up to them and shouted, "That rock man's after us. I may have broken Fausto's neck, Astoria. If I didn't, it may be a race to see which of us kills him first, Raina or me. But that's after we get back from checking out the trouble up ahead."

"Wait!" Astoria yelled after us. I reigned in Shadow.

"What? Make it quick, that rock man of his looked like it was about to attack me."

"It's not, See? It's just standing there."

"So, if Fausto gets up, he may send it after us."

"Right," Astoria said, "but he's getting up and it looks like he's holding his jaw, not his neck."

"All right, let's see to the idiot then." I agreed.

We got a little closer and saw that Fausto's whole lower face was a bloody mess. He was trying to do something with his rock man. He was flailing one arm like he was trying to tell it to stop, while his other hand supported his jaw. He was making noises, not words.

Laurealis flicked her wrist. "Wait, he's not mad at all. He's genuinely concerned and in a lot of pain, but he's not angry."

I asked, "What's that mean?"

Astoria said, "It means that you broke his jaw, and unless he can talk to the golem, it will only obey his last order."

"Fausto!" I shouted. "Can you get over here without your rock man?"

He shook his head "no".

I shook my head wondering what to do. "Astoria, can you heal my hand?"

"Of course." She began humming and a light-green light covered her hand, then moved over mine and the pain was gone. Then she laid my hand out on her thigh and set the broken bones. I was extremely glad that she'd numbed the pain. Her hand glowed dark green and the green traveled to mine. With her eyes closed in concentration, I felt the bones wiggling under my skin. Watching my bones move like that was so strange that I'm surprised I didn't run off screaming gibberish right then. I felt Raina's arm wrap around my back and calmed me enough to ease away from the panic I felt growing.

"All right, your hand's mended, but not healed. What're you going to do now?"

"Attack that rock man!"

"What? But that hand needs time to finish healing!"

Shadow and I were already charging. Preparing to leap off Shadow, I patted his back and pointed to indicate where I wanted him to run. We dodged the rock man's attack and we jumped off right behind it. I suspected the thing was extraordinarily strong, but slow.

I was right. I landed and swung my sword into its chest then backed off. It slowly turned toward me. I feinted right and went left. The damned thing was so slow it never noticed my feint. I jumped away as it swung at me. I ran past it and swung at its chest again. I didn't know if it had blood, but I figured its energy must be centered in its chest.

I was right. Those two solid hits were well placed, and it was slowing down.

Shadow, bless his heart, hammered the thing's back with his two front hooves, while I ran in front of it and used Glenfallis like an axe, chopping halfway into its chest. It began to topple, then fell to pieces.

Fausto gaped at me with wide eyes while Astoria ran to him and healed his broken jaw, much like she had healed my hand. Unlike me, he took it like he was used to it, instead of like he had never seen nor imagined such a thing in all his life.

After the repair process was over and Fausto was finished working his mouth, much like I had worked my fist, he said, "I'm impressed. Not many people can take out a

Golem as quickly as you just did. Your animal is better trained than I'd realized."

Still furious about the slave comment to Raina, I picked him up with both arms…barely. I was surprised how heavy he was. "Do you realize how close your mouth came to getting you killed just now?"

"Not really. I made a comment about an actual past event. People shouldn't get upset about their past. They should just look to their future."

Though I was angry I couldn't hold him much longer. Actually, it was like the ground was pulling him down, making him heavier. Maybe it was something to do with him being an earth mage. So, instead of dropping him, I used the last of my strength and heaved him up higher, kicking him as he dropped.

Standing over him glowering, I said, "We'll deal with this later. I'm too angry to think straight and I expect Raina is, also. Don't for a second imagine this is over. And if you ever…" My rage began surfacing again and I felt myself shudder all over as I battled to control it. "If you ever show that much disrespect to Raina again, I'll let her have her way with you while I act as backup. Do I make myself perfectly clear?"

"Perfectly, but really, why are you so upset?" He actually managed to present the air of the person wronged. I couldn't imagine how he pictured himself innocent.

"Now that this is swept under the rug for a while," I glowered at the smug or very dense little earth mage, "let's plan what we're going to do about the slavers."

Fausto exclaimed, "What! I thought you'd realized there were too many for us to do anything about!"

"Well, let's just say your last comment to Raina gave me a change of heart about the value of slaves, present or former."

Fausto was about to say something, but he looked past me to where Raina was standing behind my back. He looked from her to me and back to her and held his hands out in resignation, "All right, you win. I can't go back unless I help you and get a good report, so it looks like we die here. Do you at least have a plan?"

"Not yet, that's what we're about to do. Like my dad always said, 'Many heads make for good plans.' Ladies, do you know about the situation across the pass?"

Laurealis replied, "No." So after we spent time explaining the situation to them, the five of us produced a plan using all of our strengths. We rode forward to the pass where we saw that a winter storm had stopped the caravan. It hadn't made it to our side yet, but it was coming, and the surrounding rocks channeled the winds in the pass. They were already so powerful that all we could do was cover ours and our horses' faces and lead them through on foot while we were all tied together to not get lost from each other. The snow was blowing hard enough that we couldn't see and howling so loudly that speech was impossible. Fausto managed to work his way forward and I vaguely saw a cave in the pass to which he was pointing. I guided us in by the ropes we had tied to each other. It was a little too large, but it would do.

"Can one of you ladies light this up a bit?"

Laurealis lit up the cave with a pale light that filled it without coming from any one point. We all saw a pile of wood and tinder showing us that this cave had been used for shelter before.

"Let's leave our horses here. It'll be safer for them, and this cave is small enough that their body warmth will keep them from freezing."

"What about us?" Fausto demanded. Astoria was already laying a small fire near the horses but behind some rocks. I admired how sensitive she was to the needs of others and their limitations. The horses wouldn't accidentally knock the fire out behind the rocks and the fire would steady and warm them. I covered them with blankets. When I pulled out my sister Marsha's blanket, I paused for a moment, stroking the patterns she had worked in the cloth and remembered her.

"Duncan, what about us?" Fausto asked insistently.

"Huh?" I was jerked out of my reverie when he repeated his question.

"What about us?" I replied.

"What's going to keep us from freezing? I say we leave the slavers alone."

"We all know your opinion, and if you would keep your mouth shut more, you might get your way more often."

"So, you're going to get us all killed because I think it's stupid to risk my, I mean, our lives on a bunch of…well, uh, slaves." The worried look he cast at Raina, before he said something else foolish, did my heart good.

"The storm isn't as bad out in the open as it was in the pass. I don't see how anyone could have seen us yet. Laurealis, are you ready to make us invisible?"

"Yes," she replied. Remember to keep the ropes attached until we get close enough to listen. We may have to change plans once we get there. We'll be able to see each other, though others won't. However, the separate illusion of the more intense storm may make it more difficult for us to see each other."

"How intense is it?" I asked.

She smiled, "I made it as bad as here in the pass. Just like a real storm can do sometimes. It should be enough to make them all go inside their tents. At the very least, it should make any guards unable to see us, even if something happens to our invisibility. That should make it possible for you fighting types to have just one tent at a time to deal with."

"Wonderful. Thanks, that'll help a lot."

Once we made it to the other side, we saw twenty-seven large tents, with the one in the back far more ornate than the others. We worked our way to the fancy tent.

As we were passing one of the lesser tents, we heard, "You fool! You know you could have had any one of the five pretty girls we've picked out for our use. They're just going to the mines with the men. We'll have to move her in with our personal slaves now. Don't you remember that we get ten times as much for breeders as we do for mining slaves?"

"Yeah, but even if she does get pregnant, she won't show 'till we're long gone."

"You blithering worm! Before I was a master, I served on a caravan that sold breeders to the Asmodians, and some of them were pregnant. Yeah, we got away…for a whole month! Then when we awoke, we found ourselves surrounded by hundreds of the damned Skarg. They took the slave-master Thomas and *ate* him, slowly, right there in front of us. They had a magical necklace they put on him that stopped him from bleeding or feeling pain and stopping him from dying of shock as well. It had to have, since I've seen shock kill men who lost just a hand in battle. This guy never went into shock, when all that was left of him was his head and chest. He screamed more horribly than you can imagine!

Though he treated us well, we had to stand there and watch him for the entire day.

"The way they actually killed what was left of him was the worst. Their leader vomited out something black and semi-liquid. I don't know what it was, but it moved over to him somehow and shaped itself into a small demon who pulled something out of Thomas and absorbed it. It was his actual soul, by what he was screaming. When the thing had it all out, Thomas died. We wanted to do something, but there was no way. Think what you like, but with all those dart-thrower arms trained on us, we had to just watch him die. Then the thing moved, crawled, whatever back to the leader. The leader's body had gone to sleep when the black thing left it. When it climbed back inside him, he woke up.

"Then they made a lottery to pick six of us, one for every pregnant girl, then did the same to them. At least that didn't last six more days, I don't think any of us would have stayed sane. I'll never go through that again!" The leader declared, "If you ever pick another of the breeders for your personal enjoyment, I'll kill you. For now, move her to one of the other tents and know that you'll be fined four times her breeder price, plus I'll have you on every crap detail I can think up. Do you understand?"

The fear in his voice was apparent, "Uh, yes, sir."

"Remember, also, you idiot, they do the same thing to any of us who tell anyone who doesn't already know! You're in now as a Skarg slave trader, and you'll never get out alive, any more than I can. Outside of this caravan, no one knows about selling breeders to the Skarg. I don't know why they want women young enough to have babies, and I don't want to know. I don't know if they'll eat one of us for each person told, but I suspect that's exactly what they'd do!"

A man left the tent a moment later, his anger apparent in his stride. He strode quickly to the more ornate tent and disappeared inside. Hard as it was, I put aside my concerns for Marsha, based on what I had just learned, and motioned for Laurealis to make the wind howl more violently outside our little circle.

"Well, this changes things," I said.

Raina was in a quiet rage, and I knew slavers were about to go down under those knives in her hands. Astoria held her healer's staff more resolutely than I'd ever seen. Laurealis' emotions appeared to be reflected in her personal illusion, since it was smoking. What surprised me was that Fausto, uncaring Fausto, was wearing a frown as well, as if he were capable of human emotions.

"Yes, it certainly does," he said. Raina's mouth dropped open, and he had our attention, mainly because we were all so startled at his unexpected disdain.

"We should go in as Skarg, Laurealis, because this may be a missing clue as to why they can breed so fast. That's always been a mystery to us and discussed over many an ale since they first appeared when your homeland was overrun," he said, turning toward Raina. "I wouldn't be surprised to learn that it was your Goddess, Astoria, who let this fall onto our laps. Laurealis, can you make the five of us look like Skarg with five more in front to act as shields?" I was surprised how fast Fausto had come up with that, but looking back, it made sense.

"Yes, that'll take a little preparation, but I can do it. I wish now that I had ever actually seen a Skarg or heard an accurate description."

Raina and I were surprised, but Fausto was flabbergasted. "You're married to a Champion and never heard a description of a Skarg?"

"Well, no. I wouldn't let him bring up such unpleasantness."

He looked at her like she was a particularly low life form he'd like to squash, but all he said was, "Damned elf."

Laurealis set right to work. She pulled things out of the huge gem in her jeweled necklace that hung around her waist. Things like a mirror, ash, and two small gourds that had grown together, and more. I couldn't see how she could store stuff in a gem. I briefly wondered about the fight about the clothes when we were leaving, since she had a gem that could somehow store stuff. I figured it was a woman thing and dropped it.

Fausto and I told everyone what we knew of the Skarg. We described how they had parts that were like men, but other parts like animals or simply demonic. The parts were random. They just as easily were nothing but the ears or everything but the ears. Fausto's people had determined that they had something he called *Chaos Matter* in these strange parts, but the human parts were truly human. His people had no idea how they had come to be. What we heard was new information to all of us.

It took Laurealis almost a half hour to get everything ready, but at last she said, "Ready. Now, this illusion will hold 'till you have hit or been hit three times, ladies only once. Raina, since I expect you'll be sticking pointy things in them, I made your illusion with three tactile elements as well. The ones out front have more."

Fausto said, "Excellent. I assume that I'll do the talking then?"

I replied, "Uh, from what Dad said, the Skarg leaders tend to be more human-like, as I told Laurealis when I was describing the Skarg as I know them. The leader is the only one who talks. He's also the first target for anyone with any sense. Are you sure you want to be the first target?"

"Uh…yes, I see your point."

"The leader will be in front and pure illusion, so I'll have to control him, Laurealis said. Oh, how do I make his voice sound?"

"If he's human enough, he can sound human. If his head or vocal cords are something demonic or animal, then it will have to reflect that. I'd make him pretty human, like most of their leaders." Fausto replied.

"Good." She chanted and lit some powder she had crushed with a mortar and pestle. It exploded in a cloud of smoke. When the smoke lifted there were ten of us. By our astonished looks, I realized Raina, Fausto and I were all equally surprised by the realism of the illusion. I noted our positions, so I knew who of us the illusion belonged. Unlike the invisibility spell, we were all now affected by the spell instead of seeing each other while others couldn't.

The Skarg standing where Laurealis had been, spoke first. "We have less than an hour. I'm letting the illusion of the storm keeping these beasts in their tents become part of this illusion as well. When we open the tent, it must look real to give us an advantage."

We moved into position, and I studied our surroundings for a moment before opening the tent flap. Until I did that, we could still back out.

I was impressed by the severity of the blizzard. It was as bad as the one in the pass just a short while ago. The five of us and the five illusions were pretty human-shaped. I noticed that we all had small crossbows hanging at our sides. I raised mine, pretending to arm and cock it and one of the created Skarg's motions mimicked mine. After a moment all of us had armed and ready crossbows. I nodded my approval at the "Laurealis Skarg" to acknowledge her impressive change in the semblances. It was obvious that Laurealis had paired each of us to an illusion. I wanted to ask if they would work on the guards if needed but was scared to tip our hand just outside the tent.

I opened the tent flap, not trusting an illusion to do so.

"What the…?" exclaimed the slave master and several of his guards. A nearly-undressed nice-looking young woman was being raped by one of the men. I saw a toddler that was certainly the woman's asleep a few steps away.

The slave master recovered first. He approached the lead Skarg but stopped well short of him and bowed extremely low. "My Lord, you arrived far sooner than we had been led to expect. Are you here to pick up your delivery? I had been led to believe that we were to meet your army in several weeks in front of the city of Sharcu."

Sharcu, I realized, was the human mining city that many of the merchants were traveling to and from.

Our illusionary leader announced, "Plans have changed."

"Fine, we have many other fine slaves who would do for your travel rations. Would you like to purchase them as well?"

"Yes, that will be fine."

"Excellent," he said, pointing at the girl his men had been raping and ran his finger across his throat, then at the sleeping child and did the same.

The mother squirmed out from under the clutches of the man on top of her and screamed, "Not Dana, no!"

The man she was escaping from pulled her chin back and slit her throat. Another man murdered Dana. The leader picked her up and said, "For your dinner. The mother is for your men."

Simultaneously, all of us, illusionary and real, fired our crossbows. They were so realistic the slavers we shot thought the bolts were real and died. It never occurred to me that illusions could kill. The ladies' illusions disappeared at the same time, but the only living people left in the tent were the five of us and the dying slavers. I held open the flap and Raina and her illusion rushed out as I expected. Suddenly, when she got about twenty feet from Laurealis, her illusion just faded. Laurealis had forgotten to mention that there was a range to her spell.

I was shocked by "never hurt a fly" Astoria. Her face was filled with rage and her staff had somehow extended into a huge battle-axe. A blue nimbus aura surrounded her and the axe as she took off after Raina. Strangely, the nimbus strongly resembled a massively built elf man. Fausto and Astoria, in her blue man-shaped nimbus with her staff / battle-axe, left the tent. I tried to catch up with Raina as well.

Laurealis stamped her foot hard and waved her arms to each side and Raina disappeared. She did the same to Astoria, but nothing happened. She did it again and nothing happened. I raced on.

Astoria cut her way through the side of the nearest tent while I saw what must have been Raina opening the flap on the other side. I stepped in behind Astoria into a cloud of blood as Astoria turned into our warrior, cut the first guard in half, and turned to another.

Wiping the splattered blood from my eyes, I saw Raina appear behind the second guard who was raising his crossbow toward Astoria. She wrapped her hand around his mouth and stabbed up into his kidney, which made him unable to do anything but sink to the ground soundlessly. The tent was finished. I ran past the slaves in their chains to the flap where Raina met me at full speed. My last image of that tent was of all the prisoners' chains falling off.

The storm was terrible around the tent and Laurealis was moving it to the next to screen the noise. Astoria had cut into the next tent and was wreaking mayhem. Raina and I ran on past it, figuring she wouldn't leave much. I didn't see Fausto, but I figured Laurealis had turned him invisible. I did see the chains from the tent we had just left, race like a giant hyperactive snake and follow Astoria as we ran past to the next tent.

I took a clue from Astoria and sliced my way in while Raina went the long way. Seeing a shadow against the tent wall I placed my stroke to cut him from top to bottom, like our once-gentle priestess had done. I charged through, screaming my battle cry, a yodel our people use that terrifies most enemies. There were two other guards in the other tent, and Raina took out one with that strangely effective attack. This time he screamed. The third guard switched his attack to her but was stopped by a *Gaelaur*! He threw his shackled fists up into the guard's stomach, forcing him to fold over, and Raina finished him off. I ran to the Gaelaur who held his hands out for me to chop the chain in two.

Raina and I ran on. The illusionary storm couldn't keep up with us, but an enraged priestess wielding a huge axe and an invisible earth mage sure did. In the full flow of battle rage, I knew I was far faster and stronger than normal. Men were coming out to meet us, fortunately only a few were armed with crossbows. Against the melee, Raina and I were reigning supreme, but ranged weapons can cut any man down.

Even without her invisibility, which vanished when one guard sensed her then hit her shoulder with a crossbow bolt, Raina ruled the battle. While the guard's attention was on me, she slipped up behind them from the shadows and killed them.

Another guard closed on her, and she had to fight him. It was an uneven fight, two knives in close against a sword of greater length. I screamed my fear and rage and jumped over the prisoners between us. He looked up at my scream as I took off his head and Raina stabbed her dagger into his heart.

My heart skipped a beat when I saw blood running from a long cut that ran from between her breasts to her belly, joining the blood running from her shoulder. She had gone to her knees as soon as we killed the slaver but looked up at my gasp. "I'll live, move on. I'll catch up."

"But…?"

"Get out of here! They'll need your help!"

With one last backward glance I charged onward, screaming as I ran toward Astoria. It distracted the man she was attacking, which was all the opening she needed. She dispatched him with great skill. It was far greater than I would have expected. I mean, unless I was vastly mistaken, she was a pacifist until days ago, and she was using a battle-axe as well as I have ever seen it used. That weapon is one of the preferred weapons of my people and we have masters of its use. Perhaps that blue man shape was the cause. Its use also required great strength and she didn't seem to have the muscle for it. I put my thoughts aside as we were at the next group outside the tents and any thought, but battle, was a suicidal luxury.

Ten of them were arrayed in a battle line arced away from us. I glanced at Astoria and nodded to the far-right side of them. I hadn't noticed it till then, but the blue shadow nodded first. Her nod followed a fraction of a second later. Very strange. Before moving right, as I moved left, Fausto, bless his tiny arrogant heart, sent his chains flying into their center, tying up the middle four. I saw the Gaelaur I had freed come running out armed with a sword.

Astoria held her clenched fist straight out in front of her and cast some sort of spell that made one foe collapse, then another, before she charged. My battle cry distracted one of her opponents and two of mine. Feinting right, I spun around and hit a sword that tried to parry mine. My strength was far greater than his and I caved in the side of his helmet as my strike against his sword continued onto his head. One down, three to go. Spinning back, I faced them. I remembered a move my Dad used sometimes. I retreated a few steps, getting them to charge. Feinting right, I swung inside left, striking with my sword's pommel. My blow knocked the man into the other two. Checking my charge, I reversed directions and took off a hand and sword with an upward stroke, then spinning around, cut the other attacker in half with a reverse swing.

"Aye!" I screamed as a mace struck my leg, which suddenly wouldn't support my weight. As I fell, I felt the bone rip through my skin. I was helpless to defend against more attacks. Astoria moved forward and Fausto's chains moved to intercept them.

By the Ancient One's Hammer! Fausto went down! His chains were moving, but not attacking, and Astoria was attacking by herself. The Gaelaur was making his way to us, but it was too late. We were all going to die.

Somehow, I made it up on my uninjured left leg. That was all I could do. I could scream to distract them, but I could do no more than hop and would certainly fall. They would cut me down. I began thinking of how far my spirit would have to travel to meet my family.

Suddenly a bear roared behind the men. The distraction let Astoria and the Gaelaur take them from one side while the bear attacked the ones to the rear.

Regina

We were all sitting in the cave around a fire built by the grateful people we'd freed. The bodies of the slavers had been simply tossed outside while the bodies of the mother and daughter had been removed by grieving kin for proper burial in a cairn.

Most of the prisoners were indentured servants but several, including the other Gaelaur were truly prisoners of raids by the slavers. He was just sitting on a nearby rock studying everything, though most of his attention was focused on Duncan, which meant me, also. I didn't know if he spoke our language, but his silence and the way he was studying me was eerie.

Astoria was just sitting quietly with her legs crossed and her eyes closed.

Duncan was unconscious. His eyes were closed, and he moaned occasionally, but that may have been despite being unconscious. Astoria was waiting to heal Fausto and me after healing Duncan, who was the worst of us. I was kneeling beside the horrible wound in his thigh. He had cuts all over, but his leg was the worst. Blood had soaked his legging where the bone was protruding.

Blood had been spurting beside the wound when I reached him, but a year ago I'd been taught how to hold a spurting artery closed till a healing could be worked. I was holding one closed in his thigh as I waited for Astoria. I was expecting her to get started and saw her put her hands to her head, like she was focusing.

I was so worried about Duncan. I couldn't figure him out. I'd never met a man I couldn't get to desire me. Normally it was the opposite problem, but he rejected my every advance and ignored me when I was blatantly offering myself. I wanted him, partly for protection, but also because he was driving me to distraction with his resistance to what I was freely offering him. My thoughts also wandered to the talk I'd had with Laurealis about things more meaningful.

I was so worried. Duncan couldn't die on me. I just found him!

The women had forced their bandages on me and covered me in a blanket while they mended my ripped dress. I wouldn't leave Duncan for any reason. They dropped the dress the poor murdered mother had worn beside me. I couldn't put it on since I had to hold the artery. I didn't care that I was only covered in a blanket. I was doing what I needed to be doing.

Several had come by and laid sympathetic hands on my shoulder for a moment and asked if they could relieve me so I could put the dress on. When I nodded to Duncan and the artery I was pinching tightly, they understood and left me in peace. They would do it right and maybe they wouldn't. It did comfort me that they were keeping an eye on us.

Fausto was sitting on the other side of the fire while a woman bandaged him. He also waited for Astoria to heal him. He was drinking hot tea that the released slaves made for us all, when suddenly he stood and bellowed quite rudely,

"Well, Raina, I hope you're satisfied."

"Huh?"

"You nearly got us all killed with your stupidity."

"I did not!"

"Ha! Look down. We're both wounded; Duncan is near death and would probably die if we didn't have a healer with us. I told you, attacking sixty slavers with five was stupid! Did anyone listen? No!"

"All right, you made your point, but did you notice?"

"Notice what? That we all almost died? Yes, in fact, I did."

"No, stupid! The fact that we won. All the people are freed and as soon as Astoria can begin healing us, we'll all be fine."

"Humph," he said as he stomped off. After a minute or two, he returned and walked right up to Laurealis. "Laurealis, just where the hell were you? Raina and I did our jobs. Astoria…" he held his hand up and put it down like he didn't know what to say. "Astoria the pacifist, the healer, just where the hell did that battle-axe come from? Duncan's sword work was impressive, not flashy, but effective. He did well. Raina, you did well, too. You surprised me how well you use those knives of yours. Laurealis, you did great in the beginning of the battle, and that bear roaring from behind them at the end was great. But just where the hell were you in the middle of the fight?"

She blushed, "I, uh, I…"

"Did you run out of mana?"

"No, I, uh…"

"Out with it, woman! It couldn't be worse than if you zoned out, or something like that."

"I was throwing up."

By the Goddess, she was having a reaction to actually killing those people. A scene of me doing the same thing after my first assassination crossed my mind.

"Fausto, leave her alone."

"But she left…"

Around Fausto, I always feel like I'm on a low simmer and it takes extraordinarily little to bring me to a boil. This definitely qualified. I tried extremely hard to control myself, since I couldn't let go of Duncan's artery. I felt my anger grow into a cold rage.

"I said, leave her alone, Fausto! She couldn't help it. That was the first time she killed anyone. She knows they deserved what they got; we all do. But she's so sensitive to emotions and killing people up close and personal like that is tough for anyone. I can't imagine how much more offensive it was for her."

I glared at him for a minute and his stunned look made me realize that he must not have realized that angle.

"I guess you're so stupid and insensitive that your first killing didn't bother you at all," I said derisively.

"Uh, no, actually, it didn't. They deserved it and they got it."

He hesitated, like he wanted to say more and realized as soon as Duncan was healed, things would go badly for him. Then he shut up and just glared at me. I was amazed; he did the sensible thing and didn't say another word to me.

Turning back to Laurealis, he went on the attack again, "What are you, some kind of artist, a pacifist or something?"

"Uh, huh, both actually," she replied quietly, like she was about to throw up again.

"And you're married to one of the greatest fighters of the Age?"

"Yes," she replied demurely.

He began pacing, but stopped cold, mid-stride. He put his hand to his forehead like he had a headache. "Well, except for hanging us out to dry while you got all touchy-feely, you did well. Thank you."

I was still waiting for Astoria to begin healing Duncan. She was kneeling beside him, but she was holding her hands to both sides of her head. "Just shut up!" she yelled.

I asked her. "Who, Fausto? Is his talking distracting you?"

"I can't hear anything, you're all too loud! Just quiet down! You're driving me crazy!"

No one was saying a word. Everyone in the cave was staring at Astoria in amazement. Laurealis put her cup down and knelt behind Astoria, laying one hand on her back, the other on her arm. "Honey, what's wrong? You're so agitated. No one's shouting, well, not now anyway."

"It's the Consort! The Lady's mate! He's not had anyone listen to him for years, ok, 432 years, three months, four days, ten hours, and fifty-one minutes, ever since the last battle priest died! I hear you! Just quiet down! He's so excited about being able to talk to someone other than The Lady, that he's just going on and on."

"Is there anything you can do?"

"I'm trying! I'm trying!"

"All right, I'm right here with you. Would a song to the Lady help you focus?"

"Yes! Anything, I can't think!"

Laurealis began singing something in their native tongue that I couldn't understand. After a verse or so, Fausto began singing the notes with simple nonsense monosyllables. I was surprised that he was helping, but he's a talented musician. After another verse or two, Astoria began singing with Laurealis. Their voices were in unison for a while, then they began singing different harmony, but it sounded really good. Fausto began doing the same thing with his deep voice, going down where theirs went up, and the reverse, doing a bass harmony. Finally, Astoria held up her hand.

"Thanks. That really helped. Fausto, you surprise me. I hadn't realized that you could spontaneously harmonize like that. Harmonizing well with a song that you just heard for the first time, is impressive."

"I'm a man of many talents."

"Obviously, and tact and humility are not among them."

"So…you just got in contact with this god of yours, The Consort?" he asked.

"Yes."

"So, when you saw them murder the mother and her baby, that's when it happened. You were enraged and you, another pacifist, became a battle priest, uh priestess."

"Pretty much."

I added, "So that's where the big battle-axe came from?"

"Uh huh."

Fausto thought about that for a second. "So, you've never used a battle-axe before. I guess you, being the good little pacifist and all, have never struck another person in anger.”

She looked up all doe-eyed, “Oh no! I’d never hurt another person in anger. It would be horrible. I’d prefer to die than to…” the innocence in her eyes changed to shock. “Oh Laurie, what have I done! What have I done?” Hysteria was rising in her voice.

Fausto interrupted. “What you needed to do. It cannot be undone. Your Consort allowed it. Accept it.”

Astoria and Laurealis just sat back on separate rocks in shock.

“He’s right, in a way,” I said, “Your shock at the double murder opened yourself to your Consort. I’m sure realizing what you did must be a huge shock, but it was the perfect thing for the moment.”

Astoria just nodded and hung her head again.

“Look, I know what you’re going through is beyond anything I could imagine, but would you mind getting on with healing Duncan? He could die.”

She nodded and looked up. Her hand lit up with that red glow. The shouting must have revived Duncan and he held up his open hand, “Wait.”

“Wait? I need to heal your leg. Compound fractures are bad.”

“I know. It’s my leg that hurts, but I need to be awake. Get me something to bite down on and if you can tone the pain down without putting me to sleep, I’ll be forever in your debt. Fausto mentioned some things we need to talk about.”

Fausto said, “Duncan, it’ll wait.”

Duncan moved his hands to stand, then winced in pain and stopped. I was glad. I didn’t know how I was going to stop him, so I was about to start screaming. The other Gaelaur was beside us in an instant.

The Gaelaur was inserting a bit of stick between Duncan's teeth that he had produced from somewhere. Astoria said, "No, you're not talking to anyone," and brushed Duncan's brow. A red glow briefly surrounded her hand before flashing over to Duncan. He was instantly asleep. She waved me back a little and using a scissors-like thing she clamped and pinched the artery I was holding, finally relieving me.

She paused to lay a hand on my cheek, "You saved his life, you know. Your fast action, while I couldn't do my *real* job, saved him. Thank you." Then she nodded at the Gaelaur, and they worked like a practiced team to pull Duncan's leg straight.

As they were working, I slipped the murdered mother's dress on while I was still under a big basket that had been with the supplies looted from the slavers caravan. It was a relief to finally be able to stand.

Duncan, my Duncan, moaned into his bit. I screamed when he moaned from the pain that reached through the soft sleep, her spell had put him into. I just knew how much that had to hurt. I know my throat was sore the rest of the night and my face wet with tears when it was all over. Three of the freed women were holding me and comforting me.

The Gaelaur smiled and patted my shoulder, saying something I couldn't understand.

Astoria looked at her hands in disbelief, "Not now!" she exclaimed. "I need my spells, my healing spells!"

I stared at her in disbelief. "You don't have your healing spells?"

"No! The presence of the Consort is interfering with my communion with the Lady. Let's take care of your minor wounds. Then I can see to all the other people's needs."

"But your hand just lit up and put Duncan to sleep."

"That's an attack spell, a minor one, but still an attack spell. *Sleep*, I can do, but my major healing spells just aren't there, only minor healing spells. I just need to meditate and commune with the Lady, well, with both of them. I hope I can do that, but getting the preliminaries done will let you heal normally in case I don't get my healing spells back."

I just stared at her slack jawed. Fausto held his wounded forearm out for her to take the bolt out. The Gaelaur handed him the bit for between his teeth as well. He closed his eyes as she cut off the end of the bolt and pushed it through. She closed her eyes and began singing and her hand lit up with a pale green glow! She touched his wound as her consciousness worked inside it doing whatever it is that she does, and it began slowly closing.

I looked for a place to be private but seeing none I dropped the dress to my waist. The three women who had been watching me moved quickly toward me with a towel raised, but Fausto raised stone walls around me first for privacy. I was surprised by his thoughtfulness even in his pain.

Then Astoria did the same slow healing with my shoulder and the cut across my chest as she had with Fausto.

I winced as I bent to pick up the dress and immediately the three women surrounded me to help me dress. It was nice having earned this attention instead of just being *the poor orphan girl*. I was so tired of charity, badly as I needed it at the time. But this attention I had earned.

Immediately upon finishing with me, Astoria turned to Duncan's less serious cuts, and they began closing as well. She tried to do something with Duncan's leg, and the wounds began visibly closing. But the glow faded before much had happened other than the skin closing. The area was still red and swollen. She hung her shoulders, frustrated with the ineffectiveness of the weak spell.

"Well, this will ease the pain a little." A faint green glow emanated from her hands again. In his sleep, Duncan seemed to relax. The spell was working. She tried to do something else, and the glow faded too quickly again. She looked frustrated. "I am going to heal the other people with what little I can do as fast as I can. Then I'm going to pray and meditate."

With the help of the freed slaves, we prepared a proper camp in the cave for those hurt and weak and we all got some healing sleep. Several of the slaves had assumed leadership of their people. The Gaelaur and I stayed to watch Duncan. Astoria was deep in a trance or something. She'd been like that since doing her limited healing.

A good while after she left, Duncan woke, and he and the other Gaelaur talked a good bit. I couldn't understand a word of it.

Duncan

When I awoke, it was morning in the cave. The older and weaker slaves had moved in, with women cooking and helping them. I saw that Raina's wound was dressed but magic hadn't been used to heal it. I wasn't sure whether that comforted me or not. Magical healing could certainly be useful, and I knew by the agony I felt in my splinted leg that I hadn't been fully healed. Raina's work on my broken hand had required nothing of the sort. I wonder what happened. Getting on the move quickly is what we needed, but that obviously wasn't going to happen.

"Duncan," the older Gaelaur said, "My name is Druce. It's time we talked."

It was nice hearing my native tongue, even with his accent. He was from another Clan, but I couldn't place which one. I wasn't thinking so well.

"How'd you know my name?"

He flicked his eyes over toward Raina. "Your woman. She's been crooning your name all night. Sort of hard to miss."

"I see. So, what do you want to talk about?"

"The five of you, that's all there are?"

My head fell in shame. "Fausto, the dwarf, has already told us how stupid we were."

"Well, a good point you know," he said, chuckling.

"Yeah, I know."

We had set Druce free. I'd hoped he wouldn't be angry at me as well. I knew it was foolish, the five of us attacking so many, but we succeeded. Seemed like that would count for something.

He set his hand on my shoulder. "Look son, he's right; no point in denying it, but ignoring the odds is what heroes do. You did measurable good, *despite* the odds, as a hero should. You all should be proud of your accomplishments. You helped save hundreds of people. I gladly assisted your healer with your leg, though more care will be necessary.

"On another subject Duncan, may I ask you a personal question?"

My head had risen with his praise but now I was confused.

"Huh? Uh, I guess."

"What happened to your Warrior's queue? You fight like a man, a true and tested warrior."

I hung my head again in deep shame and felt my face redden. I'd been of the age to take the Test of Manhood for five months but put it off until the Winter Solstice. Now my family was dead, and I didn't know what to do. My Dad knew all that.

"Son? You are of age, aren't you?" "I am," I mumbled.

"Then what happened? You have a woman, and what you did yesterday certainly qualified you for Manhood, in any of the Clans."

My heart leapt in my breast, "You think so! My family was killed by Skarg two weeks before the Winter Solstice when we were going to hold my tests! I don't know what to do!"

"First, I have to know. Your woman…is it what it appears to be?"

"No, I'm not married to Raina, or even engaged to her. The Dom'barn is a one-eared mule and wouldn't act properly toward her unless Laurealis made an illusion of an engagement torc for her. Wearing it is horrible for her because of her past, for reasons I won't go into till I know you better."

"Horrible for her, for reasons you won't go into. I see." He looked me in the eye, searching for something. Either he found what he wanted to find, or didn't find what he feared, for he sighed resignedly and continued. "In that case, I won't either. You have kept the Code?"

"Yes."

"In all ways? I only doubt because of her obvious affection toward you. I find it strange that her feelings are so strong if you haven't encouraged them in any way. You know, for one who has not gone through the Ceremony of Manhood, to seek a woman is strictly forbidden."

"I have kept the Code."

He smiled broadly and moved behind me, moving rocks and bedrolls.

"Watch your leg, I'm moving you."

Confused, I aided him. When he began braiding my hair, I angrily pushed his hands away.

"Duncan, my freedom was your gift to me. You gave it to me at great risk to yourself. Let this be my gift to you. I am a Clan Do chief, a minor one, but a chief none the less. I have the right and I claim the honor to do this."

"But..."

"Duncan, you've earned it. Your genuine humility does you credit, but if it becomes false humility, then you violate the Code, and you *know* it."

I considered his words and realized he was right. I knew the Code, all twelve points of the basic Law, and the Oath as well. Dad had ensured that. "Proceed," I said after a minute of thought.

As he worked, I went over both the Sacred Promises, reciting them to myself.

When Druce finished, he moved in front of me and went to one knee, bowing his head. "Duncan, may I hold your sword?"

Lost in the majesty of the moment, I marginally noticed Raina motioning wildly to someone to come near. As I handed Glenfallis to my countryman I questioned my sanity.

I was handing my father's sword, my most precious relic to a total stranger.

"Duncan, is this your father's sword?"

Nodding yes, I kept my focus where it belonged, as if my folks and family were gathering proudly around me. Strange, I could almost feel their presence surrounding me as I focused upon the Sacred Law and Oath. But I knew that couldn't be.

"A splendid sword, indeed. Who was your father?"

"Taen, son of Camlain, son of Donneal of the Falcon Troop of the Loch Clan."

"From the Loch Clan, west of the Inland Sea, conqueror of Nuon?" The wonder in his voice did my heart good.

"The same."

"Well, now I'm not so surprised. The son of a legend is on the road to making himself a legend as well. I feel as if it is you who are doing me an honor. The story of what happened yesterday will go far and wide once I return to our people. Let us continue. Ask some of the men to help you stand. I know your Wounds of Honor will hurt, but you know as well as I, you should be on your feet."

Hearing those unique words, the way he said them in our language, made my spirit soar.

I turned to look for Raina and was astounded to see Raina, Laurealis, Astoria, Fausto, and many of the freed slaves standing all around us. I realized the background noise I'd been hearing had been Astoria translating our conversation. Two large men were already moving forward from the deep mass of people surrounding us. They carefully lifted me by my shoulders and supported me, another of them bending a knee just enough for me to rest upon.

Satisfied, Druce continued, "Duncan, son of Taen, son of Camlain, of the Falcon Troop of the Loch Clan, having satisfied the Trial of Manhood, do you accept the responsibilities of Manhood, to protect Family, Clan, and all the Gaelaur?"

Wondering if the heartbeat pounding so loudly in my ears was showing visibly through my clothes, I answered, "I do."

"Do you accept the responsibility of raising any children you may have, to honor and cherish the ancient ways?"

"I do," I know I must have been blushing, knowing that Raina was hearing this, also, but strangely proud that she should be.

"Do you swear to always protect and defend the innocent and helpless, doing so in the manner most likely to help them, putting their good above your own life, limb, and honor?"

"I do."

He dropped to his knee and head bowed to his knee, he raised Glenfallis saying, "New Man, I give you honor."

I found tears in my eyes as I replied, "Mature man, I accept the honor you give me."

The last thing I expected was to hear Astoria finish translating Druce and to see all of the freed slaves spontaneously go to one knee, and say in Francescan, "New Man, we give you honor."

At my sharp intake of breath, Druce looked up, and seeing what I was looking at, smiled broadly. I didn't know what to think.

Astoria took care of that for me. "So, now that your Ceremony of Manhood is complete," she looked to Druce. "It is complete, isn't it?" He nodded affirmatively. "Let's see to that leg."

I knew I should be fearful of her magic, but I believe that my smile must have been as broad as hers when her hands went deep green, and she touched my red and swollen leg. The pain immediately got better.

She bent over my leg, closing her eyes while concentrating intensely and manipulating things inside my leg. Her hands and my leg glowed deep green for a time. I could feel where she was working. Things were happening, moving somehow, as she worked slowly over each area. The panic at watching and feeling things moving inside me, was beginning.

But it was as though Raina sensed my fear of magic, especially when it was happening inside my own body.

She wrapped her arms around me and kissed my cheek briefly before whispering in my ear. "It'll be all right. We'll be through with this in a little while." I felt a little more in control, though Astoria wasn't finished for some time. When she looked up, she smiled. Offering me her hand for assistance, I tested my leg and feeling my strength returned, I jumped up, and laying my head back, gave a victory trill. "Thank you so much Astoria!"

"Your fear of my magic is less than it was, eh, Duncan?"

I stopped moving, stilled by her question. "You know, yes! I turned to Raina and held her hand. "It wasn't gone, and Raina, your support helped more than you know. But the fear really was less. I don't know why, but…"

"Glad to hear that. So, what's next?"

"Um, we really need to warn Sharcu of what's coming their way."

I looked at Druce and the men all around us. "Astoria, can you do the spell that taught me your language on Druce?"

"Of course. When you're ready."

"Druce, I thank you for what you've already done, but I have something else to ask of you."

Smiling, he said, "Ask away, brother."

"We need to warn the city of Sharcu that hordes of Skarg are coming their way. Since traveling fast is the priority, you're an obvious person to go. But you can't speak Francescan."

"I could lead some of these Francescans. I'm sure that some of them would be happy to warn their compatriots of the danger. We'll be safer, too."

"True, though what I was thinking might include them. It was more like making you able to talk to them."

"Huh? It takes years to learn a new tongue."

"Not with these people. Astoria here can do a spell that'll knock you out for a few days, but you'll be able to speak their tongue when you wake."

Astoria broke in, "Actually, you got two languages at once, Duncan. That's why it took three days for your brain to process the information. He'll only get one. Unless he already speaks several related languages, he'll sleep just one day or less. If he does speak several languages already, it may not force him to sleep at all."

Druce didn't hesitate before turning to Astoria. "Do it," he said.

"It'll take me a little time to get ready. Why don't you find a comfortable place to sleep? It will be a normal, though very deep sleep, so all you'll need is a place that's warm and out of the way."

"Druce, before you go, would you point out one of the Francescans I can speak to about how to get his people to a border fort manned by Dwarves?"

He motioned to one, who came over, followed by others. We discussed getting his people back to safety. Then, exhausted, I slept.

Regina

While watching the ceremony, it was good to see the huge man with the queued hair who braided Duncan's hair, and declared Duncan to be a man.

Duncan's actually a good person who has been through a lot. Strange that a man could be so gentle, yet so strong. Seeing him hurt so badly made the old feelings come back. The battle didn't help. I needed to find someplace private. Easier said than done with so many people around.

A little while later, I was behind a chest in the backside of one of the tents. With my bandages ready, I pulled up my skirts and made a long slice on my inner thigh. Watching the blood weal, I could feel the stress leaving my body along with the blood. I learned this during those horrible days in the orphanage. I made another slice and let more of the tension escape. I figured this was a four-cut session. The battle, and Duncan's wounds, well the bad one, and Astoria's inability to heal it last night made things build; I had so much pressure inside. Watching the blood escape somehow let me relax.

Feeling better, I was in the middle of wrapping the first cut with the strips of cloth that Duncan hadn't wanted me to bring along. I was glad that I had, as I'd been pushed too far.

Suddenly, Laurealis opened the flap and ran around the chest where I was hiding. Astoria was following close on her heels.

"Raina! Honey! What's going on? I tasted your building stress and then it spiked and went away! I've been so worried! I've been searching for you everywhere!"

Standing to drop my skirt to cover my legs, I hoped I had been fast enough. I kicked the bandages close to the chest, trying to hide them.

Astoria's hand glowed blue and she held it to my waist, then moved down to my knees quickly. Pushing me back onto the chest, her concern showed in her voice.

"Raina, what did you do?"

Her hand already had my skirt up to my waist.

"Oh, dear!" She was already grabbing the bandages that I hadn't succeeded in hiding and began cleaning my inner thighs. I thought I was going to die from embarrassment.

Laurealis held my hand and I felt strangely comforted. She was emoting comfort to me. I didn't want her spells. I just wanted to be alone. I was dealing with the stress simply fine, until they came in.

Astoria's hands glowed green for a short while as she passed her hands slowly over each wound. The wounds closed quickly. She dropped my skirt and I stood, only to be engulfed in Laurealis' arms. The comfort flowed into me strongly.

She changed to the sprite. I saw my mother's hand touch my shoulder. I looked over and she was there, smiling her comfort to me. Dad was there, too, just to her left. I just broke down and cried into her shoulder. Dad moved behind me and hugged me, too.

After a good cry, they disappeared. Laurealis was flying just above my head. She landed and reappeared in her normal form.

"Where are they? They were just here!"

"Where are who? It's just the three of us."

"My parents! They were just here!"

"Dear, your mind supplied the images you needed to see. I'm hoping when you are in such distress from now on, your mind will do the same thing."

"Oh…"

"Go ahead, think about what was causing you such distress. Was it the battle, or Duncan, or both?"

"Both," I answered, dismayed she could read me that way.

"Well, think about Duncan with his broken leg and you holding his artery closed."

Hesitantly, but obediently, I brought the image to mind, and my parents were standing behind me. Duncan was still there, with his thigh bone sticking out of his leg and my hand reaching inside his injured leg. I still felt the same welling of emotions about him, which is what made me hurt so badly when he hurt. Recalling the event, my pain seemed more distant. More like the pain of my parents' deaths when time had blurred the pain. It was there, I hadn't forgotten it, but I could live with it, the pain was distant. "It's better."

"Now think about the battle and your own wounds. Are they better, too?"

"Yes," I said. "They never were a problem. I don't have any problem dealing with what happens to me. It's just when…it's just when they happen to him."

Saying that made my eyes tear again. I felt my parents' presence and Laurealis took me inside one arm and sat with me on one of the chests. We talked about exactly how I felt about all the things that had been happening between Duncan and me, and all the other events since we began our journey. I felt more reassured when we produced the plan for attacking some of the other issues that I was dealing with over the next few weeks. They would be available to do whatever it was that Laurealis did, whenever I needed.

I noticed Astoria gathering up and taking my bandages away.

"Stop, I need those!"

"Do you?" she asked as she glanced at Laurealis.

"Uh…"

"Sweetie, these are a crutch, and a bad crutch at that. Cutting yourself like you did is extremely dangerous. What if you had cut too deep and hit an artery. The femoral artery is quite close to where you cut yourself. You could easily have killed yourself. And besides, crutches are only good if they're needed. Don't feel any shame from needing them, but after the need has passed, they keep you from healing. They can even give you a permanent limp. Give up this crutch or you'll never fully heal."

She looked at me firmly for a second, then left.

"But…"

Laurealis gently placed her hand on mine. "She's right, you know. Let go of whatever has caused you such stress in the past. Let it go, so it doesn't weigh you down or discolor what good things are in your future."

I could feel calm creeping into me again and knew this was a battle I was certainly going to lose. I can't fight her emotional manipulation, but I was feeling a good strong sense of anger coming on. For now, I let Astoria take my bandages, my *crutch* as she put it. I'd try to play their way, but I wasn't happy, at all.

I was doing fine with my crutch, and with Duncan. I was so confused and upset. I was glad to notice that my dead parents didn't appear to comfort me while I was emotional. I hoped they didn't reappear when I was sad either. I hate being manipulated, especially by my own emotions.

Chapter Fifteen
Past the Mountains
Fausto

I was impressed. Despite the stupidity of attacking those slavers, we did well. True, it was only because we had a healer that we weren't destroyed as an effective raiding group. But an effective leader uses the tools available to achieve the objective. I thought of Lookout Mountain and wondered how things would have turned out differently if our people had healers like Astoria with us. Losing my father still hurt.

I tried to avoid speaking with any of the freed slaves, as I felt they weren't really people anymore. Several seemed lonely or needing to talk and wouldn't let me alone. They were annoying and irritating, but the cave we were in was too small to get away.

I was already raising the first wall out of the surrounding stone to create a private room for myself, when a woman asked me, "Too good to associate with slaves, huh? Well, I was a slave holder and used to have the same opinion about them, 'till I became one. What makes you think you would have been treated any differently than I was?"

The question stopped me cold. I let the spell die and the stone slumped into a half-formed, waist high wall. Was she right? I thought about it, finally seeing the truth in her challenge. We don't have slavery in our culture, but that's probably because they just wouldn't survive where we live; all the tunnels would have to be so much larger and not economically feasible. We weren't innocent of the attitudes of slavery; it just wasn't economically practicable to practice it.

All humans recognize and practice slavery. Our ensuing talk helped me realize that their ideas had permeated our culture as well. It took someone like Duncan, who had never seen slavery, or Raina who had lived as a slave, to make me realize I had made a horrible mistake with Raina. Duncan had been right to attack me.

I held my jaw that he had managed to break through my *stone-skin* spell. The strength of that boy was incredible. Thinking of my father a short while ago made me think of what he would have said I should do when I realized I was wrong. I went to look for Raina.

"Raina, I'm sorry." I had already turned away, my duty done.

"What did you say? You mumbled."

My temper rose. Who was she, a former slave, to question me? I beat the thought down. I came to apologize for thinking things like that, but I was still influenced by such thinking… Besides, I may have mumbled. Being out of practice, I don't do apologies well.

Her hand on my shoulder brought my attention back to her, "Fausto? What did you say?"

"I said I'm sorry!"

"My, my. Sorry about what? And you can keep your voice down, I'm not that far away."

Damn, but she was the most irritating person around. I paused to collect myself. I wanted to storm off, but I decided she was *going* to accept my apology, whether she wanted to or not!

"I'm sorry for considering you a non-person because you were a slave."

Her jaw dropped. She didn't say anything for several seconds, then her face contorted into anger.

"You, the most irritating, self-righteous, arrogant bigot around, are apologizing to me? Well, glory be, the ices of Hell must be thawing! What brought this on?"

Her aggression and moving her hands around accented her attitude. Fury flashed through me. How dare she be so insolent?

She calmed, realizing she'd gone a bit too far. "Thank you for apologizing."

"Thank you for apologizing? What does that mean? Are you accepting my apology?"

She smirked; the little wench smirked.

Her expression suddenly changed to deadly serious. "Fausto, I don't like you. Your obvious contempt for me is the first of many reasons I don't like you. Telling me you considered me a non-person is just too much. I may have realized you felt that way, but saying it is quite another thing."

I had never had anyone speak to me quite that way. It was refreshing; none of the stupid dance of most conversations.

"So, I spoke words which made it hurt even more."

Surprise flashed through her eyes, "Yes, that's it. That's it exactly. Telling me you were apologizing, while insulting me even more deeply, made the apology insincere."

"I was just being honest."

"Well, sometimes honesty needs to be sugar-coated."

"Why?"

"For someone as smart as you are, you can be so stupid."

"Me, stupid?"

"About people, YES!"

Everyone within hearing distance turned to look at us.

"You've given me a lot to think about," I said as I walked off.

"You said all of that, and you're just walking away?"

"Yes."

"But you, but you..."

I was glad when I left her sputtering. She should organize her thoughts better.

Astoria

Better how things were going. That Ceremony of Manhood did Duncan a lot of good. That he has been through so much while having an emotional hand tied behind his back impressed me even more. Discovering that Raina was a cutter was surprising, but not shocking, in light of what the poor girl has been through. Laurealis hit the right thing to do to help the kids. I hoped she could do it consistently moving forward.

There were so many war orphans. Fausto, another one. Seems like he made progress as well. Our spirits were growing, praise be the Lady. My faith and spirituality are a daily companion to me. I found strength in that connection with the Lady knowing that she could work her benevolent plan through me. Life is never easy, but it would be so much more difficult without my faith.

However, what happened to me still had me unsettled. I never realized that part of why the enchanted metal core was incorporated into each staff a Priestess or Priest carried enhanced our spell abilities. But that transformation into a battle-axe, and the things I did while The Consort controlled me, were unbelievable. As a healer, the memories of what I did to those evil men are extremely disturbing. Fighting may be necessary at times, but what I did, and worse, the joy and sheer exhilaration I felt was quite disturbing.

The Consort choosing to make a new Battle Priest was yet another sign that the end of this Age was approaching. I never realized what was needed to create one. With that knowledge I needed to get more Priests and Priestesses angered enough to reach out to Him. Perhaps Laurealis could help with that when we returned. The war could still be won, with our people entering the battle in truth.

Fausto was walking toward me with his violin; his fiddle as he called it.

"Astoria, I've noticed you work your magic better to singing and music, so I thought playing together might be a promising idea. I could learn your styles to help when you have a lot of healing to perform. I know my people's music and the syncopated beats of the Firenzians, but I don't really know much about your people's music. It would be a good idea, if you have enough paper, to write some of your music.

Better yet, if you have already some written, you could let me study them. One good study and I should be able to join in when you begin singing."

My, my, something was changing in Fausto, or at least coming out. I needed to speak to Laurealis. She could practice her new technique on all the rescued people.

"Of course, Fausto. I do have paper, so I'll get a couple of songs down soon. That would be an immense help. Thank you. I'd like to get Laurealis to do something with us as well. Would you get Duncan, and we'll get started? It would probably do these people some good, too, after all they've been through."

A short while later we had all the people inside the cave, and Laurealis cast an illusion upon the open entrance, hiding all of the light and sound. She next set up mirrors around the fire, which reduced the amount of mana she would use enormously. The Francescans had gathered wood during the day and now multiple fires lit the cavern, revealing people setting on ledges and large rocks, anywhere a few hundred people could find room. Fausto's idea of entertainment this last evening together certainly hit a strong chord with these people. Fausto had also used his earth magic to improve the acoustics and to make primitive seating. I also noticed how warm it was with everyone gathered inside. It was somehow snug and special.

Laurealis began by creating illusions of a full orchestra. In the manner of our people, there were a dozen woodwinds, another dozen stringed instruments, and a few horns. It was a small orchestra. An orchestra of a hundred or more was more like home, but it did cover the deeper notes on up to the highest. She began the concert with one of our people's favorites, a tune that covered the changing of the seasons. I joined with her, singing the beautiful trilling notes that moved all over the scales.

I noticed, after several minutes, that while many people seemed to enjoy it, most everyone else looked decidedly bored. Duncan and Fausto were studying our music but hadn't joined in yet. I held up my hand to Laurealis to stop.

"Our music is too complex for them to enjoy. Let's follow Duncan or Fausto. Perhaps a simpler tune is what these people need."

Raina, bless her, immediately protested, "No, no! It was fine."

"Sweetie, is that why you were already nodding off, like most of the people here?" Laurealis asked.

"Uh, well, it was kind of hard to get into."

"Fausto or Duncan, would one of you lead us into something? We'll play backup for you. You seemed in tune with each other back at the fort."

Fausto grinned, and holding his violin all wrong, dove right into a fast tune. Duncan noticed it immediately, as did many of the people. Smiles began breaking out as they recognized the song, and the therapy of music began its own special magic. The song had a catchy beat and I joined in with my flute. Laurealis dropped all her previous illusions and elves appeared with drums and Fausto immediately smiled. Then people joined in with improvised drums, just sticks beating on each other, but it added a nice new tone to the music. I was beginning to see what he meant about distinctive styles of music. The humans' drums, while ridiculously primitive, were actually working better with this music than the wonderful drums Laurealis was illumining. The music was from their tradition, not ours. I resolved to meld with their music, so different from my own. Focusing on the repetitive chords took most of my attention. Although they were in the major chords, they were different melodies than I'd ever heard. Still, it was good music.

Pretty soon, the people began dancing and whooping in sheer exhilaration. I noticed the illusionary drums fading as Laurealis went elsewhere and I could feel her emotive dance begin. She had gone to the sprite and was now flitting about, tasting the emotions, not merely the surface ones, but the deeper ones of those currently being masked. Anyway, that's the way she described it later. I could only imagine how bad they were after all those people had been through.

Soon, her drums faded out altogether as her attention was focused entirely on her gathering of information, or so I hoped. She could be as flighty as the sprite whose form she wore and sometimes got lost in her "studies" by the sheer voyeurism of tasting emotions. I tried to get her attention between songs but failed. Finally, she flitted to hover in front of me, flushed with pleasure, focused on the task at hand. With the bad underlying emotions, if she were lost in voyeurism, she would have been sad.

"I'm ready to begin the dance in earnest. I'll keep it light and without visual effects. Their culture is so different, I'm not sure I could pull it off. But straight emotions I could do."

"So, you've gathered enough information?"

"Yes, thank the Lady, their pain is nowhere near as deep or as long term as Raina's, so that part is easy. I'm still trying to decide how to affect so many at once. It's so complex."

"Could you keep your field small and just do five or ten at a time?

"Still too complex, Astoria. I'll just have to do it one at a time and only help but a few of these people. There is so much pain here, that's why the exuberance of their dancing.

There were thoughts of mating, too, especially amongst the younger ones. I suspect that is part of their native therapy as well."

"What I do with too many patients and limited time and resources, is to triage the worst cases and focus on them. Sounds like you have to go one at a time, just as I do. So do what you can. And Laurealis, you must promise..."

"Promise what?"

"Absolutely do not worry about all those you can't treat. I've had to learn that the hard way. If you worry about those you simply couldn't get to, it can overwhelm you and destroy your effectiveness for any of them."

"I can see that." her brow furrowed, "I just hope I can."

I held out one hand. She landed on it, and I carefully touched the back of a finger gently against her cheek. "Be strong my friend."

Rgina

I had forgotten that not only was Fausto a huge jerk, but he was also a fantastic musician. As the dance was going full steam, I managed to pull Duncan off for a dance or two before he claimed exhaustion and stopped.

The change in him after that ceremony of manhood was amazing. He greeted me with so much more desire in his eyes than before. I welcomed the change in his demeanor. He was the first man, other than my papa, who had seen me as more than an object of lust. But it was so frustrating that he didn't show me any affection. It was like he respected me! I could get his body to want me, until he stopped even that. But his desire never made it to his eyes. It was like his code was more powerful than I could overcome. It made me want him all the more. At least that was over, and I could proceed with binding him to me, no matter what it took.

How could a man be like him? There he was, taking a nap. I thought he was just exhausted from his injury and had to rest. He had a little smile on his sleeping face and two orphaned toddlers going to sleep snuggled against him, one per arm. I had seen him flirting with them with smiles and looks all through the night until they came to him. Then he spent the evening talking to me while they sat in his lap. The three of them looked as content as could be, just curled and sitting there. He'd play with them sometimes, but he seemed sensitive to when they'd had enough. Men generally aren't compassionate like that, but *he* was. I couldn't understand. He'd protect me, too, and when we have kids, he'll be like my papa. Watching him with those two toddlers amazed me. Kids never just come to me like that. My determination to bind him to me increased. At last, he might not turn aside my advances.

Earlier, I noticed Laurealis holding a little baby as well. She seemed near tears as she was talking to Astoria. What was she telling Astoria?

"Yes, I'm thinking of mating with these humans," Laurealis revealed.

"Laurealis, I know you're missing Aisling, but…"

"I NEED a baby, Astoria! I'd love to have one by Kailynn, but it's so dangerous! If a baby's magic is too powerful, it can manifest early and…"

"Yes, that was so sad when Sahki's baby manifested during birth last year and immolated both of them."

"And Galatea a hundred and fifty years ago."

"Yes, they froze into a huge chunk of ice during the delivery. Galatea was barely saved, and her baby didn't make it." Astoria looked a little defeated.

"Half-breeds like Raina are still adorable and they're so much safer to bear."

"Laurealis, it's thinking like that which led to Asmodians breaking away and breeding with demons. Their excuse was that the demon's inherent chaos allowed their bodies to mutate during delivery and make it safe to carry incredibly talented children to term. The dragons, as descendants of elves, also were just individuals who gave up their Elvenkind to lay eggs to be safe from dying in childbirth. What good came of either of those choices? Both races are self-centered and evil. Sure, they can reproduce, but at what cost?"

"But I want a baby! I'm in Kaipoctouyevva and I'm getting older! Another thousand years and I won't be able to have a child! It's so rare for any of us to be fertile, and you know as well as I, a thousand years will only allow a few opportunities, maybe a dozen, to become pregnant. Kailynn loves children and would support my decision; I just know it! I'm fertile now. It would work, I could have my baby!"

"It's not just the babies here...WAIT! You're in Kaipoctouyevva!"

"So, what if I am! How does that change anything?"

"Laurealis, I know seeing all those children, with you needing to mate, is what's bringing this on. But this is apostasy! I knew Fausto and the other Earth Children believed that the destruction of the dominant human civilization marked the end of each Age. I *believe* it's always a new abandonment of the Forest Children, especially us, the most blessed of the Forest Children, which marks a different Age!"

"Maybe."

"Oh, come on, Laurealis! You know it is. The Second Age, the Lost Age, saw the long dark time, then the rise of both the Forest and the Earth Children. Then the unholy rebellion of a third of our folk to form the Asmodians occurred so they could have children safely and dependably. That happened near the end of the Second Age. The Dwarves are right; that Age, and the others since then, ended in the human's deaths feeding the Asmodians dark spells, giving them far more power. But it was our apostasy that began them!

"The Third Age, when more of our people chose a new evil way to reproduce, formed the Dragons. Then the Fourth age when yet another new apostasy occurred. One branch of the Forest Children attacked another when the Asmodians wiped out the Dragons and almost destroyed themselves in the process."

"Well, not quite."

"All right, since the Dragons have reappeared in this Age, at least two survived. But again, it was total disregard of moral and societal law! Branches of the Lir'folk, the Forest Children, fighting amongst themselves. It's obscene! This Age is marked by over a thousand of our people going off to have babies with humans. That's almost five percent of our entire population! What new evil will come with this blending?"

"But I want a baby!" She paused, then added, "I *need* a baby!" Her aching need poured through with every word.

"You know of the Lady's will, and you're willfully choosing to disobey Her. Our people learned back in the Second Age that mating with anything but our own leads to evil. I beg you, don't do it! Besides, we'll rescue Kailynn and you two can decide. You'll still be fertile. You aren't fertile often, but you still have a half year or so."

"He ran off to war because he missed Aisling! I'll give him another child! I can't face losing him again!" Her tears were streaming down her face. "I thought I lost him once and I won't lose him again! I'll give him a baby to love!"

"Good!" Astoria's hand stroked her shoulder. "But, Lauri, do it the right way please. It should be *his* child. And I remind you that he left you with two who desperately need your love and guidance.

Laurealis, I haven't asked this of you before, but the reason he left is because he knew you were ready, isn't it? And you pressed him for a baby?"

Fresh tears erupted from Laurealis, "Yes! Yes, I did! And he said that he couldn't face the risk of losing another child or worse, me, again. Then he walked out the door! Now I may never see him again! It's so unfair! I just want a baby to love, and this is the first time I've been physically capable since Aisling died!"

Astoria quietly held her friend for a while. I was about to stop eavesdropping when Laurealis looked up and asked, "How is having mixed species children evil? Raina isn't evil. She's been terribly abused, and she is dealing with a lot of anger, but she isn't evil. I simply can't accept that having babies safely with non-magical folk is evil. The Asmodians and dragons *became* evil because they turned to evil. They were after more power, and the reproduction thing was an excuse. But *they* turned. I'm not turning, and neither have those other women and men who now have *healthy* children to love and cherish. I love Raina with all my heart. I would love to have a child of my own to raise from a baby who's just like her."

Astoria sighed, "You're right, you know. I have argued much the same way with the rest of my Order. But while the act isn't evil, mixed children face so much unfair bigotry. You've seen that with Raina. Anger begets anger, and hatred begets hatred. Raina is walking a thin line between strength and rage. We've both seen times she's slipped in just a few days. My Order, and I am now beginning to concur, holds that bringing children into such conditions is in itself evil, or at least very unwise. Raina has a lot of strength, but I fear greatly for her. She's adrift. She needs an anchor to hang on to. Bringing children into the world that are so needy, well, there has to be a better way."

I resolved to prove her wrong.

Chapter Sixteen
Out of the Mountains
Fausto

I'm glad that not only is that bit of unpleasantness over, but at least I'm still in one piece. Oh, the stupidity of attacking sixty slavers, even with all the magical power we had. At least Dwarven and Elven magic is dependable. What would have happened if our magical power had been only human?

The resulting celebration last night was enjoyable. After Laurealis and Duncan dropped out, a couple of the slaves…damn it, Raina…people, took over their abandoned instruments so the dance could continue.

Images of my four companions crossed my mind. Duncan, poor bloke with that nasty wound he took; he's good with that blade of his father's. I rubbed my healed broken jaw, the one he broke through my *stone-skin* spell. Though dangerous, he's also like quartz; tough, hard, dependable, pure. I wonder how hard and pure he really is. Could be, he's a gem like Citrine or Amethyst. He's different at any rate. Duncan is pretty straightforward; he can even think…some.

Raina was furious from our last discussion. Raina's just as dangerous, but she's nowhere near as self-controlled as Duncan. She's still in the quartz group, but more like flint, not the pure crystal. She's a dark flint; brittle, sharp, easily shattered, but also easily knapped into a useful sharp-edged tool. She's one to watch out for. She's far more adept with those knives than a girl should be. It's just not right, a girl that pretty, being that good with knives. Scary. Raina's not only eye candy, but she's also good in a fight. I could do well to not get her angry at me. Girls are supposed to be soft, physically, and mentally. But Raina is cut from a different cloth.

Astoria and Laurealis, the militant pacifists. Now there's an oxymoron if there ever was one. Astoria was just a healer, a damned good one, too. Then wham, she's a battle priestess, complete with her people's warrior god controlling her moves. I understand she doesn't think that will ever happen again; it was a first manifestation of him in a ridiculously long time. All I can say is she needs practice and training. Still, we were lucky. Three casters, with one front line fighter and a backstabbing fighter, isn't the right proportion for all of us to survive. I'd much prefer to have numerous Dwarves with us. I'm still mad with Uncle Marcellus for not sending at least a company, or even just a squad. But what's done, is done.

Now Laurealis, did well at times, and what Raina said in her defense made at least some sense though I still have a tough time buying it. I just can't get a handle on either of those elves.

Still, I haven't yet decided if I'm furious with her little stunt. I know she did something. It's just that she should have asked me before she went tampering with my mind. I noticed her flitting about here and there, and now, when I think about Dad's abandonment at Lookout Mountain by the damn elves, I'm not as angry. I can hear Pa's voice, or one of my other kinfolks, telling me things like, "It'll be alright," or, "Keep your eye on the gem or you'll miss-strike it."

What was the new gem I needed to focus upon? Rescuing Kailynn, the Elven Champion, seemed to be the task at hand, the next gem to be accomplished.

I thought, "Elven Champion," with my normal mocking sarcasm, but I didn't feel it. With my anger abated, I recognized my faulty, emotional thinking for what it was. My anger was how I'd been looking at everything since the news of the disaster at Lookout Mountain hit me. Nothing could be done about the past, and I'm sure as all the Hells not going to apologize for being angry with the damned, lily-livered elves. They abandoned us, and my father died as a result. Things seem to have changed, so I turned the marred gem over and moved on.

With the aid of my considerable intellect and abilities, we could strike the new gem properly.

That decided, I moved on to aiding in rescuing Kailynn. I would scout the terrain ahead of us. First, I created a private room while everyone was still asleep in the predawn hours. I began casting arcing scans of the upcoming eastern terrain. I knew from my maps that we were at the eastern edge of this mountain range. I wish I had been more familiar with the area. I studied the strata east of us and found the deep hole that had been made when a bit of the Chaos Comet hit the Earth thirty-five thousand years ago. It broke up our single moon, creating the three orbiting rings from the remnants. A mountain formed, surrounded by a deep freshwater lake, from the core of the strike. I suspected magic was involved, and it was. The mountain has a number of vents, not the single one I would have expected from a hole punched into the soft interior of the planet. I wondered what the chaos had formed around the area. Sometimes, the chaos storm that swept the world after the impact formed benevolent creatures, sometimes malevolent. Of course, that's the nature of chaos matter; anything can be formed. Our world is filled with all manner of creatures the ancients would never have recognized. A large number of them are unlikely hybrids, giant or miniature forms of natural creatures.

I wished reading the strata could give me a reading of the life forms ahead of us, but we were prepared as best we could.

Duncan

It was a beautiful morning, cloudless and warm. The sounds of the melting snow and clumps of ice hitting the ground were a symphony as we made our way downhill. I let Shadow pick his way down yet another foothill, glad the way was easy.

Now that I'm a man, riding with Raina in front of me felt so right. We were going downhill again, and she lay back against me. Life was good, despite that we were going into new and undoubtedly dangerous country. We passed over a couple other mountains over the last weeks since we left the people we'd freed. They could work their way back to the Dwarven fort. Druce and five other men had gone on to warn Sharcu of the impending attack by the Skarg.

I peeked back over my shoulder. Astoria, Laurealis, and Fausto were working their way behind, each on their respective beasts. Astoria was riding Star, her chestnut mare, a fine spirited lady who liked Astoria's gentle hand. As the rising sun lit our healer's face, I noticed how well the earthy yellow of her skin and her green hair matched the yellow stone and bushes of our surroundings. Raina taught me that these bushes were junipers and tamarisk which meant it was drier on this side of the mountains we'd finally left behind three days earlier.

Laurealis' poor beast, Midnight, was decorated in yellow ribbons and bows in her mane and tail, matching the little yellow flowers sprouting up all around us.

Fausto was riding his stone golem as a solid rear guard and was as far from Raina as I could manage. He'd behaved himself since the slaver battle and Raina no longer chafed against the torc around her neck. I understood why she hated it, and I'll be glad when it's not necessary anymore. That blockhead flat out refused to let her off the hook when I approached him about it, at the changing of our watches. It just didn't matter to him.

And Raina is being…Raina. She's still pushy. I had to stop her twice when I woke up and she was sitting on me in an inappropriate way and being completely immodest. My thoughts shied away from those scenes, nice as they were in one sense, a sense I can't afford to indulge in until I can provide for us and any children that might come along. At least I was now confirmed as a man. One less thing to worry about. Those thoughts, and where they lead, were still distracting. We were *not* married yet; despite that cursed illusionary torc she has to wear to keep Fausto behaving himself. It was an engagement torc, true, but meaningless until I proposed marriage to her. I needed to proceed more slowly, not more quickly.

Fausto's comments, after he agreed to allow her to wear it, proved that he considered us married, despite the true situation. He thought me a fool for not taking advantage of the situation, as did she. Thinking about her smiles and kisses and her shape…maybe they were right. She heard my sigh and turned around to flash one of those heart-stopping smiles at me.

"Whatcha thinking, darling?"

This area was full of wildlife, and I hid my thoughts by indicating the pair of eagles or falcons swooping down and backing off, only to swoop back down again.

"Those eagles or falcons over there. They aren't acting right."

"Where?"

"Coming this way."

I pulled out my spyglass, and after spending a few seconds looking for the fast-moving flyers, I exclaimed, "What!? Those aren't eagles, not with necks and tails like that! Those are wyverns!"

"Wyverns? We didn't have those down in Firenzia."

"Small dragons, no breath weapon, and a poisonous tail sting. They're dangerous for their small size. They're attacking something over and over. I suspect they're angry over the defense they're facing. Something makes me feel that whatever they're attacking is intelligent, probably people."

We had been riding northeast of a high slope all morning. It wasn't like the natural slopes around us. It was very steep, but dirt mixed with rocks and boulders, not just solid rock. It was covered in the local bushes. We had been riding mostly in its shadow to keep the rising sun out of our eyes, but it was time to get over the slope. We dashed back to Fausto.

"Fausto, there's wyverns attacking something, probably people, just the other side of this hill. Can you make it so we can get across?"

"Wyverns! You want me to open the impact caldera to attack wyverns? No! No way!"

I heard a scream and watched one of the wyverns fly up with a body the size of a child in its claws, then eat it in two large bites.

"Now!" I screamed.

"Damn do-gooders," he mumbled, but he began working his magic. Shortly thereafter, the hillside collapsed to a more manageable slope. I almost bolted up right then, but I was worried about the shifting rocks and dirt. I didn't want Shadow to break a leg going up, but I was frantic about the kid I had just seen die.

Astoria and Laurealis arrived while I was holding Shadow back. He had picked up my angst and wanted to charge in as badly as I. The spell continued to work; the rocks were breaking into smaller pieces which made a path with a gentler, climbable slope for a horse.

"What's troubling?" Laurealis asked.

"Wyverns. Attacking people on the other side of this steep hill we've been riding beside. They just ate one of them, probably a kid. They might not have much time left." I lifted her off and followed her down, stringing my horse bow.

"Raina, when we get closer, I'll drop you off, so I can shoot and charge."

"You'll all be invisible. The spell will be on the saddle, so stay near it," Laurealis said.

Astoria asked, "You're sure they're people?"

"Here, come see."

I held my spyglass in position and pointed at one. "Look for the torn wing. That's why they're mad. The one they ate looked like a human child, but it happened so fast I'm not sure. Their pattern of attack looks like what I saw with my Uncle Kearney. Several wyverns were attacking a lone wagon with a group of men watching their herds. That shape I saw was so small it had to be a child."

The disturbed soil settled with an audible "harrumph", and Fausto said, "There you go, go kill yourselves. I'll be up in a minute or so."

I was back up on Shadow in an instant, pulling Raina up behind me, eager to be doing something. I couldn't tell if we were invisible from inside the spell. I heard voices following and realized that I had seen a blue glow beginning around the top of Astoria's staff as we began galloping up the slope. When we reached the top, Raina slammed her hands on my thighs and pointed.

"Look!"

Straight ahead was the lone mountain we'd seen in Astoria's vision. I was shocked at the sight. It was the right mountain, surrounded by a huge lake or inland sea with forests covering the slopes of the circular ridge surrounding everything.

There were breaks in the forest where huge rocks lay. The wyverns were mounting another attack against something behind a flat rock on the opposite and downhill side. I lifted Raina off then dismounted as well. I can shoot pretty well on horseback but getting a shot accurate enough to down a diving wyvern required far better than 'pretty well'.

It required an excellent shot, perfect timing, and a huge amount of luck.

As I aimed, I was wondering what could keep wyverns in the air. They're the toughest of the smaller dragonoids; not much more intelligent than a smart dog, but they can best about anything up to twice their own size. And there were two of them, fighting something small enough to be effective and still able to hide behind that rock.

I took my shot. I was aiming at the softer belly side where the wing joins the body and a near miss might still be effective, remembering Shala's training with the bow.

I missed the soft spot, but it was still a chest shot. I turned to leap onto Shadow and charge with my sword held as a spear, one of my people's basic attacks, but Raina was already on him. She dug in with her heels and they took off, taking the invisible spell with them. When I was outside our spell, they just disappeared. I chose to trust Raina, rather than whistle for Shadow to return. I wasn't sure he would return anyway, but I was confused. I wondered where Raina learned to ride, especially since Shadow doesn't respect any hand that isn't sure. He knows and only respects a true rider. He had a little soft feeling for her, too, I think.

I charged, screaming after them, hoping to distract the wyvern from them, or perhaps to confuse the beast. It wasn't confused…it focused solely on me.

YIKES!

Understanding the danger, I slowed. Wyverns' bodies are five to six feet long; solid, strong, and stocky. They're a powerful base for their snake-like necks tipped with a two-foot, tooth-filled head and for their even longer tails with that poisonous foot long stinger. With a four-footlong neck, the thing had as much reach as I did, and that tail could be whipped around so fast that it actually had a longer reach than me. The tail wasn't like a giant scorpion; it was as snake-like as the neck.

Wishing I had my armor, or even a shield, I approached cautiously, hoping to give Raina a chance to do whatever she was planning. Suddenly, she appeared in midair doing a back flip to land right in front of the beast. It reared back in surprise, and Raina's two daggers entered both of its eyes as deep as they could go. Shadow appeared during the attack. Invisibility illusions lose their power to fool when a creature moves when it shouldn't. Shadow slammed the beast with both his hooves, shattering its head. The tough beasts can take a while to realize they're dead. Wyverns are tough, but this one was thrashing around, dying. At least we could all stay away from its death throes.

Raina and Shadow turned and ran away as the other wyvern screamed its rage and dove on them. I ran to cover them, but I knew I'd be too late.

Then, from nowhere, a large otter scrambled on top of the rock and 'aimed' its body at the diving wyvern. It was tracking the scaly beast when something hit my head, on the inside somehow, and the wyvern lost control. It had been on a track to snatch Raina, but it just stayed on its path and crashed into the hillside thirty feet away.

As I ran to dispatch the obviously stunned creature before it regained its wits, I was surprised to find that I was running with seven otters armed with swords, shields, and crossbows scaled down to their size. They caught up with me just as I removed its head.

Shadow stayed back, but not Raina. She leapt into my arms for a kiss and hug. I pulled her off and set her down to stare at the otters surrounding us. I wondered at their obvious intelligence, and the blast, or whatever it was, that stunned me and brought down the wyvern. I'd only caught the edge of it, and it was hard on me. I could only imagine what hit the wyvern. No wonder the beast went down.

My attention returned to Raina and my concern for her safety. I sat on a rock to be more at eye level with her and said with far more scorn in my voice than I had intended, "Congratulations on a masterful job of killing one of them and almost becoming lunch for the other."

Her joyous look became hard as my anger and, to be truthful, my fear came out. My fear shamed me, but I recognized it as the cause of my anger, even as the words spilled out. She had lied to me! She was a fine rider, far too skilled to have picked it up just riding in front of me. I was hurt that she'd lied to me.

"And just when did you learn to ride like that? As I remember you were afraid of big, scary horses like Shadow."

Her smiling shrug, followed quickly by a playful finger on my nose, counting coo as my people would say, told it all. I'd been fooled. She had been hunting me, as I suspected.

My anger evaporated, and I picked her up in one arm like the child whose size she resembled, at least for my people, and tickled her. Unlike a child, she turned my play into a kiss before I knew it. I became shy because our traveling companions had joined our new four-legged otter friends. After a wonderful moment I made her sit. Half in anger, I swatted her cute little behind.

Before I was declared a man, touching her there, even with her guiding my hands, had felt so wrong that I was mortified. Now I felt a thrill as I touched her, however briefly in a "forbidden" area. Still, it wasn't enough of a thrill to not remember the reason for my anger. "Don't put yourself in such danger again. You scared me half to death."

Anger hardened her eyes briefly before she smiled mockingly and dropped to her knees, "Whatever my Master desires shall be done. This humble slave exists only to serve and please her Master in any way she can."

Her answer threw me into confusion. "Her master?" Where in the world did that come from? I put Raina and all these confusing thoughts aside. There was a time and place for everything, and I needed to think about the otters. She had crawled forward and was kissing my feet. It made goosebumps crawl all over me, that anyone could act like that. But this was an embarrassment added to the disappointment of being duped about riding horses.

"Stop it, Raina!" I scolded, perhaps a little too harshly, but it really bothered me. I stepped forward past her and with a couple of the otter people between us, turned and asked in their general direction.

"Can you speak our language?"

I heard them chirping and clicking like the natural otters they so resembled, but nothing like speech. The one who had brought down the wyvern had a slightly wider face than the others. He looked up at me and I heard his voice in my head.

"Stranger, you have our thanks."

I sat, weak kneed, flabbergasted by speech inside my head, but without his mouth moving.

"You spoke to me. How do I speak to you like that?"

A little chuckle filled my head. *"My friend, you speak in your mind when you talk. I merely reply in the manner of the Chriptagar, of which I am one."*

"You speak in my mind. Uh, can all of you do this mind talk?"

"Duncan, what is going on? Astoria asked as she leaped off Star and raced toward me. What are these otters doing surrounding you?" Laurealis was right behind her on Midnight.

Suddenly, Laurealis reigned in the horse. "Astoria, these otters are intelligent! Duncan is speaking with one who is emoting as though he's in command. Leave him alone."

"So, the rest of your people come. No, there is one more. Duncan, you have our thanks. We will be watching you."

"Wait! Who are you? We're going to rescue someone in yon mountain! What can you tell us of it?"

"Beware of Her. She has filled the whole valley with her progeny. Your only safe route is to leave. Leave your friend, there is no hope for him, and you will die as well. I read your stubbornness. If you must, the safest, well, the least unsafe route I should say, lies under the water. But your kind can't travel like ours."

"Her? Who is She?"

They all just disappeared into the water.

"Where did you go? Did I do something wrong? Please come back!"

One of them, the leader I saw, resurfaced.

"It is dangerous for us to stay on the hard ground. History tells us that long ago, this whole place belonged to us, but then She came."

"Again, who is She?"

"The Chaos Dragon. For a long time, she lived with the Ancient One, a fire dragon, as his mate. They filled this whole area with their children. Fortunately, most of them

flew or wandered off. We killed the ones who ventured into our water, so an uneasy truce was formed. The water is ours; the land and air are theirs. The wyverns are too stupid to understand the situation, so we have to clean them out from time to time."

"Those two could have killed you. Especially those like you. I gather you're special."

"I am a Chriptagar, a mind user, an officer, a chief or noble is the closest term you would understand. The girl with you knows of nobles. She can explain the differences between your chiefs and her nobles. We are the only ones capable of mentally speaking to other races. The psychic blast that brought down the second of the foes is just one of our powers."

"You are a Chriptagar. What is your species called?"

"My, you are young and full of questions. We are the Grupptara. One of those monsters attacked a village and we came hastily, too hastily it turns out, as it had a mate. We will return tonight with a means to float you across the water. You must be ready to spend the night in the water. If you must protect your belongings, make use of the time to do so. Again, you have our thanks, young Duncan, and Raina. We have a place of haven for your beasts. I see they mean a great deal to you. They will be safe. May the waters always support you and the fish always fall into your hand."

I stood when he first stuck his nose and eyes out of the water. I sat again, flabbergasted by the entire experience. Raina returned, and acting more normal, just laid her hand on my shoulder. It steadied me. Fausto also joined us, so I explained what had taken place, since the Chriptagar had only spoken to Raina and me. I don't know if it was because he could only speak to two of us at a time, or because we were the only two who killed the wyverns.

Regina

Fausto and Laurealis were trying to work out a waterproofing spell. It seemed Laurealis, though she's an illusionist, had the talent to be a mage as well. She lacked the interest 'till now, so of course, she lacked the training.

Fausto, an earth-mage, couldn't manipulate mana properly to cast spells dealing with anything but earth and metals. He could make thin stone cases for our packs that would, of course, sink like stone.

It turned out that while at least most mages are as empathic as Laurealis, one can choose not to use that gift. Fausto doesn't "feel" his way through a spell, he's as empathic as a rock, but he's real smart. He explained something to Laurealis, but I missed about every third word. It was about the theory of how to cast the spell to waterproof our stuff.

I searched for Duncan, crawling over the rocks, and watching the skies. I could hear him talking to Shadow about *me*!

"I wish that I could be like you and just be a stallion and she be my mare. But I can't. You live by just eating grass and fighting or running. I have to find a way to support us, especially after the babies start coming."

Babies! How many does he want?

"Shadow, it's just so complicated. I'm beginning to realize that what I'm feeling is more than just desire. Oh, lust is there, all right. Just like when you find a beautiful mare and you're filled with longing…and you just can't wait to be with her. I feel that, too. Everything she does is like magic to me. Her smile, I just live to see that smile." *Ahh, ok, I'll smile more. Thanks.*

"Her hair, her eyes. Her eyes are full of mischief and fun, except when she's so hurt that I just need to step in to protect her. Her body. Shadow, what can I say about her body? I ache at night when I go to sleep alone, in the morning when I wake up alone and most of all; I ache during the day when she is so close, so touchable, yet so distant because we aren't *engaged*. When I swatted her behind a little while ago for being non-observant in combat, well, it made me dream of doing a lot more."

Wonder of wonders; I couldn't wait to hear more.

"Shadow, I *love* her."

I drew a sharp breath, too sharp. He heard me. He couldn't hear like I could, but he has a hunter's instincts. I saw a stick caught securely in the rocks, so I placed my foot in it and tripped, taking care to ensure that I fell so that two very strategic areas of my white blouse were dirt covered. It had belonged to the dead slave woman and had a fairly low cleavage, probably to make feeding her baby easier.

He knelt to help me up, his eyes staying well south of my face.

We stood together. I made sure that I stayed close to him and brushed my blouse off to ensure his eyes stayed where I wanted them.

"Raina, are you all right?"

While boys and men used to frequently annoy me, they were talking to me while their eyes remained locked in place about six inches below my collarbone. Now however, I was extremely glad for Duncan's eyes on me, any part of me, instead of his HORSE.

"No, I'm fine. I was looking for you and tripped, that's all. Looks like you found me instead of me finding you."

Matching my actions to my thoughts, I began worrying with the hopefully inconsequential stains on my blouse, pulling it out to give Duncan an unobstructed view.

"Oh no!" I said as I noticed that the stains weren't so unsubstantial. I pulled my blouse even further out from my belly to brush it clean and to keep Duncan's attention solely on me.

"I hate this. My blouse is ruined, and I so wanted you to think I was pretty."

I looked back up at him to flash that smile he liked so much, and the *ungrateful* lout wasn't even looking! He was standing very tall and very pointedly ignoring me by staring at something in the distance! I was speechless. I stood and brushed my dress off. He looked down and smiled at me.

"But you are pretty. It doesn't matter that your clothes got dirty. You could be dressed in mud and rags and still be beautiful."

That was better, and even sincere. This Duncan was certainly not the ordinary sleaze I always had to deal with. Time for a new tactic since his wind of purity was so strong.

I took his hand, "Walk with me?"

"Sure," he turned us back to return to Shadow.

"Raina?"

"Yes, honey." He paused for the barest moment.

"I'm confused. What was that whole bit about Master and slave? I know you're wearing an illusion of a marriage torc, but we both know it's just a fake to encourage Fausto to behave himself. You're not a slave. Our people are free, and the very idea of slavery is revolting to us."

I paused to think, then with just the right amount of righteous indignation in my voice, I responded. "You dare to ask me that? You ordered me around as if I were your personal slave! I've heard that tone enough to know what it sounds like. Is that all I am to you, your slave? At least you're better than most! You at least have some feelings for me, I think."

"But, but…"

The thicker I laid it on, the more he sputtered. I was bowing down to fully prostrate myself and kiss his feet, as I had learned to do so well in the past.

"I do have feelings for you!"

I bolted upright and let my anger boil over, "Do you? You have more feelings for your horse than you do for me, and he's just a dumb animal!" I realized too late that I'd gone too far. Words once spoken cannot be retrieved.

The glare directed at me and the loving look he gave Shadow said it all.

"Now just a minute!" he said, anger and hurt in his voice.

He abandoned me and went to Shadow who was just a few feet away and gave him a big hug. Shadow responded like I had seen many times. He put his head over Duncan's back, hugging his master as well.

Duncan stayed like that with eyes closed for a minute; I guessed that he was gathering his thoughts, like he did so often. When he responded, he sounded angry, but controlled.

"Shadow's a smart horse; one like you have never seen. He's also loyal and has done nothing to deserve being called dumb."

He went back to petting Shadow's head and neck.

"Duncan, I'm sorry. Shadow is a very smart horse. I saw how he helped you attack Fausto's sandman. Very impressive. Do you forgive me?" I asked in my sweetest, most innocent voice with my head hung. I walked over and patted the horse's shoulder. Inwardly, I was gritting my teeth. I couldn't *believe* he loved his horse more than me. My previous act of anger was changing and growing into the real thing.

Still, back to the act; I wasn't going this far to get a protector and fall short. Duncan was upset and I'd lost a lot of ground. I looked up at him full of humble contriteness and he crumbled.

"Yes, I forgive you."

I beamed my brightest smile, thinking about how nice it was that he'd revealed my most potent weapon. He relaxed. I went back on the attack.

"I was wrong to insult Shadow, but I did it because I'm jealous."

"Jealous? Of a horse?"

"Yes! You talk to him, groom him, hug him all the time. Why wouldn't I be jealous? You show him more affection than you've ever shown me."

"But, but…" he sputtered.

I began crying in my anger, surprising myself, especially with the words that I heard spilling unplanned out of my mouth. It wasn't supposed to be happening this way.

"If you want a horse as your first wife, go ahead! But I will not be a second wife to one."

"What? Huh? …we don't have second wives. What's that?"

"Bad custom, forget it. Now, how is it going to be? Now you know I can ride. I just wanted to spend time with you, be next to you. Is that such a bad thing? But if Shadow is all you want, I'll leave you two in peace."

I turned to go, my tears not so much an act. I'd had to push a lot harder than I'd expected after I lost so much ground to Shadow. It made me aware that my feelings were far more real than I realized. Not only was I playing a dangerous game with Duncan's feelings, but I was also losing control and my own real feelings were visible.

Duncan finally broke and brought me back to the real world.

"Wait!"

He laid his hand gently on my shoulder. I pushed it off, split between wanting to slap him and hug him. Now I was the one confused.

He turned me around. I let my instincts guide me as I tried resisting him, knowing that against his strength, it was useless. He would feel my resistance and anger, I hoped. It felt like the perfect reaction, maybe because so much of it was real, not an act. I sure wasn't running away. Honesty was taking hold.

His face was crestfallen. He held my face, my whole head really, in his huge hands. I sniffed, my tears on hold, wondering how deeply he'd swallowed the hook. I wondered if I'd swallowed a hook as well.

"Raina, the three words I'm about to say are the three most sacred words I know how to say. Lots of people may say them and not mean them. I don't. I've been waiting to say them until I was sure they were true."

He cleared his throat and wiped his hands on his thighs and took my hands in his. I wished he'd get on with it.

"Raina…I love you."

The sureness in his voice and eyes were so different from the dozens, no hundreds of times I'd heard those same words before. His eyes were so real, intense, and genuine, my heart melted.

I threw my arms around him and pushed him over, "I love you, too." The strange part was, I realized I really did.

I kissed and hugged him over and over, 'till he rolled us over. I found I wasn't fearing him. He was so huge that I was fearful of him, of his size, but not of him. I realized I did love him. And more than just giving him what my experience said he should want, I owed him for his protection. I was beginning to look forward to what was coming. I was confused. My past kept flashing before me, then I would see his eyes.

Those clear, steady eyes gazed into mine while he held my arms down. He didn't realize that the emotions boiling through me were holding me far more strongly than his unbreakable grip. I, the huntress, the lioness, was caught, and it was wonderful.

"Since we know how I feel, I want to ask you one more thing." He pulled me up to a sitting position.

"Yes?"

"Stay still for a second. This thing needs to be off for this question." He reached for my neck with his knife.

I felt him take that damned wire in his fingers and cut it from my neck. He took my hand and opened my fingers, dropping that cursed wire on my palm. I stared at it, confused. I thought I had to wear that horrible symbol of my slavery to men as long as Fausto was with us.

"Will you marry me?"

The battle was over? I had been manipulating him to this exact goal, and I realized I wanted this, too. I'd been willing to give him what all guys want, so I would have protection and would never have to go through the hell of those five horrible years ever again. He took that awful thing off my neck to set me free so I could tell him "no" if I chose.

I pulled his face down to mine and kissed him slow and gentle. When he began pulling back in his shyness and caution, I said, "No, you're not pulling back anymore. I'm yours, completely. You're mine, as well, and you're not ever going to pull away from me again. Now let's finish this promise properly."

After a kiss that should have set him on fire with desire, I slipped the straps of my dirndl dress off my shoulders, pulling it down so I could remove my blouse.

"Wait! What are you doing?"

I smiled. "Trust me. You want me to do this."

He took my wrists in his hands. "No, not right now. This can wait."

"What? I thought you loved me!"

"I do. That's why this can wait."

"But…why?" I was completely confused.

"Raina, I love you for you, not just your body. Yes, you're beautiful, but you're my friend first."

I plopped onto a rock, my legs suddenly no more solid than jelly. He looked strangely compassionate at me, as though he really cared. Men aren't compassionate. Savage beasts, yes. Fierce defenders of what they consider theirs, yes. Compassionate, no, unless I'd been wrong all this time.

He pulled me to his chest and just hugged me. I tried to be strong. Strength was all that had held me up ever since Mama died. I couldn't think. I tried to stifle the tears, but they began and wouldn't stop. He just sighed, picked me up and sat on a rock to let me have my little cry. He confused me so much; he didn't act like a guy should. After a while, I dried my face and looked up at him, smiling weakly. I felt spent.

He took my hand again, saying, "Raina, I know next to nothing about your past. And if I did, I might not understand why it hurt you so deeply. There are things my folks and our troop taught me that I don't really understand, but I accept. One of those is that you have to love and accept your life-mate, before you cross the line into intimacy. What I mean is that I must know you, know you far better than I know you now, and that's what our engagement is all about. I don't know, but your past was so bad that you think I need to be *bought* to be nice to you. I don't.

"I don't know what your past will do between us, but I do know this; you'll never have to fear me. Yes, I want you badly, but right now, it…well, it just feels wrong to take what you seem to be offering. I know I'm saying it wrong…"

I put my finger over his lips. "Shush," I whispered, then I hugged him. "And you're saying it just right."

He cuddled with me for a few minutes longer. I suspect he was counting the minutes because he was always in motion. While sitting like we were was heavenly for me, I felt him tensing and relaxing several times before he suddenly stood and gently put me down. His unreal sensitivity toward me and my needs just made me love him more.

He looked in his saddlebag and pulled something out. He held out his sister's sachet and a leather thong and quickly tied it off and began to hold it over my head.

Realizing what he was doing, I reacted without thinking. "No! That's all you have left of Aisling! I can't accept that!"

"But…Raina, the reason I want you to have this is that it IS so special. This torc is my gift to you for our engagement. I want it to be special, as special as you are to me. I know it won't last and when we get to my people, we'll get a more proper torc to let people know of our engagement. I want you to know how special you are to me."

I let him put it on me. I didn't know what to say. I just hugged him, my tears of joy covering my face.

We spent more time together, talking about the strange otter people and finally made our way back to the others near the mid-day meal. Duncan had mentioned that we'd have to try to get some sleep that afternoon, since the otter people said we'd be trying to cross the water to that mountain in the evening. Since Duncan, Fausto and I ate meat, we looked for Fausto first.

Astoria

Fausto and Laurealis were spending their morning hours working out a spell to waterproof our gear, while I chose to spend the time in much-needed meditation and rest. When I was at peace for what was to come, confronting the Consort, I felt His presence and saw Him smiling at me in my mind's eye.

"My Lord Consort, I worship you, but we need to talk."

"Any time, my dear Child."

"I cannot be the battle Priestess that you want me to be."

Dead silence.

"I'm a healer, not a fighter."

The silence continued. It looked like I was going to have to monologue and see where things went. I could feel

His presence, but he was allowing me to work this one out on my own.

"When the slavers murdered that mother and her child, for *food* to feed what they believed were Skarg, I was enraged. That was a holy anger, a righteous anger. Your Spirit filled me and gave me the strength and skill to wield the axe that you created from my healer's staff. Because of your intervention, we succeeded in freeing innocent people who were doomed. For that, I thank you and praise you."

"You're welcome."

"But I'm not a fighter, I'm a healer. I fight in my own way. I fight to save lives. I understand the fighters on our side fight for lives as much as I, but I can't willingly kill.

"I have chosen you as you have chosen me, child. You are my first dedicated worshiper of this Age."

I sighed, accepting my fate. After a moment, I continued. "I know the creation of battle priests has always been one of the signs of an End Time, and you have chosen me to begin that tradition. But I can't be a battle priestess. I heal people. I CAN'T stay who I am and become a fighter. When we return, I will help Laurealis show all of our people what we have seen and initiate those who choose to fight."

"You are a gifted healer, Astoria. But who says you have to remain what you are?"

I saw in my mind's eye the Lady leaning over His shoulder and whispering in His ear. He nodded and smiled at her.

"Still, for now, I agree. You will bring me active believers, and my Lady and I will be with you for comfort and guidance."

He faded and I prayed a prayer of thanksgiving to the Lady, hoping that He couldn't hear my prayers.

"*Child, why wouldn't my Consort be welcome to hear your prayers?*"

"My Lady, I've always been yours to command. This feels like I'm betraying you. When He first chose me to fight and I couldn't heal anymore, I…I was so scared. I was terrified that our relationship had been broken."

"*My Child, I know your fears. Your fear is what blocked your ability to cast your major healing spells. You must master your fear since you have been chosen to lead the Order of Sachos.*"

"The Protector of Mankind?"

"*Yes, my dear. As you have been my Hand, now you must become our Hammer. You will know fear and you will conquer it.*"

"But…yes, my Lady. Let it be as you wish."

Her Presence faded and I sank deeper into meditation, absorbing every moment of my Gods' message to me.

Fausto

With Laurealis we finally finished working out a spell to waterproof our stuff. I'm still amazed that a featherhead like her can walk and chew food at the same time, much less cast a spell. Still, she is a proficient caster. She feels her way through the spell, rather than understanding it. I don't see how that works, but I've been told that I'm not the most sensitive person, so maybe our methods simply differ. It's a fact that she's an accomplished illusionist, and emotive dancer par excellence.

Heading to a more private place to get a reading; none of this touchy-feely stuff for me, I needed to know things. I wanted a reading on that mountain up ahead that Astoria recognized from her vision.

I came across Duncan doing something. That vixen, Raina was with him. Oh, the sacrifices I've made for the unity of the group.

"So, Duncan, what are you doing?" I asked in my friendliest voice.

"You mean, 'How are we wasting your time?" the vixen asked.

Duncan waved his hand like he was patting something down. "Calm down, he wasn't being nasty. We're working on something to waterproof our things for the crossing. I know you do that wonderful magic. It's just that I trust the tried and true more. We're rendering the fat from several rabbits into grease to rub down our gear and my leather clothing. While the fat is boiling down, we're sewing the skins into additional coverings for the saddlebags."

"You're doing that. I'm just watching," Raina added.

"Please don't beat yourself up like that. You're helping. You can't know what you haven't learned. That'll change. Just keep the fire going at that heat and keep stirring to keep it from burning, while I finish cleaning the skins."

I saw what they were doing, and it made sense, especially the part about trusting the tried and true.

Raising a bit of cooked rabbit toward me Duncan asked, "Care for a bit of roasted rabbit?"

Suspicious of kindness, I accepted carefully. "Uh, sure."

Not familiar with wild rabbit, I took a test bite. "It's good," I replied while licking my fingers. "Thanks."

Since he was being nice, I decided to explore what he was doing a little closer.

"So… you've done this kind of thing before?"

"Sure. Well, it's not that complicated, just follow the steps. Bring your things over and work with us, and we'll do everything at the same time. I would do Laurealis' and Astoria's, too, but Laurealis would pitch a fit using dead animals to make life easier, or something like that."

Chuckling, I agreed, "She does seem a bit adamant about not killing poor innocent animals, doesn't she?"

Duncan changed the subject. "What do you think the Grupptara will be doing tonight?"

"The Grupptara, what's that?"

"The Otter people. Their leader told us that in his mind speech," the vixen replied.

"Don't know. Wouldn't be surprised if they used something to let us travel underwater. They do live in the water, after all."

We ate in silence for a few minutes, then Raina said, "Fausto, you were so nice in the tavern at first, then you made that wisecrack about how much money I'd bring. I'm still furious about that."

I was confused, "Why are you furious that I thought that you would be able to demand a high, probably a very high, dowry?"

"That's what you meant? I thought you meant that I was still… that I was a whore."

"Well, it's true that you dress like I imagine one would dress. I mean, you shamelessly expose your ankles with that dress, and your dress doesn't cover all of you up to your neck, like a proper dress should."

I could see her anger was growing quickly. I hurried on, "Our people don't allow women to do things like sell themselves. We take care of our own. We don't abandon them because of the hand life has dealt them. We have heard stories of how human cultures do things like that. But no, what I meant was that you seemed like a very desirable girl, one any man would be lucky to find, and would pay a great deal of money and goods to her family as a dowry."

"So… when I reacted angrily and cut off your beard, you reacted as if you were the one offended."

"Of course. I WAS the one offended."

Duncan broke in, to calm things. "My, my. It seems we owe each other apologies, me included." He stood. "Fausto, I'm sorry for my bad impressions of you. Seems we got off to a bad start." He offered his hand to shake mine.

I shook his hand and turned to Raina, "I'm sorry our cultures made my comment appear to be other than I intended. I hadn't realized that I had called you a whore by my comment and all that comment would dredge up from your past. I beg your forgiveness."

She glared at me.

Duncan looked down at her. "Raina, what's happened after that comment came about in large part because of that initial misunderstanding. He unwittingly insulted you deeply, and you did the same to him by cutting off his beard. He didn't know what his remark would mean to you, you didn't know what his beard meant to him."

She glared back at him and crossing her arms pouting defiance.

"Raina!"

She looked up at Duncan, fear now in her eyes.

"This tension has gone on long enough. Apologize now! I respect your pain, but the pain is mutual, and this has gone on long enough!"

"What will you do if I don't?"

"Spank you."

"You wouldn't."

"Try me."

She smiled and said very teasingly, "No."

Duncan turned to me and said, "This may take a few minutes."

Raina yelped and took off, Duncan hard on her heels. They disappeared behind the boulders, though I could still hear their running and her yell out an occasional, "Ha!" After several minutes, the scuffling stopped and I heard Duncan's even counting to five, each count punctuated by a loud spank and a squeal.

A few minutes later, they came back hand in hand and Raina glanced back up at Duncan and rubbed her backside. She then looked at me and said, "Fausto, I'm sorry, too. Let's try to start over again, all right?"

"Fine by me. I sure don't want to have my jaw broken again," I said, rubbing my jaw.

Duncan smirked, "Well, for my part, I don't want to break my hand on your jaw. Hardest jaw I've ever hit. It felt like a rock."

"It was rock, you dummy. I'm an earth mage. Think. Why wouldn't I make an armor of stone?"

"Uh—I don't know. Never had much dealing with all this magic."

"I've noticed. As for me, I've never had much dealing with someone who could swing a hard-enough punch to break a *stone-skin* spell."

"Enough of this mutual admiration society." Raina interjected. "Fausto, why do you always seem to have a chip on your shoulder?"

"I don't. Why do you think I do?" Duncan cleared his throat pointedly.

"Oh well, perhaps I have been a tad touchy."

"A tad, like these boulders all over are a tad larger than gravel." Duncan added.

"You don't understand, I miss my father so much. If the damned elves had just helped, he wouldn't have died. We were so close. You just can't imagine what it's like to lose your folks."

I must have said the wrong thing again. Both of them looked highly offended, especially Raina.

"By the Lady! You…"

Duncan's large hand caressed her shoulder, "Hang on."

"Fausto, we each lost our entire family to the Skarg. Don't you remember from the tavern?"

"Uh, well, I wasn't exactly listening. I was thinking about my family. Lookout Mountain only fell a few months ago."

 Duncan's voice calmed. "Well, I can understand that. My family was killed only two and half months ago."

We all seemed to calm our defenses and spent an hour getting to know each other better while we finished waterproofing all our gear. He told his story, and she began telling her story. She was more talkative once she stopped thinking of sticking one of her daggers into my backside. I was impressed. What they'd gone through made my troubles seem less intense and they'd taken it much better. I couldn't imagine having to do a mercy killing on my own sister, especially if I were as close as Duncan and she were. I was shamed by how I had acted. Their actions taught me something. Respect. After they left to show the two elves Raina's new makeshift torc, I spent a lot of time in thought.

Raina

After having such a surprise from Fausto, we left to find Laurealis and Astoria. I couldn't wait to show them the sachet that Duncan gave me to replace that horrid THING I'd been wearing around my neck. I couldn't get over that sweet Duncan wanted me to wear something so precious to him. It made me feel…well, wonderful.

We found them behind another of the huge rocks near the lake. Laurealis looked at me, then at my engagement torc, not that horrid illusionary thing that I had been wearing. Her face, and somehow, her whole body lit up.

"Raina! Did he, did he propose to you?"

Her excitement surprised me. I didn't know whether to show my excitement or get ready to be scolded. I felt guilty feeling so happy while her husband was in mortal danger. Yet, here I was, asking to get rid of something she'd made to help me out. I was feeling a bit shy, and a little, hopeful smile grew on my face. I began thinking that this wouldn't be as bad as I'd feared.

"He did! Oh, how wonderful!"

The world around us exploded in pink, followed by flowers of all kinds and colors, showering all of us. By the time I could see through all the joyful colors and flowers, I found myself engulfed in all six feet of a Laurealis hug. She immediately pulled me away and the world faded to just our small little group as I told her and Astoria about the whole afternoon; not once, but three times, constantly interrupted by their questions and comments. We had a delightful time.

Chapter Seventeen
Crossing the Water
Fausto

I arrived at the spot where we were to meet the Otter people, only to see Laurealis and Astoria still making a big deal about Duncan and Raina's engagement. I beat down my initial irritation and tried to join in the good spirits with everyone else. The Grupptara had come by earlier and led Duncan, Raina, and the horses to a cave by the water where they would be safe from wyverns and other dangers. I stayed back and pondered what Duncan had done to win the hand of the fair maid, Raina.

A furry head popped out of the water, then another, and another. The Chriptagar popped his head up and Duncan and Raina turned to face him like he was talking to them. They'd explained how things seemed to work with this new folk.

"Okay everyone! Let's get over to the water. They're ready," Duncan announced.

As we moved down to the water's edge, we saw a most unusual thing appear. It was a boat, an upside-down boat, but its faded pink color was the most surprising thing about it. I've seen very few boats, but pink? It looked faded and it was long and thin, like it was made to cut through the water had it been right-side up.

Laurealis tried the spell we discussed earlier, but she failed. I guess she just didn't understand it. Although water isn't my element, I tried the spell myself. The idea was to use centrifugal force to keep a barrier of air around us, thereby keeping everything dry. It also caused a waterspout to form, which agitated the otters. The leader made a lot of noise and my waterspout dissipated.

"Just how is she supposed to stay dry now?" I demanded.

"Oh, my things," Laurealis wailed. She stepped out of the water and pointed her finger at her small stack and twirled it until all the water swished out, drying it instantly.

"If you knew how to do that all along, why didn't you say so?" I demanded.

"Oh, that little spell? I just couldn't follow what you were trying to say. I've known how to clean my clothes for, oh...well, since I was a little girl. You wouldn't expect me to not know how to clean my clothes, would you?"

"Argh! Scatterbrained elves, can't you follow the simplest of discussions?"

When everyone glared at me, I realized I should have stayed quiet. "Sorry."

Duncan directed us to the strange craft at the beach. Not being able to determine its construction or composition by direct observation, I did an analytical spell upon it and discovered it was fibrous. The most surprising thing was that the fibers were glass, refined silicon dioxide with some significant impurities. This was obviously a First Age artifact. I couldn't imagine the skill that allowed something thirty-five thousand years old to survive to the present time. That it was a fibrous glass held together by a strong glue, proved to be so strong, well, surprised isn't an adequate word.

Everyone else waded into the water to get under the overturned boat. I tried, I really did, but my feet wouldn't move. I'm not scared of water, per se, but getting into a body of water, well, I just couldn't do it. I froze right at the water's edge and couldn't force myself to go forward another step. "Hey, Fausto!" Duncan called. "Come on!"

My heart raced. I tried to stick a toe in. I failed.

"Fausto! Quit diddling. We need to go!"

Astoria turned around to see what the problem was. "Oh dear, I had completely forgotten about Dwarven hydrophobia."

Duncan began splashing his way back to me. "If you won't come on your own, I'll carry you!"

I began preparing an earth wall spell.

Astoria grabbed Duncan's arm. "Wait. He can't help it."

"What do you mean? He's just being his normal mulish self." His expression changed as he pondered our healer's words. "Isn't he?"

"Duncan, I know from your clear aura that you are guileless and free of fear." She paused for a brief second to let that sink in. "However, when we were in the Dwarven border fort, your aura was clouding with fear the longer we were inside. You have claustrophobia, a fear of small spaces or being enclosed."

"But…"

She placed her hand on his arm, "It's all right. You've described how you grew up in wagons with storage spaces, drawers, closets, and such. You had older brothers. It's not hard to imagine how your claustrophobia developed."

Duncan just stood there looking confused. I lessened my preparedness to defend myself as I found myself eavesdropping on their conversation, wondering where it was going.

"Fausto's issues stem from a different source," Laurealis continued. "His people are semi-elemental in their very nature. They can't get away from the source of their nature, the ground. That's why they can't ride horses. It puts them completely in the element of air. Fausto can ride on his golem because it's made of earth. For this purpose, it doesn't matter whether it's earth, stone, or metal. What matters is its origin. Crossing a stream isn't an issue; their feet are on the ground. It's swimming that puts them in a completely different element.

A look of understanding came to Duncan's face. "So, since it's so basic a part of him, he can't fight it, and why I can deal with being in small spaces."

She gave him one of her looks.

He smiled, "Well, to some extent, anyway. It's a lot better if I can get outside for a breath of air every now and then."

She returned his smile, "Exactly."

"So, what are we going to do about Fausto?"

"This."

She turned back to me. I began getting an awfully bad feeling about what was coming.

Astoria was voluptuous and coming out of the water her multiple layers of thin fabric were clinging to her in all the right places; it grabbed my attention. She looked like an off-color vision of loveliness.

However, my concerns about what she was about to do were quickly growing. The calm and steady smile she had fixed upon me was getting me very worried. Without my consciously willing it, I found myself backing up, fearful of this beautiful woman approaching me.

"Fausto?"

"Yes? What are you planning to do?"

"Are we doing this the easy way or the hard way?"

I backed into a boulder and worked my way around it, getting it between us. It helped a little, but not enough.

"Doing what the easy or hard way?"

"Crossing the water."

"I won't go. I'll…a… I'll stay here. I can't get into that… that water."

"Oh, dear, but you must."

Her calling me dear made my heart flutter a moment, but there was no way I was going into the water, though I couldn't find myself doing something aggressive against her, even to defend myself from her.

"I'll, I'll go around. There must be a way around. There's always a way around."

"But we can't leave you out here."

Duncan was on the land, "Fausto, you know you can't stay here."

When I turned back to Astoria, her hand turned red, and I was so sleepy.

Duncan

Astoria cast her *sleep* spell when Fausto looked at me. I was close enough to catch him as he fell. Strange how much lighter he seemed. I guess that attraction to the earth thing she was describing worked in more than one way. He may have been actively pulling himself to the ground when I tried to pick him up before the slaver battle. He was lighter now and a more manageable weight.

I explained our problem to the Chriptagar, the Grupptara noble. He helped with a magical bubble of air, while I manhandled Fausto into the water and tied him securely in place with his head in the airspace at the top of the strange canoe. It was so much better constructed than ours, as were all First Age artifacts that had survived to the present. In our main city, built between two of the inland seas, we had seen many broken artifacts, but the ones that survived were always well constructed.

I turned my attention back to this immeasurably valuable artifact as we each in turn dove under the craft and came up into a bubble of air that the craft held for us. The cross pieces were made of a strange metal that showed no rust even though it had been submerged for thousands of years. Ropes had been braided with wide parts which served as footrests. They had even taken the radically different heights of our various party members into account. Raina, well, Raina and Fausto had one of their own, as did the taller members of our group.

When we were all inside the canoe and our gear settled, Raina spoke. "All right, listen. I'm telling you this as the nobleman is telling me. The air will be kept fresh, so we can breathe. Laurealis, if you can, make a *light* spell, but hide it with illusion so the wyverns don't see us from overhead."

"I can do that," she replied.

She gave our space a general light, which was better in one way, but far, far worse in another. I could see how small the space was.

"Everyone comfortable?" Raina asked. I kept my mouth shut. Astoria might know about my shameful fear, but there was no need for anyone else to know. Hearing no objections, Raina said, "Then start paddling."

I was glad to begin. Although the air had warmed up with the beginning of spring here at the lower elevations, the water was still quite cool. The exercise helped warm me, and I'm sure everyone else, to safer levels. Well, except for unconscious Fausto. I saw Astoria cast some spell on him, so he's probably fine, too. Then she prayed with me about my fear of being enclosed. When the inside of the canoe was suffused with light, my fear was far less then it would have been normally. I was in the middle and in front of her, so I turned my head and mouthed my thanks. She just smiled and nodded.

After we had been underway for a few minutes, Raina spoke softly. "We'll be dropped off near a main gate, so staying as invisible as we are now is important. The main defenders we'll run into are kobolds, dragon-like humanoids that stand about as tall as the Grupptara, about three and half feet. There are various dragons that live in the mountain as well, but the Grupptara won't be able to help us once we're away from the water. They will surround the island mountain, because they're not highly effective against the wyverns and other dragons and dragonoids on dry land. They do know about a huge lake in the center of the mountain that is open to the inland sea, but it's protected from them by obstructions. They suspect that's where we'll need to swim, err, head toward.

"Sorry, translating what's said in your head can get a bit confusing," she added, smiling sheepishly.

We spent the rest of our time discussing plans based upon this limited information. The next hour passed quickly.

When we were approaching the island, Astoria said, "Duncan, you'll have to get Fausto up to land, and Laurealis, you'll have to dry him off. I definitely do not want him to realize he's been in the water."

"Makes sense," Laurealis said. I just nodded, as she was behind me.

When my feet touched the bottom again, being the tallest, I took the weight on my shoulders. It would have been much easier had Fausto's weight not been part of it. He weighed many times what the canoe did by itself.

Laurealis cautioned us, "Raina, stay close when you slip out. We're all invisible within twenty feet of me. Remember the wyvern fight when you ran off and your illusion disappeared."

"Uh, yeah. Gotcha."

Then she gracefully slipped into swimming beside me.

I saw the otters dropping their guy lines and swimming off to form a group around us. I hadn't known they were helping us. Thinking about it, I had wondered why Fausto's weight wasn't putting more drag against us. I looked for the Chirtagar's face markings to thank him, but it was too dark.

"I hear your thanks. The help was our thanks for your unsolicited aid when we were overmatched by the wyverns. I

only wish we could assist you inside, but we are no match for dragons on land. We would die for no purpose."

"You've done enough, my friend. I, all of us, thank you. Getting across to save our friend is something we couldn't have done so easily, or so well, without your help. It is enough."

"Remember to return our canoe to us."

"As you wish."

All the otters, the Grupptara, slipped quietly below the surface and disappeared. With the ladies out, I shifted my grip and manhandled Fausto and the boat to shore. After removing him and laying him out, I shoved the upright canoe off into the water. It was a sleek craft which shot out over thirty feet before the Grupptara swarmed over one side, capsizing it as they and their treasure disappeared under the waves.

"May the waters always, uh, something and fish always fall into your hands, my friends," I thought after them.

May the waters always support you, my land walking friend, and the fish always fall into your hands.

I could hear the laughter in his mind voice and my poor memory of his blessing. I briefly wished I could spend more time with these interesting creatures. I knew the business at hand. I only hoped we all survived. I noticed a strange sensation on my skin and all my clothing was dried and clean. It was stiffer as well. Of all the people I know, Laurealis is the person least familiar with leather.

When I turned around, everyone else was dry as well.

Chapter Eighteen
Into the Lair
Fausto

When I awoke, I quickly realized I was on the other side of the lake.

Instantly incensed, I spoke. "How dare…," I began, when Laurealis pointed at me, and my voice went silent. I fumed anyway.

"Yes, I know we brought you here against your will," she said.

When I naturally wanted to protest, she continued. "However, it was in line with our deal originally. You were to help us rescue my husband."

I nodded curtly, obviously not happy, but accepting the situation.

"Now, before I release the *silence* spell on you, I need you to understand some things."

She waited for my nod before speaking again.

"We are on a kobold infested island. The Chaos Dragon is holding Kailynn and there are probably other dragons as well."

My normally happy and cordial attitude was quickly turning sour at the thought of our certain death.

"Now that you know, realize this; Illusions are all about odds. I make things look, sound, even smell as lifelike as I can. But I can't remember every single detail. We don't dare push things too much because, if it fails, one of them will hear us. Once one hears us, it will tell the others. They'll all notice the petty things that aren't quite right and see through the illusion."

Duncan said, quietly, "Nothing to fear from those little guys. I could take down three or four with just one swing."

"Out here, maybe." I corrected before realizing that the *silence* spell was still in place. I looked at Laurealis to release the spell, which she did.

I repeated, "Duncan, sure you could, out here. But their tunnels aren't going to be much taller than they are. You'll be crawling once we get out of the dragon tunnels, my giant friend. Or would you prefer to run into a dragon on its turf? Don't forget that kobolds like to use poisoned crossbows. Oh, and poisoned blow darts, as well."

Now that I had a voice, I quickly cast a spell I suspected would prove useful.

"Nothing for it but to investigate," Raina said. "Fausto, do you have a spell that will let you find the traps, especially if they affect the stone, like pit traps and such?"

"Already cast. But before we all get ourselves killed; would someone explain to me why we're all going to get ourselves killed? We were going to rescue Kailynn, which was fine before we found out that he was being held by dragons. And not just any dragon, the Chaos Dragon. I mean, of all the creatures in the whole world, you're going up against the biggest, meanest monster of them all. Why? What hope have we of succeeding?"

They all looked at each other like no one had thought it through. I was about to launch into an impassioned speech for self-preservation when Astoria spoke up.

"Fausto, I understand your fears. They're legitimate. I began by supporting my best friend in her moment of need. However, I have had peace about this entire mission since it was first decided upon. That *peace*, especially about something this dangerous, means that I am in The Lady's Will. I'm not saying that some of us may not die or be seriously injured. I am saying that doing this mission is what The Lady, and now Her Consort, desire of me. Therefore, I'm going. Also, since She so wants me to go, I believe the mission will succeed. Whether I live or die is in The Lady's hands. I am at peace. So, while I came to simply support my friend in her moment of greatest need, without that ` peace I would have spoken out against the mission."

"Oh… uh… that is all well and good for you. I can see that, and it does reassure me that you've thought this through. Still, you're a priestess, I'm not. Laurealis, I assume you're going because it's your husband out there. I can buy that for you, but again, not for me."

"I gave my word," Duncan said, "that I would help rescue Kailynn. While it set me back that we would have to face dragons, our raiding party proved itself against the slavers. If you'll remember, you believed that one to be impossible as well."

"Good point. Still, dragons and slavers aren't the same."

"No, they aren't," Duncan continued. "They are one against a group, and a weakness we can exploit. We are a powerful group, but there's not many of us. Had the slavers hit us all at once, we're the ones who would still be out there near that pass. Same thing here. We have to think our way through, one step at a time."

Raina slipped inside Duncan's arm. "Where he leads, I will follow."

"Even to death? Raina, I understand Duncan's reasoning, but isn't that a bit trite, 'Where he leads, I will follow?' If he leads you over a cliff, you'll jump with him?"

"He's the first," she cast a quick glance at Laurealis, "well, the second good thing that happened to me in years. I trust him. If he were jumping off the cliff, I believe that he would have seen something I hadn't. Even if that weren't true, right now, life wouldn't be worth living without him. So yes, I'd jump with him." She hugged him and he returned the light embrace.

"Wow! I can't argue with that kind of faith, love, whatever it is. Astoria, your faith is built on something I don't truly comprehend, but I can respect it. Duncan, your point is cogent. Keep together, isolate the enemy. It worked once, and since it looks like you're all set in your ways for one reason or another, I guess I have no choice."

Duncan broke the thoughtful pause. "On that note, let's move out. We're supposed to go to the central cavern?"

"Well, I've already mapped out a good bit of this mountain before you knocked me out and brought me here against my will. I'm still not happy about that, but I do realize that it's the only way you could have gotten me over here. Now, follow me and get ready to crawl. I'm going to summon my mount."

After a few minutes, I had a bit of work adapting the spell, a proper mount for exploring a kobold infestation rose out of the rock.

"Yuck!" Raina exclaimed.

"Eee-ooo! It's a spider," Astoria said, a bare second after Raina screamed.

"I SAID quiet," Laurealis hissed as she pulled more lamb's wool out of her locket and made arcane motions over them.

"Sorry," Raina said, "but why a spider?"

"One, I must have my head below three and half feet if I want to avoid a headache. Two, I'll need to be able to go straight up or down while still casting spells. My mount gives me that ability."

"Wow! That actually makes sense. Could you make one for me?" she asked.

"Sorry, I can only control one at a time. Besides, you're the only one who wouldn't be stretched out flat. The others are all too tall. You'd do better climbing on behind me, since you'll be closer to being able to operate normally than your big bruiser boyfriend will be."

That was the second time I traveled invisibly, but without the screening snowstorm to provide the illusion to us that we couldn't be seen. It made this time seem so much stranger. We could see the kobolds, but even though we weren't hiding, they were just going about their business with their grunting and growling speech punctuating their actions. We stayed near the edge of the water, on a gravel beach. A sand beach would have left footprints, but a rock one would have been as bad, if Laurealis hadn't had her drying spell. The black volcanic basalt would have shown our wet footprints like a huge sign.

I had already "read" that the way we were going was clear. I stopped us as we huddled out of the foot traffic next to the cliff face before working our way to the left and the entrance.

"Raina," I whispered, "Look for a trip wire or a release mechanism just this side of the entrance. There's hollow space behind the wall there."

After working her way over cautiously, we all understood Laurealis' warning about pushing the limits of her illusionary invisibility.

She found another on the way and after pointing it out, found and pointed out the one that I had indicated. That was humbling; discovering that I couldn't do this by myself. I looked up as we approached the first trip wire. It led up to a stick that was holding back a rockslide, which I quietly solidified. Blasted Kobolds.

Working our way inward using this style, Raina and I found several more traps before we found a kobold tunnel that looked completely clear.

"This looks clear, but we'll soon be running into company this way."

"We fight the kobolds now or after we've run into a trap that we missed. As many traps as there are, I think that I'd prefer to risk fighting the little runts." Duncan said.

"I concur. I've been thinking about things I could do in these tight spaces. I just hope there isn't an earth mage on their side."

The ladies looked at each other and nodded, then turned toward me and nodded affirmatively. I took the lead through the tiny corridor, Raina following close behind. With the lack of traps, we made quick progress. My Earth Child ability to always be oriented to the earth's magnetic field aided enormously with making choices at intersections.

Combined with "reading" the tunnels, we were halfway there before we ran into our first group of kobolds.

I barely realized they were there until I saw the cloud of darts coming our way. I 'pulled' the wall in front of us. Using a different spell, I looked through the inch-thick wall. They were turning into a side tunnel. Clapping my hands together, the walls responded with alacrity, crushing the miserable creatures within. Surprised at the ease of "molding" this stone, I closed off the side corridors and widened ours enough for Raina to run crouched over. This helped the others, but I feared to do more.

"Hey! This is great!" Raina said. "Why don't you make it big enough for Duncan and everyone else?"

"Because I narrowed some of the side tunnels to do that. That sort of advertised our presence. Doing enough to make room for the big people would affect a generous portion of the mountain, I fear. Also, I didn't have time to fully analyze the effects on the structure of the surrounding rock forms. If I do too much rearranging, I could inadvertently bring the mountain down on our heads."

"Gotcha. Thanks for what you did."

For once, it was nice getting thanked for what I did for others.

"Come on, let's keep moving," I hated the grouchiness I heard in my voice, even as I said it. She really had meant well.

"Ooh, disgusting!" Trust Laurealis to be grossed out by the blood stains. The rock had been far more responsive than I had realized, and she was crawling through the remnants of fifty or so crushed kobolds. At least it wasn't any of our blood, gore, and stench.

I kept closing off the side tunnels and widening the corridor when I could. I was patting myself on the back for successfully avoiding more combat when we entered a large cavern.

"Oh, shattered gems!" I wailed. A large dragon was waiting for us there. I could swear it was chuckling, though that was hard to tell with its draconian face. I had feared that molding the stone would give us away. It looks like it had.

It stood twenty feet tall to the top of its spine, with a double row of ridge plates lining its entire backbone. Its long tail ended in a group of nasty looking spines. Its eyes, at the end of an equally long neck, gleamed with intelligence.

Duncan charged, I watched horrified as a wide, deep hole opened in front of him. I spied a large rock. Using a spell, I threw it at Duncan, and while it was moving rapidly toward him, I closed my fists hard, which crushed the flying boulder. I molded it into a sling to lift him out and throw him near the dragon's left rear flank.

The dragon snapped its head back and shrieked its rage. Another stone-seat, fashioned to throw Raina to the other flank, collapsed as I lost focus at the sheer volume of sound.

The sound finally ended. I began fashioning another stone-seat, but I couldn't hear a thing. I saw Raina's mouth moving, but I couldn't hear her. She bumped the side of her head, obviously as deaf as I was.

So that's the way it was going to be. Damn beast wasn't using just magic and now I'm deaf. Well, I am my father's son. We never backed down from a fight and this one was going to be spectacular against an earth mage dragon. I am a Son of the Earth!

I cracked all my knuckles and snapped my neck in new resolve. I bet that THING had more raw power than me, but I was smarter and faster thinking.

I threw a dozen boulders at it, half at its head, knowing they would miss. The others, including one the size of a wagon, I threw at the base of its neck. Almost immediately, I threw Raina to the other flank.

"Take that, Beast!" I screamed. Of course, I couldn't hear a thing, but hopefully the beast could. Duncan hamstrung it as my boulder hit it square in the breastbone, causing it to unleash another volley of sonic defense.

I couldn't hear the screech; I could feel it. We got it's blood up good, but it was hard to think, hard to do anything with that overwhelming sensation.

The dragon made a slinging motion, and half the floor of the cave came racing toward me, with Duncan and some of the hundreds of gathered kobolds still on it. I crushed the center of it, so it turned into fine sand. There was no way I was stopping that much solid mass. The ensuing sandstorm was bad, but at least it wasn't solid.

By the time I dug my way up through the sand which had settled a couple of feet above my head, the kobolds were in full retreat as the dragon flailed about in pain and rage. I may have broken its breastbone after all. Duncan must have jumped off; the kobolds that rode on that rock were moaning or dead behind me. Duncan was in good shape, just climbing up over the ten feet deep by seventy feet wide circle of rock the dragon had thrown at me. By the size of that hole, I may have underestimated its anger. Well, at least the beast wasn't paying attention to Duncan or to Raina racing up that long neck…it wasn't paying attention to anything but me.

That mouth was HUGE! And all teeth!

Parts of my hastily pulled up wall hit me as it shattered. At least it stopped the damned beast, though he looked dizzy. Two feet of stone wall shattered with all the power of that strike. I think those rocks must have broken half the bones in my body. I could move, but oh it hurt!

I stumbled to my feet, sort of. Astoria knelt to support me. Laurealis was doing something. The dragon was just reeling, seemingly without purpose. A bit like I felt at the moment!

Raina was hanging on to one of the spade-like structures going up its spine. She then got a second hand firmly back on its neck. A courageous warrior, that girl!

A sphere of darkness formed around the beast's head. Laurealis!

Raina ran up to its head and disappeared into the darkness. Duncan was out and charging. One great swing of that splendid sword and dragon entrails spewed out from that mighty cut. Raina emerged from the darkness around its head, knife blades drawn and bloody. Duncan looked like he dodged the blood and entrails. Dragon blood could be quite corrosive. I'll have to check their weapons for damage.

The beast's head reeled back and forth several times while Raina held on for dear life. Duncan ran out, sheathed his sword, and held his arms out for her. She was thirty feet up and she jumped without hesitation! He caught her and ran back to me and the two ladies with his foolish, brave warrior in his arms.

I must have looked bad because Astoria laid me down. She ran a diagnostic spell over me.

"How bad is it, priestess?" I was sure I was fatally injured.

She looked surprised. She ran the diagnostic on her own ears and her hands turned dark green while she focused for several minutes. Next, she did the same to my ears. I could hear again!

"So, how bad is it, priestess? How many bones are broken?" I felt horrible, like half the bones of my body had been shattered.

"Bad? With your Earth Child bones? Why, you're going to have to try harder than that to break your bones."

"They aren't broken? They sure feel like it."

"Oh, you silly boy, they're just bruised."

"Bruised!"

She cast a spell that stopped the pain. "Don't worry about being a wimp. Bruised bones hurt as much as broken ones. They're just easier to heal. No time for a proper repair job at the moment. All I can do is stop the pain, so take it easy on stopping rocks with your body, all right?"

"I'll try."

She smiled and poked me. "You do that. When this is all done, I'll heal you properly. But stopping the pain is all I can do for now, with all the dangers everywhere. I don't think we can stop for the several hours of intense concentration it will take to heal you properly."

Her smile disappeared, and she looked directly at me. "I'm serious about the injuries. You shouldn't feel any pain now. If you do, I'll stop it, but that doesn't mean you aren't injured. And don't you give me any of that nonsense about tough Earth Children. If you do, I'll remove the pain suppressant spell and let you tell me how tough you are then. Understand?"

"Uh, yes ma'am. I'll still be able to ride my mount and cast spells, right?"

She was all smiles again; funny how attractive she is when she smiles like that. Can't understand why she thinks she's fat. Voluptuous, yes, but not fat. She looks like a tall strangely colored Earth Child.

"Yes," she chuckled. "You'll be able to hold your own again, since you don't have to do a lot of walking."

I noticed that Duncan and Raina appeared to be ten feet tall and really formidable. It must be an illusion of Laurealis.' They were backing off the hundreds of kobolds with threats and feints. Duncan had his head about him as they obviously realized the real danger of numbers of weaker foes against a few stronger fighters. Laurealis turned into the sprite, and I felt a little bit of fear. The kobolds that it was focused against obviously felt its full force as they fled.

I stood and straightened my clothing.

"Well, time to find the treasure."

Duncan stood in front of me, fists on his hips, "You must be kidding," he suggested.

"Huh? Move. Let me just do this spell…"

"We are NOT finding and lugging treasure around. We have a job to do…or have you forgotten why we came here? This place is way too dangerous to go hunting for treasure."

"Just move out of my way."

When he didn't move, I did. Moving the thin stone cap aside, I saw several gold statues and chalices, as well as some jewelry."

Scooping it into my purse, I said, "See, easy as one, two, and three."

Finished collecting my reward, I added, "It's there for the taking." I noticed that I didn't have to tell Raina twice. She was gleefully filling her pack with treasure as well. Duncan, unimpressed with treasure, asked, "Which way?"

I got my bearings and sat atop my mount again as we set off once more.

"Wait!" Astoria demanded. "Fausto, didn't you tell us one night about your travel guide? You said, as you were thumbing through it, that there was a bit about dragons."

My face felt like it was on fire in my embarrassment. "Uh, yes, I did. I totally forgot about it. Wish we'd remembered it earlier. Just give me a second to thumb through, yes, this book."

I pulled out a thin book, <u>A Travel Guide for the Rough Country</u>.

"Where is it? Where is it? Ah, here. 'While dragons are rare, one must always be aware of them. Preparation is the best defense against most of them, so the following review should prove helpful.

"'Red dragons, most common, use fire breath which can heat walls and burn ballista bolts in midair…distract before firing.

"'White dragons use cold breath which can block tunnels and ballista terminals with ice if air is humid…keep sledgehammers available to clear.

"'Blue dragons use lightning breath, the thunderclap of which can be as dangerous in unstable tunnels as the lighting…reinforce walls.

"'Black dragons, the most dangerous, use poisonous gas, which sinks…small cracks will let gas in. Find a way to seal all cracks and kill quickly or flee.

"'It is rumored that some dragons may speak or even cast spells. This has not been confirmed, except in the writings of Barkalonae from the early Fifth Age.

"'Finally, remember all dragons will generally scream loudly in challenge before attacking. This scream in closed spaces will deafen…Plug your ears.'"

"Oops," I said, just as everyone else accusingly said, "Fausto!" Raina said rather acidly, "Wouldn't that have been a little helpful to know BEFORE we were all deafened by that thing's scream? Or hit by a spell casting dragon? Do you think spell casting dragons are confirmed now?"

"Confirmed… Yes! We need to collect a scale or two and some blood and possibly, no, absolutely, a few claw tips."

Duncan quickly said, "No, we can't afford the time to just confirm a, what did you call it, a travel guide?"

"Duncan, we are, in effect, scouts. It's the job of scouts to bring back and confirm new vital information. I really don't care what you think; I'm doing my duty by my people. The earth mage dragon scale will be proof of their existence. The blood and claws will be further proof."

"And the value of dragon parts has nothing to do with your doing your *duty*, I take it," Astoria said, the humor in her voice showing through.

"The fact," I replied, "that my people's craftsmen will probably be able to make it into a shield that I can cast my spells through, is simply a reward for doing my duty."

"Right," she said, her voice dripping sarcasm. "Still, as much as I doubt your actual motivation, you have a valid point. Duncan, you are our leader, but I concur with Fausto. We should collect some parts from each dragon as we are able. The rarer the dragon, the more valuable the information we bring about it. We can stop arguments by simply bringing forth a scale or claw. If we run into one of the poisonous dragons, I would especially love getting some of the poison to try to develop an antitoxin."

"Thank you, Astoria. Well, Fausto, you get your wish. How long a piece of claw do you need? I can cut it off more easily than you, I imagine."

I was delighted. I was expecting more arguments from him, "Try about two feet. Oh, and can you get a tooth or two? The teeth are the hardest part of our bodies and I imagine the same might be true of dragon's bodies. Glass is inert to most acids."

I had a horrid thought and quickly looked inside my pack.

"Oh! Shattered gems!"

That dragon had hit me so hard that my flasks were just glass dust and shards in my backpack. Well, nothing for it, but to put it back together.

Before working on the flasks, I sealed the entire cavern. I hoped there weren't two earth mage dragons, but we'd be safe from anything else. Our presence must have been announced pretty well by that fight, especially by the shrieks of the dragon.

Finished with securing our space, I concentrated as I worked on making three new thicker flasks out of the six flasks I had carried in here. I had only recently learned this mending spell and as easily as earth magic was to work here, I didn't want the slightest crack or weakness for the corrosive blood to work on. Carrying a leaking flask of dragon blood on my back didn't bring pleasant pictures to mind.

When I finished with the thicker flasks, I took the further precaution of molding volcanic basalt cinders around the flasks as well. This increased the weight, but it was a porous rock that would crush before my precious flasks were destroyed again, plus it's an inert stone. Hopefully, the caustic blood wouldn't burn through it if it did leak. I took the additional precaution of smoothing and bonding the basalt molecularly to the glass, so there would be no slipping, and therefore scratching. Each flask was a single unit, not two that could move against each other. At last, I would have a less dangerous way to transport dragon blood.

Of course, now I had to collect it. None of us were adept with telekinesis. We tried several things, but the stuff was just too corrosive. Finally, I made a funnel with a long-pointed bottom out of some nearby quartz to stick in between the beast's scales. This finally solved all the issues of getting to the blood without getting any on us. I was satisfied, one flask was filled and two more remained.

The collection of dragon parts, especially the blood had taken us perhaps an hour.

Duncan said, "Come on, we've wasted enough time here."

I knew we were coming into a different region of the mountain, the open cliffs and water region that Astoria saw in her vision, but I had no way of knowing what was waiting for us. The problem was to get to the central lake where we needed to go, we couldn't stay in the safety of the earth any longer. It was open to the sky and an aerie. A dragon flew out as I watched. Laurealis had made us invisible again, so we slipped along silently. The area was composed of cliffs with small caves for dragons smaller than the earth mage dragon we had already encountered. To our left, the cliffs dropped off into the water forty or fifty feet away, giving us a nice space to walk or a safe landing ground for the inhabitants.

We traveled past several sleeping dragons of different shapes, sizes, and colors. Just like my travel guide described, there were black, wingless ones that smelled of chlorine, lots of red winged ones that smelled of sulfur, and pale, pale blue ones that were frigid with the cold they radiated. The further we walked the more varieties of dragon we saw. Oh, for the Fourth Age when they say only fire drakes existed. An earth mage dragon was bad, but I was worried about what else we might encounter before we found Kailynn.

The illusion of invisibility worked wonderfully; none of them noticed us. That is, until we passed another red dragon who was asleep, though her offspring were not. There were three little ones, six to seven feet long, tails included. They were playing, and we tried rushing past them, but one of them ran out, the other two fast on its tail. It ran over Raina, who went down without slowing it a bit.

Duncan drew his sword and had its head off a heartbeat later, in one smooth motion. His eyes blazing his anger, he dropped his sword and threw its corpse off Raina before wading into the fray with its siblings. One of the others screamed its fear, but fortunately, Duncan cut the scream off short with another quick decapitation. The third followed its siblings into headless silence a second later, but that single cutoff scream was still enough to wake the mother, her fury fully aroused.

It is fortunate that dragons seem to want to screech or roar before they attack, since as her head went up to scream her rage, Duncan's huge sword sliced halfway through her neck, silencing her as effectively as her brood. Nice and neat. Astoria had to patch up several bone-deep gouges that Raina had suffered when the hatchling ran her over. I'm sure Raina wouldn't agree, but what does Raina ever agree to, except for looting dragon treasure?

This one didn't have any treasure worth looting. A few coins, but given the sheer number of dragons living here, I guess that's to be expected. Not even I wanted to stop to collect more than a hastily cut off claw. There were just too many dragons! I knew we were invisible, but we just had the limits of invisibility rather forcefully demonstrated to us.

I hoped we didn't run into any more dragon hatchlings whose three-inch claws cut deep. I cringed, remembering seeing Raina's gouged thigh bone from the three evenly spaced claw cuts before they started filling with blood. One thing I'll give the lassie, she has heart. She never made a sound, beyond the initial muffled grunt when she was bowled over while Duncan dealt with mama dragon. Her face showed the pain she was in before Astoria could heal her. Had she screamed like one would have expected, like I would have, all the dragons would have attacked us. I'd really like to meet a girl like her one day.

I made a stone bridge across the water at a narrower point, and we made more progress to the center where I was beginning to sense a massive source of Chaos. I suspected that possibly a chunk of the original Chaos Comet was here, under the lake we were heading toward. Unlike the elves, my peoples' mana came directly from the dust of the Chaos Comet and was far stronger around large concentrations of it. All of our homelands had chunks of the original Comet deep in our caves. By the strength of my magic, I knew there was one here as well, and I had a direct line to it. I just had to be sensitive to the "heat" coming from it. I had to focus; it was like noticing a distant source of heat in a warm room and my heavy use of earth magic was creating its own heat.

I was intoxicated by the sheer power I felt. I noticed Duncan sweating and looking somewhat fidgety, and Raina laying her calming hand on his arm. A moment later, she took his hand into hers. I remembered my own fear at crossing the lake, and knew I had the power to easily help him. I looked at Duncan and smiled briefly. The earth parted before me as I bore a large hole in the cliff, one large enough for Duncan and the elves to walk through easily.

"Keep your magic use down, Fausto." Astoria cautioned me. "We don't want to attract the attention of something even more dangerous than the earth mage dragon you drew before."

"Hey, I didn't…"

"Fausto, your intent is appreciated, but don't be stupid."

Ouch! That hurt, especially since she was right. I didn't change the tunnel back, that would use more magic, but I didn't make any more extra wide tunnels, either. I decided to try going up about fifteen degrees, since we were supposed to be well above the lake.

"Have you all noticed that the temperature seems to be going down, the further up we go?" asked Raina.

"Uh, now that you mention it, yes." I replied.

"Remember those icy blue cold drakes we saw?" Duncan added.

"Yes…"

"Well, this may be silly, but we only felt the cold a little way away from those and they were twenty to thirty feet long."

Astoria said, "Fausto, I think that we should change…"

I had been focused on sensing the earth and hadn't really been paying attention for the last few minutes. There was a ramp on the other side of a wall I was about to break into, and I wanted to connect with it. After one more chamber, we'd be into the central lake chamber. I only realized what was being said as I broke into a new chamber. A blast of arctic cold quickly dropped the temperature twenty or more degrees.

"Uh, oh, I think you're right."

As I was speaking, Raina squealed and disappeared from sight. I was right behind her and arrived at the opening an instant later. The ramp that I sensed was icy slick, and she slid down quickly. Something big was at the base of the long slope and there was a light source behind it. Duncan crawled up beside me just in time to see that the big something was a huge ice drake as it raised its nearly white head. It must have been awakened by Raina crashing against its front paws that had been folded in front, supporting its head as it slept.

I widened the hole to something we could all use. Duncan leapt through before I could do anything for the footing, and immediately began sliding as well. I made hundreds of small blunt spikes rise through the ice, hoping to give him traction.

Fortunately, the ancient dragon appeared to be yawning rather than preparing to challenge us with its deafening roar. Raina noticed the better footing, once my little spikes broke up the ice, and began climbing back up.

Duncan slid too far down and was moving too fast on his backside to stop, even after I improved the traction. The dragon noticed them about the time Duncan slid into Raina, knocking them both back. The Drake took a deep breath, and

I threw a group of large rocks at its head and neck. I couldn't aim for its breastbone for fear I would hit Raina and Duncan.

It dodged several rocks as a sphere of darkness appeared around its horn covered head. Laurealis was turning into a tactical wizard, I thought, just as her spell was dispelled.

Raina tried stabbing its foot, but she didn't even make it through the thick ice that was part of its armor. It raised that foot and Duncan changed his swing from attempting to hamstring it, to attacking the foot coming at him. He did succeed in cutting off half of that foot, but then that same foot swatted him. He was thrown back twenty feet against the side of the cave and didn't get up.

I managed to create a shelter around him by throwing about ten feet of stone up into the air just as a massive icy blast widened into a cone at least ten feet wide. It splattered over the stone, freezing everything within a hundred feet of where it struck. The icy stone ramp was about a hundred feet long, so we got cold fast. I looked for Raina and couldn't find her.

"Foolish humans, I'll pick my teeth with your bones!"

Great, this dragon could talk. It could probably cast utility spells, as well as its icy breath, like that *dispel magic* spell it had obviously cast on Laurealis' *darkness* spell. At least it wasn't coming up the slope with that damaged foot. It leaned against a wall to favor the injury.

The beast poked at Duncan's cave with the undamaged foot that was at least four feet wide.

A fire drake came walking in behind it and fired its breath weapon at the wounded beast and the illusion disappeared.

"You think to trick me with illusions? How foolish!" it said, amused.

"An elf and a dwarf, yummy," the dragon said. "No, two elves and a dwarf. Even better."

I drove a huge earthen spike into its less protected belly. Not as good as I thought. The ice armor was too thick. The spike actually lifted the dragon up a few feet and I discovered Raina had been thrown by the impact and was hanging by a horn. She had been climbing up its neck to its head.

I had to think! I couldn't jar it too much, and I had to keep its attention to give her a chance.

I began raising sharp spikes up under its feet, forcing it back. It would swat at them, breaking them and I would bring more up under its remaining front foot. Backing it away from us would distract it from noticing Raina, and she might be able to stab its eye like she had the other dragon. Laurealis tried an emotional attack, but Raina almost lost her grip, so she had to stop. Her illusions just didn't work, and she didn't seem able to hide us either, because we were spread apart.

Then I saw Kailynn, or some humanoid, hanging suspended in midair, naked, and looking right at us.

"Kai! Honey, we're coming for you!" Laurealis shouted. She tried several more spells in quick succession. The only one that did any good was her cleaning spell. A small patch of the dragon's head near an eye appeared to be whiter and the ice armor looked to be thinner.

"What did Kai' tell me to do first?" she thought aloud. "Yes, summon the elemental fires."

"Good, Laurealis. Fire is the best thing to use against an ice drake," I reminded her.

"Yes, yes, now let me remember how to do this. Kai' taught this to me a thousand years ago. I hated it. Now I can't remember how to do it."

I shut up, except for casting my own spells, as I forced the beast to move with its injured foot to distract it, so we had some relief from those icy blasts. It hadn't cast any spells, except to dispel Laurealis' illusions.

Duncan was up on his knees, rubbing his head and back. I hoped he would be up and functioning soon.

A firebolt struck just over Duncan's head! Laurealis was using the apprentice move I had seen humans use to pull the fire out in a backhanded swing, instead of a more controlled point-and-shoot or throwing move. She really was an apprentice mage at one time, still was, really.

Another firebolt just missed my ear as it flew past, striking the beast square in the chest.

Seeing the dragon set for another volley, "Not at my pet fire mage you don't," I shouted as I threw up a stone wall just in time to stop another icy breath attack that was coming our way.

"Laurealis, you're aiming like an apprentice, just point and let it go! You're going to get us all killed with your bad aim!"

"I AM an apprentice, you idiot! I stopped practicing a thousand years ago! There wasn't anything I was willing to hurt, so practicing fire bolts made no sense. Now I have something worth killing for! I'm trying, but I can't make it go out of my finger yet. I have to pull it out!"

"Then pull more carefully!"

"I'm trying!"

"Fine, now get ready. I'm going to drop the wall just before you cast your next firebolt. We may have to do this every time that beast fires its breath weapon at us."

Her next firebolt exploded harmlessly against the far cave wall, illuminating it briefly. An idea crossed my mind. I began shaping the far cave walls into smooth sides, between raising up earth spikes under the beast's feet and defending us with stone walls. As firebolt after firebolt splashed all over the cave, with only about one in three actually hitting the beast, I began smoothing walls into a glasslike surface. With walking the beast around on its injured foot, we had a faster rate of fire, because I didn't have to raise up the stone wall as often.

The next time I did, I shouted, "Laurealis! Do firebolts and let them bounce into the beast. The walls are smooth enough to help you now, I hope!"

She had been settling down as she fired, with unbelievable amounts of mana available. She really was an incredibly powerful illusionist and emotive dancer, and the power transferred over, even if the skills were nothing alike. The little yellow flame that had first appeared, flickering weakly in her hand, was now a strong blue flame, sure and true. The intensity of the firebolts was reflecting that focus as they changed in color from yellow to red, then to blue. Their size shrank and speed increased as the color changed as well. The cavern was getting to normal temperature, quickly.

Her next firebolt went wide, as expected, but it bounced. A little fine tuning and I'd make sure her shots hit the cold dragon somewhere.

Then, out of nowhere, Raina stabbed it in the eye, where that earlier spell had thinned the ice. The dragon reacted violently, swinging its head back and forth rapidly with Raina holding on somehow. It was only for a few seconds, but that was time enough to cast a powdered stone seat to catch her when she flew off like a slingshot. I landed her beside Duncan and began really using my magic offensively against the beast, hitting it with high-speed boulders as well as big spikes from underneath. I was trying to keep it off balance enough to prevent another ice attack against us or crushing my two friends.

I realized they really were friends, surprising as that sounds.

Laurealis' next shot bounced off the wall a time or two, weakening it, but it hit the cold breather in the flank, causing it to spin around and impaling a foot on one of my stone spikes. With Raina away, I pulled three spikes up from the floor, into its belly and this time, one of them penetrated. The firebolts must have thinned the ice armor enough to let me get through.

The impaled and trapped dragon looked back to the cavern opening and saw Kailynn hanging there. Casting a baleful eye back at its tormentors, it drew a deep breath to freeze Kailynn.

"Noooooo!" Laurealis screamed out her horror. She then did something I'd never seen before; no one would be foolish or desperate enough to try it. She turned her left hand, the one with the elemental fire in it, toward the dragon, and somehow increased how much elemental fire she was summoning, while screaming her rage the entire time. The blue elemental fire didn't shoot a bolt, it just lengthened to nearly a hundred feet. Screaming now in pain as well as rage, she walked down to the beast and began burning it to death. It roared and screamed, and we all lost our hearing, but who would be victorious quickly became obvious.

The beast tried backing away, its remaining eye rolling in fear, but I stopped that with stone shackles over its feet and tail. Our peace lover turned warrior, Laurealis, didn't stop till its head was charred black.

The uncontrolled use of elemental fire was affecting Laurealis as well, in a horrible way. Her arm was becoming flame as she continued to burn the dragon. Her screams of rage became screams of agony. She wouldn't stop, despite what it was doing to her. I had to admire her tenacity; it was worthy of my people. She was going to save her man, even if it killed her.

The elemental flame was consuming her, changing her. I remembered my lessons about the dangers of the elements summoned from their appropriate plane or dimension. By the Smith. I was watching a magical elemental accident occurring before my very eyes!

When it was finally dead, or when she finally quit killing the dead beast, she couldn't put the fire out.

"Make it stop! Make it stop! Oh, Goddess! Make it stop! It's burning me alive!"

The flame had died back, but the hand was definitely aflame, a hand-shaped blue flame. It wasn't focused anymore, but from her hand to her elbow she was covered in blue flame. I could see right through her hand. Her whole body was affected, but the hand was the worst. The pure chaotic elements were dangerous things to mess around with, even earth, which was the safest of them. I didn't know what to do.

Astoria, brave heart that she was, was right there singing something as she tried spell after spell. She was openly crying while she cast her desperate spells, though she seemed as clueless as I would have been.

Helpless to aid them, I turned my attention to the others, who seemed uninjured.

"Duncan, we can't do anything with them. Help me with Kailynn and let's get out of here."

"Sure thing. And Fausto?"

"Yes?"

"Thanks. You saved my life back there. I was out of it, but I saw the ice everywhere around me like that THING had breathed at me. You're all right."

"Uh, yeah. Uh, well, you big dummy, you're welcome. Charging a dragon that size…stupidest thing I've ever seen."

I've never had anyone thank me like that before, well, except for Raina. It made me uncomfortable, especially now that it had happened twice in such quick succession. "Come on," I said, with more irritation than I really felt.

I studied the spells holding Kailynn and satisfied that he wouldn't be harmed when I crushed the crystals holding them. I supported him with a bed of sand over stone, for when he fell, and squeezed my fists, crushing all four crystals at once.

My stone bed worked perfectly, stopping his drop of a hundred feet into the lake below. However, the mana that had been holding him was suddenly released. The energy wasn't well-controlled, but it may have been enough to be noticed by one of the dragons.

His appearance surprised me, I had expected him to be well-muscled, but he looked emaciated, and his hair was white. His skin was a light blue green, but it didn't look healthy. His left wrist was a mess. It looked like it had been cut to the bone and just left to become infected, or not, depending upon how lucky the poor bloke was.

My sand bed carried him inside and laid him beside the two elf women.

"Honey, we came for you," Laurealis said through her whimpers and cries. She reached her good hand out to hold his and he squeezed hers. His eyes never opened, though he appeared to relax a little.

Astoria finished the spell she was casting, which did nothing for Laurealis' hand, and ran her hands through her hair. After only a moment of apparent frustration, she looked inside her bag and pulled out an ornate box. Opening it, she took a pinch of a yellow powder and pulled open Kailynn's mouth, wiping it under his tongue.

"Hold his head up, Duncan."

Kailynn opened his eyes as Duncan began handling his head. As soon as he was stable, Astoria held the box of pollen near his chest for him to see. When he tried and failed to bring his hand up, she closed one nostril and brought some pollen up to the open one for him to inhale. She motioned for Duncan to hold him up straighter.

He took one good sniff and lay back so Duncan, after glancing at Astoria, could lay him back down. She smiled, and at more of the half crying, half whimpering noise from Laurealis, looked worriedly back at her.

Suddenly, Kailynn began sneezing. What was significantly different was that he moved his arms with speed, first to stabilize himself, then to cover his nose.

"Nasty way to get the Talu pollen back into your system," he commented. "But it works. Thank you, my friends."

"Raina, please get him food and water," Astoria directed. Raina didn't hesitate.

After another bout of sneezing, Kailynn said, "Earth mage, treasure," pointing to one of the walls I had molded smooth. Surprised, I searched the stone, and finding a small chink, I exposed the treasure.

"Wow, now that's a treasure!" I said.

I had to dodge a green gauntlet that flew from the treasure to Kaylynn's left wrist. The gauntlet flared a white halo. First his small clothes appeared, then the thicker cloth of his padding appeared, and next, an exceptionally fine chain hauberk covered his arm to his elbows and down to his knees. Finally, the finest armor that I have ever seen appeared on him. It consisted of shining bands of fine steel, I believe, covered in gem quality gleaming green enamel. He had finely worked gloves with a strange black material that served the purpose of leather on the inside surfaces. There was a big white flower that floated in front of the bands like a sigil, not attached to any of them, but solid and striking.

His vambrace had flanges that could be weapons, or aids to parrying. His helm was open faced, but I could discern a magical shield protecting his exposed skin.

The bands covering his torso were about five inches in width and the one over his heart began regular pulsations of light. At each pulse, he appeared stronger, or at least, his color was less yellow. I can't describe why he looked healthier, other than maybe more vibrant? I mean, I read my people's health by their color, and his color wasn't anything like my people. But somehow, he did look better.

"Thank you, Angalis. Your healing was desperately needed."

He appeared to be listening to something.

"Quickly, she's coming! Darling, I wish we had time for each other, but the Chaos Dragon is coming. I know you're suffering terribly from your accident with the elemental fire, but I can't get you out of here yet. I can barely stand; I'm so weak, much less work magic."

The edges of the opening over the lake, where I had just brought Kailynn through, grew multi-colored. The micas, quartz, feldspars, and other minerals degraded to simpler forms, even to gases, then collapsed as the internal crystalline structure holding them together failed. They left a hole over forty feet wide. I assumed it was from a single enormous chaos breath weapon or something. Terrifying. Those of us who were mobile backed away. I felt tremendous guilt leaving Laurealis and Duncan holding Kailynn there. But the implications of that breath weapon, compared to freezing or frying, left me weak-kneed. Added to that, the sheer size of the area affected was more than I could face.

The nose and tip of the head of the Chaos Dragon appeared at the bottom of the newly widened entrance. It was huge. The white tendrils that grew out of the sides of the head on the upper jaw were as long as its head. They began just behind the nostrils and were in sharp contrast to the black iridescence of the rest of the head. As it continued to rapidly move into the cave, I could finally see the entire head, all twenty-five feet long by ten feet wide of pure malevolence. I backed into the wall with Raina and Astoria and pulled the stone in from each side so that we only had a one-foot archer window to look through. The three of us crowded in order of height to look at the horror coming into the cavern with our three friends in the open. In preparation for making them a hidey hole as well, I used a powdered stone bed and moved them away from the dead ice drake to the opposite side of the cavern, right beside us.

Chapter Nineteen
The Chaos Dragon
Ereshkigl

In my sleep I felt the release of the bonds holding my future mate and I woke infuriated. How *dare* someone release my intended before I said so? And I will never release him until he either dies or agrees to become a dragon and my mate. He has the power; he would be a fine mate. Climbing up the sheer cliff walls, my fury grew. My pet was gone! If Rigiljo let my pet go, I would eat *him*!

The entrance to Rigiljo's roost was too small for me, so I let go a breath to not only make it possible to see, but to announce my presence and ill temper in no uncertain terms.

The first thing I saw was Rigiljo's corpse, burned horribly. What little remained of his head was charcoal and still glowing. Rigiljo was the most ancient dragon I had. He had carefully starved himself to remain smaller than me so as to be no threat. Who could have done this to my most loyal and cautiously humble servant?

I felt an intense primordial heat. A fire elemental! Who summoned a fire elemental? I saw an elf, one of those cursed ones who had been a thorn in my side since before I became as I am now. Making a delightful cacophony because of her pain, she stood with her arm engulfed in blue fire.

I breathed in deeply, preparing to cover the entire room with my breath and avenge dear, sweet Rigiljo.

From the source of the flame I heard, "I just got him back! Now leave us alone! Oh Goddess! It burns!" Her flaming hand, the one that must have killed dear, sweet Rigiljo was becoming a more intense blue. I drew in breath as she approached me. Oh, how I love hearing lesser creatures howl in pain.

There were several other intruders I saw scattering. Obviously, one was an earth mage, hiding as a stone.

A large human with a sword came charging at me. I ignored the insignificant bug as I watched the elemental elf burn in agony.

The human creature cut off my right nostril and tendril!

Oppressors Bane! The metal covering the ancient Paladain's holy weapon was burned off as it cut me, and I recognized the sword that had taken off my leg in my former life.

A moment later the creature, still screaming, pointed her arm at me and burned me. The pain was so intense, I instinctively retreated and dove into the cooling waters hundreds of feet below me.

Duncan

I felt Glenfallis go light as the badly corroded blade fell off after striking the monster. At least it held together long enough to strike a true blow. I regretted destroying father's sword, but, like him, it had gone out nobly. One couldn't ask for more.

I was glad that only a whiff of the huge dragon's breath had hit Laurealis and didn't move past her. Because it was hurt so badly, it didn't exhale as fully as the ice drake had just a short while ago. She didn't go down, so I dashed to the edge of the cave only to see the dragon disappear into the water. It wasn't shaped like the dragons that we'd already fought, but more like the black ones that smelled of some strange poison. They were long, like a snake, with short legs and tendrils around the end of their snouts. Strange how dragons have so many forms. This one was huge. The water was hundreds of feet below us and its head was already deep under water. All I saw were the two *pink* hind legs and long snake-like tail follow the rest of its body into the clear water. That thing was definitely the source of Astoria's sense of foreboding she felt when she did the spell in the bowl of water.

Laurealis and I had successfully backed the monster out of the cave, but I didn't know what to do next. It wasn't out of the fight, and I wasn't sure how to get out of there if that huge black thing summoned all the other dragons.

Suddenly, something was happening to the pommel of my now bladeless sword. I was saving it, since it had been the sword of my father and his father before him, back into the mists of time. It had become badly pitted with the corrosive blood of these horrid dragons and was destroyed, but now… with almost no weight, I noticed the blade wasn't destroyed after all. It was clear, like glass, and Glenfallis' pommel had become too hot to hold.

I dropped it, but it didn't hit the ground, it flew up and into a defensive stance against me. How could a sword hold itself up was beyond me, and worse, I somehow knew it was studying me.

I studied it as well. I wondered, what magic is this and who's behind it?

I could feel a weak connection with it. It reminded me a little of the way that language spell worked in my head. The metal that had covered it, which the strange connection let me know was a disguise, was now gone. Revealed was a clear blade, like perfect crystal, pulsating with light energy.

I moved around a little and the sword moved with me, countering my moves. This went on for a minute or two, while we danced with each other, each forcing the other to move one way or another. Finally, I won the skirmish when I feigned left and dove under, grabbing the handle with both hands. The fight wasn't over, as the sword almost took off my foot before I got it out of the way. Who would ever believe that I was fighting with a sword not wielded by someone?

Expecting a fight now, I was ready. Well, less unready.

It twisted and turned, and I held it away from me. Finally, one of our gyrations forced it into a stone. I had expected to use the stone to help me control it by holding the tip in place, giving me leverage. Instead, it slid into the stone, cutting it as easily as if it were butter. But then it appeared to be captured by the stone. Not hard, but I could finally do more than react. I had the upper hand at last.

I *thought* I had the upper hand. The sword flew out of the stone, punching me in the belly with its pommel. While I gasped for the breath driven from me, it flew straight up into the air. I got a second hand onto the cross guard and pulled it back. It responded by charging my belly again, but this time I flexed uninjured. I threw it to the ground and held it down with a knee. Finally, a break.

Before I could catch my breath, it dissolved the stone under my other foot, and when I fell, it flew off. Worse, it turned invisible.

Fausto, watching the theatrics, poked fun at me. "So, what happened to your sword? Looks like it's getting the better of you." Raina giggled. I could feel my face turning red.

"Want a little help?" he offered.

"Yes!"

Still smirking, he threw a cloud of dust into the air so I could see the sword. I lunged, the sword dodged and turned visible, then flew over and spanked Fausto.

He blustered and trapped it under tons of stone. Stone disappeared from one end in just a large enough shape for the sword to escape. It flew out and struck Fausto hard on the head and he fell to one knee.

"All right, all right! I quit! Duncan, it's your sword…I think. YOU tame it!"

While it was dealing with Fausto, I grabbed it and slammed it flat sided into a boulder. It was like it bounced…right back into my forehead, stunning me.

"By the Ancient One's Beard, what are you? How can a sword do such things?"

"Oh, talk canst thou? Full of wonder, am I! That's what thou art supposed to do. What am I? What are you?

Until I taste your blood, how can I know if thou hast the right blood to become my master?"

"Have the right blood to become your master? What? Taste my blood?"

"What! Not only canst thou barely speak Paladain, but thou also canst hear me clearly either? Art thou daft, or stupid?"

"Neither. I've never encountered anything like you before."

It sank itself into the stone, pulsating red, instead of a 'friendly' light blue.

"Don't lie to me, boy. I just tasted one of the ancient foes, Ereshkigal, Queen of the Asmodians. For thou to be fighting the likes of her, thou must have met masterful magic. And not just swords like me, but a host of other things. She's a master of chaos. But she be far more, she hast become a dragon."

"The queen of the Asmodians? But she, it, is a dragon. I'm so confused."

The sword began pulsating more strongly and it was humming now. No, it was vibrating, strongly enough to hum.

"We are in great danger. I must taste thy blood before the contest of wills can begin."

The sword vibrated strongly enough to shake itself free of both the stone and my hands.

"And I will taste thee…now! Hold out thy hand!"

The sword slipped rapidly from the stone, and while my hands were still in position to hold it, it sliced both palms. It reversed itself then, laying itself into my grip. I tried to move my hands and was unable. It somehow held onto them with its pommel while my blood ran into its black, leatherlike grip.

We stayed like that for at least a minute. *"So, thou art Paladain. Fine, thou hast passed the first test and thou shalt live. Now, master me…if thou can."* Then, the blasted sword laughed and in a surprising move, spanked the side of my thigh…hard.

I growled. The sword howled with laughter.

"Sword, my family has always called you Glenfallis. Is that your name, or just one some ancestor of mine gave you?"

Ouch! It bonked me on my forehead. With all the weight of the disguising metal gone, the sword weighed next to nothing, and it made up for it with blinding speed.

"What dost thou know? The boy does have a brain! Good question, and yes, thy ancestors were accurate in their memory of my name. Glenfallis, at your service, maybe. The way this is going, I think thou art going to be in MY service. Fight me, boy!"

"My name's Duncan, son of Taen, son of Camlain, NOT boy!"

"Very good, so the weakling boy has a name. So, tell me Duncan, son of Taen, son of Camlain, how long has it been since the People, the Paladain, gave up training their children in discipline. Dost thee still wet thy bed?"

Though angry, I emptied my head of all thoughts but to hold the sword still.

"Ha, thou must do better than that, boy!"

It pulled me straight forward, then sideways, right over a rock that I'm sure it knew was there. I tripped, naturally, so it dragged me several feet…face first into another boulder. I stopped it and stood, better braced this time, while blood ran down onto my lips from my broken nose. The pain was blinding, but I wasn't about to let go.

"You…will…do…as…I…command!"

"Oh, that be much better. Thee almost had me there…seriously, thou art not going to wet my sheath during thy sleep art thou?"

I sighed, closed my eyes, and curled my shoulders, releasing tension as I surrendered my pride and tried cooperation.

"Glenfallis, I am to be your human half. We have a battle to fight, together. We must become partners. You have much to teach me. I have the blood of my fathers and the strength of my arms to help us defeat the evil of this world, from dragons to Asmodians, from Skarg to just bad humans. Now stop this, and let's move forward, together."

"Well said, Duncan. I agree. I thank thee for the chance to serve again." He said, solemnly, this time with all the sarcasm gone.

I "heard" singing in my head. I saw things, too. Men, lots of men singing. They were riding large horses, covered in chainmail barding, like my people did, marching in rank after rank. Their armor was different from ours. It stirred a memory, like I had heard it long ago, though I couldn't remember ever doing so. Could it be a racial memory? I heard the elders discussing the concept with my father one night when I was supposed to be asleep. Strange.

> *It's an honor to serve, to fight for what's right.*
> *To march to the fore, to lay down my life,*
> *Leaving all else behind, to right every wrong.*
> *It's an honor, an honor to serve.*

I felt tears come to my eyes. My heart surged with feelings of courage, of the desperate fight against unnumbered foes to protect the innocent. I remembered the stories of the battles and sacrifices my people made over the generations.

Mixed in among my memories were vivid scenes of people who wore armor like ours; hard men bringing their wounded with them as we have always done. "Leave no man behind." They were the last survivors of their race, the Paladain. They had been a troop on a scouting mission who watched their last castle fall to city sized chunks of ice, just as Raina told me the human cities suffered five years ago. They fought and successfully destroyed the last of those harrying them so they could hide themselves in the endless prairies. They were the early Gaelaur! The name Paladain had been completely forgotten, perhaps to help them hide? My thoughts distracted me, and I missed parts as the strange vision continued.

As their leader lay on his deathbed, pale and suffering from terrible wounds, a warrior in glowing green armor stepped forward from the group gathered round and knelt by his side. Kailynn? Indeed, it was a much younger Kailynn!

"Captain Harailt, it is no trouble. It will be an honor to serve, to watch over and protect your people as your people watched over and protected so many in their time."

Kailynn is the Watcher! I hadn't realized…

"Uh, Duncan, who or what be the Skarg?" Glenfallis asked.

My thoughts were scattered.

"Huh? Oh, they're the new creatures of darkness and chaos, demon-men. The elves call them *Soulless Ones*. They killed Raina's and my families. Fausto's father, too, though that was part of an army with Asmodians as well."

I looked up to see everyone gathered round me. Raina was smiling.

A thought crossed my mind, it could think at me, could I think at it?

"Of course, thee can," I felt, or heard it sigh.

Would you mind if I sheathed you? I thought at Glenfallis.

"Why? Oh, just so thou can hug that female fleshie." He chuckled.

I sheathed him and Raina rushed into my arms and kissed me full on the lips, despite everyone being right there looking at us. I held her back, "Raina!" I said, shocked, embarrassed, and proud all at the same time. Her affirmation of me in every ounce of her being did strangely wonderful things to me. Apparently Glenfallis allowed the others to 'listen' in on his historical tale.

She locked her hands in the hair behind my ears and looked me right in the eyes.

"Your sword has turned into an artifact of legend, and you need to be rewarded. Now let me reward my hero." "Uh, all right."

She hissed in my ear, "I'll make you regret it if you ever turn me away again."

I was still considering what she said as she took my face and kissed me again. I blushed, but I didn't back away. I did not, most definitely did not, want to find out exactly how she was going to make me regret it. At least, that's what I told myself as I thoroughly enjoyed what Raina was doing to me.

"Hey, hero! How does it feel to be wrapped around a little fleshie finger?"

"Oh, shut up!" I thought back at him.

Ereshkigal

I couldn't believe how badly those two soft skins injured me so quickly, one with a sword from legend, and the other with elemental flame. Both of my Tendrils of Law were gone, so I couldn't heal myself. One was almost burned off and the other was cut off below its base, so it wouldn't grow back without help. My left eye was blind, and I was choking on my own blood from my missing nostril. After the initial pain subsided, I summoned Shulpec, my only earth mage.

When he didn't respond, I called for the servants while I waited in the cooling waters, trying vainly to ease the pain on the left side of my face, while not choking on my own blood from the right side. As they streamed into the room I sneezed, and blood blew out on a number of them, killing them. That was unfortunate, but I had no control. The pain and the lack of control were making me terribly irritable. They backed away, giving me room.

"I need Shulpec, now!" I roared.

Several of my kobold servants immediately and obediently dashed off. One of the others, the ruler, I couldn't remember his name, stepped forward. He waved the others back and they disappeared into the nooks and crevices in my lowest nest. It took only a moment for the cavern to empty.

"My Lady, Shulpec is dead, killed by those same soft-skins that committed sacrilege upon your holy body."

I breathed upon him, stopping the bad news. Well, there's nothing left but to move to Plan Two. I summoned a water elemental to neutralize the demi-fire elemental who had done this to me.

Duncan

Suddenly, water began filling the room from the cavern entrance. How?

Laurealis screamed, "Oh that hurts."

She ran up onto a rock, splashing as she ran. An enormous amount of water was filling the cavern. It was already a foot deep.

"Water elemental," Fausto said. "I was wondering what the dragon would do next. It's been close to an hour."

"Well, I'm now enough of a fire elemental, according to Kai', that water hurts badly."

Being preoccupied, I hadn't paid much attention to her, but she'd changed. That breath weapon had stabilized her. She was still lilac colored, but her left hand was blue, and she had a faint aura of blue flame around her entire body. It was fortunate that since her clothes were illusionary anyway, she was still dressed as she had been. I'm sure that any clothes would have been burned to a crisp, she was so hot. So, obviously, she still had her illusion abilities.

A mass of the water rose up, like a wave with eyes, and shot a bolt of water at Laurealis. Fausto countered with an earth wall.

Laurealis seemed to be biding her time by climbing higher on the rocks.

The water elemental moved with the speed of a wave, coming up right to the base of the rocks Laurealis was climbing and engulfed her in water.

She screamed and activated whatever she did with that hand of hers and boiled the water elemental to death. The water itself was quickly getting ridiculously hot, and we all climbed up and out of it. It wouldn't be any better to be parboiled by an ally than by an enemy. I saw Kailynn having trouble, he was so weak, so I splashed my way to him, threw him over my shoulder, and looked for a place to climb. There was nowhere to go. Fausto had smoothed the walls to focus Laurealis' earlier firebolts, and it was smooth enough to shine.

A stone stairway grew out of the wall with a landing about ten feet up and I nodded my thanks to Fausto as I climbed. As I gently laid Kailynn down, the water began streaming out as rapidly as it had flowed in. My feet were burning from being soaked with near boiling water. I rapidly took my boots off. That helped, but I was still badly scalded.

I saw Raina's pack moving with the water. I jumped down and rolled to collect it, and any other things of ours that the water might be carrying out. I was barefoot, but I was by far the closest. The water was only warm, but to my scalded feet, it felt like fire. I made it to her bags and gathered them to my chest before I fell, unable to take the pain anymore. Laying on my back, I held my feet up and just closed my eyes, trying not to scream.

Everyone was gathered in a little circle around me as Astoria healed my scalded feet. It was fortunate Astoria was such an accomplished healer. Burns hurt so incredibly more than cuts.

As she finished, Laurealis began complaining, "I'm so hungry. I can't believe how much I'm eating." She had broken into her pack and the food was flaming as soon as it entered her mouth. She wasn't even really chewing before she crammed in more food. It was mere moments before all her food was gone.

Kailynn replied, "Laurealis, it's your new nature. You're burning all your energy at a prodigious rate." "Well, we only have so much food. What will I eat? We still haven't found a way to get out of here without going through hundreds of dragons, and I'm so desperately hungry."

I almost volunteered that there was a huge amount of dragon meat, though I thought better of it. With the heat she produced, I expected the corrosive nature of the flesh would be burned away. While elves couldn't eat meat, she probably could now since she wasn't exactly an elf anymore.

"Fausto, what about rock? Are there any rocks in here that would burn? If so, I bet that she could burn them and get energy, call it food or whatever."

"No, nothing here. Nothing that could be burned normally, anyway. I doubt even Laurealis could burn it. Not without using more energy than she got from doing so.

I know!" he said, snapping his fingers. "We couldn't eat it, it's too corrosive, but I bet she could." He pointed at the ice dragon that I had been thinking about moments earlier. I backed away, expecting a huge explosion, possibly in more than just words.

"How could you even suggest such a thing!? I'm a Shala'lir. That thing is meat! Poisonous meat! Poisonous and corrosive! Look what it did to Duncan's sword! Ugh!"

Astoria weighed in. "He makes a good point, dear. Your metabolism has increased to the point that you need to eat vast amounts, as fire does. You look slimmer than you did before you burned up the water elemental, so you're obviously burning up your food at a rapid rate, like Kailynn said. Maybe you should try it."

"You, too?" She was shaking in her rage and her light blue flame aura had grown from an inch to three or four inches.

"But I'm so hungry. I feel like I'm starving. Oh Kailynn, wouldn't that be the way it goes; I rescue you from starving to death, then starve to death myself?"

"I'm so worried about you," he said, though he didn't reach out to her like one would expect. I wouldn't either, she felt as hot as a live coal.

"What am I going to do?" she wailed as she sat on one of the wet rocks. The rock quickly dried in a widening radius around her. She looked up at the dead dragon then back at her feet.

"I was only trying to save my husband and look what happened to me," despair filling her voice. Bitter tears began streaming from her. As she wailed, her body shook with her crying, though no tears actually showed because they evaporated.

"*Duncan?*"

"Yes," I replied to Glenfallis.

"*We have to find a way out of here.*"

"What do you propose?"

"*I am attempting to contact one of the several Elven Champions that I knew during the Fourth Age.*"

"You can do that?"

"*Duncan, would I have proposed something I could not do?*"

"Uh, no?"

"*Duncan, please stop proving that thou art an idiot and start thinking.*"

"I'm still getting used to a hunk of something shaped like a sword, having a mind. You're constantly surprising me with your abilities, humility not being one of them"

"I am magnificent, aren't I?"

"So, do I need to do anything to help you?"

"Don't get into a fight or something requiring my immediate attention and move over to near Kailynn so thee, and therefore I, can see him and the dead ice drake at the same time."

"Fine."

After doing so, I settled back to rest. Glenfallis began pulsating in yellow, blue, and white.

Bedros

I was conducting weapons practice with my apprentice Galen when the summons arrived. I had a strong image of Kailynn, looking horrible, backed up by a dead dragon, perhaps an ice drake, except there was no ice. It had been burned so badly its head was simply a dull glowing ember. Most unusual.

I sat, shocked. The image was sent by my ancient friend, Glenfallis. I hadn't heard from him since the End of the Fourth Age. I thought he'd been destroyed along with everything else of the Paladain. This was momentous.

Standing abruptly, I announced, "Galen, we have a mission. Kailynn's been found. Go, get gear for climbing and caving. We'll need travel rations and we have at least one severely injured Champion. We'll need high energy rations, as well as bland bread. I don't think we have any, so borrow from somewhere. He looks like he hasn't eaten since he disappeared last month."

I sat to meditate upon the image I was sent. I needed to memorize the location. Once I contacted the rest of the Champions, I would be teleporting all of us, so I needed to have my coordinates absolutely correct. The slightest error could have disastrous consequences.

Kailynn

My long watch over the remnants of the Paladain was nearing an end, now that Glenfallis, one of their legendary swords that I had the Earth Children disguise, was now unveiled. I could see the drain of mana that it was pulling from Ereshkigal. I wonder why it needed all that mana.

What to do about Laurealis? As flighty as she could be, she never handled major change well. She had no choice in this though. I supposed she would just have a number of cries, and I would try to support her as best I could.

It had been over an hour I think since I ate that first apple. Time for another. I was still so weak from the last month of starvation; all I could do was think. I hate being useless.

The water began welling up again, another water elemental!

"Fausto! The entrance! Close it off if you please!"

Laurealis ran toward the rapidly closing entrance, when Fausto, then Raina, was knocked down into the couple of inches of water that had already made it into our cavern, despite Fausto's quick action. A weak air elemental was in the cave. Weak, but so fast that it was hard to see, much less hit. A combination attack of several elementals! It seemed the Chaos Dragon was well enough to think.

Fausto stood to begin closing off the entrance, as the water continued to pour in. Laurealis screamed from landing in the water. As she regained her feet, her temper became far worse. Her face contorted in her rage, and she held out her left hand and boiled the water as it tried to pour in. She was winning. She was boiling the water faster than it could enter!

Fausto was almost finished with the entrance when the air elemental knocked the knees out from under my valiant, infuriated wife. She landed hard on her back, knocking the breath from her.

I had to try something! I couldn't let it keep her in the water, but I couldn't stand either. "Laurealis!" I tried crying, despairing at my weak voice.

Fausto yelled, "Hey, Duncan! A little help over here!"

"What can I do?"

"Use the sword! It's magical. Kill the air elemental!" I shouted, as loudly as I could.

"What?" Duncan asked.

Raina shouted up in his face. "The sword! Use the magic sword! Kill the air elemental!"

A roughly humanoid form thrust itself from the floor and hit Fausto's newly built wall. A wall of water washed over my beloved just as she was standing. Fausto was bowled over, as well.

"Laurealis!"

Infuriated, I tried to stand—I landed on my chest and face when my legs gave out.

When I was able to turn my head to see again, Raina was pulling me out of the rising waters. I saw Fausto in a desperate battle with the earth elemental, mainly because he kept getting sucker punched by the air elemental. He was far more powerful than his foe but was having a tough time getting his spells off.

Duncan had just killed a water elemental, one of a group, with a mighty two-handed blow.

Astoria! When did she get a battle-axe and learn to use it like that? Ah, I could see the Consort helping her. So, she was of the Order of Sachos, a battle priestess, which explained how she could fight so effectively. I wasn't aware that the Order of Sachos had been restored.

I fumed privately, thinking about the reason I was banished.

I could see that I was proven correct. The Order of Sachos was a sign of End Times. Perhaps I would be invited back early, especially if becoming a demi-fire elemental brought Laurealis out of Kaipoctouyevva.

I summoned a rope from my left vambrace, the pocket dimension where I kept all my gear.

"Raina, I don't know if this will resist burning long enough to haul Laurealis out of there, but you must get her out of the water."

She surveyed the bedlam around us, then dashed off into the middle of it. Tiny little girl, but she had grit far greater than her size. My heart and prayers were with her as she fashioned a loop while standing on a rock. Then she splashed her way in, dodging a lumbering earth elemental. It was slow, but it's immensely powerful swing would be deadly. She sprinted to a rock and dived out over the water to where Laurealis had been submerged for at least fifteen seconds.

That damned air elemental hit Reina in the face. She spun up and over, landing face first in the water herself. I hoped she was conscious. She had hit the water hard. She could drown like that, which meant Laurealis would, also.

I tried fashioning a ball of void. The most difficult of the elements to work. I gave it all my focus. That air elemental was going to die.

Void was best, void was best, I kept telling myself as I tried and tried to summon and form the void.

The trouble was, I used my katas to work my magic, but I was too weak to stand, much less do a kata. I couldn't ground myself either. If Laurealis died…I choked at the half-formed thought and the nearly summoned void dissipated. I felt the drain upon my core mana since I hadn't been able to ground myself. If she died, I just didn't care if using ungrounded magic killed me as well.

I began again.

Raina hauled Laurealis out of the water and her flame was out. I couldn't see if she was breathing! Raina dashed over and cut off some of the dead dragon's flesh from where one of the fire bolts had cut through its armored hide. She screamed, holding her hands in pain. Taking care with her burned hands and to avoid letting the blood touch her; she wrapped several pounds of dragon flesh in her dress, wrapping it up from the bottom to near her waist so she could carry it.

She walked quickly back, and dropping it, cut off a little bite-sized piece of the meat with her dagger. Despite the obvious pain in her hands, she lifted my beloved's head and placed it in her mouth. After a moment, Laurealis opened her eyes and began chewing. Then she snatched the meat from Raina and buried her face in it, eating ravenously.

I looked back at the battle. Fausto, in a rage, yanked his hands apart and the earth elemental flew into pieces. I waited a moment, expecting it to reform, but it was dispelled. Astoria was battling the last water elemental and Duncan was running around the cavern chasing that blasted air elemental. That was the last thing I saw. I had worn myself out trying to cast a spell, but it looked like we had won with no losses.

Duncan

I kept chasing that blasted air elemental all over the cavern.

"Stop!" Glenfallis screamed in my head. *"Hey, Dummy. Thou art supposed to be the one giving orders, remember? Dost thou not remember that I can use void to disintegrate stone?"*

"Uh, I remember you made stone go away. I didn't know the stuff about void and disintegration."

"How didst thee survive to eighteen? Point me at the elemental, instead of running around after something both quicker and faster than thee, and let my spell hit it." You can do that?

"YES!"

I aimed and pointed. Shoot, I commanded. A black bolt, about the size and speed of an arrow, shot from the sword. Our first shot missed, but missing everyone as it soared high. A chunk of stone the size of my fist disappeared. The second shot hit the ice drake corpse, where Laurealis was actually eating the meat. She never noticed, though a head sized portion of the corpse disappeared only a few feet away from her.

I began focusing, aiming where it would be, not the easiest task in the world since it changed directions constantly. It was like shooting a bird on wing, a task I had given up as futile until my step Uncle Kearney taught me how to aim ahead of the target. He was a legendary archer and my father's best friend. An image of his body ripped in half flashed briefly across my mind as I tried to use his methods to kill this invisible *bird*. Finally, on the eighth shot, we hit it. It simply ceased to exist.

Nothing else was attacking us. Kailynn was passed out, but Astoria was beside him and not looking frantic. Our plight seemed less bad. I remembered seeing Astoria beside Raina for a moment, casting a spell before she moved over to Kailynn.

Laurealis continued feasting upon the ice drake. Raina was nearly in tears. Her dress had a series of holes in it that began near the ground and got smaller as they rose to her upper thighs where she must have carried that corrosive meat to feed and save Laurealis. At ankle level, the front of her dress was just gone, then another smaller hole at her knees, and finally, the smallest hole, still as wide as her legs and six to eight inches high in the middle of her thighs. In fact, most of her legs were visible up to the middle of her thighs. There was really only a couple of inch-wide strips of cloth linking the sides and back of her dress at the knees, with more holes around her ankles and calves where she handled the nasty meat.

As I got closer, I saw that her upper thighs were severely burned, and she was crying. She seemed more upset about the dress than I thought she'd be from those horrible burns. I suppose Astoria had done one of her pain relief spells before checking out Kailynn.

I asked, "Why are you crying?"

"My dress is ruined!"

"True, but Laurealis can hide it with a spell, and you'll be able to patch it, well, replace it as soon as this is over."

"You're not angry?"

"About what?"

"You want me to be shy and modest. With my dress like this, I can't be."

I took a deep breath. "I don't care about the holes in your dress. I wouldn't care if all your clothes were destroyed, as long as you weren't hurt. I hate that you're burned so badly. You fought like a true warrior. I'm so proud of you."

"What! I tried so hard to dress modestly and properly for you and you'd prefer to see me without any clothes, just naked! How dare you!"

"Huh? I like the way you dress. I was trying to say…"

"So now you want me to just rip the dress off above the holes? Is that what you're saying?"

"No! Just leave it alone and get it patched or get a new one when we get out of here. Or when Laurealis finishes eating, let her cast an illusion over the holes…"

"I try so hard and you just don't care!" she screamed over my words.

"It'll be fine." I don't think she even heard. I never met anyone so adept at twisting words into meaning so opposite of the original intent.

She charged me, flailing at me with both fists, once. She moaned briefly, then holding her right hand with her left, changed to kicking my shins and elbowing me with her left elbow. As I caught her wrists, I was very thankful she didn't pull out her knife. I noticed, looking past her, the handle and badly corroded blade of one of her knives was lying discarded on the ground.

"Raina, didn't you ruin your dress while saving Laurealis' life? Getting her the food she needed?"

"Well, yes."

"Then why would I be angry? You did what you needed to do. You followed the code that I follow. Part of that is to help other people, regardless of the cost to yourself." I touched my forehead to hers. "You make me proud. Immensely proud."

"Do you really mean that?"

"With all my heart."

She looked at me hard, and with a lot of suspicion, but finally laid her head against my chest. She winced when her thighs touched me, so I went to one knee so she could sit on my leg and held her head to my chest as she calmed down.

I finally looked up to discuss getting us out of here when I noticed Laurealis sobbing as she continued to use her left hand to cut off pieces of meat with a controlled flame.

"This is so wrong. I can't believe I'm doing this." Tears were pouring down her face as she ate. She couldn't stop eating, her body was demanding so much energy. But the shame of doing what she had despised for so long was tearing her apart. My heart broke for her.

She saw me looking at her over Raina's head. "You probably think that this is funny. Well, it isn't! I hope you're proud of what I'm having to go through." Not again!

"I'm sorry that you're having to go through this. I know how much you despise eating meat. Perhaps you can now understand better why I have to eat meat, also?"

I groaned, knowing what was likely to happen next.

She threw the meat at us, hitting Raina square in the back. I hoped it wouldn't eat a hole in her dress there, also! Her dress, nor her back!

I snatched Raina up and carried her over to a fairly deep puddle and dropped her in, hoping to stop the meat from eating a hole through her dress into her back. I rubbed her back down hard, with her still under water. Then I turned her over and to my immense relief, there was no damage, well, not much in the back of her dress. I couldn't see her back and only a little of the white shirt thing that she wore under her dress. I was quick enough. Apparently, burning the meat off like Laurealis was doing, destroyed most of the corrosiveness before it hit Raina, I was so relieved.

"Just what did you do that for!?" Raina began screaming.

"I tried so hard to be nice to you," Laurealis joined in, "despite your filthy eating habits. Now I've been reduced to your level, you're laughing at me!"

I just sighed and sat with my hands over my ears, trying to ignore the two women screaming at me. They screamed for several minutes before Fausto jumped in. "Hey, at least now you know how good meat tastes."

Laurealis moved from screaming at me to screaming at him. Raina had stopped screaming at me as well, in shock at Fausto's incredibly callous remark. It seems he can't help himself!

Astoria looked up from where she was beside Kailynn. "Dear, they're just trying to help."

Laurealis looked at her best friend in shock, "Not you, too." She looked at the three of us in turn and finally broke down into tears.

Fausto then turned to Raina and demanded, "So why are you mad at him?"

"Just look at what he did! He just snatched me up and threw me into the filthy water! He just ruined what was left of my dress!"

"He saved your dress, and probably your life."
"What?"

"Didn't you see what Laurealis threw into the middle of your back?"

Raina followed his finger to the meat lying where they had been standing a moment earlier.

"Look at your dress." Fausto said, as he pointed at the series of holes between her legs.

"Oh." At least she had the decency to blush.

"We have to get out of here," Fausto reminded us.

"I know, but Glenfallis has contacted another Champion who may be able to teleport straight here. Should we leave with him on the way?"

"Yes," Fausto countered. "We were all hurt in that last encounter. That dragon will send another bunch of elementals much larger than that group, since that group was larger than the first. We need to get out of here before she realizes we've defeated them as well. The Champion should be able to fend for himself, and perhaps Glenfallis can give him an update."

"Do you have a plan?" I asked.

"Yes. You go pick up Kailynn. He tried to cast a void spell, after Raina got knocked for that spin before she fetched Laurealis out of the water. That must be what exhausted him so badly. You watch him and let everyone lean on you. We're about to have a bumpy ride."

"Works for me."

I collected Kailynn on my lap and sat. Raina held onto my back and wrapped her legs around my waist. Astoria was on one side and Fausto on the other. He had warned me to secure him, so I grabbed his belt at the small of his back. Laurealis was a problem. Finally, now that she was well-fed, we discovered that she had more control over her temperature, and we placed her in Kailynn's lap. He still had his armor on in case she lost control and heated up.

Fausto made a sled with sides, then moved us to the wall which he opened up. We shot rapidly into a tunnel that formed just ahead of us. It was a harrowing ride as he would turn us, sometimes rapidly, in different directions. The little space we were in was illuminated by Laurealis, but we couldn't see more than twenty feet ahead of us as the tunnel formed. It felt like we were moving at a fast gallop. At one point, I glanced behind us. The tunnel was closing behind us as rapidly as it formed in front. Now I began worrying about what would happen if Fausto lost control. How would we get out? Realizing there was nothing we could do, my grip on Fausto's belt tightened.

My fear of small spaces hadn't been so bad when I was crawling. I was doing something. This was another thing altogether.

Finally, we popped out into the brightness of open air, then we rode an avalanche down the side of the mountain. At least there was no chance of anything lying in ambush for us. We were moving too fast, and the avalanche would kill anything in our way. I felt relieved; we were finally back out in the open air. The space we were travelling through had been horrifically close.

To my terror, when we had almost reached the water, we disappeared under the ground again, and went down a long way. I tried closing my eyes, but it didn't help. I knew we were not only under the ground, but under the lake! I worked extremely hard at keeping myself under control, hearing Raina telling me that it would be all right and to calm down. I realized that I had been screaming. I kept secure grips on Fausto and Astoria as we swayed and rocked all around. When we surfaced a final time, Fausto collapsed, totally spent. I wasn't much better. I was covered in a cold sweat, which I'm sure reeked strongly of my fear. I stood unsteadily and surveyed our surroundings, working to put my fear behind me. Fear was a thing to be mastered. I was ashamed that it had mastered me.

Fausto impressed me. He had drained himself, but he had gotten us out of there. I stood to look around and discovered muscle cramps from how hard and how long I had been hunkered down.

After a minute, I sat to try to work out the stiffness. Astoria, bless her, moved over behind, and began massaging my neck while I sat with my eyes closed. After a minute or two, the pain left, and I was fine. I sat up straighter to stand and Astoria demanded, "Just what do you think you're doing?"

"Uh, getting up to go get the others under cover, and to get our horses."

"Not yet. Hold your arm out."

She ripped the cut sleeve a little wider and healed the gash that had bled through when I was thrown against a rock during the fight.

"I don't see any place else that bled through. Is there anything not bleeding that might slow us down? Speak now or hold your complaints 'till we're safe, when you'll strip and let me investigate you fully, the same as I'll do for everyone else."

"Uh, no ma'am. Nothing else that won't wait."

"Good. Raina, your turn. Sit up on that rock and pull your dress up and let me check your burns."

Raina complied, and I turned my back to give her some privacy after the barest glimpse of her beautiful legs. The large burns on the front of her thighs held my attention far more than the beauty of her legs. They worried me.

Astoria whispered in Raina's ear, "Thank you, dear, for saving Laurealis. That was so brave. You were perfect." Then she gasped, loudly. "By the Lady! Raina! You should have told me how severely burned you were. I knew you were in pain, so I relieved it before moving on. You only blistered a little, but I'm not surprised at your temper now. Let me see your hands."

I wanted to turn around; I was concerned but restrained myself. Then Astoria said, "Dear me. Only one was severely burned; good. Well, we're going to stop the pain right away. I used almost all of my material components for burns on Laurealis and Duncan. I'll heal your hand, but your legs will have to wait. They're not as bad as your hand. I'm sorry, but you just sit there, and I'll do something to help them begin healing. We'll heal you properly as soon as we can."

"Duncan, silly, you can look." Raina chided me. "You're going to be seeing a lot more of me in the future anyway, and I want you over here with me."

I laid my hand on her shoulder. She smiled back up at me as Astoria stripped off her outer robe, the yellow one.

"Laurealis, would you be a dear and clean this, and what I'm about to cut off of Raina's dress."

"Of course. I know your *sterilization* spell works a lot better on clean items."

"Stand, Raina. I need to cut away a lot of what's left of your dress. I can't have it rubbing against the bandages you're about to be wearing. Just be brave a little longer."

I stood behind Astoria as she worked on getting Raina's dress out of the way. Starting just above the top burned area of the dress, she cut the dress off at an angle which left space on either side of the burns and tapered down to just behind her knees. It looked far more practical than the remnants of the dress had been. I smiled; glad she wouldn't be tripping over the awkwardness of her ruined dress anymore. Raina just looked at me the whole time.

Astoria now rubbed some alcohol on her hands and a red glow surrounded them. She did the same over Raina's burns. Next, she pulled a short wide bottle of a salve out of her backpack and very carefully wiped it over Raina's burned hand, and the last little bit on one thigh. Focusing on Raina's hand with her own hand glowing medium green, the blisters collapsed back into the skin and a lot of skin just flaked off and fell away. Then the red just faded into pink and finally into the normal color of her skin. Astoria then did the same thing on the little bit of thigh burn that had the salve on it, with the same results. Though the skin didn't look as severely burned, it certainly didn't just flake off the same way.

Taking a deep breath, Astoria went back into her trance again, only this time her hand glowed dark green and results weren't quick. The smaller blisters slowly sank back into the skin and disappeared. Several were already close to an inch in diameter, so they only shrank to a half inch. The skin was still red and inflamed.

Finally, Astoria opened her eyes, her weariness showing, before she smiled, "Well, it's time to wrap your legs. I think we can forego that step with your hand; it's fully healed, not even any stiffness. But your legs need to be dressed and kept dry. We'll change them every day till we can finish the job."

She took her sheer, yellow robe from Laurealis' waiting arm and cut and ripped it into foot wide strips. She next wrapped the bandages several layers deep around Raina's thighs, taking care to keep them stable over the burns. Raina winced every time the cloth shifted. I offered her my finger to squeeze and the wincing stopped. Her courage was admirable.

"The pain suppressant spell works fine with the base level of pain, but as you're discovering, spikes of pain are still going to occur. I'm being as gentle as possible, consistent with a proper wrapping."

"I know, I've been healed lots of times from worse injuries than this. You have a very gentle touch. Just finish it up, please."

Astoria cast a sharp look at Raina but said nothing. Next, she wrapped strips of Raina's dress material over the yellow dressings and stored the leftovers of both materials into the jeweled locket with a bird image engraved in it.

"These will begin healing, but they'll still hurt a lot when the pain suppressant spell wears off, as I guess you're aware of from your last comment. Now, promise me you'll let me know the moment you begin feeling any pain again. I don't want our brave girl to feel any pain."

At Raina's quick nod, Astoria said, "Good. I promise we'll finish healing you as soon as we can, and you won't have any scarring, or my name isn't Astoria. You're so brave and I want to thank you again. Your black eye, where that horrid air elemental hit you so hard, isn't critical, so it'll wait. I need to conserve my mana for things that will slow us down, like your pain.

She touched her eye and smiled sadly, nodding. It really was developing into an intense black eye. Another war wound from saving her friend, a small price to pay. After hearing what Astoria said, I was worried about her burns. I resolved to never say a word, no matter how badly scarred she might be. They didn't look so bad; but I've never been burned like that so I can't judge how bad they were. They were Wounds of Honor, gained in the saving of a companion's life.

Then I realized we were near where we had left our horses. Fausto's impressive skills and knowledge of the surrounding terrain left me speechless.

"Raina, would you come with me? Let's let everyone get hidden while we get the horses and let Fausto and Kailynn rest."

I reached for her hand, knowing I would have to be gentle, but she folded her hands inside her underarms.

What now? I wondered.

"So, the reason you didn't care if I was naked was that you think I'm ugly," she stated firmly.

By the Ancient One's beard! I thought everything was fine, but she continues to only see everything through negative eyes. "What?"

"Just say it. I can handle it. You think I'm ugly."

"But you're beautiful, cat ears and all." As soon as the words were out, I knew I'd spoken without thinking.

"So, it's the ears that make me look ugly to you? Well, that explains why you said, 'why would I want to kiss you.'"

"Huh? When did I say that?"

"When you made the tea for me after you made that horrible comment about me being a brown cat."

I had to scratch my head on that one, "Oh, I remember now. But I only said that because I was upset about Aisling. I didn't mean it."

"Then why'd you bring it up again?" she asked, her voice rising again.

I groaned inwardly, not again.

"Honey, you're beautiful, and I can't wait 'till the appropriate time to see your pretty legs healed and healthy. Happy?"

"No! I don't believe you! You think I'm ugly!"

I sighed heavily. "Please Raina, not now. We have to get our horses and get out of here! Now let's go! I was just trying to spend time with you, but if you want to go back, then do so. We don't have time for this!"

Astoria stepped up behind Raina and touched her shoulder with that red glow. She caught Raina as she fell, already asleep.

"Duncan, get the horses. I could tell she was getting ready for a good blow, and we can't have her screaming drawing dragons towards us. You will learn to control your tongue, or at least not get her riled up."

"Astoria, I have a lot to learn, but she needs to learn another viewpoint as well. Being confrontational to elicit kindness will get old real fast." I hung my head and walked off toward the cave where our horses were hidden.

The Grupptara noble was there and most helpful. I brought him up to date on the evening's events, which took a surprisingly brief time with their mind speech. I left riding Shadow and leading the other two by lead lines.

Raina

When I awoke, I was under the big rock where Duncan had placed Kailynn and Fausto to rest peacefully.

"Raina, you have to give Duncan a break," Astoria stated, with Laurealis right behind her. It seemed I was going to get a lecture.

"Why? He keeps pushing me off and making comments like he thinks I'm ugly." I crossed my arms, stubbornly refusing to give up my anger. I was glad I didn't hurt anymore. I realized that a part of my earlier irritability was caused by the pain. Still…

"Really? What comments?" Laurealis asked.

"He didn't care if my whole dress, my only dress, the one you bought for me, was destroyed and I was left naked. It was a nice dress, and I liked it. I still like the cut of it. I thought Duncan did, too. Despite what he said, his eyes showed how much he liked it. Still, he didn't care if all my clothes were destroyed."

"Yes, and what else? He explained his feelings, Raina. He was so proud of your self-sacrifice, that losing something replaceable, like your clothing, just didn't matter. I agree with him. I'll happily get a new dress for you, as many as you want, for saving my friend. And he's a young man in love; he's going to notice those legs of yours. You should be concerned if he didn't!"

"He wouldn't kiss me because of my ears."

"He actually said that? Seeing how he looks at you and strokes your ear, makes me doubt that."

"Really?"

"Was this when you both first met, and you had already decided he was going to be yours, whether he wanted you yet or not?" Laurealis asked.

I shook my head no but changed it to yes. Perhaps she had a point.

"What else?" Astoria asked.

"Dear, what else? I know you're holding back." Laurealis added.

"I hate you for feeling my emotions, or seeing my aura, or however you're doing it! Yes, there's something else!

"He got himself thrown halfway across that damned cave, and I just found him. I can't lose him. It's all so unfair and I hate him for getting hurt again!"

Laurealis' arms were already wrapping around me as I cried hard into her shoulder. It wasn't until later when I calmed down that I realized she was merely very warm to the touch. The only thing she was doing to protect me from her heat was keeping her left hand away from me. I felt a lot better and a bit ashamed for taking my fears out on Duncan that way.

Duncan

When I returned with the horses, Raina was awake and talking with Astoria and Laurealis.

I jumped off, looping the two lead lines to Shadow's saddle horn. In defense, I held up my arms just in time to catch Raina as she was already in mid-air leaping into my arms, sideways to protect her legs. She was so like a female cougar; agile, graceful, and oh so deadly. After an exuberant kiss, I said, "Come, my love, we must see how long before we can move out of here."

"There's no rush. Well, there is, but there's nothing we can do until Fausto wakes up. He totally drained his personal mana in that mad dash out of the mountain. He has to sleep it off. Kailynn as well."

"Why don't you ladies give him some of that pollen stuff, like you gave Kailynn?"

"Different races. His people absorb mana differently than ours. He pulls it in from the ground. 'Dom'barn' means *Earth Children*, you see?"

"Oh."

Laurealis smiled broadly, "Since we have some time and the men are hidden under the ledge of this big rock with us, why don't you two kids go over to the other side of this rock and spend some time getting to understand each other better? My illusion will cover us all."

Raina hopped down smiling and led me to a slightly smaller ledge on the other side where we proceeded to do exactly that, secure in our privacy.

Laurealis

When the kids were gone to enjoy themselves for the first time since he proposed to her, I was finally ready to talk through what had happened to me with Astoria. However, when I finished with the last touches of my covering illusion, she was bent over Kailynn, kneading his belly. Her hands had their deep green glow as she worked on my beloved. He's lost so much weight, though his color was already better.

Looking at him, I could certainly understand why Raina was so worried about seeing her man getting hurt again. I almost told her that it doesn't get any better over time, when her man gets himself hurt. Maturity just helps us express it better.

"What are you doing?" I asked.

She was deep in a healing focus and didn't answer for a moment. "Give me a few minutes, Laurie. He's fine, but I'm just making sure he recovers as quickly as possible from his starvation. A little extra work now and his digestive tract will be restored and working better. Hopefully, we can get a full meal into him. He'll be awake soon, I think. Would you prepare a meal for him? I think we can let him have a normal meal now."

"Gladly." I settled back to wait, working on controlling my body's temperature. I didn't want to cook the fruits and vegetables with a touch. After a while, I had confirmed that if I was calm, my body temperature was normal. I realized my emotions were a key to using my new ability. I could have burned Raina badly, if that weren't the case. Thinking back to my heat control problems, being able to manage my temperature meant I didn't have to eat such enormous amounts of whatever was at hand. I was so humiliated by what had occurred inside the cavern, I just put it aside. The very thought of eating meat still nauseated me.

I understood why it happened, and my irritation at Raina for her presumption was fading rapidly. But it still upset me a lot that I had fallen to such depravities.

Seeing motion above us, I saw dragons flying up out of the mountain. I almost projected my voice around the rock to warn Duncan and Raina, but hesitated. The dragons were a long way away and wouldn't be able to find us easily, even those with True Sight. True Sight only worked on small areas. Spells to detect illusionary magic in a large area, especially of the highest order as mine, didn't exist. You couldn't see with True Sight; it was a spell or ability for tightly focused searching. Even with a large number of dragons, they would have to be looking right at us to even have a chance of detecting us. I would give the young lovers more time. Duncan didn't have armor to wear, just his clothes. And knowing him, probably no more than his shirt would need to be put back on, which wouldn't take much time. We'd be fine.

"Astoria," I asked, "how long do you think Fausto will need to recharge his mana? The dragons are out and looking for us."

"Well, eight hours is probably what he'll need to mostly recharge, but four will do him a lot of good. The way I understand it, it's just another function of sleep. An elf would meditate and recharge much quicker. But dwarves don't seem to use meditation as much as we do. Let's just play it safe and give them all as much time as we can."

Bedros

I had immediately used the abilities built into our armor to speak to the other four Champions, leaving Kailynn out of the loop for a moment. It took about a quarter hour for everyone to respond to me. Even though a Champion was down, we were too far away to get to our Hall any quicker. I was the specialist in teleportation and air manipulation, so I would bring us all together.

Linked by our armor, we all turned invisible for our transport to the mountain where we knew Kailynn was being held. We were quite aware of where the Chaos Dragon had made her lair as she repopulated the earth with her foul brood. We also knew that Kailynn and his rescuers had been in another battle but were still alive. We were all excited that our brother had turned up alive a month after we lost all communication with him, though we were puzzled as to whom his rescuers might be.

We were the only ones I could think of, both powerful enough and martial enough, to do something so insane.

All we were certain of was that teleporting into the heart of the Chaos Dragon's Lair would be near suicidal, and the reason we'd never removed her and her vermin before. I brought us to the west side of the mountain and hundreds of feet up.

Their escape had stirred up the dragons, like a stick stirring an ant hill. There were dozens of dragons flying about with more exiting the various aeries every few seconds.

"Kailynn! Brother! Where are you?" several of us thought as soon as we appeared. The obvious answer occurred to all of us simultaneously.

"He's out. Let's stay together so I can bring us quickly to wherever they may be," I thought through my armor to the other Champions. We all knew better than to use verbal speech. Our armor could also communicate via our thoughts.

While all were equal in our group, I was the nominal leader, since I had summoned us.

"Any ideas?" I thought. *"His group is in hiding, thank the Lady, but how do we find them?"*

"Watch the dragons, Bedros." Pancros cautioned. *"It looks like they're all coming out and I've always maintained that there may be at least a thousand of them in this mountain. With the True Sight that most of them have, they'll find him sooner than we will. We'll have to act quickly once he's located."*

"He's right." Obelix concurred.

"We should create a diversion to help them escape. What if they're on the move now?" Cougar asked.

"Cougar, no one doubts your courage, just your sanity." I said. *"Galen, what do you say?"*

"Wait."

"I agree. Let's keep alert for any indication from the dragons of where Kailynn and his rescuers might be. They're obviously powerful, but they're probably much the worse for wear after coming through that mountain. I'm extremely curious how they managed to do it, and how many they lost doing so."

The ancient proverb states, "Hurry up and wait." And wait we did. We had arrived just past dawn four hours earlier. Pancros, my dear wife, was proven correct, though her numbers were low. There were well over a thousand of the beasts filling the air around us, not including the five hundred or so wyverns that also inhabited the ancient forest. Then, in the manner of these things, everything happened at once.

A smaller fire drake, only fifteen feet long, screamed from the deep forest surrounding the lake and dived. All the other drakes screamed and followed.

Just as we were about to go there, the Chaos Dragon herself appeared in front of us. "Going somewhere, boys?" She released her breath weapon, a horrible thing of pure chaos that mutated everything it touched. It could cause masses of horrible cancers and other random growths, like extra limbs, or worse, as the poor victim died, sometimes slowly, sometimes quickly.

I instantly pulled a powerful wind to blow it right back into her face, her horribly burned and injured face. The rescuers had done well I thought, and that just finished her off. Then I realized the chaos matter of her breath was healing her!

"Cougar! Pancros! Galen! I'm moving you down there to help Kailynn! Obelix and I have Her Majesty."

Obelix quietly said, "Touch of Death," and released the arrow he had just armed with his most powerful attack spell, I teleported half our party to aid Kailynn and his rescuers.

As can happen when fighting exceptionally powerful foes, the spell fizzled, most likely due to a *dispel magic* spell from our foe. Still, the arrow sank deeply into her eye, the one growing back from that once horrible burn.

I teleported to beside her other eye using the power of the wind to speed my attack. I took out her remaining eye and teleported back to Obelix, just as another breath blast covered the area where he'd been.

Pointing to a spot above her left front flank to warn him, I teleported us as he armed another arrow, "Touch of Destruction." Blast him having to *say* his spells! She heard him and bludgeoned us with her enormous head. Stunned, we fell.

Kailynn

I was awake but was still too weak to do anything. I had been brought up to date about our plight as I ate as much as I could force into my shrunken stomach. I was trying to get food in quickly so my depleted body could recover enough energy to not require my being carried to escape. My heart sank seeing the numbers facing us. It was only a matter of time 'till we were discovered. Fighting out of an enclosed space, while it left no retreat, also hadn't allowed the Chaos Dragon to have any room to maneuver.

A small fire drake screamed; its body barely larger than a wyvern.

"This is it," I shouted and stood, relieved to discover that my legs held firm under me. Well, somewhat firm. I leaned against the rock we'd been hiding under before they collapsed again. Laurealis effectively warned Duncan and Raina by manipulating sound to reach around the huge boulder between us.

Fausto, the doughty earth mage who had done so well earlier, woke as well.

Screaming its rage, the fire drake dove at Duncan, who had stepped out in front. Duncan sidestepped its flaming breath and cut its head off halfway down its neck. Able to observe him better, now that my beloved wasn't in immediate danger of drowning, I noted that the boy was good with that sword. He would be better. I would see to his training.

Laurealis' blue flames were back in a big way. A black chlorine drake who had a long body with tendrils like the Chaos Dragon, had crept up behind us. I tried to move into a kata to cast the necessary spells to climb or fly away from that stinking gas, but I didn't yet have the strength. At least, with the help of the boulder, I stayed on my feet.

Raina jumped on its upper leg, distracting it while she ran up its neck and plunged her knife into its eye. As it rose up, injured, and angered, she jumped off, rolling under our rock. Then Laurealis, my peaceful Laurealis, fried its head, sealing its poison inside and killing it.

Raina held up her knife, now rapidly corroding into useless rust, and tossed it aside. "Damn, that was my last knife. I guess I just hide now," she said in defeat.

I couldn't fight, but that was something I could do something about. I pulled a matched set of daggers, short swords to her, out of my pocket dimension and shouted, "Raina, come here! I have something for you!"

She dove off the boulder and rolled, coming to stand right in front of me. Her Lir'folk heritage showed clearly in her cat-like agility.

"These blades are magical enough to not be corroded by dragon blood. They have a few other special properties you might like as well."

She flashed a uniquely beautiful smile; I could see why Duncan was so drawn to her.

"What properties?" she asked, inspecting the blades carefully.

"Bleeding. Wounds made with these don't stop bleeding and their nature can divert your aim up to a few inches to find an artery which they can sense is close. Work with them and they'll make you far more effective. They're intelligent enough to help you strike true, but they're focused. They're stubborn about wanting to cause lots of bleeding. It's why I quit using them. They might cause problems with that eye strike you seem to prefer."

"Can they cut through dragon hide? My steel daggers couldn't. That's why I went for the eyes. It was the only place I could think of where I had a chance of doing something."

"Beautiful, agile, AND smart; Duncan doesn't stand a chance against you, does he?"

She flashed that wonderful smile again. "Nope." She half jumped, half climbed back onto the rock and under a fallen log, to await another chance to strike from her ambush point.

I liked that little slip of a girl.

"Kailynn! It's good to see you," came a voice from the edge of our hiding places.

"Cougar? Pancros? Galen, if you're here then Bedros is as well, and probably Obelix. Well, it's about time you showed up. You left me hanging over that bloody lake for a stinking month!" I couldn't help my anger. I'd been stewing up there for a long time.

"We tried! We couldn't find you. We were beginning to think you were dead," Pancros pleaded.

"No time for this," Cougar said as he turned into his wild form of the cougar he had taken as his name. Racing through the forest, it was like a wind was following him. The trees rustled and became active. He may not have come for me, but at least he was now willing to do his part.

A wyvern dove in through the trees, followed by two more in a straight line. The trees hit the small dragonoid with their branches, knocking them to the ground. Then roots flew out of the ground, wrapping the downed wyverns rapidly enough to hold them immobile. Then the gruesome part began, and the roots grew into the captive dragonoids. First, their scales were forced apart as the roots grew. Within minutes the wyverns would be dead, roots running through all parts of their bodies, absorbing nutrients from anywhere moist enough to hold nourishment.

As all that happened, three greater dragons, and a half dozen wyverns, flew into the little space we were defending.

Bedros

We fell a couple of hundred feet before I came to, and another hundred before I regained control of our flight and moved us out of the way of another blast from attacking dragons. We were now visible to some of the dragons. They must have been looking when the Chaos Dragon hit us. While

True Sight isn't so good for searching, it's great once you've spotted something.

I needed clouds to add to an almost clear day. As Obelix released shot after shot, taking down three dragons quickly, I looked for a convenient bank of clouds or something to obscure us long enough to become invisible to the four dragons defending their queen.

Obelix got one shot off at the queen, a *Touch of Flesh Destruction* arrow that hit her squarely between the eyes! While it wasn't enough to kill her, she was looking grayer than her normal iridescent black with pink legs. She flew off, her four bodyguards going with her.

"Obelix, let's go finish her off. Great shot!"

"No, I'm going after her escort. She's hurt and running. Her escort is the danger now."

"You have a point. Fine, the escort it is."

We dashed down to a mere hundred feet from the nearest one. I thought through my armor, *"I'm going to stop its flight for a second for you to aim better."*

"No, you just keep steady. I'll be fine."

His arrow flew and so did we. There was no way I was staying within a hundred feet of dragons, one hundred to two hundred feet long, in the case of the Chaos Dragon. He had let fly a *Touch of Death* at an ice drake, but we left too quickly to see what happened.

My fast departure also didn't allow me the time to notice the small little fire drake a couple of hundred feet above us. I only barely managed to dodge it. Obelix proved as steady as his name and calmly shot between its closing wings. Nothing we know of could pierce dragon wings. A lot of the dragons' magic is focused on the bones and skin of their bat-like wings. Even Obelixs' shot from twenty feet away would have been deflected. Fortunately, his aim was true, landing between the soft shoulder muscles. Another creature of evil took the long fall to crash and burn.

"Where to now, Obelix?"

He smiled grimly, "Under them."

I took my bearings and flew us in a slightly winding path to under the three remaining dragons guarding their queen. The fourth guard, the ice drake Obelix shot before we retreated, was about to hit the water. Dead ice drakes don't swim so well.

Seeing how effectively Obelix was at taking down the dragons, I decided to focus only on flying and dodging any huge heads, dragon parts, or attacks coming our way. We couldn't afford to let any of the creatures, especially the ones using magic, get a fix on us again. Even with our armor, we wouldn't be a match for the beasts.

We were behind and slightly under them to let my friend's arrow penetrate between the scales. One was built more like the Chaos Dragon, long and serpentine, with no wings. This type used spells to fly and were casters, not breathers, and far more dangerous.

"Touch of Death," Obelix whispered. I hoped the dragon hadn't heard us. Unfortunately, the legendary hearing of dragons was to prove our bane.

Lights burst open all around us, blinding us and covering the area in *sparkle dust*. The dust got its name from the way it covered everything with sparkles. It is also a wonderful way to spot invisible things, like we had been a moment earlier. I couldn't help but name the event the Obelix effect.

Obelix again let his arrow fly true, slipping up under a scale and delivering its spell directly to the dragon's flesh in a brief burst of black destructive energy. There was no time to see how badly the dragon was hurt. We had only a moment before every dragon up there was going to be coming for us.

I used the wind to shove a big fire drake into the queen, hoping for the best. The blind and injured Chaos Dragon reacted poorly to being shoved and bit the head off her nearest remaining guard.

Only one left, but no more time for mayhem. All the nearby dragons were diving for us, rage blazing in their eyes as they sought to defend their queen, or to just kill their tormentors. Either way, we dove fast for the ground. My improvised plan was to come to earth near Galen and hope my training with his preferred spells would pay off. He worked with time, speeding things up and slowing them down.

Pancros

A combat illusionist, I had already multiplied images of myself and all the others to a dozen each, except for Cougar, whom that really irritated. While doing so, to add to the confusion, I made changes to each, so they appeared to be different. Next, I chose the nearest of the big, bad lizards to gift with an illusion of pain. It's a difficult illusion to master, but oh so effective. Dragons are hard to fool, especially with things they can see. But intense pain is something older creatures are so familiar with, that the illusions hold. You never know where the pain illusion will show up, since it works on an old injury or arthritis, which most old creatures suffer from.

That one went down groaning holding its forepaw with the other. No deafening dragon screams either, just whimpering.

I turned to the next, only to see its feet sink into the earth, trapping it. One of the many boulders scattered around flew into its breast, hard enough to break it. I realized we had an earth mage on our side. I decided to build upon his success and cast illusionary pain to compound the pain it was already feeling, hoping to completely disable it with pain.

I noticed Laurealis, the illusionist wife of Kailynn, with actual flame all over her body. No time for speculation about how. She burned my first pained dragon's head to a charred cinder. The large human, with his clear sword, took off the head of the one the earth mage had wounded. A powerful team, indeed.

The third dragon was wasting its breath on a couple of my duplicate illusions.

A half-breed girl leapt out from under some rock and debris. She raced up the leg of the third dragon and stabbed it several times where its color changed from its deep blue dorsal color to its lighter blue ventral color. She then leapt off and raced away. Blood spurted from the obvious arterial wound. I was impressed.

Astoria appeared from hiding as a battle priestess of the Order of Sachos! The blue nimbus of the Consort was clearly visible, wielding the battle-axe, the Order's weapon of choice. It's a good thing the Consort was guiding her. I'm sure the Astoria I knew wouldn't know which end of a battle-axe to hold, nor have the strength to wield. She dispatched the bleeding dragon with ease.

Cougar's trees were dealing with the wyverns to a substantial extent, while dragons were diving all around us.

It was Galen doing a speed spell. We didn't need the dragons sped up!

"Galen, stop! You're speeding up the dragons!"

He ignored me and completed his spell. It was a large area spell that hit everything above twenty feet. The dragons' speed increased dramatically. They were too close to the ground to change direction and crashed headfirst in the ground, rather than pulling out of their dives.

A hundred dragons hit the ground hard enough to incapacitate and kill many of them outright. So that was his plan. Cougar's tamed trees immediately began working on the host of groaning and barely moving dragons, immobilizing then killing them.

Bedros and Obelix must have already been near the ground since they were moving at a normal speed, for Bedros. He was flying fast, but his movements were normal speed.

Then the Sparkle dust filled the area! That's why he came down.

Two dragons were winging their way over the water toward Bedros when the first one slowed suddenly and the rear one sped up, crashing into him. The results were predictable for creatures as prideful and demanding of their personal space as dragons. The battle was short and effective, leaving both less able to attack us, the slowed one permanently so. The less injured of the two suddenly collapsed.

I felt an odd kind of pressure in my head. Looking at the nearby water I saw several otters' heads just sticking up out of it. Did we have a new race of allies? So many surprises, so many enemies! Victory was still up for grabs.

Kailynn

The battle was progressing well. We hadn't lost anyone, and we had taken down hundreds of dragons and at least two hundred wyverns. There was still the better part of a thousand dragons left, and hundreds of wyverns. Praise the Lady, the Chaos Dragon had not come back out of her mountain. The odds were still impossible, and everyone was exhausted, though the dragons kept coming. Cougar's forest was mostly burned down for at least a half mile around us, though it was filled with dead and dying wyverns and dragons. Breathing through the smoke was difficult.

I began crawling; it was easier than walking to the horses. I planned on mounting one so we could leave as soon as Bedros was able to get us all together. Trouble was, we were spreading out, not staying together. I doubted anyone could shout loud enough to be heard over the incredible bedlam and noise of dragons fighting and screaming, and the high-pitched keening of their dead and dying. I couldn't seem to get their attention through the armor's intrinsic speech. There was too much background noise.

I spotted Laurealis and began my crawl toward her. She would listen to me and had the ability to speak to everyone through her proficiency in sound illusions.

Everyone continued to have success. Raina dashed out to slice an artery, that her new knives helped her locate, right behind the rear leg of one drake pausing to cast her breathe weapon at some of Pancros' illusions. When the creature was well sliced, she rolled backward, and dashed back under cover. It appeared her burned legs weren't hampering her too much. She was really good at striking from ambushes. The gift of those knives would be permanent.

Laurealis was focusing on ice drakes. Admirably, she was using illusion to bring them in with a tempting false target of her, projected thirty feet from her actual location, and facing the wrong way. One was almost comical in how it crept up behind and drew in breath with a loud whooshing sound. Only then did she let loose with her focused blue flame from up close. The drake never knew what hit it. I chuckled, as the next thing she did was consume several large tree branches. Her core temperature was so hot that merely grabbing the branches burned them off the tree. She could eat her preferred vegetation quickly while searching for another target. No more eating dragon flesh for my fastidious beauty.

Obelix found a location with his back covered and was releasing shot after shot using his sorcerer's spells with perfect accuracy. No one handled a bow like Obelix.

Instinctively, Duncan set himself up to cover his back. Archers are so vulnerable when something gets close to them, especially from their blind backside. He used his sword as a distance weapon himself. Any dragon approaching the pair from behind Obelix received a bolt of void, which would disintegrate a head sized portion of flesh. While not as effective as Obelix, aimed well, it would at least chase the creature away.

Cougar's original trees had been burned down. He ran past the burnt-out area, and using a far more powerful spell, animated some of the forest giants. The trees were truly animated, striding purposefully to wreak mayhem on their foes. I knew how much pain it cost him to cast that spell, as each uprooted ancient tree would die. He, the caretaker of all forests, had destroyed a substantial portion of this one.

He was now spending his time sowing seeds of an improved tough green briar he had bred, then speeding its growth to be a net that grew right over a dragon's feet and tail or anything else within ten feet of the ground. That was how he was defending his doomed forest giants from any threat on the ground. Then one of the melee fighters, or a team of otters, could take it out. Otters, with little crossbows and swords, dashed out of the water to execute a trapped drake. The otter folk were taking many losses, but they were indomitable.

The trees, obviously under Cougar's control, were using a new technique. They were throwing masses of the huge, animated vines into the air at the lower dragons and the vines were tying up the dragon's wings. Once the dragons were on the ground, they were far easier to deal with. He smiled grimly as he noticed the otters working with him to kill those he downed near the waters' edge. The dragons avoided even flying over the water. It seemed this was a long-term war between them and the otters.

Galen was using his speed spells more effectively than ever, especially since he was merely Bedros' apprentice. All of our people were sped up and he had an interesting way of combining his slow and fast spells to cause collisions and let the greater drakes' own mass injure or kill them.

Another caster drake threw sparkle dust over the area, blinding us momentarily. Worse, Pancros' illusionary duplicates all disappeared, leaving her in the open and blinded. A fire drake reached down and engulfed her head and chest, lifting her twenty feet off the ground. Another drake bit her lower half and they proceeded to have a tug of war, held up only by the strength of her armor. Hearing her scream through our armor's communications, I was sure my friend was already dead, and there was nothing that could be done.

The armor itself was screaming in all of the Champion's heads, incapacitating us as the intelligent armor was attempting to heal its dead master and save itself. The two dragons pulled against each other, pushing, and clawing as they fought over their half of their stubbornly intact prize. They reared up, half flying in their rage and greed to better use all four of their claws.

Suddenly the armor gave way and my friend's corpse separated. The armor, the wonderfully powerful armor that had taken at least a thousand years to craft had one last surprise for these monsters who had slain my friend and Bedros' wife. It exploded, its intense magic released in an astonishing display of colors and strange effects. Half of both of the two dragons who had slain Pancros simply disappeared, their magic joining the armor's and, I suppose, Pancros' as well. The balance of their bodies joined the magical pyrotechnic explosion which continued to consume the intensely concentrated mana of their bodies. However, the effects didn't stop there.

Bits of magic, pure chaos, fizzed and dashed first one way, then another 'till they impacted with something, a tree, a dragon, nearly my Laurealis. She dove behind a rock, which was transformed into a giant stone grasshopper. Perhaps one had been on the rock. Anything living they hit was transformed or joined with things around them, generally lethally. One exception I saw was a dragon with half of a rear leg joined with and partially transformed into the rock it had been standing beside. I dodged a bolt myself, which then turned ninety degrees to fly straight up.

Duncan stopped attacking and, looking completely shocked, held his sword up into the air. On second thought, I believe that the artifact sword was controlling Duncan. The sword pulsed in a burst of colors and all the multicolored streaks of Chaos Light dashing this way and that, suddenly streaked right into the sword.

I held my breath wondering what would happen and praying for all I was worth to Sachos the Warrior for the sword to be able to control all that raw power.

A green light formed in the hilt and pulsed upward through the blade, becoming a brilliant beacon that disappeared high in the sky. I was renewed, I could stand! The others all felt the same way, renewed in mind and spirit. The wyverns fled, routed by the powerful beacon that was pulsating between red and green. The dragons didn't leave, but they retreated to a high watch several hundred feet above us. Except for Obelix, we couldn't reach them, and they couldn't reach us. He was taking his time aiming, but each shot, three to four per minute from an endless supply of arrows, brought down a dragon.

I looked for Bedros, hoping he was functional, he could fly us up there. But no, with the loss of his wife, he was crumpled beside a tree, emotionally broken. Astoria reached him and pulled him to her shoulder. She waved Laurealis off.

Duncan, or rather, Glenfallis had another surprise for us. He began releasing bolts of void like he had earlier, but their size had grown from crossbow size to ballista size. The range increase was impressive as well. The largest dragon, a beast of better than a hundred feet long, was flying near the top of the dragon horde. It must have thought that it was safe with all the other dragons between it and the new menace.

The ballista-like void bolt simply disintegrated its chest. Its limbs flew apart from the power of the impact. While that bolt was wending its message of doom to the largest dragon, Glenfallis or Duncan, must have been aiming because a second huge bolt shot out from the sword's point and hit another large dragon on the other side of the flock. It exploded within seconds of the first one's death.

Obelix had actually hit more dragons because he started earlier, but when a third bolt hit and disintegrated another of the ancient dragons, the dragons broke and fled to the mountain. The dragons that Glenfallis killed died a far more horrific death than merely falling. You could see right through their chests. With their morale already damaged by the first spell, the effect of seeing their comrades die in such a particularly gruesome way was more than they could handle.

Glenfallis nicked two more before they reached the mountain, ensuring their continued flight. Duncan then sheathed his sword, dropped to his knees, and sprawled face down to the ground.

I ran two steps, and feeling my exhaustion returning quickly, slowed to a walk. I was at least forty feet away, but I could hear Raina asking him, terror mixed with the concern in her voice, "Duncan! Are you all right? Speak to me, please be all right!"

He held his head down for a moment longer before he sprang for her, playfully catching her in his arms for a jubilant fling into the air. Catching her, they kissed for a long time. The rest of us had gathered around them by then.

"So," Laurealis asked again for all of us, "Are you feeling…?"

"Wonderful! I was merely thanking God for our victory."

Feeling the need to assess damages I spoke quietly. "Now that we have a moment—wait! Where are you going?" I cried out after the couple running for the water.

Feeling faint I chose dignity and sat quickly rather than fall, as my legs were giving way under me.

Astoria, looking over Bedros' shoulder, yelled, "Stop! Don't get your dressings wet!" but it was too late. The children, young adults rather, were bowing and laughing with a huge group of otters who had surfaced all around them. One of them climbed up Duncan's back to his shoulder and appeared to be having a conversation with them. After a few minutes, they all three bowed their heads to one another and the otter dove into the water.

Duncan and Raina kissed again and held hands as they waded out to the beach where we were waiting for them. Fausto had considerately formed a stone chair with legs with which he walked me down to the beach with everyone else.

Raina was the spokesperson for the couple. "We just had to thank them for all of their help. We asked if there was anything more we could do for them. They just said, "No, you and your people have given us a tremendous victory. Leave now while you may. Ereshkigal is hurt, but she will certainly heal. Then all of us must be in hiding. Your people must be far, far away."

Cougar exclaimed, "Ereshkigal! She was the queen of the Asmodians for ten thousand years! She died near the end of the Fourth Age, or so we thought. How could she be the Chaos Dragon?"

"Glenfallis recognized her soul when I wounded her the first time," said Duncan. "He recognized her as the Asmodian queen, so she is both the former Asmodian queen and the current dragon queen. If you'll give us minute, we'll go back and ask Drrriptor... Well, I can't say his name. I can think it, but I can't say it. My mouth can't move that way. But

I can ask the Chirpatgar noble we were talking to about what he knows."

Astoria furiously pushed her way in front of Raina and me, saying, "You can go out there again if you wish, but you, young lady, are staying right here to let Laurealis clean and dry your bandages and the rest of your clothes. Get out of them and give them to her. NOW! Then you lay down right now on that rock over there while I check out how well you are healing. You are NOT getting an infection in those burns, you hear me!"

"Yes, ma'am." Raina replied, totally abashed.

"Duncan," I said, "you talk to your nobleman while Astoria deals with Raina. The rest of us will make plans for getting us out of here fast. I agree with your nobleman friend completely."

Chapter Twenty
Escape
Regina

Astoria's demands and most of all, her genuine rage, unnerved me. I was moving to comply with her demands when Laurealis made illusionary modesty walls for me so I could undress in front of only the ladies rather than those strange men. I did that often enough in the past, but I didn't really want to. Once I realized I couldn't see out, so they couldn't see in, I relaxed.

"Now you just be a dear," Laurealis said, "and hand me all those wet things and I'll clean and dry them."

"Yes, that's good. As soon as you get those off, let's get these bandages off and see what we see." Astoria was practicing her bedside manner with me, now that I was doing what she wanted me to do. I just wanted them to shut up and let me hear what plans were being discussed. I just knew that the adults were going to separate Duncan and me. This reminded me so much of six years ago when lots of strange men were making plans for me. Even though they had seemed as sincere as these men, I had ended up in that horrible *orphanage*. The ladies just kept on prattling on and on. Yes, several of the blisters had broken and bled and I'd gotten them wet. But I'd done what needed doing and I wasn't about to let Astoria make me feel guilty about it.

Astoria had to replace the bandages. This meant that she had to rip up the bottom half of the green robe. She was down to just two intact robes. The old bandages had been too fouled from blood and other burn discharges for her to reuse.

"If you keep opening these wounds like this, you're going to have my legs as bare as yours," she joked. I only barely appreciated the humor. I was still upset about having to bare so much of my legs. It brought up bad memories. On the other hand, Duncan's eyes were spending a lot more time on me than they ever had before. It might be a promising idea to leave it like it was.

"Seriously, Raina, I know this damage came from fighting for our lives, and I understand why it occurred, but try as much as possible to *not* put pressure on these wounds. If I had all my normal supplies, it would be different. But just try to be more careful, all right, honey?" she smiled hopefully as she spoke.

"I will try. I really will."

She then turned serious. "You *absolutely* will not get these dressings wet again. And walking out into a non-sterile body of water like that is simply unimaginable. That wasn't fighting for your life; that was just foolishness. I'm serious, Raina. Keep these dressings dry. Outright wounds, I can deal with. Infections are another thing altogether and can cost you your legs. Keep them dry and clean. Do you hear?"

Her fear came through loud and clear, "Yes ma'am. I'll be good."

"Raina, I hate to interrupt Astoria's scolding," Laurealis said, "but, I'm making new hemlines in your dress where Astoria butchered it."

"How? You said you don't have any sewing stuff.

"Oh, dear, I'm not adding anything to your clothes. I'm simply reusing the material that's there. I'm just using a little hemline spell to keep the edges from fraying any further than they already have. It will make your dress a half inch shorter, but with Duncan around, I doubt that'll upset you very much.

"I know you've noticed where he's been looking." She smiled as she nodded her head toward his voice coming through the modesty screen.

I laughed. "Well, put that way, I guess you're right." I handled the back of the dress, which was now five inches shorter from fraying, so that it was squared off instead of tapered and noticeably short. It was folded over Laurealis' arm. "I hadn't realized how badly frayed this had become. Thank you."

"Thank *you*, Raina. I'm sorry I didn't say so before, but I really do thank you. I know forcing that horrible meat down my throat saved my life. You did it despite how badly it was hurting you and my reaction was just petty. When we return to Anthopoulos, I'll get anything you want, anything at all."

Raina smiled. "After all you've done for me?"

"No, I was just doing what I needed to do."

"Oh, pooh!" she said, stroking my cheek.

"There's nothing I can do about making the hemlines longer, the material's gone. I wouldn't do anything about that anyway since that was done so your bandages wouldn't be brushed by clothing. But I can do other changes in your clothing. Is there anything that you'd like me to do?"

Her comment about the shorter hemline had made me think of the changes that I'd been contemplating since just before Duncan proposed to me. I told her of the changes I'd like to see in my blouse. They were changes that would keep Duncan's eyes on me even more. He may be modest, but his eyes certainly weren't. A wolf's appetite was smoldering inside Mr. Prim and Proper, and I planned to bring it out. There was no one else out here, so I was safe. But his eyes had given me hints of what he liked to see. Fine, when we got back to civilization, he would be well-trained to keep his eyes on me, where they belonged.

Speaking of Duncan, the discussion outside suddenly intruded upon our conversation.

"What do you mean you can't take Shadow or the other horses with us? Shadow will die out here within a day." Duncan's anger was well and truly up.

"We're all exhausted." Bedros countered, "Our mana is all but gone. We would have lost the battle within another half hour simply from having no more spells to cast. Horses have a lot of mass."

"I'll not let my friend and companion die," Duncan replied.

"YOUR friend and companion? MY friend and companion, my WIFE for several thousand years, Pancros, just died saving your ungrateful hide! And you're upset about horses!"

Galen volunteered, "I can long-door us all in several jumps to the mountains. Then we can continue this discussion. Master, I know you're exhausted. I'm exhausted.

Bedros, I'm so sorry that I simply can't turn time back. I used all our stashed Talu pollen, then used virtually all our mana anyway in that battle. I know you're heartbroken, but can you help me by splitting the jumps with me? I can manage the horses for several jumps and after we're rested, we'll be able to think more clearly. Tempers are high right now."

"Out of the mouths of babes," Kailynn added. "He's right."

"Oh, all right," Bedros conceded. There was a general noise of agreement amongst the men.

Bedros stuck his head inside to ask, "How much longer, Astoria?"

I was shocked. All my feelings of comfort just evaporated as I jerked my legs out of Astoria's hands and snatched my dress from Laurealis as I covered myself. Fortunately, I was wearing my lower small clothes. But my blouse was lying on a nearby rock waiting for Laurealis to work on it, since she'd proved she still didn't have full control of her flames. When her temper went up, so did her flames.

A flaming Laurealis leapt in front to defend me. "Bedros, how dare you! She is not an elf! She was raised by a human mother! Why do you think I put up this modesty screen?"

"I don't know. I've seen bad wounds before." His eyes must have seen my legs before I pulled them up close to my body, "So what?" He must have gotten a good look at me in the instant it took to cover myself. I tried to make myself even smaller.

"Get out! Humans, especially human girls have lots of taboos about letting the opposite gender see their naked bodies. Now get out!"

"But why? I don't care what she does or doesn't have on. I just want us to get out of here before the dragons come back." He backed partially out through the illusionary wall.

"Get out!"

"All right! I'm out!" he said from the other side of the wall. "Women!"

"Men!" the three of us said in unison.

Astoria finished more healing of my broken blisters and redressing them a short while later. Laurealis finished drying and hemming my dress and dried my small clothes as well. She finished with my blouse, and I slipped it on quickly before any more of the elven men decided to stick their heads through the wall.

"These are hastily done, but we have to hurry." she said as she finished. I finished dressing as quickly as I could. It was nice to be clean and I couldn't wait to see Duncan's reaction.

Laurealis dropped the illusionary walls. "All right Galen, we're ready."

I saw Fausto, Duncan, and a couple of the elves packing Fausto's other two blood flasks and as many dragon parts as they could into their packs and onto the horses. Duncan had to calm the horses. They certainly didn't like the smell of the baggage being loaded on them. I agreed and sympathized with them fully.

The elves were packing dragon parts differently. They were holding various dragon parts over their left vambraces and saying something or making a motion and the parts just disappeared. I remembered Kailynn pulling my magical knives out of his vambrace like that. And come to think of it, Laurealis pulling stuff out of her big locket. Even Astoria had a jeweled locket that did the same thing. I looked back at the

Champions loading up dragon parts. Their vambraces seemed to hold so much. They just kept loading things in, yet it didn't seem to have any weight. I wished I had a pack like that, convenient. Laurealis' locket would be even better. That's what I'd ask her for.

We waited another fifteen minutes while the men finished packing scales, claws, and teeth into their various places. The elves finally ended up using Fausto's stone funnel and pouring dragon blood into their vambraces directly. Bedros used his telekinetic powers to keep the blood in a tightly controlled stream as it flowed out of the dragons, one per Champion. That was so the blood would be pure once they got it to the smiths of both races.

Duncan asked, "Why is it so important to keep the blood pure, or even to collect it at all? I can understand keeping the scales, like Fausto said, shields can be made out of them that are really hard and spells can be cast through them. But why the blood?"

"Because both elven and dwarven smiths and magicians can do a lot with it," Kailynn answered. "I fully expect an attack upon one of our major cities in the near future and they may be able to create and test ways to neutralize dragon's blood."

He indicated the dragon corpses surrounding us, "Now that we know that the vengeful Ereshkigal is the Dragon Queen I believe we can predict a counterattack, first upon Anthopoulos, then upon Chorisala because of Fausto, then possibly upon one of the human cities. It depends upon whether she recognized Duncan as Gaelaur, or she just assumes that the human that cut her so badly is from Francesca. Regardless, we must make defenses for ourselves and the Dom'barn. Much as I appreciate your rescuing me, I fear that you have unleashed a fearsome fate upon many." Astoria stepped through the modesty wall and placed her hand on Kailynn's arm. "I sense the work of The Lady in all that has occurred today. What happened today was destined. We must have faith in Her Benevolence."

"Benevolence? Tell that to Pancros." Bedros muttered bitterly.

"Bedros, I'm so sorry for your loss. We all mourn her, you most of all. But I stand by what I said. I can feel the Lady's Peace pouring over me. When we stop and you can pray, I'm sure you will feel it as well. We have completed the first of a particularly important part of Her Plan."

"And Her Ladyship's Plan included my wife's death?" Bedros demanded. "I want nothing to do with it! Or Her!"

"Let's rest, then continue this conversation. We're all exhausted."

She fixed him with a stare. They glared at each other for several seconds. Tears pooled in the corners of Bedros' eyes. Finally, he hung his head and Astoria almost leapt to enfold him in her arms.

"Know the Lady's Comfort, my friend. Be at peace.
We'll get through this together."

Duncan

The walls disappeared while Astoria and Bedros were facing off and I saw Raina on the rock. I liked how her repaired dress looked. The edges of her dress were neater, and it was light green instead of the brown that it had been. It was immodest, but she couldn't help that. I liked how immodest it was.

I glanced over at Bedros and Astoria and felt guilty for feeling so happy when he was so broken. He was holding his grief in, but his arm was wrapped tightly around Astoria as if he couldn't take a step without her support. I knew how he felt.

"Honey, get down. I have to help Kailynn."

"But Cougar and Obelix are taking care of him already."

"True."

"Come on Shadow." I guided him over to Laurealis' horse, Midnight. Now that Kailynn was mounted and tied on, I took her reins to steady and guide her. With both of us on Shadow and Bedros mounted behind Astoria on Star I figured we were taking as little space as possible. I hoped that the familiarity of being ridden would calm the horses.

Galen made some arcane motions and a black doorlike portal opened before us. When I moved directly in front of it, the black disappeared, and we had a clear view of the top of the ridge through the *Long Door*. It looked like it was just a few feet away. Very strange. Stepping through, we gathered on the other side. Galen came through last and closed the door before turning to scan the mountains to the west. There was a high hill to the northwest. He opened a door there, even though it was miles away.

"How can he do that? That's so much further away?" Raina asked no one in particular.

Kailynn answered, "It's a line-of-sight spell. If you can see it, you can *Long Door* there. We generally travel that way. We cast a *fly* or even a simple *levitation* spell, *Long Door* to mid-air a long way up, then open another Door at the end of our line of sight. It doesn't use nearly the mana that teleporting uses, but even more important, you don't have to be extremely familiar with the site like you have to be with teleportation."

"Ah, thank you."

Galen next moved us to one of the nearer mountains.

"That's about it for me. I have one more *Door* in me before I must rest. Look around here and try to find a good spot to spend the night."

I dismounted and looked around, climbing in the nearby rocks. I could see a cave across the valley.

"Over there, do you see that dark area? Looks like a cave to me. There's a nice patch of grass near it for the horses."

"Yes," Galen said. "I'll get us over there, but that's it. There's nothing left 'till I rest."

"Fine," I said, "Let me go first and I'll dismount and check it out."

"I'll have your back," Raina added.

We *Long-Doored* over, and Raina and I dismounted. Pulling out Glenfallis, I asked him in my head, *"Glenfallis do you have any more surprises that would be useful in here, like a small light or something?"*

"Good, good, you're learning to think. Yes, I can make a light. We'll see what else is needed once we're inside."

We stepped inside, cautiously. Nothing. Continuing further, we found nothing but the old remains of what may have a bear's lair. Glenfallis' light was gentle, so we weren't blinded. How convenient. We stepped back out.

"It's fine. We'll rest here."

The magic-using types all were exhausted, so I volunteered for the first watch with Raina for second.

After our camp was set up, I noticed a couple of missing people.

"Laurealis, where are Astoria and Bedros? They came in with us, but they aren't here now."

"She pulled the *Cloak of Mourning* over them."

"*Cloak of Mourning*?" Raina asked. "Well, if it hides her and Bedros that well, why didn't she use it back in the Dragon Lair?"

"She can only use it when the Lady let's her. She's using it now to give Bedros the privacy he needs while he mourns the loss of his wife, Pancros. They first started seeing each other during the End of the Third Age. They've been together for a long time."

"Will we be able to find them if we need them?"

"No. Nothing can find them, not True Sight, not even groups of people crawling around feeling their way for them. They will move around where the mourners are without even realizing it. Only when the cloak is released twelve hours later do the tracks show where people had crawled or walked around them without even knowing it. When the Lady allows that spell to be used, she makes sure they are protected. I expect she pulled a lesser Cloak over us as well, even though her attention was primarily focused on the person in greatest need, Bedros. Keep your watch, but I expect that with that spell in effect, we will have a peaceful night. Nothing, not dragons, not panthers, not bears, or even soulless ones will be able to find us tonight."

"That would be nice. So, they'll stay in there for twelve hours from a little before dusk. And we'll see them in the morning. I'm curious. Was there anything to what Astoria said about this all being what her goddess wanted?"

"That's not the kind of comment she would make unless it were true. Her faith is deep, and she walks and talks constantly with The Lady."

"What does she do inside her *Cloak of Mourning*?"

"What goes on inside the *Cloak* is holy and is not spoken of. Anything is allowed."

Raina asked, "Anything? Do I hear hanky-panky?" Laurealis began to show some ire and her flames ignited. They were still only a bare glow, but she was definitely irritated.

"If that were what is needed. She will do whatever the mourner needs. It is not spoken of. Occasionally, when the *Cloak* is raised, the mourner has passed the Veil as well to join the one they were grieving for. How far a priest or priestess will go to help the mourner is in The Lady's Hands."

"But…"

"Enough, Raina!"

"Alright, all right. Calm down. I'm sorry I asked." Raina turned and sat on a nearby rock, head on her hands, fuming.

I kissed her goodnight, "Get some sleep, dear. I'll wake you about midnight."

It took a while for her to calm down, but she did finally go lay down. After an uneventful night, I looked for Astoria and Bedros. They still weren't in sight or out from under that cloak spell. Raina was making breakfast for us all. I was getting so tired of fruits and vegetables, but at least I still had some jerky. I slipped a little to Raina and went outside to eat more. The elven breakfast was good, but not filling, and I still enjoyed meals with them. Their meals were fun times with lots of banter and laughing. I thought today might be different, but that was to be expected with a spouse's death.

Fausto stepped outside with me. I passed him a piece of jerky and bit off a piece myself. He held his floppy wide brimmed hat, rubbing the brim between his fingers, passing it between his hands and looking shy, as if he were trying to form a question. A shy Fausto was not something I thought I'd ever see.

"Ah, Duncan?"

"Yes?"

"I know you and Raina will be going to your homeland and I was wondering. I was wondering…"

Now I was intrigued, what could be making cocksure Fausto so shy?

"Well, we need to go by Chorisala and Anthopolis to warn my people and the elves of the danger from the dragons. But after that…"

"Fausto, spit it out. What has you so tongue tied?"

"I want to travel with you! I know Raina hates me, and probably has reason," he said, regret in his tone. "Everyone else seems to, but you accept me as I am. I'm exiled from my people because I rub people the wrong way and, and…"

"It's alright," I found myself saying. "You're trying to change, and you need more time. You saved our lives several times back there. Yes, you can travel with us. I'll talk with Raina. You behave yourself around her, you hear?"

Relief poured over his face, "Thank you. I promise you won't regret it."

I already did. What possessed me to say that? What will Raina say?

"Stuck thy foot in that time, did thy not, meat-bag?"

"Not you, too?"

"Boy, thee did the right thing. I'll be right there with thee."

Fausto

Duncan's a good man. I couldn't imagine what I would do if it weren't for him. I did pity him having to speak to Raina.

"You what? I can't believe you are letting that, that BEAST travel with us!"

Duncan said something, but I couldn't hear what it was.

"No! I just won't let you!"

Again, I couldn't hear Duncan's response, except that it was calm. This went on for better than ten minutes. Abruptly, Duncan exploded.

"Woman! I gave my word! Fausto is coming with me! Are you?"

"Of course, I'm coming with you. What a silly question!"

"Why do you always have to push things to the limit, only to make it seem like the outcome was already decided? This conversation is over."

Duncan stormed out of the cave and marched down to Shadow and began currying him. Raina came running out and followed him down.

"Leave me alone."

"But…"

"No! Go back inside. Pack or whatever, but I'm too angry to speak now."

"But Astoria and Bedros…"

"No! Wait, what did you say?"

"Astoria and Bedros are back," she answered.

"Well, why didn't you say so? Sorry, you tried. Alright, I'll be there in a minute. Walk with me?"

"Of course."

The elves began singing one of their four-part harmony songs. It was beautiful the way the voices interwove like that. It was definitely head music, not heart, but I suppose it spoke to their hearts. I was used to earthier music that came from the heart as Dwarven musicians like to say.

I waited for Duncan and Raina, so we'd all enter together. The elves stopped singing and Astoria stepped forward.

She greeted us with, "Bedros has become a Priest of Sachos."

"Excellent," Duncan said, "Why such a major decision now. I was always taught to not make any major decisions while your emotions are strongly influenced by something like grief. I may be wrong, but…"

"No, that is excellent advice. But first, no one may become a priest until after they have suffered enough for The Lady to deem it necessary for them to require the *Cloak of Mourning*. Two, we spent a long time in there. Time lasts for as long as needed in the *Cloak of Mourning*, so he's had days to make his decision. By the way, when's breakfast? I'm starving, as I'm sure Bedros is, also."

"True, I am." Bedros replied. "After we eat, it's time to go. Duncan, I see everyone else has eaten, so if you would bring the horses up here it would save time."

"Sure."

"And, Duncan, I'm sorry for snapping at you about them earlier."

"Bedros, it was nothing. When I lost my family and everyone I knew, I snapped sometimes, too. I've already forgotten the incident and you should, too. It's in the past."

"Thank you."

While Bedros was eating his various fruits, I went to him and asked, "Uh, sir, what are your plans for getting us out of here? Could you drop me off at Chorisala first?" "What? Chorisala? No, we have wounded. First, we go to Anthopoulos and get Raina fixed up and leave Kailynn to recover. Then, we all go to Chorisala."

He continued eating. I began to believe that they had spent several days of their time inside the *Cloak of Mourning*. His whole countenance had changed as if he had processed much of his initial grief.

"Fausto, I need you to change this room to something I can make into a proper teleportation chamber. Would you smooth the floor to a ridable surface? It needs to be just rough enough to give the horses traction. I will need to have a few more changes made for this room to be unique."

"I could do that while you're making your pentagram. You just need some features to make it easier to memorize, right?"

"Yes, just something to make it truly unique."

We each went about our business while everyone else packed the horses outside. I made a point of staying outside his lines as I pulled out individual pieces of stone to mold. I finished each of the four statues just before dusk, then I cast an enchantment in them to predispose them to receiving light spells.

"Bedros, would it help if I lit these? I don't want to disturb you, but it's getting dark."

"Yes, fine, fine. Some light would help. Now, I must be alone."

When he finished, near midnight, he had an extraordinarily complex pentagram surrounded by a symbol filled circle. I could feel its power. I could recognize some protections in it, but most of it was far beyond my rather limited knowledge of teleportation. I recognized that I was in the presence of a master to create such a powerful pentagram from nothing but chalk in less than a day. I understood he was probably making this to be a jumping off point to attack the dragons again, should that ever prove necessary. Good long-range planning. I was impressed.

Bedros looked up at what I had done. For the first time, he smiled.

"That's great, Fausto. That's a red dragon and one is white. This one is black. That last one is blue. Great, you lined the room for the portal to lead us here with the four main populations of dragons; genuinely nice work."

"Thank you."

"Well, there's just one more thing to do."

"What's that?"

"Use it, of course," he chuckled. "Hey, Obelix and Cougar! Get everyone in here. We're going home. No doubt, an interesting future awaits us!"

Index

The Races

- Lir'folk- A group of three races, with pointed ears and cat eyes. Commonly known as elves, the name means *Blessed Ones*. All three races are magical in nature and must occasionally breathe or ingest the pollen of the Talu tree to maintain their health.

- Shala'lir- The most magical of the Lir' folk, are between six and seven feet tall. Their skin, eyes, and hair are of all imaginable colors. At their pinnacle they were great warriors and magicians. Something has prevented them from reproducing for the last several thousand years and their numbers continue to decline.

- Hama'lir- A magical people who live on the east side of the eastern continent near where a chunk of the Chaos Comet landed after its collision with the moon. The event destroyed the humanities First civilization and magic came to the world, leading to the rapid evolution of many new races of people and new living organisms. Their magic tends to focus on weather and water. They are the most capable sailors in the world since their magic also includes powerful defenses against the great sea monsters.

- Tala'lir- Sylvan/ wood elf and the smallest of the Lir' folk. Their magical ability to disappear within their forest is aided by their dark earth tone colors.

- Lir' folk derivative races:

  o Asmodians- A third of the elves left near the end of the Second Age. They worship the demon Asmodius, whose first generation after the rift were exclusively hybrids with demons, rich with Chaos

Matter. The Chaos Matter would enable more live births, as the mother could survive an uncontrolled manifestation of an infant's potent magic. Different kingdoms exist on different continents. Each kingdom is constantly active in various power plays with each other.

o   Dragons- Isolated elven masters of magic who transformed themselves on lizard models to separate the mother from the egg so an exceptionally magical child wouldn't inadvertently kill both itself and its mother. First seen during the Third Age, and almost eliminated by the Asmodians during the Fourth Age.

•   Dom'barn-The Earth Children are short, stout masters of many crafts. Numerous tribes live in mountain chains around the world where large pieces of the Chaos Comet landed.

•   Humans- Survivors of every earth age and creators of many nations. They have been virtually eliminated many times, first by the comet, then by the Asmodians at the end of every Age.

Some of the Human Nations
(Western side of northwestern continent only)

• Francesca- Capital; Lergenze. The most powerful of the nations on the west side of the continent of Manora, occupying a huge, extremely fertile valley.

• Arcea- A powerful trading kingdom whose capital and largest city of a half million souls Bourbesonne, was completely destroyed. Due to horrible diseases and curses, it will remain uninhabitable for the near future. The ruthless destruction of Bourbesonne became a rallying cry for the remainder of the seven major human nations located nearby, the elves, and dwarves to fight the Asmodians.

• Koranidor- The worlds' most metropolitan city-state, built by the dwarves and financed by Bourbesonne. Run by the very lawful dwarves, organized crime is deep underground. The city is a melting pot, with traces of all the world's diverse cultures and races. Almost anything can be found in Koranidor.

• The Gaelaur Clans of Detrota. The loose confederation of traveling herders, tradesmen, and defenders of traditional values. Large, fierce warriors, known for their equally formidable warhorses, the heavy chainmail and half-plate armor that both horse and rider wear, and for the Great Wagons they travel in. Their Great Wagons are forty-eight-foot-long masterpieces of construction, requiring up to sixty oxen or even more horses to pull them.

Major Characters

- Raina- A choleric and sanguine seventeen-year-old female war orphan, half Tala'lir, half human, of Firenzian descent. Street smart; a bold and cunning survivor.
- Duncan- A phlegmatic and melancholy sixteen-year-old war orphan of one of the Gaelaur clans from the prairies just south of the ice sheets. A master of his fathers' enchanted sword.
- Laurealis- A beautiful, sanguine, and melancholy Shala'lir artist, sculptor, singer, illusionist, and emotive dancer who adopted Raina and Duncan with her husband Kailynn.
- Kailynn- Shala'lir Champion and Laurealis' grieving husband.
- Astoria- A rotund Hama'lir Priestess of The Lady. A healer and close friend of Laurealis.
- Fausto- An insensitive, Dom'barn earth mage. An exiled war orphan.

Minor Characters

- Marcellus- Fausto's uncle who exiled him. A Tribune, commanding a major border fort.
- Ereshkigal- Originally queen of the Asmodians, now Queen of the dragons.
- Pancros- Champion, combat illusionist, and wife of Bedros.
- Bedros- Champion, master of teleportation and air magic, and Pancros' husband.
- Cougar- Champion, Forest Mage.
- Obelix- Champion, Master Archer, Archer Mage.

- Galen- Apprentice of Bedros, Time Mage.
- Asmodeus- A demon lord from about 40,000 years in the future. Being male, he absorbs energy, and especially likes spiritual energy, such as that found in souls.
- Cluentha'I'zul- A female demon lord. She is the size of a large moon. She attempted to destroy the Earth by wrapping herself with the moon and ramming the Earth. She failed to destroy the Earth and nearly killed herself.
- King Nergalis- Asmodian king for over twelve thousand years. Possibly the most powerful mage in the world.
- Sharra- Daughter of Erishkigal and a minor lord of another dimension. She is the stepdaughter of Nergalis who replaced her mother as the Asmodian queen and his wife.
- Tiamora- The living remnant of Cluentha'I'zul. After four Ages and thirty-five thousand years, she has regained power, and eventually sentience, through absorbing millions of human souls at the End of every Age.

About the Author

JERRY BRIDGES

Jerry is a proud graduate of LSU School of Horticulture and has been a practicing horticulturist for most of forty years. He began his practice in Baton Rouge, but when that city experienced 48 percent unemployment, he moved back to his ancestral home of Columbia, SC. After many years there, he followed work to Beaufort, SC.

An avid gamer, his writing is based around the magic system found in one of his favorite Role-Playing Games. Jerry reads constantly, accompanied by his dog beside him and his cat on his lap. He is a proud husband to Vickie for 37 years and father of four incredible children. A committed Christian, he is an active member of his church choir.

About the Artist

CURTIS DRESSER

Curtis Dresser is a professionally trained illustrator and designer, with experience in novel illustration, graphic design, narrative and comic book illustration, concept art, and website design. He has worked for multiple publishers including Dynamite Comics and Dwarf Star Comics, along with many other private contractors, with over 10 years of experience in the commercial field.

www.ingramcontent.com/pod-product-compliance
Lightning Source LLC
Chambersburg PA
CBHW062101290726

48975CB00001B/72